MAR

D0481719

NO LONGER PROPERTY OF
THE SEATTLE PUBLIC LIBRARY

Road of the Lost

ALSO BY NAFIZA AZAD

The Candle and the Flame
The Wild Ones

Road of the Lost

NAFIZA AZAD

MARGARET K. McELDERRY BOOKS

New York   London   Toronto   Sydney   New Delhi

MARGARET K. McELDERRY BOOKS
An imprint of Simon & Schuster Children's Publishing Division
1230 Avenue of the Americas, New York, New York 10020

This book is a work of fiction. Any references to historical events, real people, or real places are used fictitiously. Other names, characters, places, and events are products of the author's imagination, and any resemblance to actual events or places or persons, living or dead, is entirely coincidental.

Text © 2022 by Nafiza Azad
Jacket photography by Atelier Sommerland/stock.adobe.com
Jacket design by Sonia Chaghatzbanian © 2022 by Simon & Schuster, Inc.

All rights reserved, including the right of reproduction in whole or in part in any form.

MARGARET K. McELDERRY BOOKS is a trademark of Simon & Schuster, Inc.
For information about special discounts for bulk purchases, please contact Simon & Schuster Special Sales at 1-866-506-1949 or business@simonandschuster.com.
The Simon & Schuster Speakers Bureau can bring authors to your live event. For more information or to book an event, contact the Simon & Schuster Speakers Bureau at 1-866-248-3049 or visit our website at www.simonspeakers.com.
Interior design by Irene Metaxatos
The text for this book was set in Baskerville MT.
Manufactured in the United States of America
First Edition
10 9 8 7 6 5 4 3 2 1
Library of Congress Cataloging-in-Publication Data
Names: Azad, Nafiza, author.
Title: Road of the lost / Nafiza Azad.
Description: First edition. | New York : Margaret K. McElderry Books, [2022] | Audience: Ages 14 up. | Audience: Grades 10–12. | Summary: Croi is compelled by a summoning spell to leave her home in the Wilde Forest and travel into the Otherworld, where the enchantment that made her into a brownie begins to break, revealing her true identity, her hidden magick, and her forgotten heritage.
Identifiers: LCCN 2022005558 (print) | LCCN 2022005559 (ebook) | ISBN 9781534484993 (hardcover) | ISBN 9781534485013 (ebook)
Subjects: CYAC: Fairies—Fiction. | Identity—Fiction. | Kings, queens, rulers, etc.—Fiction. | Magic—Fiction. | Fantasy. | LCGFT: Fantasy fiction. | Novels.
Classification: LCC PZ7.1.A987 Ro 2022 (print) | LCC PZ7.1.A987 (ebook) | DDC [Fic]—dc23
LC record available at https://lccn.loc.gov/2022005558
LC ebook record available at https://lccn.loc.gov/2022005559

To Katelyn Detweiler.
Thanks for taking a chance on a
smart-mouthed brownie-something
and her creator.

CAST OF CHARACTERS

THE HUMAN WORLD
Croi/Fiadh
The Hag/Blanaid

TALAMH FAE
Tinder (pixie)
Uaine (dryad)
Enya (dryad)
Irial/the Robber Prince (fae)
Saraid/the Robber Queen (fae)
The Forever King (fae)
Daithi (fae)
Caolan (catkin)
Mabh (fae)
Monca (brownie)
Nuala (fae)
Lugid/the Usurper (fae)

TINE FAE
Aodh/Tine King (fae)
Lorcan (fae)
Ceara/Fire Princess (fae)

"A person often meets his destiny on the road he took to avoid it."

—LA FONTAINE

ACT ONE

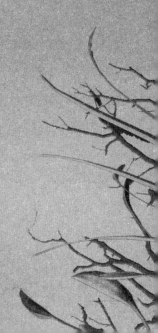

ONE

A *HINT OF RED. AN ALLURING CURVE. THE ANTICIPA-*tion of sweetness.

The apple promises and Croi falls. Eyes wide open and hand grasping. The fruit seller has no idea that one of his apples has gone missing. He is far too busy hawking his wares to notice. Besides, it wouldn't matter even if he did. He can't see her nor the apple she's currently holding. Folding herself under his cart, Croi settles in the shadows to enjoy the fruit as it should be enjoyed. With quick, crisp bites and spurts of juice dribbling down her chin.

The apple is gone too soon, and Croi emerges from under the cart, looking at the other apples, wondering if she should take another one. She decides against it, however, when she looks around the market. There are too many other things to taste here. She takes a step and then skips back, narrowly avoiding a dirty little human. There are many, too many, in the market. It is their forest after all.

Croi is not supposed to be here in this sticky, stinky collection of moving humans. The rich ones try to mask their stench with perfumes. They sacrifice flowers and the bees mourn. The poor ones cannot afford the floral sacrifices, so theirs, at least, is an honest stink.

Across from the fruit seller is an old woman with far too many toffee sticks. Out of the goodness of her heart, Croi eases her burden. The merchant beside the bakery that sells honey buns has colorful scarves on display. Croi takes a few and thanks him, but he can't hear her, so he doesn't respond. She doesn't mind his rudeness.

The market is her favorite place in the human city. Set up by the big gates that lead out, it is always full of sounds, smells, and colors. The smells are not always pleasant, but the colors frequently dance in the sunshine. Humans set up shop in any space they can find. Sometimes they quarrel in loud, ugly voices. Croi learns the language they speak by studying the shapes their mouths make as they throw words at each other.

She has been frequenting the human city for thirteen of the (almost) seventeen years she has been alive. Not once have the humans seen her walking among them. The animals are much more sensitive to her presence. A cat meows from her perch on a wooden fence when Croi passes it. She responds to it with a hiss. Meows don't make music for her.

The Hag told Croi this morning that she is no longer allowed to visit the human city. She stood up tall, pretending to be a mountain, and said in her grandest voice, "You cannot, Croi. A little brownie will be discovered much too quickly. It isn't safe there."

"But I've been there many times before! Down the river path, through the hole in the wall, and into the grounds of the castle. The humans *never* see me!" Croi was mutinous.

"You must stop now," the Hag commanded. She looked at Croi with her stormy eyes, and Croi became a boat about to be capsized.

"Why?" Croi wailed.

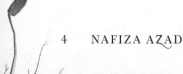

"No questions," the Hag said, and turned away.

She says not to ask questions, but every time Croi glimpses herself in the mirror, all she sees are questions. Her body makes no sense to her at all. Her fingers, arms, and shoulders are whys, her torso and legs are hows, and her head is a who. Her body is a billion questions she keeps asking the universe. So far, it hasn't replied.

She follows a little human boy through myriad alleyways to a shabby house near the city wall, not far from the market. She peeks through the open door of the house and sees him clamber onto the lap of a human woman sitting on a chair. She is a mother. Humans have them. They hold, they kiss, and they love. Brownies don't. Well, *this* brownie doesn't. She has a Hag who is part stone, part memory, and part tree. The Hag doesn't hold, doesn't kiss, and she most certainly doesn't love. The Hag teaches and expects Croi to learn. She commands and knows Croi will obey.

The sun climbs the sky and the day gets hotter. Croi leaves the human child to his business and returns to the market, where she continues collecting various tasties. But the market gets too crowded, so she abandons it and follows the main avenue deeper into the human city. As she moves away from the city gates, the houses get bigger and bigger until she reaches the castle, which is the biggest of them all. Croi has glimpsed the king and the queen here and there on her meanderings through the castle grounds, but only once has she seen them make their way through the city with white handkerchiefs pressed to their noses as if they don't stink as well.

The city is surrounded by a gray wall that keeps humans within and the Wilde Forest, where Croi lives, without. Humans don't venture into the forest; the Hag says they're not allowed. The Hag doesn't ever visit the human city. Perhaps it is beneath her dignity to go through the little hole in the wall. Well, Croi doesn't think the Hag would fit even if she tried.

The city has a rapid pulse. Everyone here is in a frenzy to breathe, to live, to couple, and to gobble. A maelstrom of emotions eddy in the air: hunger, greed, and lust are more common than others. What would it be like to live here forever, trapped within the metal and the stone, captive to decay?

Croi stands against a fence and watches human children shrieking with laughter as they play a game of chance by the road. Would the people here accept her? Would she want them to?

After a minute or so, she starts walking and doesn't stop until she reaches the castle. As usual, the entrance is crowded. Guards stand in front of the horde of people seeking audience with the king. There's no point in waiting; people won't make way for Croi no matter how long she waits. So she shoves her way through the crowd, stepping on feet and pinching any flesh available. Humans react quite quickly to pain.

Once she has crossed the sea of people, Croi starts running. She runs until there is no breath in her. She runs until she can breathe again. Slipping into the inner grounds of the castle, she walks unseen through hallways and outer corridors until she reaches her destination: a forgotten courtyard in an older part of the castle. The place usually sees very few visitors, so the air is still and dank here. A sad fountain spews up rusty water in the middle of the courtyard while a few straggly trees wearily lift their branches in obeisance to a distant sky.

Croi is not concerned with the dilapidated state of the courtyard. Her attention is on the stone maid half hidden behind the trees on the right. The stone maid is frozen midmotion; both hands have lifted her voluminous skirts to aid her running. One foot is arched on the ground while the other is lifted in a step. She is looking back, her features petrified in an expression of anguish.

Croi was six when she crawled through the hole in the city wall and into the castle grounds for the first time. As soon as she got to her feet and regained her bearings, she found herself pulled forward entirely

against her will. She walked without knowing where she was going until she ended up in this courtyard, in front of the stone maid. At first she was confused, not knowing why she was called to this place. Then she looked into the stone maid's eyes and met a horrific truth there; someone, alive and aware, looked at her through the stone maid's blank eyes. Croi immediately returned to the Wilde Forest, found the Hag, and demanded she help the stone maid. The Hag refused, saying that some magick was beyond her. Croi, teary and apologetic, returned to the human city, clutched the stone maid's hand, and cried.

It was at that moment that Croi first felt warmth in her hands. Though the stone maiden can't speak using words, she makes herself clear by warming Croi's hands. The stone maid became Croi's only friend, a confidante, and someone to love—Croi, who is lacking in people, human or kin, adopted her. She tells the stone maid all her secrets, all her complaints, and all the dreams she is brewing for the future. Of course, she hasn't stopped trying to break the curse on the stone maid, but she has even less magick than the Hag. Croi hasn't given up, however. Someone out there will know how to free the stone maid.

Today, like other days, she presents her stony friend with the bounty she harvested from the market and is just about to launch into a protracted complaint about the Hag's tyranny when a side door opens and two human maids emerge into the courtyard. They are carrying pails of water, scrubbing brushes, and soap.

"Oh my, I completely forgot this place existed," one of them, red-haired and blue-eyed, says. "How did the King of the West come upon it?"

"Matilda from the right-wing drawing room says she saw him take a walk after luncheon. Presumably, he came upon the old king's court-yard then," the blond one replies.

"Right. I heard that the Old King forbade people from using this place. But he's gone now, and the queen has her own rules," her companion says in a lowered voice.

"Can she simply give away the stone maid, though?"

"Who's going to tell her she can't? Anyway, the King of the West took a fancy to the stone maid, and the queen is only too willing to please him. We are in no position to be asking questions. You know that already. Let's clean the stone lass up and get her ready. I hear she's being moved tomorrow."

Hearing that, Croi turns in alarm and loses grip of a pack of toffee she was holding. It falls away from her, becoming visible in the process, and falls to the ground with a crisp sound. The maids startle. They look at the packet of toffee that has suddenly appeared, pale, and flee the place immediately after. Croi doesn't care about their hysterics. She's much more concerned about this unexpected danger to her friend.

She paces in front of the fountain, trying to think of a way to save the stone maid. She can do almost no magick; in fact, the only thing magickal about her is her invisibility to humans—Croi comes to a standstill and turns to the stone maid in excitement. She clutches the statue's cold hand. "What if I make you invisible to humans, like me? If the human queen can't see you, she can't give you away, right?"

Croi rubs her sticky fingers on her equally sticky chin.

"The only problem is, I don't know how." She holds the stone maid's hand tightly. "Do you? Can you try to tell me?"

For a moment, nothing happens. Then the hand that Croi is clutching heats; some sort of current passes through the maid's stone hand and into Croi. She stares at the stone maid, bewildered for a second, before a sharp pain in her chest has her gasping. It feels as though there is a hot rock in her chest, trying to burn its way out. The pain is so intense that she squats on the floor and rocks back and forth.

The discomfort fades after a long while, leaving Croi flushed and

weak on the cobbled ground. She gets up jerkily and scowls at the stone maiden. "What did you do to me?" She shudders. "I've never hurt that much before."

Of course, no reply is forthcoming. Croi rubs her chest, torn between wanting to leave immediately and feeling like she has to stay.

"All right. How . . . ?"

She gapes at the stone maiden. There's a spell glowing hot in her mind. A spell that tells her how to make the stone maid invisible.

"If you could do that, why haven't you told me how to turn you back into flesh and blood?" Croi asks the stone maid. "Oh well, I suppose it's not that easy. Perhaps you don't know how to break the curse on yourself either. Anyway, I forgive you for the pain. Let me try this. I don't promise anything however." She stands in front of the stone maid, places a hand on the maid's stone dress that is covered by a thin layer of green moss, clears her throat, and pronounces the strange chant that appeared in her head. It is in a language she has never heard before. Nothing happens. She tries it again. Nothing happens. She tries it one last time, and this time, her chest throbs sharply once before her fingertips heat. Croi looks up into the stone maid's eyes. She pushes a few potted plants in front of the stone maid, scatters some gravel around the area. "I think it's done."

Only, there's no way to check. No sooner does Croi have this thought than the side door opens once again and the two maids who were scared off reappear. This time they are accompanied by two burly footmen.

"Look, there's the toffee that appeared suddenly! I wasn't lying," the redhead says, pointing.

"The statue's missing!" the other maid suddenly shrieks. "It's no longer there!"

Croi tunes out the flurry among the servants and grins gleefully at the stone maid. "I succeeded!" She chortles, forgetting the pain. "Wait till I tell the Hag I did magick!" She pauses. "No, maybe that wouldn't be the best idea. After all, she told me I am not allowed to come here anymore." More humans enter the courtyard as she speaks, looking for the missing statue.

Croi leaves the courtyard after promising the stone maid to come see her again the next day. Feeling good about her success with the spell, she runs through the immense castle grounds. She passes pavilions full of people and runs through a maze, leaving holes in the hedges. Finally, she comes to the rose gardens at the back of the castle. There, she finds more people. Courtiers are arranged around a princeling like the feathers in a peacock's tail. Croi is distracted and still running; perhaps that's why she runs straight into the princeling. He careens and would have fallen, too, had it not been for a quick-thinking attendant who rushes to steady him. The princeling looks around, as do his attendants, for the missile that almost knocked him over, made him stumble, and, for a lightning second, stole his dignity. They're looking for Croi.

She stands frozen, like the stone maid she needs to save, staring at the princeling they call Prince *Charming*, with his blue doublet and the shiny buttons that don't show her reflection and the white pants that mold his parts in ways that cause the maids to stare and giggle. The air crackles like it does before a storm, and that's when it happens.

Invisibility is supposed to be Croi's magick, and her magick is not supposed to fail. But fail it does. People look in Croi's direction and they see her.

They *see* her.

A short, plump creature with long, straight brown hair, wearing a baggy dress that looks like the bark of a tree (only because it is) and scarves the color of dusk wrapped around her neck. They see a brownie with eyes the brown of a chocolate pudding. A brownie with a round face, a button nose, large pointed ears, sharp teeth, and brown

skin. They see someone who is very obviously not human like them.

Nobody moves, nobody speaks, and for a second nobody even breathes. Then hysteria conquers the masses. Someone screams and someone else swoons. Croi stands, fixed in place, too surprised to move. The princeling is calling for guards. Croi can hear them running around the corner; she knows they have their shiny sharp swords at the ready.

She takes a breath of the suddenly suffocating air and squeezes her eyes shut.

TWO

ONE SECOND PASSES, TAUT WITH THE POSSIBILITY OF death. Then the air crackles one more time, and Croi is able to breathe again. Her magick has reasserted itself.

Bewilderment shades the expressions of the humans. They blink and rub their eyes, distrusting their minds. Croi is invisible to humans again. Whispers crowd the tense air when the soldiers point their swords and find that there's nothing to poke.

Croi slips away from the crowd, barely suppressing the urge to run. What if she bumps into someone else? Brownies are supposed to be unfailingly invisible to humans! Why did that change? How? Humans don't truly believe in kin except as figments of their fancies. This disbelief strengthens their inability to fathom kin.

But they saw her! She saw herself reflected in their eyes! Croi doesn't know the hows or the whys of it, but she rarely does about anything, so she's not very bothered. What thrills her is the fact that for the very first time in her (almost) seventeen years of life, someone other than the Hag *saw* her. Of course, their reaction after seeing her leaves something to be desired, but that's unimportant. What matters is that, just for a moment, she existed fully in the human world.

Suddenly Croi remembers the stone maid and hastens her steps. She slips behind the rosebush, wiggles through the hole in the castle walls, and enters the leafy embrace of the Wilde Forest. Sharp relief hits her and she takes a deep breath, drinking in the smell of the forest. Just as she is beginning to calm, a sudden pain stabs in her chest, and she falls to her knees, her palms flat on the ground.

The forest throbs underneath her hands. The pain fades after a moment, but Croi doesn't remove her hands from the ground. She's too busy feeling the forest breathe. It is alive in a different way than the human city. Where the city is animated due to the people living in it, the forest owes its life not to the beings that call it home but to something deeper, something wilder, something Croi doesn't yet have the words for.

She gets to her feet after a while and looks up at the forest ceiling, trying to tell the time from the visible patches of the sky. A bunch of gringits the size of the wild pears she likes to eat are hanging from an oak tree. When they see her looking, they make rude gestures at her. Croi can't speak Gringit, but she can click her tongue in a way that infuriates them. So, she does. They chitter excitedly, blending into the leaves with their green skin and gravity-defying green hair. Their sharp, pointy ears spread on either side of their heads like wings. The two antennae on their foreheads are currently quivering with rage. Before they can galvanize into action, Croi flees. As gringits are territorial and don't ever venture too far from the tree they call their own, she is sure they won't follow her.

Leaving the gringits behind, she follows the river path, avoiding the thorny attentions of the blackberry bushes growing alongside it.

The river sings constantly. Croi wonders if the fish ever get tired of its song. Stepping off the river path, she ventures deeper into the forest, past three giant willow trees, a clearing filled with blue delphiniums and giant white butterflies, and onto a well-worn path lined on either side by wildflowers. The path leads to a clearing surrounded by four trees whose branches Croi has borrowed to form the roof of the dwelling she shares with the Hag. She stuck moss in between the holes in the roof to keep out the rain.

Croi and her guardian used to live in a cave, but then she discovered the human city and houses. She can't build a house in the Wilde Forest, but this shelter functions similarly to one. The dwelling is just one large room divided into three parts: a space to eat, a space to learn, and a space to sleep. The Hag doesn't eat, and she doesn't sleep in the way Croi sleeps. The dwelling is filled with colorful gewgaws Croi picked up from the human city. There's no furniture, just cushions, scarves, and sparkly things including a handheld mirror. Flowers grow inside, outside, and around the dwelling. Flower sprites love Croi, so they try to be as close to her as possible. Though they don't speak the same language as her and her attempts at befriending them have been met with bewilderment, having them around makes her feel less lonely.

A cow and two chickens live at the back of the dwelling. Croi gives the cow delicious grass, and the cow provides milk in return. The chickens lay eggs when the mood strikes them, and Croi has to fight for every single one. She moves past the dwelling into an area more densely populated by trees than the rest of the forest.

And there Croi finds her.

The Hag is standing under a tree with large waxy leaves. In the fractured light that filters through the gaps in the forest canopy, she seems as strange to Croi as Croi must have seemed to the humans. She is so still and so silent that at this moment, the Hag is no different

from a tree. Tall with smooth, unmarked cheeks made of stone, and eyes, when they are open, the green of a seedling pierced by sunlight. Her limbs are made of a mixture of stone and wood. Her hair is a ropy brown mess on her head. Her stone-and-wood body is swathed in a silver cloak that she never takes off, not even to wash. She smells like the forest, like something green and growing.

"I told you your excursions to the human city are no longer allowed." The Hag opens her eyes suddenly, startling Croi.

"You did tell me that, and I also told you that I can't abandon my friend in the city," Croi replies immediately.

"She's made of stone," the Hag says.

"So are you," Croi replies.

"We are not the same," the Hag says slowly. Her voice has no inflection and her face no expression.

"I agree. You're not the same," Croi says. "She, though infrequently, gives me warmth. You, on the other hand, are always cold."

A bunch of gringits peek out from the shadowy depths of a tree beside the Hag, but they are too afraid to make any sound; the Hag has a way of silencing even the loudest of creatures.

Croi looks up at the Hag, irritated by her unchanging mien. "Don't worry. I won't ask you to save her. I can do that all by myself. Today, I made her invis—" Too late, Croi realizes that she should have kept her spellcasting a secret.

"You made her what?" the Hag asks, her slow drawl somehow even more menacing than usual.

A long moment, punctuated by the squawks of birds in the forest, passes. Croi exhales loudly. "I made her invisible. She taught me how." She peers at the Hag, afraid of her reaction. She has forgotten; the Hag has no emotions.

"Is that all that happened?" The Hag's words contain no rancor, but Croi's face drains of color. She bites her lip, knowing that if the

Hag finds out that she became visible to humans, she'll make sure Croi never sets foot in the human city again. Never see those fever-burning frenetic humans. Never again feel the thrill of the market. Never see the stone maid, ever again. Never feel her warmth, have her company. The narrow corners of Croi's loneliness will suffocate her.

"Tell me," the Hag demands. "Clearly."

Croi cannot lie. She has tried, many, many times, but her tongue refuses to cooperate.

"Did your magick fail?" the Hag asks, a compulsion in her voice that makes a mockery out of Croi's resistance.

"Just a bare moment," Croi spits out. She draws away from the Hag, folding her arms around herself. "A tiny moment. Less than a second. I blinked and it was back."

She avoids the Hag's gaze. The guardian looks at Croi from her great height and sighs. The trees surrounding them echo the sound.

"Follow me," the Hag says, and starts walking without another word.

Unable to disobey, Croi follows. The Hag takes her to a part of the Wilde Forest she has never been to before. In fact, Croi has only explored a tiny portion of the forest, as the Hag won't let her run around as she pleases. She says there are too many dangerous things in the Wilde Forest that will make meals out of little brownies.

Tall, thin poplar trees grow in two straight lines in this part of the forest. Between these two lines is a corridor filled with verdant grass and little else. The Hag pulls Croi back when she would have ambled into the corridor.

"Why?" Croi looks at her. "Is there a monster I can't see waiting to eat me?"

The Hag gives her a piercing look in reply. Croi huffs at her in resentment and turns her attention to the gringit-infested tree behind her. The gringits are hanging upside down from the branches, making

faces at her. Croi sneers at them when the Hag isn't looking.

"Croi," the Hag says, and she immediately comes to attention. "Go, stand in the corridor for a moment."

Croi narrows her eyes and looks at the Hag suspiciously. After preventing her from entering the corridor, the Hag now ordered her to go there. She hesitates.

"Go!"

Croi takes a breath and walks out of the cover provided by the trees and onto the grass. For a moment, she feels nothing. Then she senses a breeze laving her face, playing with her hair, and ruffling her dress. This breeze is somehow weighted with smells that she cannot identify. It brings a sweetness both to her tongue and to her heart, pricking it awake, making it hurt, hope, and grieve. Her eyes fill and spill over without her permission. Croi's limbs are heavy, but her insides feel like they've been shocked. What's happening to her?

"Croi," the Hag calls from the side. "That's enough. Come back."

No way. Croi has decided to live in this corridor from now on.

"Croi," the Hag says again. "I won't repeat myself."

Because Croi is a good brownie and fears what the Hag will do to her, she, very reluctantly, returns to where her guardian waits.

"What was that?" she asks the Hag with wide eyes.

"That . . ." For the first time ever, the Hag seems to be at a loss for words. Her face is still expressionless but her eyes are deep. She clears her throat. "That is the smell of home. Of magick. Of the Otherworld."

"Hag," Croi says, following her back to the dwelling. "If the Otherworld is home, what are we doing here? Did you do something bad and were exiled? But if you were exiled, why did you bring me with you? Where is my family? Did you kidnap me?"

She asks the Hag these questions periodically, hoping that one day the Hag will be annoyed enough to answer. This hasn't happened yet, but Croi hasn't given up hope. She is confident that one day she'll anger the Hag into answering.

"Are you sure you can't help me rescue the stone maid?" Croi asks one more time before they reach the dwelling.

The Hag enters the shelter without replying, and with a sigh, Croi follows her. The flower sprites cavort when they see her, and the air gets heavier with the scent of blossoms.

"Here." The Hag takes out two books from somewhere on her body and holds them out to Croi.

The brownie tries to figure out where exactly her guardian had been keeping the books. She hadn't noticed any bulges.

"Croi," the Hag says. A very faint exasperation colors her voice.

"Have you realized that you call my name a bit too much?" Croi asks her.

"Take the books," the Hag says. Oh.

The books are heavy and very ornate. The first one is thick with gold-edged pages. The title of the volume is *A Compendium of the Peoples and the Magicks of the Otherworld*. The edges of the pages of the other book are black. The title of the book, written in gold on the equally black cover, is: *The Talamh Crown*.

The first book Croi can understand, but the second one? She looks at the book and then at the Hag with not a little confusion on her face. The Hag doesn't say anything, so she puts the first book on the cushion and tries to open the second one. No matter how much she pulls, the cover doesn't budge.

"Your book is broken," she finally tells the Hag.

"As I have taught you before, the Otherworld is divided into four elemental kingdoms," the Hag says, ignoring Croi's words. "Talamh or Earth kingdom, Aer or Air kingdom, Uisce or Water kingdom, and Tine or Fire kingdom."

"Why aren't there queendoms? Are there only kings?" Croi asks.

"Regardless of the gender of the ruling monarch, the lands separated by the elemental magicks are known as kingdoms," the Hag says patiently.

"There's something very wrong with that," Croi mutters.

"The book you are holding contains details about the monarchs of the Talamh kingdom. You will be able to read it soon." The Hag gives Croi a look she can't interpret.

"But I am a brownie. You said that only fae can be kings and queens, remember?" Croi reminds the Hag, just in case she has forgotten. "Why do I need to worry about the monarchs of elemental kingdoms?"

"Ask me no questions," the Hag says, and this time Croi cannot hold back a rude snort.

"What kind of a teacher allows no questions? A bad one!" Croi crosses her arms.

"Sleep early. I will see you tomorrow morning. Don't leave before you see me." The Hag gives Croi another opaque look and leaves, melting into the forest as Croi watches from the door of the dwelling. Don't leave? Where would she go? Unless the Hag doesn't mind her going to the human city, but somehow Croi doubts that.

She squats down at the entrance and sighs deeply. The magick of the Otherworld . . . Would there be someone in the Otherworld who would help her save the stone maid? Will the stone maid be able to survive until Croi can find someone to help her? A flower sprite chitters at Croi loudly, and she jumps, startled. The cow bays, reminding her that she needs to milk it. Croi gets to her feet and busies herself with the business of living.

The sun is high in the sky when she finally sits down in front of the dwelling, among the flowers and the sprites that live in them. She shares a bottle of fruit juice she filched from the market along with some pastries the baker put out. Once full, she brings out the books the Hag gave her, and under the waning light of the day, opens the one that can be opened. The thick, creamy first page doesn't have a single mark on it. The second page has the oddest table of contents she has ever seen, though admittedly she hasn't seen many. The chapter titles and page numbers zoom around the page as if undecided where they will appear in the book. Croi clears her throat sternly and the writing calms down; the words and numbers slink back to their proper places.

"Brownies" appears on page sixty-four, so Croi turns to the page and reads. This is what the book has to say about brownies:

1. They are domestic.

Obviously a lie. Croi detests housework.

2. They are fiercely loyal.

Croi suspects this one as well. She would betray the Hag in a heartbeat.

3. They live in large extended families usually in a brownie village.

Presumably large families mean more than one large Hag.

4. They have a fondness for sweets.

This is the only one that rings true. Croi is dangerous around pastries. The bakers in the city keep setting mousetraps, and Croi keeps avoiding them.

She peruses the page, and the illustrated brownies at the bottom giggle at her. She rewards them with a frown.

Croi taps her chin and thinks. Perhaps the reason her parents abandoned her into the dubious care of the Hag is because she has very few of the qualities innate to brownies. Maybe the Hag accepted her as her own out of the goodness of her heart.

Somehow, Croi doubts that.

For one thing, she doubts the Hag even has a heart.

Her thoughts return to the problem of the stone maid again. Croi hopes the spell holds and the humans continue being unable to see her.

She flips through the pages, wondering if there is anything in the book that will help her free the maid. Not finding anything, she goes back to the beginning.

A separate table of contents marks the section on magick. The page is shiny, and the illustrations slither around as though looking for the most comfortable spot.

Distill the Night into a Cloak of Darkness
Charm the Wings Off a Butterfly
Hex a Fire Fae
Cast Glamour on Kin

There is a fingerprint beside the Glamour spell as if the Hag tapped her finger on the title. Curious, Croi turns the pages to the spell and reads. Glamour, the Hag has taught her, is the magick kin do on themselves to appear in a shape other than what they are. With Glamour, a brownie could make herself look human—not that Croi would ever do that. The only magick Croi can lay claim to is her invisibility. . . . Well, she can't be too certain about the invisibility, either.

She reads ahead and is surprised. She didn't know that kin could do Glamour on other kin without their permission. She turns to the spell excitedly. If she could, she'd Glamour the Hag into a bunny. The Hag wouldn't be amused, but—Croi grins to herself—it would be an excellent adventure. However, no matter how much she tries, Croi can't read the spell. The words shimmer and slouch, completely frustrating her. Finally, she bangs the book shut and shoves it aside.

The day's light slowly fades, yielding to the stars gradually blinking awake. A sliver of a moon hangs ponderously in the sky. The flower sprites lean against Croi, their small bodies providing pockets of warmth. The birds have fallen silent, and the crickets now preside over the music. Croi reaches for peace but it eludes her. Intense melancholy suddenly tries to drown her; this melancholy is accompanied by terror at the thought of spending seventeen more years in this stagnant state. She shifts and fidgets, feeling like the skin she is in has become unable to contain the person she is becoming.

Croi sighs a little and sprawls on the ground among the flowers in front of the dwelling. As she has done many times before, she will sleep outside, collecting stardust in the shadows cast by her body.

The snores of the flower sprites soothe her, and Croi closes her eyes, conceding to the demands of the darkness. When she opens her eyes again, it is in a sunny clearing in a forest. A long, wide table stands in front of her, groaning under the weight of numerous dishes, like scones with dollops of cream on them and steam as evidence of their freshness. Chicken, roasted, fried, and stewed; potatoes, crispy and baked; bread, savory and sweet; and so much more. All these things are Croi's favorites. She steps toward the table, her eyes wide and her mouth full of water.

She knows very well she is dreaming because such bounty will only occur in her dreams. She won't complain, however. At least her subconscious gets to feast.

"You must be very hungry," a voice says just as she is about to reach for a chicken leg.

THREE

OWERING ABOVE HER IS A BOY, FAE FROM THE POINTED shape of his ears. Because this is a dream, his edges are blurred, but the rest of him is clearly visible. His nose is straight and thin, and his forehead is narrow and elegant. Croi is momentarily fascinated by the shape of his lips. They are full and look firm. She wonders what they would feel like if she kisses him. Bewildered by her thoughts, she shakes herself. Is this fae boy casting some sort of enchantment on her? Maybe his lips are magick.

"Who are you, and what are you doing in my dream?" Croi takes a step back. She looks at the full table and turns to the boy suspiciously. "I hope you don't think I'm going to share my food with you."

"It's just dream food," the boy points out with a grin. He has dimples and a really nice voice. But these two things are not enough for her to forgive his trespass.

"It's *my* dream food. If you want to eat, you should dream up your own food. It is very rude to go uninvited into other people's dreams, you know." Croi crosses her arms and tries to look stern. It is a difficult prospect since she is only as tall as the boy's thigh.

"I do apologize for invading your dream. I most certainly don't plan to steal your food," the boy says, bowing formally.

"I will think about accepting your apology." The trouble with tall people, Croi decides, is that talking to them is painful. She addresses her words to the boy's belly. If she can't see his face, she won't be tempted by him.

"My name is Irial," the boy says after a short hesitation.

"Hello, Irial. Why are you in my dream?" Croi asks. Then, because she can't help it, she picks up a meat bun and takes a bite. For dream food, it is delicious.

"I'm looking for the Forever King's descendant," Irial says softly.

Croi blinks, wondering who this Forever King is. "In dreams?"

"It's a scrying spell. It uses dreams . . ." He trails off, seeing her disbelieving face. He clears his throat. "Anyway, are you?"

"Why are you looking for the Forever King's descendant anyway?" Croi asks instead of answering Irial's question. Though only in a dream, this is the first time she has talked to anyone besides the Hag, and she wants to prolong the experience.

Irial's eyes narrow at the question. He coughs slightly, perhaps trying to find the best answer. "I . . . It's complicated. There's no point telling you. You won't even remember this conversation happened," he mutters, and Croi raises her eyebrows.

"Why not?"

"The spell will erase your memories afterward," he confesses.

"In that case, you should tell me *all* your secrets." Croi leans forward, her eyes gleaming. "Since I won't remember them, or you for that matter, go ahead and get things off your chest. Vent!"

Irial doesn't seem to need much persuasion. After a minute or so of pondering, he sits down on a wooden stump and pats the space beside him. Croi obliges and sits down, her head tilted to listen. He clears his throat and begins. "My mother is the nominal queen of Talamh. They call her 'the Robber Queen' because they think she stole the throne."

"Did she?" Croi asks, forgetting to eat probably for the first time in her life.

"It would be better if she had. At least that would mean she wants the throne she's stuck with," Irial says, his voice bitter.

"Why doesn't she abdicate? Can't fae monarchs do that?"

"There are reasons she can't. Reasons I am not allowed to say. But I've noticed that she has become more secretive with the approach of the Saol ceremony. She has frequent meetings I am not invited to, conversations with her allies. She is making plans for something that she won't tell me about, and that worries me." Irial sighs, leaning back to stare at the forest canopy. Croi's dreamscape is quite detailed.

"What do you think she'll do?" Croi asks.

"I don't know what she *can* do." Irial frowns. "If we make it through the Saol ceremony, she will be stuck as queen for many more years. I heard her crying herself to sleep one night, and when I asked her ladies-in-waiting, they said it was a common occurrence. The Talamh throne, for all that she sits on it, is not hers. So, I thought that if I found the Forever King's heir, we could hand them the crown. Are you his heir?"

Croi makes a face at him. "I'm assuming this Forever King was fae?"

"Yes, of course. All monarchs are fae," Irial replies.

Croi remembers the Hag's lesson and sneers. "I'm not even fae. How could I be his descendant?"

Irial shrugs. "I just thought you were Glamoured to look like a brownie."

His words fall on Croi the way a knife falls on the neck of a chicken before it becomes food. It has almost the same effect. Croi wakes up gasping, her heart galloping in her chest.

Cold sweat dots her forehead as an unwanted realization blankets her horizons. The Hag doesn't do things without reason, so the books have more meaning than she accorded them. The Glamour spell is a sly presence within her, a burr snagging on her insides. Irial's words have unwittingly answered the question Croi doesn't recall asking.

She sits up, feeling uncomfortable. Her tiniest toe hurts suddenly. Engrossed in the idea that she might be under a Glamour, Croi initially dismisses the pain as petty discomfort.

Then the pain becomes deeper, becomes an ache. All the bones in her feet are waking. Their awakening affects the rest of the bones in her body, which feel as though they are sitting up and stretching, trying to move out of the flesh that confines them.

White-hot agony stretches from her toes to her ankles, journeys up her legs to her thighs. Her hip bones creak a protest before her back arches as her spine rebels against the shape it has been forced into. The pain travels down her shoulders, thrums through her elbows before scorching her fingertips. Her skull tries to reconstruct itself, and that is when everything goes dark for a few minutes.

When Croi comes to, she is lying facedown on the ground, her fingers sunk into the soil. Her body spasms, a broken marionette of some diabolical puppeteer. She takes a deep gasping breath and trembles. A taste of tears lingers on her tongue, a taste of the earth.

As the pain fades, the absence of sound becomes louder. Her throat is raw, her cheeks are wet, and her heart is a mess. She tries to get to her feet but her knees buckle. The flower sprites cling to her, chittering in high-pitched voices, trying to provide comfort. However, she doesn't have the strength to respond to their goodwill. She tries to stand up again and succeeds this time. The ground seems farther away now than it did before. She takes a step toward the dwelling and

stumbles. To settle her fawn legs, she stands still for a moment, trying to understand what just happened to her. Her mind retreats from thinking about the pain; it's a monster she doesn't want to provoke. What if it returns?

Croi lifts her hands and stares at her fingers. They look longer in the starlight. Something rustles in the forest close by, and she startles, peering into the darkness. The trees that surround the dwelling seem unfriendly all of a sudden. She is so desperately alone. Even if she screams for mercy, no one will hear. She resolutely turns her back to the trees and enters the dwelling, lies down on some blankets in a corner, and shuts her eyes.

The sun spilling into the dwelling through the spaces in the branches wakes Croi up the next morning. The light intrudes in all the shadowed corners of the room and seeps through the thin blanket she is hiding under. A direction echoes in her head when her eyes yield to the inevitable and flutter open. There is a tug in her middle as though someone has begun pulling on a rope attached there. Her feet seem bent on answering a summons her ears can't hear. She sits up, her chest hurting. She gets up without even thinking about moving. Her hands wash her face, clean her teeth, and feed her fruits while her mind tries to regain control of her suddenly rogue body. She doesn't know what is happening to her. Is this what unraveling feels like?

Did the Hag know that a summons would come for her this morning? Croi milks the cow, battles the hens for eggs, and packs a bag, all without choosing to. Her newly awakened bones demand, and her brain insists on answering.

Her packed bag contains stolen bread, a flask of water, gaudy scarves she took from a merchant in the human city, and a spare dress made of green bark. She packs the book detailing the peoples of the Otherworld and leaves the one she can't read, the one titled *The Talamh Crown*, behind.

The bag is slung over her shoulder, and she is poised to walk away when she grits her teeth and digs her feet into the earthen floor. Croi has spent a lot of her hours in this dwelling, sunk many minutes into the ground here. Surely she has forged a bond to this land that should anchor her until the Hag returns. She pulls herself to the middle of the dwelling, her body fighting against the direction she's moving in. The flower sprites hold on to her with their slight bodies, trying to keep her stationary. Time passes, and the urge to leave becomes so intense that she is standing and walking to the entrance without realizing it. At the last moment, her arms go around the trunk of one of the trees that form a pillar of her dwelling. She holds on tight and exerts all her will over a body that seems determined to betray her.

It is then that she feels the Hag's presence. The guardian feels like the lack of pain, like deliverance from this compulsion to move. She feels like safety.

She emerges from the trees like an answer to Croi's unspoken prayers. Her steps are unhurried; she moves with the grace unique to her. She flows up the path, through the garden, and comes to stop in front of the not-brownie.

Croi looks up at her and feels hot tears slip down her cheeks. Despite their prickly relationship, the Hag is her only family.

"You're still here," the Hag says, her face expressionless as always. "I expected you to have already left."

"What?" Her words shock Croi still, until pain lances through her. This pain has nothing to do with her bones and everything to do with her heart. "You knew . . . ?" she whispers, then laughs. Of course she did. Her words yesterday prove as much. Croi takes a shaky breath. "What's happening to me?"

"I left you the books for a reason, Croi." The Hag's eyes are infinitely old, and in this moment of half-truths and impending abandonment, Croi can feel her guardian's age in her bones.

"Someone Glamoured me?" she croaks. "You?"

"No. This is not my work," the Hag says.

"Then who?" Croi demands.

The Hag doesn't reply.

"The person who placed a summoning spell on me?" she tries again, but it's no use.

The urge to walk away becomes more intense, and she gets more desperate.

"I really am not a brownie?" She begs for an answer. "You said I was! We cannot lie!"

"I did not lie, child. You *were* a brownie. However, you are no longer one."

"If not a brownie, what am I?"

"You will find out."

"I want to know now."

"It is not allowed."

"Whose law are you following?"

"I cannot say," she replies in the same uninflected voice. Croi cannot read a single emotion from her.

"You cannot say?" Croi repeats, her voice thick with tears. She laughs a little. "Of course you can't. I should have known. Is there *anything* you want to say to me?"

The Hag turns her head for a moment before speaking. "Tell the princess I did my part. I have paid off my debt. Tell her I owe her nothing more."

Time, that trickster, freezes. Croi looks at the Hag, standing serene in front of her. Unaffected and cold, like always.

"I was a debt to you? That's all?" Her voice cracks and she sucks in a breath, trying to keep her emotions in check. The Hag doesn't like it when she is too excitable. "What if I promise to always listen to you? I will be so quiet, it will be like I don't exist. I will never go to the human city again, all right? I will stay right here every day. Please don't make me go like this. Please!"

The Hag doesn't meet her eyes. "Do not tell anyone about yourself. Do not trust anyone. The forest paths are far more sinister than you think them to be. Be aware and be alert because the forest will no longer recognize you as kin. While the Glamour is in the process of breaking, you are not kin but something in between. Until the spell is broken, the forest will consider you a stranger." The Hag stops speaking, hesitates, and finally meets Croi's eyes. "I will remember you."

Then she turns and walks away, leaving Croi looking after her, like a fool.

She used to play a game when she was little. She would try to find the softness in the Hag's eyes. The softness would be a good enough substitute for the love she was sure the Hag would never be capable of. Croi was sure she would catch her unawares one day and see the emotion on her face, in her eyes. She was certain she would at the very least hear it in her voice. It took some years before Croi finally understood. You cannot expect softness from a creature made of stone.

Croi lets go of the tree trunk, and her feet start moving. She looks back once and murmurs a farewell to the garden, to the flower sprites, to the dwelling, and to the Croi who lived there.

Her goodbye tastes of pain, feels like forever, and smells like the earth, wet from the rain.

FOUR

THE WILDE FOREST IS A STRANGER TO HER NOW. CROI no longer knows her curves, and the forest, in turn, shows her no softness. Croi stumbles over roots, slips on muddy patches, and is attacked by briars. She suspects the vines of harboring sinister plans and the trees, with their coarse barks, of providing less comfort than they used to.

The pull in the middle of her stomach is steady and no longer as intense as it was before she started walking. Her feet seem to know where to go, so she lets them carry her away. Who is this princess the Hag mentioned? Could she be Croi's mother? The word "mother," however, is too strange. Her tongue curls around the unfamiliar syllables; the expected sweetness is missing.

Why would a mother put a Glamour on her own child? Cast a summoning spell? Croi hasn't met any kin mothers, so she's not sure, but human mothers don't seem to hurt their children as a rule. Croi dismisses the idea. The princess the Hag mentioned cannot possibly be her mother. Surely no mother would be that cruel to her child.

She sucks in a breath and thinks of the stone maid. Will the stone maid think she has been abandoned? Will the stone maid hate her? Croi rubs her eyes when they sting. Her steps are slow and her feet drag, but the summoning spell pulls her forward regardless.

As she walks deeper into the forest, she thinks about the kin she might meet on her journey. All she knows about them is what she has learned from the books. How should she talk to them? What if she says the wrong thing and angers them? Croi has learned the correct etiquette, but theory is different from practice. Angry faces don't bother her much, but what if their anger moves their hands and they try to hurt her?

When the light in the forest dims and a chill finds its way under her dress, Croi comes across a hollow in a wide-trunked tree and examines it curiously. She has always had an amicable relationship with trees. Perhaps it's because she is—no, she *was*—the Hag's own, but she has always felt warmth emanating from them. Now that she has left the Hag—no, now that she has been thrown away by the Hag—they have become alien to her. But she has no other place to go, and she'd much rather be in the hollow than on the ground, so she shrugs and crawls in. It's a snug fit, and she has to curl up tight, but she is safe and warm. Exhaustion slides its gnarly fingers up her body. She hurts all over, but it is the uncertainty about who she is, what she is, that makes her shiver. She tries to curl up into as small a not-brownie as she can. Fear is an unfamiliar emotion. It resides in her chest, and when she pokes at it, it bites her insides.

She is not a brownie. But if not a brownie, what is she? Not a human. The Hag would never keep her around if she were one. Perhaps she is a sylph or maybe a goblin. A centaur? Croi doesn't fancy being part horse, though. She would like to be a pixie, but they're tiny, so she'd be shrinking instead of growing taller.

She has been living a lie for almost seventeen years. No wonder her body didn't . . . doesn't make sense to her.

The thoughts are distressing, so she decides to think about food instead. Chicken, roasted with sweet onions, garlic, and rosemary; baked potatoes sprinkled with salt, herbs, and cheese; savory vegetable stew. Sweet cakes dripping with honey and custard tarts hot from the oven. Apple cider, delicious whether chilled or warm. Her stomach growls its longings, and her mouth waters.

All she has are slightly squashed berries, some stale bread, and tepid water. No one would call that a feast. She deflates and hugs herself in the hollow, deciding that her need for sleep is far greater than her need for food. Just as she is on the cusp of unconsciousness, the pain hits again.

She grits her teeth, determined to be braver tonight. Biting down on an orange scarf helps to drown her screams. The pain is doing its best to splinter her like wood under an axe. The moment of agony stretches halfway to forever, and just when she thinks the pain is gone, it returns.

Croi doesn't know how long the pain continues—minutes may have been screamed into hours—but when it ends, she is draped over the roots of an obliging tree. Sitting up hurts, breathing hurts. *Existing* hurts.

The human city has old human women who linger in the streets or in the doorways of their homes, their joints swollen by age. Croi is not old, but her bones have already become unfriendly. She leans against the tree for a while, waiting for the pain to ease. It doesn't. A twig digging into the small of her back becomes unendurable, so she stands up and realizes that she will no longer fit into the tree hollow. She has grown again. Hunger quakes her insides, so she eats her berries and bread and curls up by the roots of the tree. The forest is singing itself night melodies, and she lets them lull her to sleep.

The dream finds Croi fleeing from a murder of trees. They are determined to spill her blood, and she . . . She has four feet? Croi stops running abruptly when she realizes that in addition to four feet, she also has a tail and a large bulky body. She is currently a centaur.

"Are you the descendant of the Forever King?" The question is as familiar as the voice speaking it.

Croi turns around with some difficulty to see the blurry form of her nocturnal visitor, Irial. "Why are you in my dream again?"

"Again?" He walks closer to her, and his incredibly beautiful face appears before her. "It's you? Weren't you a brownie last time? You . . . remember me?"

"It turns out that you are very difficult to forget," Croi tells him, feeling her heart beat faster. It's not him that fascinates her. To be honest, anyone who has a face like his would make her heart race. Her tail moves in accordance with her thoughts. Croi freezes at the feeling of a tail. She tries to move it again, but it refuses to obey her mental commands.

"You're not supposed to be able to remember!" Irial sounds upset. Croi glances at him and finds the fae's face conspicuously missing the little smile that seemed to have a home in his eyes. "Your memories are supposed to fade as soon as you wake up. That's the specialty of the scrying spell I use."

"Clearly your spell is faulty because I remember every single word you said," Croi says, enjoying the flustered look on his face. "Don't worry, I won't tell anyone. I mean, I only have trees around me, and I don't think they care about the politics of an Otherworld kingdom."

"Where are you?" Irial doesn't look convinced by her reassurance.

"In the human world. Before you ask, I've never been to the Otherworld, but I reckon that's where I'm headed. I have a summoning spell on me. Hmm. How about this? Since you told me your secrets, I will tell you mine. Deal?"

"Thank you?" Croi doesn't know why his thank-you is a question, but before she can ask, Irial speaks. "Why are you a centaur right now? Is that your true shape?" His question returns Croi immediately to the bleak circumstances she had just managed to forget.

She blanches at his question. "I hope not. It turns out you jinxed me."

"Jinxed you?" Irial wrinkles his face at the accusation. "How?"

"You guessed it right. I *am* Glamoured, except I don't know what my true shape is. It's not a brownie, and I'm hoping it isn't a centaur."

"Are you sure you're not a centaur?" Irial asks.

"No? How can I be sure of something like that? Should I try eating grass? Do centaurs eat grass?" Croi looks at the grass on the ground but doesn't find it appetizing in the least.

"No. They're carnivores," Irial replies.

"Do you know any?"

"Yes, there was an envoy from the herd living in the Glas Plains two summers ago. They brought along some of their artisans to send to the School—" Croi listens to Irial speak and feels sadder. She doesn't know the places he speaks of.

"It must be nice to know who you are and where you belong," she says softly, interrupting him.

"Not really." Irial knots his fingers together, a sneer on his face. "You can't belong to a place when you're always treated like an outsider."

"If we're going to compete about who between us is more pitiful, I will remind you that you at least know what shape is natural to you. I don't." Croi sniffs, overwhelmed by sudden self-pity.

Irial's face softens, and he pats her on the back. "Do you want to talk about it?"

"What do you think I'm doing right now?" She rolls her eyes at him. "Is your mother still being secretive? Did you talk to her?"

It is Irial's turn to sigh. He runs a hand through his hair. Croi wonders if his hair is as soft as it looks. Then she decides she needs to concentrate on more important things, like what's happening to her body.

"I asked her what she's grappling with, and she told me that I don't need to worry about anything. That she'll keep me safe." He scowls. "I'm her only child and the only other person in our family. Why won't she trust me a little more?"

Croi considers his question carefully. "Perhaps she thinks the less you know, the safer you will be?"

"But I don't even know what the danger is! What is she wary about?" He clenches his fists, frustration evident in the stiff set of his shoulders.

"I can't help you with that. Sorry." Croi really is. For some reason, she thinks she wouldn't mind helping Irial figure things out.

"No, this isn't your problem. I'm the one who's sorry. You're going through enough as it is. Do you know who cast the summoning spell on you?" Irial asks, and Croi shrugs.

"Nope. The Hag, the creature who raised me, only called her 'the princess.' Do I look like I know royalty? Wait, I *do* know royalty! Your mother is a queen, so you must be a prince. What do they call you?" Croi huffs, and her throat makes a strange horse noise. Her cheeks go red. At least she thinks they go red. She's not sure whether centaurs can blush.

Irial bows his head; his eyes are bleak. "The Robber Prince."

"Sounds dashing," Croi says. He gives her an uncertain look. "No, really. It's better than being called something like the Potato Prince, right?" She coaxes a reluctant smile out of him. "Anyway, why do you keep appearing in my dreams? I've already told you that I'm not the Forever King's descendant."

"I know, but the spell keeps on sending me to you," Irial says, and shrugs.

"Do you think I could be the Forever King's descendant under my Glamour?" Croi says. "That would mean I have a family, wouldn't it?"

Irial's eyes narrow, and a bitter expression settles uneasily on his face. "I hope you aren't. We'll become enemies if you are."

"Why?" Croi asks.

He avoids her eyes. "The Forever King's family and mine have . . . Well, my mother *is called* the Robber Queen, remember?"

"Ah, right. People think she stole the Talamh crown."

"You can say that."

"But why would that make us enemies? The Forever King is gone and I never knew him. Whatever happened was between the dead. You and I are still alive." Croi blinks at the fae who is looking gob-smacked by her words. "No?"

"Yes. You are right." He gives her the sweetest smile—well, all right, the only smile she has ever received—and Croi finds her heart racing again. "Thank you."

"What for?"

Instead of replying, Irial gives her centaur self a hug. It's awkward, but he smells like sunshine on a summer day. Croi takes a deep breath, trying to savor the feeling of her first hug. But perhaps she's too excited because the dream cracks at this moment and morning arrives in a clamor of birdsong. No matter how tightly Croi holds on to sleep, it flees, leaving her no choice but to wake. Finally, reluctantly, Croi opens her eyes, and when she does, the world explodes.

FIVE

HE COLORS ARE RIOTING.

The green flings itself off the leaves of the trees and assaults Croi's eyes. The brown of the barks fractures into a thousand shades. Patches of blue visible through the forest canopy shimmer smugly. White flowers are bewitching in their purity. Shades of red and orange undulate while threads of acid pink knot the veins of leaves. Sunlight separates into golden motes and then comes together in a flash. Blinded, Croi squeezes her eyes closed and concentrates on breathing.

She is not certain she can remember how.

Croi takes a deep breath and pushes all thoughts aside; she opens her eyes slowly, ready to close them again if the colors refuse to behave. A moment passes. Everything is still too bright and painfully intense, but the green eventually settles down and the brown stops dancing. The reds and oranges still glow, however, and the white flowers pierce her eyes.

She looks around, drinking in the Wilde Forest around her. It feels like a new place. With her changed eyes, she can see farther than she could before; the nooks, the hollows, and the dips no longer hide secrets. Light refracts in strange ways and reveals things that weren't previously visible. Croi's changed eyes paint a new picture of the forest, a clearer, brighter picture. She looks up and sees the leaves high in the trees that shine as though they're infused with light. The smallest plant has a shine. Even the ants are shining.

The soles of her feet prickle. When she looks down, she finds silver-brown lines dissecting the forest floor; these visible, yet intangible, lines crisscross and intersect in random directions. Her eyes widen when she sees several green-brown strands wrapped around her middle and leading off into the distance. These strands are damaged; there are holes in the wider ones, as if they were burnt by something strong. Though tense, the strands are not currently pulling her but have the potential to. When Croi tries to break them, they sting her fingers. This is the summoning spell.

Croi glares at the strands, calling them a filthy word she learned in the human world. The word doesn't do anything to the strands, but uttering it does make her feel better. She wonders how Irial would react to the word and decides to teach it to him the next time he appears.

She brings up a hand to scratch the itch on her nose and goes still when she realizes that *she* is glowing too. Unlike everything else that is lit by one kind of light, she is lit by two. One of the strands is green with brown bits, much like pebbles, in it, and the other is an orange, with yellow in places. The strands spark when she looks at them, but they avoid her when she tries to touch them. They are clearly tangible, but they just don't let her touch them. Even as they travel through the veins in her body.

She tries for a long while until her stomach rumbles, sourly reminding her of her obligations to it. Sorely, she gives up on the two strands. Perhaps when the Glamour breaks further, she'll be able to touch them.

Breakfast is staler bread and sips of water. Croi empties the flask, but it does nothing to slake her thirst. She pats the tree she spent the night with and thanks it like the Hag has taught her to. Next, she sniffs the air and follows the direction of the moisture.

Finding a stream, she drinks until she's content, and refills her flask. She returns to the forest and takes two steps forward when a strange vertigo hits her. She sways, throwing her arms out, desperately trying to find purchase, but it's no use. She falls forward.

Her face hits the grass-covered ground, and though the impact isn't especially painful—not as painful as her growing bones are, anyway—it still hurts. She sits up with some difficulty and a lot of consternation before looking around. Her mouth drops open. Where she is now isn't where she was a minute ago. Somehow, during that period of swaying and dizziness, she was transported to a clearing in a part of the Wilde Forest she doesn't recognize. The clearing isn't especially large, but it is ringed by trees of a species Croi hasn't seen before. The most conspicuous of them has wide and thick branches, which grants it a majesty uncommon to trees in a forest. Its leaves are a curious green shot with gold veins. It is refulgent, glowing brighter than any other tree nearby. Croi gets to her feet and walks to it, poking at its trunk, a little curious about the texture of its bark.

All of a sudden, three images are transmitted into her mind: tall, robed fae; dead trees; empty space. Croi gapes at the tree, comprehending what it's telling. This isn't a natural clearing but a fae-made one. For what purposes?

Croi pokes the tree again, but no other images follow the first three. In the midst of poking and thinking, the summoning spell decides her reprieve is over and starts pulling at her feet again. The strands of the magick yank her, forcing her to walk forward right until she

reaches the end of the clearing. Her foot is raised to take another step when her body bumps into a barrier that she can barely see. Motes of white magick are layered around the perimeter of the clearing. Croi is thrown back from the sudden collision. Her feet drag her forward, and once again, her body is unable to pass the barrier.

She looks around the clearing, feeling the air in her chest dry. Her heart pounds and her forehead becomes damp with sweat. She squints at the magick motes in the air, and they reorganize themselves to create a fine netlike structure, effectively trapping her in.

SIX

NAUSEA COLORS EVERYTHING GRAY FOR A MOMENT before the summoning spell renews its efforts to move her body. Despair, chalky and pervasive, grips Croi; she gives up fighting and once again becomes a broken marionette to the summoning spell's puppet master, her body moving forward and being repelled by the barrier over and over again. This occurs half a dozen times before the tree with the gold-and-green leaves sends out a tensile vein, which winds around Croi's wrist and, with unexpected strength, drags her away from the edge of the clearing and closer to itself.

Croi stumbles and grabs a low-lying branch of the tree, not even feeling the splinter that digs into the soft skin between her thumb and her forefinger. She is exhausted at this moment, tired of this world, tired of the hundred different shades of pain her body seems determined to learn, tired of it all. She slumps against the tree.

The air inside the clearing gets heavier, pressing against her skin, making it difficult to breathe. The vine squeezes her wrist tight, and Croi turns, trying to pull herself free. She glances at the tree, and what she sees has her forgetting the vine completely.

The surface of the tree trunk is rippling as though something alive underneath it is struggling to get out. Croi watches breathlessly as a face sculpted by golden strands of magick becomes outlined on the tree trunk. First to appear are thick lips, high cheekbones, large eyes that are closed, and a pointed chin. Then slender limbs push out of the tree, and with an audible pop, a body is birthed. This creature has the shape of a woman, but her face doesn't know age the way human faces do. Her hair is dark and ropy, threaded with green tendrils, leaves, and vines. Her skin is the ashy gray of the tree trunk, and she's clothed in linked leaves that reveal more than they hide. She smells green, like the forest around them, like the Hag Croi left behind.

The dryad opens her eyes; they are the same golden green as her leaves. She takes a deep breath and smiles widely. Sharp, pointy teeth give her smile a dangerous edge. They also alarm Croi. The dryad twirls around, once, and then again. She spreads her arms and embraces the air. Done, she turns to Croi and looks her over with an intensely curious gaze.

The tree creature is ablaze with a light that is the exact golden green that her eyes and the leaves of her tree are.

"Well, well, well." The dryad lingers over each word. Her voice sounds like an afternoon breeze rustling the leaves of a poplar tree. She speaks Faerish. "I have caught a little maybe. A very strange little maybe."

Caught things don't last very long. Humans usually eat what they catch. *Croi* eats what she catches. And what does she mean by a "little maybe"? Croi decides that she does not like this kin.

The tree creature stares at Croi's eyes a moment too long. Her smile slips, leaving her face cold and inhuman. Then she regains her equanimity and grace, moving in front of Croi, looking her up and down. "Whatever shall I do with you?"

She rubs her hands together with the same expression on her face that Croi makes when she sees a table full of food. Croi's heart is a stone in the sea.

"What are you, little maybe?" The dryad comes nearer and sniffs the air around Croi, who hasn't bathed for a while now. The smell should be ripe. Croi meets the dryad's eyes, and the summoning spell falters under the tree creature's regard. Her feet stop moving. The dryad's face creases. "I'm trying to read your blood, but there is an obstruction. . . ."

Blood? Suddenly the splinter in Croi's hand digs deeper, and the dryad closes her eyes as if relishing some flavor on her tongue.

She shakes her head after a while, looking frustrated. "Your blood tastes as though I know it. I feel as though I should know its name, but strangely, I can't speak it. Is what you are a secret?" Her eyes are bright. "I do so love secrets. Tell me." She moves closer to Croi with each sentence until her face is barely a breath away.

"I used to be the Hag's brownie," Croi offers.

"The Hag?" The dryad's voice drops several octaves, and a peculiar expression arranges her features. A story is limned on that face. This dryad has her own secrets.

"The Hag of the Wilde Forest? Perhaps you know her?" Croi hopes the Hag's name and reputation are enough to save her.

"You *used* to be the Hag's brownie?" The dryad eyes her. "Are you no longer? Why can't I recognize you as kin?"

"I'm no longer the Hag's, nor am I a brownie," Croi replies after a long moment. That particular betrayal is far too fresh to speak of.

"What are you, then?"

Croi shrugs. "I have no idea."

The dryad doesn't seem to believe her words. A second later, the splinter burrows farther into her flesh. Croi hisses her pain, but the dryad's face clears.

"It turns out that your blood is heavily magicked, and with dragon magick at that. Hmm. A Glamouring this strong has to be done with the aid of dragon magick. Who has been consorting with dragons without my knowledge? But, ah! The Glamour is breaking, is it not?"

Croi stares at the dryad wide-eyed. "Did you say 'dragon magick'? No, more importantly, do you know what I am underneath this Glamour?"

The dryad gives her a long look, something suspiciously like pity flitting through her eyes. In the end, however, she doesn't answer Croi's questions and lifts a shoulder in a languid shrug. "You will find out when you need to."

Croi scoffs. Here is someone else who doesn't want to answer her questions. "Did someone trap you in here?" she asks the older kin instead.

"Trap me?" The dryad's laughter is a rich concoction of confidence and power. "No one can trap *me*. I am the keeper of this clearing, little maybe. I take care of the humans who wander where they should not."

"But why are you holding *me*? I'm not human!" Croi is greatly offended.

"You aren't, but as I said, I can't tell if you are kin. The magick can't either, so it brought you to this clearing for my evaluation," the dryad explains.

"Now that you know I'm kin, can you let me go?" Croi shakes the wrist the vine is wrapped around.

"If I don't hold you, you will be walking to wherever the spell is summoning you." Croi winces, unable to deny the tree creature's words. "Who is summoning you?"

Croi doesn't reply. She doesn't know the answer.

The dryad doesn't appear to mind Croi's silence. She beams at her and walks around the tree, nearly skipping, infused with a glee Croi cannot understand. "You don't have to answer. I will eventually find out." She laughs out loud, her pleasure in being alive evident. "This is all very exciting. I haven't been out of my tree in nearly a millennium. I have a lot to thank you for."

"If you're so thankful, will you satisfy a curiosity of mine?" This is really not the right time, but Croi will seize any opportunity she can.

"All right. Go ahead and ask." The dryad inclines her head.

"If a flesh-and-blood kin was turned into stone, would you be able to break the spell and return her to her original form?" Croi asks.

"Who is the kin trapped in the stone body?" The dryad comes to a stop in front of Croi, and the full force of her power hits Croi in her empty stomach. The dryad is old, far older than the Hag; her accumulated years are an uncomfortable weight on Croi's shoulders. The flippancy drains away from her eyes, and she looks at Croi seriously for the very first time. "How long has the kin been stone?" the dryad asks. A cricket chirps to punctuate the question.

"I don't know," Croi replies. "She has been stone in all the time I've known her. About eleven years."

"How do you know she's kin?" the dryad asks next.

"She's alive underneath the stone." Croi looks at the dryad with bright eyes. "Can you break the spell on her?"

The dryad frowns. Croi waits, her fingers curled into fists. After a while, the dryad clicks her tongue and shakes her head.

"You can't?" Croi asks. She shouldn't have gotten her hopes up.

However, contrary to her expectations, the dryad says, "I can. I just don't have a reason to."

"You need to have a reason to help someone?" Croi growls. "Do you, like the Hag, not have a heart either?"

The dryad swoops in, invading her space once more; Croi moves back, only to press against the tree trunk. Her heart is running amok

in her chest, but she refuses to show her fear. The dryad raises a finger and presses it to Croi's cheek. Immediately, there's a crackling sound, and the smell of burnt wood infuses the air. The dryad springs back, holding her finger to her chest in a gesture of protection.

"A shield." She narrows her eyes. "Who are you?"

At Croi's silence, she asks again, "What is your name, little maybe?"

Croi doesn't speak. Names have power, and she has too little of it to start giving it away.

"If you don't tell me, I will leave you in this clearing, trapped and vulnerable to whatever horrors the forest dreams up." The dryad's threat is accompanied by a sweet smile. Croi sucks in a breath. "Do you know what happens when you resist a summoning spell?"

"No. What happens?" Croi asks in a shaky whisper.

"It tears you apart. Limb by limb." The dryad's voice drops a decibel. "Do you think you can endure the pain? Is that the end you're looking for?"

Croi bows her head, hating her traitorous eyes for filling with tears. A part of her is unsurprised by the forecast of pain. It has become her constant companion, more reliable than anyone she could have called her own.

"You just need to tell me your name," the dryad coaxes. "I will set you free."

Croi looks at the tree creature, alien and unknown. She knows better than to ask for kindness.

The dryad doesn't say another word, simply stands in front of Croi, so still she might as well have returned to her tree. Croi thinks of staying here forever, frozen in time, lost in time. She shudders; she wouldn't last a day.

"Croi. My name is Croi." She hands over the only thing she truly owns. If it means getting out of this clearing, she will make the sacrifice.

"Croi," the dryad repeats. On her tongue, the name is not just a sound but a touch, a power, a summons. The breeze that had been playing with the leaves dies down, and the insects stop their chittering. Even the trees seem to hold their collective breath. She says it again. "Croi."

Croi's bones twinge. That is the only warning.

She sags against the tree, her eyes squeezing shut as they begin to prickle. The prickles intensify until her eyes feel like they're being pierced by needles after being scrubbed by sand. Her insides shift, hesitate, and then shift again. Her throat burns. Her head feels like it will burst, and her fingers are hot like they're on fire. Her soles twist and her feet are reformed. The world slips away, and Croi falls into the familiar dark place where pain reigns supreme.

Soft words spoken in a language Croi doesn't understand but has heard before bring her back. Something has changed. The knowledge is a cold realization. She can feel the difference within, a butterfly's wings tickling her on the wrong side of her skin. She is no longer alone in her body.

SEVEN

THE DRYAD DID SOMETHING TO HER. SHE CALLED CROI by her name—no, she didn't just speak out the name. She *called* Croi and all of Croi answered. Not just the not-brownie she is, but also the other Croi, the one who beats like a heart somewhere inside this Glamoured body. She can feel this other her now. She is a warmth in Croi's chest and a whisper in her mind, as alive and aware as she is. Has this other Croi been trapped inside her, just like the stone maid is trapped inside her stone body? Croi flushes cold at the thought.

"Take a breath," the hoarse voice of the dryad commands.

Croi takes two.

"Who are you, little maybe?" the dryad whispers in her ear, wheedling. "Won't you tell me?" She is smiling, perhaps in anticipation of Croi's answer.

"No," Croi says, then blinks. "Do I sound different?"

The dryad peers at Croi, too close once again. She looks into

Croi's eyes, her own narrowed as if in thought. She hums a little before retreating.

"Yes. Your voice changed. The good thing is that you are no longer a little maybe. Your Glamour broke a little more. The forest will still not be able to, but I can recognize you as kin now."

Croi gives the dryad a sharp look. "What kind of kin?"

"I can't tell you that. I'm sorry," the dryad says, looking anything but.

"All right. Fine. Let me go now." Croi gives up trying to get answers from her. It seems that she is really not compatible with tree creatures.

"Croi . . . ," the dryad says again, entirely without warning, her voice catching onto the end of the syllable, the sound lingering in the air. A chill sweeps over Croi's suddenly fevered skin, and her body jerks. A command is laced through the sound her name makes on the dryad's lips. She is trying to claim Croi's name as her own. Croi lifts her head and looks at the tree creature. The light keeping the dryad ablaze surges in response to Croi's attention.

"Croi." And again.

Broken not-brownie, Glamoured, fractured, hurting not-brownie, abandoned not-brownie. Her legs point in a direction she doesn't want to go, and her body is coming apart, trying to assume a shape Croi isn't sure it can. And now, yet another being with power tries to steal her from herself.

Croi has never felt this fire before, never before tasted this rage. She isn't sure how she does it, but suddenly she opens her mouth, and she wills the dryad's light to herself. Though she is deaf to the light's song, Croi knows somehow that it will listen to hers. She is singing to the light with words that she forgets as soon as she speaks them, and the light responds sluggishly. It spills through the dryad's ashy skin and bleeds through her eyes. The dryad's light tries to make *Croi* shine.

The dryad screams, the sound of trees falling in storms, and scrambles backward, away from Croi.

When she can't hold it any longer, Croi lets go of the dryad's light, and it slithers back to her. Dimmer. Muted. Croi watches as fear settles on the tree creature's face. It is her turn to smile. If power is the only language the dryad can comprehend, Croi will learn to speak it.

EIGHT

OBSERVE:
One very surprised dryad, lying on the ground with limbs awkwardly splayed; two halves of one Croi, still held prisoner by the tree; and the silent forest, judging them both.

Croi doesn't take her eyes off the dryad, whose glowing orbs do not move from her face. They are at an impasse. Croi's not sure how she called the dryad's light to her or if she can do it again. She has to hope that the idea of losing her light frightens the dryad enough that she won't try to claim Croi's name anymore.

The trunk of the tree is rough behind Croi's back; twigs dig into her hips. Her face is somehow crusted with mud. The tree-bark dress she's wearing is filthy and suddenly short, and her soles hurt. Her hunger is a hollow ache and fatigue a heavy weight on her shoulders. Yet she has never felt as alive as she does at this moment, in front of someone who can destroy her so completely that even yesterday wouldn't remember her name.

"Uaine," the dryad breathes after one moment turgid with silence. *Oon-ya*. Croi looks at her cautiously, stiffening in case she tries something else.

Her incomprehension must have made itself clear because the dryad adds, "My name. Uaine." She rests her elbows on knees she has drawn up to her chest, props her face on her hands, and looks up at Croi. "I'm giving it to you."

Giving it? Like dessert?

"Will you accept it?" A glint in the dryad's eyes warns against complacency.

"Why?" First the dryad tries to steal Croi's name. Now she offers Croi hers. No one just *offers* their name. At least that's what the Hag has taught her.

"Consider it a test." The dryad seems to have recovered her equilibrium. Was she not scared at all? She gets up from the ground and stalks over. Croi tries to keep her face blank and fails miserably. "Are you brave enough to take it?"

Brave? Croi is absolutely sure she is no such thing. But if she doesn't take the dryad's name, what else can she do? She cannot stay here, tethered to this tree forever. Besides, how many other ways can she break? How much more can she hurt?

So before she can consider the consequences, she speaks the name, and even before the second syllable leaves her mouth, she knows she has made a mistake. Too late, she remembers the Hag's warning: true names can only be taken by those who are stronger than the person whose name they are speaking.

The dryad is ancient—numbers surrender their meaning in the face of her age. Her experiences are vast and varied; they have rubbed the curves of her name smooth and sweetened the sound of it. On Croi's lips, her name becomes a living thing and presses down. Croi sees visions of grand halls and gatherings of kin. She sees two faces, much like the dryad's, laughing together. She experiences the numerous farewells the dryad has made in her life, the pulsing moments of joy and the barbed notes of despair. Croi sags against the tree trunk; she's drowning, or she may be burning as the essence of everything the dryad is tries to subsume all that Croi is. She feels both too full and too small. Uaine's name stretches itself all around her and then sinks deeper, through her skin and into her blood. The moment the name reaches Croi's blood, a peculiar knowing fills her. Her chest throbs once, and the heaviness of the dryad's name dissipates as though she has held it before, if not on her tongue then in her blood. The name finds a place in Croi's chest, somewhere near her heart, to call home.

Croi breathes heavily, too shocked to do anything more. She's still alive. That much she's certain of. Just in case, she pinches herself. Yes, it hurts. So she's definitely alive, which means she survived taking the dryad's name. She has no idea how she managed this feat, but she's not going to complain. She can still feel the name in her chest—like a hot needle. Uncomfortable but not impossible. She swallows and looks at the dryad, foolish pride lifting her chin.

Croi expects her to be angry, but Uaine confounds her. She smiles—no, a smile is a rather pallid description; she beams at Croi, her light reacting to her suddenly ebullient mood and brightening.

"What now?" Croi asks, readying herself.

"Now I will tell you a story," the dryad says, sitting back down on the ground and getting comfortable.

"Story?" Croi frowns. "A tale?"

"Some people would call it a legend and others, history. Will you listen?"

"Do I have a choice?"

"No, not really." Uaine smiles sweetly.

"In that case, I'm all ears," Croi replies.

"Once upon a time, I had two sisters—" Uaine begins.

"Do you no longer?" Croi interrupts. The dryad gives her a long stare. "I'm just asking. Sorry. Please continue."

"My sisters and I protected the magick of Talamh and the lives of the kin who call it home," the dryad says softly.

"Oh no." Croi closes her eyes and holds up her free hand to hide her face.

"What?" Uaine says flatly.

"I'm getting ready for the twist. It's obvious you no longer protect Talamh and your sisters are nowhere to be seen." Croi keeps her eyes closed. "Go on!"

"Things happened. My sisters and I broke up. My youngest sister remained in Talamh while my middle sister and I left," Uaine finishes.

Croi opens her eyes. "That's it? That's your story?"

"What else did you expect?"

"Well, you started it with so much pomp . . ." She trails off when she sees Uaine's glare. "Why are you telling me this *story* anyway?" Her emphasis on the word makes a question out of it.

The frivolity fades from Uaine's face, and her regard for Croi becomes serious. "You say you've spent your entire life in the human world, yes?" Croi nods and she continues. "What do you know about the Otherworld? To be specific, do you know the origin of the four elemental kingdoms of the Otherworld?"

Croi nods. She had been reluctant to learn, but the Hag had taught her anyway. She recites obediently, "The great warrior Fionar and her companions, tired of the constant bloodshed among the kin as they grappled for power and the right to rule the Otherworld, sacrificed themselves to separate the one magick into four different magicks, thereby severing the united lands of the Otherworld into four different elemental kingdoms."

"And the Saol ceremony?" Uaine prompts in a decidedly Hag-ish way. Croi gives her a sharp look but decides to continue being obedient. Uaine's teeth are very sharp.

"The Saol ceremony is conducted every seventeen years to ensure the elemental magicks remain separated." Croi regurgitates what the Hag taught her.

"And the HeartStones?" Uaine raises an eyebrow.

Croi sighs but faithfully narrates. "The HeartStones are conduits through which the monarch of a kingdom bonds to the elemental magick of the kingdom. Without the HeartStone, the monarch of the kingdom will not be able to bond to the magick. If the monarch is unable to bond to the elemental magick, the magick cycle, where magick that a kin is born with returns to the land after they die, will break. Once the magick cycle breaks, kin will start dying in large numbers. As if this isn't grave enough, the Saol ceremony will be impossible without the HeartStones of all four elemental kingdoms. If the Saol ceremony is not completed, the four elemental kingdoms will cease to exist as the lands will unite once again and chaos will reign as it did once before. In simpler terms, without a HeartStone, life will be terrible and no one will be happy."

Uaine nods, satisfied. "So, the Talamh HeartStone is missing."

"You . . . *what*?" Croi gapes at the dryad. "No, wait, the earth HeartStone is missing? Are you sure? How do you know?"

"My sister sent word," Uaine replies.

"Which sister?"

"The one who resides in Talamh Caisleán. She awoke not long ago in preparation for the Saol ceremony and found the HeartStone missing."

"How did she tell you?"

"She sent word through magick. Yes, little kin, it's entirely possible to do that."

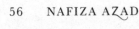

"But if the HeartStone is missing, won't . . . ? Has she searched everywhere?" Croi looks at Uaine with wide eyes.

"As much as she can," the dryad replies.

"Does she know who took it?" Croi asks.

"No," Uaine answers.

"Will the human world be affected?" Croi knows what shape home takes.

"The Otherworld is linked to the human world through the Wilde Forest, so the human world will not be spared the effects of whatever happens there," Uaine says.

"So"—Croi swallows—"what are you going to do?"

Uaine smiles at her and Croi has an ominous feeling. "To save the Otherworld, the human world, and yourself, you will need to help me."

"It's not that I don't want to help save the world." Croi coughs. "In fact, there's nothing I would rather do, but in case you haven't noticed, I am currently under the throes of a summoning spell."

"Oh, don't worry about that. I will break it for you," Uaine replies casually.

Croi croaks again. "You will what?"

"I will break it. A little summoning spell is not difficult for me to break."

Croi wets her lips, her throat suddenly dry. Does she dare hope?

"Of course, I will only do so on the condition that you will help me," the dryad adds.

"How can I help you?"

Uaine pauses and her eyes sweep the clearing, looking across a distance Croi can't fathom, at something she can't see. The dryad's eyes grow filmy with an immeasurable sadness before she turns back to Croi.

"By taking my SoulSeed to my sister."

There's a gravity to her words that Croi can't comprehend. She scrunches up her face and thinks hard. Has the Hag ever mentioned SoulSeeds before? She can't remember, but then again, she didn't always pay attention to the lessons the Hag taught.

"SoulSeeds are a secret held only by the dryads and those to whom they are loyal," Uaine elaborates. "It is what the humans would call a soul, and it contains everything we are, in the form of a seed. It is also the only way we can be moved from one place to another without dying."

"Why do you need to go to your sister?" Croi angles the dryad a glance. "There's no guarantee you will be able to find the HeartStone even if you take the risk and return."

The dryad smiles slightly at her words. "My sister might be the protector of the Talamh HeartStone, but I am the only one who can sense its presence. The HeartStone and I are made of the same vein of magick, you see."

"Not really, I don't," Croi replies, ignoring the dryad's stiffening face. "Aren't your sisters made of the same magick?"

Uaine presses her hand to her head as if Croi has made it hurt. "I cannot explain the intricacies of magick to you. You wouldn't ask the sky to explain its existence to a little cloud."

Croi makes a face at Uaine's analogy. "Rude."

"The question is, will you take my SoulSeed to my sister?" Uaine asks again.

"You're willing to trust me with it?" Croi looks disbelieving.

"No, of course not," Uaine says, shaking her head firmly just in case Croi doesn't know what "no" means. "I will require your word."

Croi wrinkles her nose and ponders. If she agrees to do what Uaine wants her to, she will just be exchanging one binding for another. Right now, though not insistent, she can feel the tug of the summoning spell in her bones. The pain that accompanies the spell pulses softly.

While the summoning spell tugs at her, hurts her, Uaine's binding would be a painless tether. If she gives the dryad her word, she will need to keep it. The Hag told horrible stories about the consequences of breaking one's word. There are many, and they involve agony and humiliation. But to be able to move as she pleases, as she wishes . . . Is there anything she wouldn't give for that?

"What will you do, little kin? Will you help me save the world?" The dryad stands in front of Croi with her hands on her hips, waiting for her answer.

NINE

CROI IS QUITE CERTAIN THAT SHE DOESN'T REALLY care for the fate of the world. It hasn't treated her very well in the short time she has been alive, so she feels no compunction in ignoring its needs. What she can't live with is the summoning spell.

Choose, the dryad says. As if there is a choice to be made. Is there anyone in any of the worlds who would choose to be a puppet?

"If you can break the spell . . ." Croi pauses, feeling her heart beat wildly in her chest. "I will do what you ask me to."

Uaine's lips stretch in a crafty smile, and she looks disturbingly pleased. Croi stares at the dryad, and beyond her she suddenly glimpses her destiny: dark and deadly, poised like a spider, waiting to engulf her in its web. She shakes herself and the image disappears.

"What happens if I lose the SoulSeed or some misfortune befalls it?" Croi knows herself well enough to want to be prepared for such eventualities.

"I die," Uaine replies simply. "You will not lose it."

There is no mirth on her face, no teasing look in her eyes, just a cold command that reminds Croi, once again, of the Hag.

"What if the circumstances are beyond my control? Will I still be breaking my word?"

"Yes."

Croi is not surprised by the dryad's answer. She shouldn't have expected anything else. This world is never fair to her. She sighs and looks around.

The hours have been passing, and the waning afternoon is stealing whatever daylight remains in the Wilde Forest. Shadows stick to the dryad, cleaving to her curves and shading her with their darkness. Croi shivers. Though the days are still warm in the grasp of summer, autumn sends her greetings on the tails of sudden breezes.

"There is one more thing you need to know," Uaine says. "When I remove the summoning spell, the protective shield around you will also be removed."

Croi smirks. "A protective shield? To stop others from causing me pain so she, whoever she is, can be the only one to hurt me? I don't care. Break it."

"You are decided," Uaine confirms, the comment more question than statement. Croi nods. "You give your word that you will take my SoulSeed to my sister who lives in Talamh Caisleán?"

"Where in Talamh Caisleán?" It is better to have her location clear before she gives her word.

"In the central hall of the Caisleán," Uaine replies.

"How much time do I have to get your SoulSeed there?"

"Before the Saol ceremony, so"—the dryad pauses, thinking—"nine days. Any more questions?" Croi shakes her head. "So? Do you give your word?"

"Yes," Croi replies. "I give my word that in exchange for breaking the summoning spell, I, Croi, will take your SoulSeed to your sister who lives in the central hall of Talamh Caisleán."

"Good. I will break the spell now," Uaine says, more warmly, now that Croi has decided to dance to her tune.

"Will it hurt?" Croi asks belatedly.

"Does not everything?" the dryad replies.

She stands in front of Croi, looking down at the damaged green-brown strands wrapped around Croi's torso and leading off into the distance. The dryad brings up her right hand, palm facing Croi. Her golden-green light, her magick, for what else can it be, brightens and surges when she spits out words in a language Croi remembers speaking but doesn't yet comprehend.

These words are all sharp angles and polished edges. For a long moment, nothing happens. Then, the green-brown threads wrapped around Croi twitch and grow unbearably taut. She is yanked forward violently, but Uaine's tree holds her firmly.

There's no give, and the spell is pulled tight between Croi and whoever is calling her—so tight that the distance melts away and for a second, just a blink, Croi can see the being who cast this spell, the one whom the Hag called the princess. It is a fleeting look, and all Croi is able to keep from this glimpse is the memory of the fae woman's eyes: a light brown, flecked with black and red, and ringed by forest green, and her damaged magick, green-brown strands with holes in them.

Croi goes warm and then cold. She feels as though she wants to both laugh and cry. Then she blinks and the person is gone. The spell cannot withstand the pressure put on it by Uaine's magick and breaks, severing their connection. The threads dissolve in the air. She is left with the echoes of the fae's emotions: desperation, regret, shock, and finally rage. There is no sweet tang of love or any bittersweet taste of longing. Whoever that fae was, Croi refuses to believe she is her mother.

"It is done," Uaine says, the tension flowing from her face.

It is. The incessant tug is gone. Croi no longer feels any urge to move. Her body is hers once again. It takes her a moment, however, to move on from the glimpse of the fae she saw. Her chest twinges sharply and she rubs it. "Can you remove your vine from around my wrist?" She shakes off the sudden melancholy and asks as sweetly as she can.

Uaine purses her lips, then the vine falls away from Croi's wrist. She takes one cautious step away from the tree. There's no pull; her limbs don't do their puppet dance. So she takes another step and another one and soon she's dancing. She laughs raucously and the birds scold her. She whirls round and round until she falls to the ground, out of breath.

"Are you done?" Uaine asks. She's leaning against her tree now, looking as though she'd like to disappear into its trunk again. Branches have rearranged themselves to form a bower for her.

"Maybe." Croi gives a hum of contentment and makes herself comfortable on the ground.

"Do you know how to get to the Talamh Caisleán?" Uaine asks.

"No." Croi scrunches up her face. "How do I get there?"

In response, Uaine looks her over. The dryad's gaze is cool and measuring as if the person she's looking at is not Croi but someone else. Croi frowns. She doesn't like the dryad's look.

"Stop looking at me like that," she tells the tree creature.

"Like what?" Uaine raises an eyebrow.

"Like you ordered a meaty stew and the waiter gave you a piece of cabbage instead. I'm not cabbage!"

Uaine grins suddenly, her earlier gloom dissipating as suddenly as it arrived. "This Hag you mention, did she teach you a great many things?"

"No, she wasn't a very good teacher," Croi replies. "She also didn't give me the answer to a very important question."

"And what question was that?"

"Why do the fae get to rule the Otherworld? Why can't brownies rule?"

"Brownies, being kinder, would be much better rulers," Uaine says. "Alas, brownie magick is not up to the task of ruling an elemental kingdom. Fae magick is." She glances at Croi. "You don't know why, do you?"

"Since you know I don't, why do you need to ask?" Croi grumbles.

"Well, it's not important at the moment. You will find out why when you need to." Uaine gives Croi a probing look.

"What is it?" Croi nods. "Are you thinking I'm not up to the task of transporting your SoulSeed? You should have thought of that before I gave my word! You aren't going to change your mind now, are you?"

The dryad doesn't reply and Croi gets more anxious.

"These Caisleáns aren't places I can easily waltz into . . . right?" She thinks of Irial and brightens. He lives in the Caisleán. He can help her find the central hall. As for getting to the Caisleán, she'll find a way.

"The high fae live in the Caisleáns, so no, they're not places you can simply dance into," Uaine replies.

"What are high fae? Are there low fae? Why do you all have to make life so complicated?" Croi tries to run her hands through her hair, but it's too tangled, so she gives up.

"High fae are those descended from the ranks of Fionar and her companions," Uaine says, as if this is all general knowledge. "Lesser fae are those whose original forms are beasts of various kinds."

"What kind of a person was Fionar?" Croi asks with some interest.

"Why are you asking me?" Uaine frowns.

"You're old enough to have known her, right?" The dryad's age actually has a physical weight. Interacting with her is exhausting because her age translates to power. She's like cheese; the older it is, the riper it is. Croi smirks to herself at the thought.

"I am," Uaine says softly. "She was an idealist and a pacifist. She gave up her magick and her life for peace. Not many kin could do that."

"*I* certainly couldn't do that," Croi replies. "One last question. How do you know which elemental kingdom you belong to? Can you choose?"

"Didn't your Hag teach you this?" Uaine asks.

"She might have, but at that time, I didn't think it necessary for me to know," Croi mutters, chagrin coloring her cheeks red.

"By the magick you wield. Kin can only wield one elemental magick. That's why Fionar's sundering works so well." Uaine sweeps a glance over Croi. "The eyes of kin are usually a giveaway too. Talamh kin have eyes ringed by different shades of green and brown, as those of Talamh wield earth magick."

Croi's stomach growls loudly in the silence that follows the dryad's words, and she rubs her stomach. It has suffered. "How do I get to the Otherworld from here?"

"Follow the magick," Uaine says.

"That simple?" Croi looks at her doubtfully.

"You will find out," she says.

"For your sake, I hope you're right. Now give me your SoulSeed, and I will be on my way."

The dryad seems to shrink in on herself for a second before she straightens. "If my sister isn't around and there is no time, plant my SoulSeed in the earth."

"I will do my best. What is your sister's name?"

"You won't need it."

Croi holds out her hand for the SoulSeed. Uaine looks at Croi's outstretched hand and then at her tree. She takes a step closer to it and embraces it for a long moment. Croi lets her hand fall back to her side. The dryad moves away from the tree and stands in front of Croi, who starts at the look in her eyes. Terror tinges the tree creature's irises dark. The dryad takes a deep shuddering breath, and before Croi can say or do anything, she plunges a hand tipped with sharp nails into her own chest.

There is a scream. It may have been Croi's. Or the dryad's. Croi watches, shock turning her limbs to stone, not knowing what to do.

Only a few seconds pass, or perhaps an entire lifetime, before the dryad wrenches her hand out of her chest and holds it out to Croi. In her hand is a seed, the size of a small human's fist, covered in green sap. It is pulsing softly; the dryad's gold-green magick runs in veins around the surface of it.

"Take it," the dryad says, her voice torn and ragged, her eyes stormy and wet. "Take it," she begs.

TEN

WE ARE WORDS, CROI. BREATHING WORDS, WALKING words, words come to life, and words become flesh and blood. When we gather, we have meaning, we tell stories. But sometimes, we come undone. And sometimes"—Uaine looks at Croi, her eyes glittering—"our stories end."

She is sitting on the forest floor as though her body won't support her anymore. Trembling, the dryad presses her cheek against her tree trunk. She is diminished. The magick has left her body and now resides inside Croi's pack, wrapped in one of the diaphanous scarves she filched from the market.

"Get my SoulSeed to my sister." Uaine's voice is a mere rustle. Her eyes find Croi's and hold on. "You must not fail me."

Croi laughs slightly, and the dryad raises her eyebrow in question. "You speak as though I have the strength to resist anyone with more power than me. Sure, I am going to exert all effort to get your

SoulSeed to where it should go, but I might still fail in the end. You speak in absolutes. Have you forgotten that you initially called me 'little maybe'?"

Uaine shrugs, the gesture not as eloquent as it would have been half an hour ago.

"Why do you take this risk?" Croi asks. "You don't know who I am or what I am." Of course, Croi doesn't know who she is either, but she's not the one handing her heart to strangers.

"Because there isn't anyone else around," Uaine replies, looking at Croi with her head tilted to one side. A grimace contorts the dryad's features and she convulses in pain. "I will sleep now." Uaine uses the lower branches of her tree to pull herself up. Croi gets to her feet as well. Uaine faces her tree and shudders.

She turns around as though she has forgotten something, and Croi stiffens, wondering if the dryad has more commands for her. She watches Uaine reach for a majesty that is no longer present. The dryad's composure slips, and, looking haunted, she takes a step toward Croi, stretching out a hand toward the not-brownie's pack. Croi stands still, some previously dormant instinct for survival rooting her in place. The dryad stops before her hand touches the pack and squeezes her eyes shut. Her hand falls back to her side. She presses the palm of her other hand to her chest, right above where her SoulSeed used to reside.

She opens her eyes, and pain tinges her voice rough as she commands once again, "Don't fail me. Please." With that, she is gone, melting back into her tree as though she never was.

For the space of two heartbeats, Croi doesn't move. Her eyes are stuck to the surface of the tree trunk. Is Uaine really gone? Croi doesn't know how to get to Talamh Caisleán. Or where in Talamh the Caisleán is. She doesn't even know how to get to the Otherworld. What does it mean to follow the magick?

After a while, Croi realizes that no matter how long she stares at the tree, Uaine will not return. She picks up her pack, slings it over one shoulder, and exhales. The clearing is suddenly gloomy, each moment sinister in its stillness.

She knows better than to stay here, but her body has learned fear too well. What if she takes one step and the summoning spell returns, pulling at her again? Five minutes pass as Croi stands, hesitating. Then Uaine's tree groans, the sound a clear expression of pain. Startled, Croi takes an instinctive step away.

The first step didn't hurt, so she takes another one. The summoning spell doesn't spring back to renew its command on her limbs. She's free to move.

Croi quickly leaves the dryad's clearing and walks swiftly, putting distance between herself and Uaine. Though the Glamour has broken further, the forest remains unkind to her. Any insect that can bite her, does. Thorns seek her out just to get their bloody due, and branches belligerently present themselves as obstacles. Even the tree roots don't leave her alone. She walks, tripping and falling, until the light in the forest dims and hunger hollows her.

Sighing wearily, she looks around. She's far enough from the dryad, so she might as well stop for the night. A tree with overhanging branches catches her attention. Croi picks up a stick and stalks under it, making enough noise that any critters and slithery beasts know to leave. Setting her pack gently down by a fallen log, she brushes the ground beside it and settles there. She leans against the log and draws her legs up to her chest. Her body aches as if one of the carts in the human city rolled over it. Night will blanket the forest soon, but darkness has no meaning to her changed eyes. She can see as clearly as though it were day.

The forest is, contradictorily, both full of sounds and silent. If she were to disappear at this moment, would anyone know that she's missing? Would anyone care? Did the stone maid wonder why Croi didn't come back? Does she think she has been abandoned?

Croi opens her pack and gently takes out the scarf that's wrapped around Uaine's SoulSeed. She unwraps it. The SoulSeed pulses softly, casting golden-green light and illuminating the surroundings. It feels far heavier than it should. She rewraps it and places it carefully back into the pack. The dryad will certainly know if she goes missing. She will care.

This is not much reassurance, but it helps. Croi feels a little peace for the first time in hours and closes her eyes.

The onslaught of rain brings pain and a stinging awareness; Croi opens her eyes reluctantly. The darkness in front of her is broken sporadically by flashes of lightning. Croi tries to raise a hand to shield herself from the rain and realizes that she can't move. Terror has her struggling, which leads to successive discoveries. She is dreaming, and in this dream, she is a tree.

A tree!

Croi wonders if she can pop out of the tree like Uaine, but alas, she has no such blessings. So she stands in place, slowly going out of her mind, wondering when she will wake up and whether her dream visitor will make an appearance. After all, every time she has had a lucid dream, Irial has visited her.

She is not disappointed. Lightning strikes the tree in front of her, splitting its trunk into two. The fae boy emerges through the crack in the tree. For a moment, his eyes are clearly visible. They are soft shades of green and dark shades of brown with just a little dash of yellow as if some of the sun lives in them. His eyes are ringed by a dark earthy brown.

The moment fades and Irial's face blurs slightly. Croi decides the blurriness is a good thing as the fae's beauty addles her already muddled mind. Still, he's a new friend. She smiles at him before remembering that she is a tree and doesn't really have a face. Wait, does she have a face? What about eyes? No, if she didn't have eyes, how could she see Irial?

Irial walks over. "You're a tree today?"

Croi sighs. "So it seems. By the way, do I have a face? Is it on the tree trunk? Does it look incredibly strange?"

Irial looks at her, then immediately averts his eyes, biting his lip, before asking, "Can I not answer that question?"

"Why not?" Croi demands.

"Just . . . trust me on this. All right?" he pleads softly.

"The less I know, the less hurt I will be?" Croi says.

"Yes, well . . ." He ducks his head. "Yes."

"All right. You are forbidden from mentioning my tree phase ever again," Croi says.

Irial stills. "Do you think we'll know each other for a long time?"

"Why? Can't we?" Croi tries to narrow her eyes at the fae but finds that her eyes won't cooperate. Being a tree is hard on her nerves. "I don't make friends easily, so I'd like to keep the one I have. Anyway, still no luck with the Forever King's heir?"

Irial shakes his head, looking glum. He stands in front of Croi, the tree, but the rain doesn't fall on him.

According to Uaine, the Talamh HeartStone is missing. Croi probably knows the reason behind the Robber Queen's secretiveness. Should she tell Irial that she knows that the HeartStone is not in Talamh? But he has no reason to trust her. They've not even met other than in dreams.

"My mother betrothed the girl I like to the one friend I have," he confesses in a voice so low, it is almost indistinguishable from the sound of the rain.

Croi feels an uncomfortable prickle in her heart. He has someone he likes. Why this makes her feel prickly, she doesn't know, but it does. She doesn't like the feeling.

"When I asked her why, she told me that I had no future with Brianna, so I might as well let her be with someone else." He bites his lips again, punishing them. Croi wonders if she should protest, then decides not to. They're his lips after all. He has the right to abuse them. "It almost feels like she's preparing for our end," he whispers.

"Try to keep yourself alive until I reach the Caisleán," Croi commands him.

Irial sucks in a breath. "You're coming to the Caisleán?"

"I met a dryad who broke the summoning spell on me in exchange for a task I need to finish for her. That task can only be carried out at the Caisleán. Don't worry, my task doesn't involve any blood," Croi reports.

"Why are you telling me all this?" Irial asks.

Croi forgets she's a tree and tries to shrug. "I don't think you intend me harm."

"I don't," Irial says.

"Besides, even if you intended me harm, you can't exactly reach me. It's nice to have someone to tell secrets to. I feel like an overfull teapot, about to overflow. Telling you eases me." Croi sneezes and her branches creak. "I don't have a nose, but I can sneeze. Dreams are illogical."

"How will you get from the human world to the Otherworld?" Irial asks, ignoring her last few words.

"I have no idea. Uaine said to follow the magick, whatever that means," she grumbles.

"Who?" Irial sounds startled.

"That's the name of the dryad I told you about," Croi elaborates. "Do you know what she means?" The fae doesn't reply. "Oi!"

"Sorry. I don't." Irial looks at Croi long enough that she feels uncomfortable.

"Am I a good-looking tree?" she asks him.

He grins suddenly, his face lighting up. Croi shudders at his beauty. Her heart can barely handle it.

"The best," Irial says.

Croi beams. At that moment, the dreamscape shakes.

"I've overstayed," Irial says. "Your mind is trying to expel me. I'll visit you again."

His form shimmers and disappears, and Croi returns to being a tree all by herself. She closes her eyes and sinks deeper into her consciousness.

The noise wakes Croi before she's ready. Something is banging at a branch in the tree above her while a thousand insects seem to be chittering right in her ear. She opens her eyes reluctantly and looks up. On the branch closest to the ground is a small bird with a sharp beak and a brilliant array of feathers. Croi wonders what wrong the branch did to deserve the holes gouged into it. The bird must feel her eyes on it because it gives her a quick glance before it resumes pecking.

The sound increases in volume and reverberates in her head, temporarily drowning out all other noise. Then she hears the soft sounds of small footsteps and swings her gaze around to where a centipede is crawling under a log. Croi's hearing is normally sharp, but even she doesn't mark her hours by the footsteps of critters.

Croi's heart races at the thought of having to live her life in a constant din. All the sounds of the world try to crowd inside her head at the same time. She panics a little, not knowing what to do and how to make the noise stop. Clamping her hands over her ears doesn't help. She closes her eyes as though not seeing the world means not being able to hear it. That doesn't work either. She tries to remember what silence sounds like.

At that moment, she remembers the evenings she spent with the Hag in the dwelling. The Hag's silences—unwelcome then—are memories she cleaves to now. They were soothing silences, soft, not full of unsaid words but empty. Croi breathes in once, then again, removes her hands from her ears slowly, exhaling with relief. The noise has receded somewhat. The volume is muted, but the knowledge that one thought is all it will take to increase it resides in her bones.

She gathers her meager belongings and dusts herself off. Croi thanks the tree for providing her with shelter before she starts searching for food. She breaks fast on tart berries from a thorny bush. They're not very filling, but there is nothing else. Croi has run out of water, but as always, she knows which direction a river lies, so she sets off toward it. The ground inclines and soon she's breathing heavily. About thirty minutes later, her efforts pay off as the trees thin to reveal a river that falls a short distance to a mostly still pool before trickling away through some gaps in the rocks to caverns underneath. In a moment of curiosity, Croi finds the stillest part of the river.

She takes a breath, finds some courage, and closes her eyes. Then, before she can change her mind, before the courage flees, she leans over the water, opens her eyes, and looks down at her reflection.

ELEVEN

ONE WEEK AGO, CROI HAD BROWN HAIR, BROWN SKIN, and brown eyes filled with the sun. On her face was a snub nose and plump cheeks. Two round ears grew close to her head. Her lips were wide and often stretched in a smile. Her face hadn't been remarkable, but because it was hers, she had liked it.

The girl in the river has a face sculpted by nightmares. She sports a misshapen bump for a nose and mottled brown-orange skin. Her forehead is too wide and her mouth is too small. The bottom of her face boasts a suggestion of a chin.

Her eyes, which were originally a light brown, have undergone drastic changes. A shimmery gold iris surrounds the black pupil, which itself is ringed twice: the inner ring is the orange of ember, and the outer ring is thicker and a light green, like new shoots on a plant. Croi's eyes are strange, beautiful, and entirely out of place on her face.

Where did her old face go? Who is this staring up at her? Croi doesn't like the look in the multicolored eyes of the girl in the river.

Croi looks away from her reflection, feeling sore on the inside. Dipping her flask into the water destroys the girl staring back at her and gains her a measure of peace. If she can't see her face, she can pretend it isn't hers.

A thought occurs to her and Croi pauses. How can she ask others to look at her when *she* can't stand to look at herself?

She opens her pack and riffles through the scarves in there before selecting a black one with silver threads woven through. She wraps it around the lower half of her face, including her unfortunate nose. Then she finds some dark mud on the riverbank and applies it liberally to her forehead and whatever skin is showing above the scarf. If she's going to be ugly, she may as well go all the way.

When she's done, Croi washes her hands and stands up. The ground seems farther away now than it did yesterday. Croi lifts her leg and examines her knee. She looks as gangly as a colt. Heh. She makes her way back into the forest and doesn't fall down once on her way downhill. As far as she's concerned, this is a victory.

Her stomach growls, complaining about its current state of emptiness. She pats it comfortingly, asking it to endure. It's not like she can conjure food out of nothing. Croi looks at the ground, noticing the pale strands of magick that rise from the surface of the earth. She follows these farther into the forest, choosing to go where the strands are more numerous and the magick thicker. She has been walking for an hour when a sweet fragrance assails her. Led by her nose, she squeezes her way through a dense thicket and comes out in a small meadow populated by long green grass tipped with feathery pink flowers.

The Hag has often told her to think before she acts, but hunger has its own set of rules. The berries she scrounged for in the morning are long gone. Before Croi realizes what she is doing, a stalk of a pink feathery flower is melting on her tongue. It is sweet but lightly so, invigorating her taste buds and filling her in the same way a full meal would. A sliver of rationality prevents Croi from eating another stalk of the candy grass. She makes herself wait a minute, figuring that this time is long enough for adverse effects, should there be any, to make themselves known. When nothing happens, Croi releases her inner glutton.

Half an hour later, she is finally satiated. The patch of candy grass has been all but decimated. Croi wipes her sticky fingers on her shabby dress and notices that the magick under the grass patch is particularly dense. She packs the remaining stalks of grass and places them in her bag and is about to continue deeper into the forest when the discordant squawks of gringits attract her attention.

She follows the sounds to a tall tree not far from the candy grass meadow and peers up. On a branch high up, thirty or so gringits have surrounded a shining creature Croi hasn't seen outside of books. The pixie's hair is a rich red and her skin is a pale green. She has silvery wings, which don't seem to be helping her very much at this moment.

The pixie is scratched, pale, and desperately trying to defend herself against the overwhelming numbers of the gringits. Croi considers the choices before her. She can walk away, pretending that she hasn't seen the pixie, and no one will know any better. Or she can take on the wrath of the gringits and try to save the pixie. She's tempted to walk away, but alas, her conscience is determined and won't let her.

Heaving a sigh, she climbs the tree, ignoring the warning chitters from the gringits who see her coming. Gringits are vicious by nature, and upon seeing her approach, they swarm toward her, biting and pinching. Croi mutters all the curses she picked up in the human city and others she has made up. By dint of sheer stubbornness, she finally reaches the branch the pixie is on and realizes that the poor creature is bound to the tree with a vine. The same vine is around her hands and legs. Croi reaches out to free her from her constraints when a large gringit rushes at her, a finger tipped with a sharp nail extended like a sword. His nail slices the soft part of Croi's arm, and blood rushes out. Croi hisses, clamping her hand over the wound, but it's too late. A drop or two of the blood falls on the branch. The gringit, emboldened by his success, rushes at her again. At this moment, the tree they are on groans in a strange, deep voice. The gringits all freeze. When the tree groans again, they scream and flee.

Croi perches precariously on the branch high above the forest floor. She looks at the tiny pixie, who blinks brown eyes ringed by a thick dark green at her for a long moment before slumping over in a faint.

TWELVE

CROI SITS ASTRIDE THE BRANCH OF THE TREE AND considers her options once again. The tree scared away the gringits, so there is no immediate threat from them. Therefore, no one can blame her if she simply leaves the pixie to the elements. It's not like she owes the creature anything. However, if she leaves the pixie unconscious and something worse than the gringits comes around . . . Croi sighs. Scruples are very annoying things to possess.

She pokes at the pixie with a twig, but the pixie doesn't respond. The pixie's magick, green infused with brown, is pale and lethargic, almost as if it is running out. Croi opens her pack and carefully extracts a stalk of candy grass from it. She tears a little bit of the feathered flower and puts it on top of the pixie's mouth. It melts into liquid immediately, and the pixie swallows it. Her magick brightens a bit a moment later. Encouraged, Croi feeds the pixie more, stopping only when her magick stops brightening. The pixie remains unconscious, however. Croi cuts the vines constraining her and leans back against the trunk of the tree, content to wait for the creature to wake up.

It occurs to her suddenly that she hasn't checked on Uaine's Soul-Seed today. She takes it out of her pack, unwraps it, and examines it. It's a bit dimmer than it was yesterday.

"Where do I go now, Uaine?" she addresses the SoulSeed. She doesn't expect an answer and she doesn't get one. Exhaling, she closes her eyes against the monotonous landscape of the forest. With her eyes closed, she hears the sounds of the forest more clearly, and for a few minutes, she soaks in the various sounds made by the living creatures. On a whim, she starts listening with her changed hearing, and what she hears makes Croi gasp.

What she had thought of as noise is actually a song. The forest is singing a song. The flora and the fauna each have their own melodies, but instead of being discordant, they harmonize. Croi opens her eyes and looks around. It is the magick that takes the different melodies and puts them together into one song: the forest's song. Croi listens to the forest singing for a long while and gradually realizes that there's a different sound, a different song being sung somewhere in the forest. She takes out another scarf from her bag, ties it into a sling that she puts around her neck, and gently transfers the pixie over. Then she climbs down the tree and follows the sound, walking for a long time before finally reaching the place the new song is coming from.

At the foot of a hill are two tall trees standing like sentries, two arm spans apart. The new song swells here. With a jolt, Croi realizes that this new tune is the Song of the Earth, of Talamh magick. She sang a bit of this song to stop Uaine from eating her, name first. Many slender saplings surround these two trees. At least she thinks they are saplings. When she moves closer, these saplings stir and wake, their bodies transforming into long, thin creatures with no feet and long arms. The heads of these creatures are shorn, and their eyes are blanketed white. As if they sense Croi, they extend their arms to prevent her from passing through the portal.

Croi comes to a sudden halt before backing away. Her footsteps cease only when she is a safe distance away from the creatures. Her heart is pounding and her palms are wet. What is she supposed to do now? How can she sneak past them?

Consult the book.

Book? What book?

The book the Hag gave us.

Oh. That book. Croi brings the pack that she is carrying on one shoulder to the front, opens it, then stops short, and her mouth drops open. The pack falls to the ground, almost overturning the pixie out of the sling that hangs around Croi's neck.

"Who are you?"

I am you. The other half to our whole.

A cold breeze prickles the back of Croi's neck. She sits down on the ground abruptly, feeling her heart speed up in accompaniment to the fear that suddenly chews at her insides. She knows, even though she doesn't want to, who this voice is. She felt the butterfly tickle when Uaine tried to claim her name. She felt the alien presence within her. Uaine woke this voice inside of her. No, that's not right. She didn't *wake* her; the dryad simply allowed this voice a way to be heard. Croi swallows.

Do I scare you?

It would be a lie to say no, but Croi's dignity is disappearing far too quickly for her to respond to the question. "What do you want from me?"

What could I want from you?

Croi thinks about it. "Don't you hate me? I'm the one on the outside while you've remained in the dark, unheard, unknown, for so long."

I don't hate you. Hating you would be like hating the sun for being hot. The sun didn't choose to be hot, and you didn't choose to be our face. It would be a lie, however, to say I haven't resented you over the years.

"I'm sorry," Croi says.

Why are you sorry? You weren't the one who made us like this. I am saving my hate for the kin who did.

"That so-called princess the Hag mentioned? Do you remember what she looked like?"

No. But I remember her dragon-damaged magick. There can't be too many kin walking around with damaged magick.

Croi thinks of the glimpse she had of the kin who cast the summoning spell on her. She thinks of the look in the kin's eyes, and her lips flatten. "Do you think we'll find her? Do you think she'll find us?"

How could she not? She halved us for a reason. The voice pauses, then continues, lighter now. *You are taking my presence better than I thought you would.*

"My . . . *Our* body is changing into an entirely different shape. In comparison, a voice in my head is almost normal." Croi shrugs.

She picks up her pack and takes out the book of spells and peoples of the Otherworld.

"It would help if I knew what these creatures are called," she mutters out loud.

"Roods." A high-pitched voice answers her. For a second, Croi thinks it is the voice inside her that's speaking, but the comment is accompanied by a tug at her dress. When she looks down, she sees the pixie blinking bright eyes at her. "They are guardians of the portal to the Otherworld."

"Hello," Croi says. "You're finally awake."

"Thank you for saving me," the pixie says, and bows formally. "My name is Rosiana, but you may call me Tinder. All my friends do."

At the mention of friends, Croi thinks of her stone maid. If she

finds another friend, is she betraying the stone maid? "Are we friends?"

"You saved my life. I hope you will be my friend," the pixie says, flushing a sweet red.

"Let's get to know each other first, and see if we can become friends," Croi replies. The pixie nods eagerly. She flies up and settles on Croi's shoulder. She doesn't ask any questions, though Croi can see her curiosity on her face. "What is a pixie doing in the human world?"

Tinder scrunches up her face and looks embarrassed. "I learned the spell to open a door into the human world and tried it, but I underestimated the amount of magick it would require. I got stuck here, and then I was attacked by those beasts," she mutters darkly. "If my magick wasn't exhausted, I would have pixed the whole lot."

"So you don't have any way to go back to the Otherworld other than through the portal?" Croi asks.

The pixie nods sadly.

Croi opens the book and looks through the table of contents before finding the entry on Roods. They are filed under "Dangerous" and also "Fatal." The book notes that Roods prevent non-kin from entering the Otherworld. Since she is currently in an in-between phase, the Roods don't recognize her, thus their actions earlier.

"Huh." Croi looks at the thin saplings who seem barely strong enough to slap flies. "You should be able to move past them since you are considered kin," she says to the pixie.

Tinder shakes her head. "My magick is almost gone. Going through the portal by myself would extinguish me."

"I guess I will save your life again," Croi replies, and looks at the book. "To move past Roods, see the spell 'Distill the Night into a Cloak of Darkness,'" she reads out loud. She flips the pages to the spell, wondering what it will ask for. To her surprise, there are only two instructions.

1. Wait for darkness to fall.

2. Recite these words three times immediately after
   darkness falls.

The Cloak of Darkness doesn't just hide kin from view but also hides their essence. The Roods won't be able to see or sense anyone wearing the Cloak of Darkness. The only problem is that Croi can't read the language the spell is written in. She tries many times until, with no small amount of frustration, she sets the book aside.

Ask the pixie to read it.

"Can you read the spell?" Croi asks out loud. Tinder peers at the words before nodding cautiously.

"But I have no magick," she says, her head drooping.

"If I give you my magick, could you?" Croi looks down at her hands, and the magicks in her speed up, coiling around her body at dizzying speeds.

Tinder looks startled. "How would you give me your magick?"

"Just answer the question."

"Yeah. If I can use your magick, I can cast the spell." Tinder looks wary. "But there's no way you can give me your magick. It doesn't work like that."

"Leave it to me." Croi affects an ease she doesn't feel. "Let's wait for the night. Are you hungry?" She gives the pixie a bit more of the candy grass still remaining in her pack. As the pixie eats, she speaks about her life in the pixie meadow she was born in. Croi learns about the pixie's friends, her many enemies and rivalries. Tinder talks about her favorite sibling and her least favorite brother. Croi listens quietly, the shifting time hiding her envy.

Someday, we will have a family too.

"Do you think we'll ever be that lucky?" Croi communicates to her other self with a thought.

Why not?

For some reason, Croi thinks of Irial at this moment and wonders

if he will be a part of her family, then shakes her head to dislodge thoughts of the fae prince.

She finds a stream nearby to slake her thirst and washes the mud off her face. The pixie looks at her curiously, so Croi shows her the face she has been hiding under the veil. Tinder flies up and pats her cheek.

"Did someone hurt you?" she asks.

Croi smiles, her first smile in a very long while. "Yeah," she replies. "Someone did."

The hours pass swiftly and soon the sun is sinking. Croi gets ready; she doesn't know if she can give her magick to the pixie, but she will try. As soon as it is dark, she brings her hands up, and the green magick in her pools in her cupped palms.

"Are you ready?" Croi asks the pixie. Tinder looks nervous but nods. Croi asks her to raise her palms, and she transfers her magick to the pixie. Tinder gasps and hurriedly casts the spell. Soon Croi feels a slice of the night enveloping her; the darkness becomes tangible. The cloak is slight, but it covers both Croi and Tinder. It also has a voluminous hood. Croi scoops Tinder up and places her on her shoulder under the cloak. She takes a deep breath.

The portal shimmers in the night, a liquid gold curtain veiling the secrets of a different world. Croi takes a look around the forest, trying to see if it still feels like home. It doesn't. The darkness obscures trees she doesn't know in a part of the forest she is unfamiliar with.

"Hold your breath," she whispers to the pixie.

Run straight. Run through. Run true.

Croi, hidden in the cloak, starts running. She tears through the night and approaches the portal. As she passes the Roods, the hood of the cloak falls, revealing her head. The Roods screech, extending their hands to stop her, but it is too late. They are left with the disintegrating cloak. Croi is through the portal and into the Otherworld.

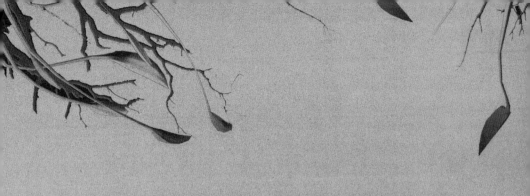

ACT TWO

THIRTEEN

A MOUNTAIN, SO TALL ITS PEAK BRUSHES THE SKY, IS the first thing Croi sees when she emerges into the Otherworld. In the next second, fear, irrational and sudden, swallows her in one rapid gulp.

A beast slumbers in the depths of these mountains. If he awakens, we will die.

Panic nips at Croi's feet. In response, she turns to flee, back through the portal, back into the arms of the Wilde Forest, ruled by the need to survive. But when she turns around, she discovers that the portal has disappeared. She stands alone on a narrow, dark road. Behind her is the mountain with the beast in its belly, and in front of her is a forest, full of seemingly hostile shadows. The skies above are full of stars Croi doesn't recognize, and the air is tainted by a stink whose origins she doesn't dare to investigate. Fear squeezes her heart tightly, and she squats down, trying to make herself smaller and less of a target.

"Aahhh!" The forgotten pixie is unseated by Croi's movements and almost falls. Thankfully, Croi reacts quickly, catching Tinder with a hand. One look at the pixie diminishes her fear. The little creature's magick is weak, her movements a fraction too languid to be healthy. Croi leaves the road and finds a bush to crawl into. She has no idea where they are, and though the darkness in the Otherworld is not impossible to navigate, she would much rather not. She feeds the barely conscious pixie candy grass before placing her in a nest made of leaves and twigs. She curls up in the hedge beside her charge. Sleep won't bother her, not this close to the beast in the mountain. Croi folds her arms around her chest, careful not to disturb the pixie, and waits for the pain. It arrives an hour later; Croi stuffs a scarf in her mouth to stifle the screams it brings. When the pain leaves, she's supine on the ground, destroyed.

Hours later, Croi opens her eyes to sunlight filtering through the straggly branches of the bush she took shelter in the night before. Tinder is stirring. Croi sits up cautiously and finds that she has grown tall enough that the bush has become very uncomfortable. She wraps a scarf around her face as a veil and crawls out of the temporary shelter. A few minutes later, the pixie follows.

It is very early in the morning, but the newness of the day does nothing to the gloom that blankets the surroundings. There is no magick anywhere here. Even the rocks are bereft of magick. Croi looks at the mountain cautiously and blinks. Now she knows where the magick has gone.

Move cautiously. Don't wake the beast.

Croi doesn't need her other self's warning, but she accepts it. "Do you know where we are?" she asks the pixie.

Tinder looks around, her delicate face distressed. Without answering and as if unaware of the beast, she flies up the road toward the mountain. Croi follows her, walking softly. They soon arrive at a cluster of dwellings at the foot of the mountain; these are constructed from

wood and grass. The air trembles here as it does in the aftermath of great violence. Croi stops walking, not wanting to take another step into the village, but Tinder seems determined to explore. Finally she mutters a human curse and follows the pixie. The village is obviously empty; a silence has sunk into the bones of this place. Withered gardens decorate the front yards of these dwellings. Broken windows and cracked walls pay homage to decades of neglect. Tinder flies into a dwelling whose front door has been ripped off, and Croi reluctantly walks in after her.

The dwelling contains the detritus of a life abandoned unexpectedly: A table containing plates that used to be full of food that has now shriveled into stains on their surfaces. Unmade beds, the blankets having long become havens for rats; books opened to pages where the ink has faded; time stealing the untold stories. Croi and Tinder visit five dwellings, and in all of them they see evidence of an abrupt end. What happened to the kin who dwelled here? Why are there echoes of screams in the air? Why are the sleeping beast and the mountain that contains him so glutted with magick?

Tinder is crying, unable to explain the reason for her tears. The despair in the air is so sharp, it almost draws blood. Croi puts the pixie in the sling, where she shrinks into as small a ball as she can. She walks out of the village and takes the road to the edge of the unfamiliar forest.

"Let's talk," she finally says, keeping her voice low. They're still within hearing distance of the mountain.

The pixie pokes her head out of the sling and looks at Croi. Her pupils contract and she gulps. Her nose is as red as her eyes, but she's still annoyingly beautiful. Croi tightens the scarf around her face.

"Why are there two rings around your eyes? Are you Talamh or Tine?" Tinder asks both questions without pausing.

"Why are you asking me now?" Croi tilts her head curiously.

"I'm feeling better now," the pixie confesses. "When I feel better, I ask questions."

"Your luck is bad because I don't feel like answering questions," Croi replies. She doesn't know the answer to the question anyway.

"Oh. That's . . . I will accept that. You can tell me when you feel like answering questions. I've never seen anyone with double rings." A few more tears slip out of her eyes, and she wipes them unceremoniously, pretending they don't exist.

"Who lived in the village?" Croi doesn't need to specify which one.

Tinder takes a deep breath and shudders. "This is Areed, the home of the blue-horned fauns. They used to mine the mountain for magick stones. We learned that in history."

"Their disappearance doesn't seem like history," Croi comments.

"Yeah. It happened only twenty years ago. Apparently, they all died because of some disease," Tinder says hesitantly. "The Forever King sealed off this village, but I guess his magick faded with his death."

"Did what you see seem like they died of disease? What kind of disease would kill them all at the same time?" Croi says. She knows what happened to these blue-horned fauns. They were eaten by the beast in the mountain.

"I . . . don't know what to think. If what I see is the truth, then it seems like we were lied to. But how can that be possible? Kin can't lie."

Truth has many shapes and sizes.

"Could the beast be classified a disease?" Croi asks her other self.

When you are desperate, anything can be a disease. Croi can feel the scorn in her other self's words.

"You saved my life again. I don't think I would have survived too long in the human world. I owe you a life debt. You can ask me for anything." The pixie, unaware of the conversation occurring inside Croi's head, sketches a wobbly bow in the air.

"Really?" Croi smiles a little. "Anything at all?"

"Yes. Of course." The pixie's wings flutter in the air behind her as she bobs up and down in front of Croi.

"Can you lead me to the Talamh Caisleán? I must be there before the Saol ceremony," Croi adds.

"The Talamh Caisleán?" Tinder hesitates. "Do you really need to go there?"

"Yes." Although she'd much rather not. But she gave her word and she must keep it. Of course, seeing Irial will be a reward.

"All right. I can do that. But we're very far from the Caisleán right now. We're on the outer edges of the Talamh, and starting from here, it will take us two months to get to our destination. The Saol ceremony will be over long before then." The pixie brings out a small bag, and from it she extracts a square piece of paper with a thorn on it. "This will be unpleasant, but invoking this spell will move us directly to the pixie meadow, which is much closer to the Caisleán than here. My mom makes me carry one just in case I get lost on my travels." She looks at Croi and correctly reads the question on her face. "The spell doesn't work in the human world. I tried many times!"

Croi nods, accepting Tinder's answer.

"I need you to hold me so you get transported along with me," the pixie says. Croi obeys. The pixie tears the piece of paper, and Croi takes one last look at the mountain before they disappear.

FOURTEEN

THE SKY, A CERULEAN MONSTER STRETCHING ITS FINGER- tips to infinity, greets Croi on the other side.

She and the pixie are both a bit worse for wear after the experience of traveling a long distance in such a short time. Croi sinks down to her haunches to calm her queasy stomach. The pixie pats her on the back; Croi thinks she's trying to be comforting. She stands up after a moment, and the pixie squeaks, flying back.

"Did you grow taller?"

"Yes."

"I shouldn't ask why, right?"

"You learn fast." Croi beams. "Do you travel like that often?"

"No. Only sometimes," Tinder replies. "Only when I need to get home quicker."

At the word "home," Croi looks around. They are in the largest meadow Croi has ever been in. It is lit by splashes of color from the flowers. Honeysuckles scent the air. Dog violets, purple and cheerful, nod gaily alongside cuckooflowers while primrose and wood anemones each command different sections of the meadow. Wildflowers she can't identify grow in scattered clusters. A breeze plays with the flower petals, and long grass rustles in response. However, no flower sprites pop their heads out of the flowers to beam toothily at her. Are the flowers in the Otherworld always so quiet?

Far off in the distance, she sees the forest that surrounds the meadow on all sides. Is it still called the Wilde Forest here? Suddenly uncertain, she looks around. The place they were in the night before was entirely devoid of magick, but dense lines of magick fill everything living in the meadow. The magick here is many times stronger than it is in the human world.

"Where is home?" Croi asks, looking around.

Tinder points at a green mound where flowers grow densely. As soon as she does, six pixie soldiers perched precariously on honey hornets emerge from the mound, flying straight toward them. Croi tenses, raising her arms just in case they try to prick her with the sharp twigs they're holding.

"Don't worry, they won't do anything to you," Tinder says, but Croi isn't convinced.

"My lady, the queen asks that you return and report to her," one of the pixie soldiers says. He is tiny, the size of Croi's forefinger, but his size doesn't detract from the ferocity in his voice and face.

"Do you want to come with me while I—" Tinder starts.

"My lady," the other soldier interrupts, making it apparent that Croi isn't invited.

Tinder's lips tighten in a flat line. She takes off a necklace and hands it to Croi. "I won't ask you to wait for me. Keep this necklace near, and I will find you."

Without giving Croi time to reply, she flies away, heading to the mound with her magick sparking. Croi watches her go until one of the pixie soldiers pokes her.

She looks down at them.

"We will escort you out of the meadow," the pixie soldier with a mole under one of his eyes says. The rest are taciturn, hoarding their words like jewels.

"I don't need an escort," Croi tells them.

It soon becomes clear that she has no choice in the matter as the hornet-riding soldiers surround her without another word, herding her away from the pixie mound. Croi grumbles quietly but starts walking.

After a while and with another look at her eyes, the chatty soldier asks, "What are you?"

Croi has come to hate this question. Why can't people ask something else? "I am a not-brownie," she finally answers. The soldier frowns, clearly dissatisfied with her answer, but he stops asking.

The meadow seems endless; they walk silently for hours before they reach the end of it. Well, Croi walks. The soldiers ride their hornets. Why they need hornets when they have perfectly functioning wings is a question Croi doesn't dare ask.

The soldiers stop at the edge of the forest. The talkative one flies up to Croi's eyes. "Go and don't look back. Go and don't return. We won't be kind if we see you again." With that, they pull the reins of their hornets and fly away.

Croi watches them leave, then turns to stare at the forest, the darkness yawning before her. She has misgivings. She has so many misgivings that she's almost spilling over with them, but there's no way to go but forward. It takes her only one step into the tree-infested place to understand how different it is from the Wilde Forest she knows and loves.

This forest has the same trees as the Wilde Forest: ash, poplar, beech, rowan, and oak. It has the same kinds of vines winding around

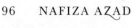

branches, and the same kinds of flowers blooming here and there. However, the leaves in this forest glisten wetly even though it isn't raining. Whatever light manages to shine through the canopy is pallid, like the sun cannot be bothered to light the world inside the forest. In the pixie's meadow outside, the sun is bright and sparkly.

The magick, too, is different. Though the strands of it are thicker than in the human world, they're less intense compared to the pixie meadow. The undergrowth of this forest, unlike the Wilde Forest, has been cleared as though many feet have walked across it, and perhaps they have. It is colder, too, inside this forest, so cold that it could be winter and not autumn waiting in the eaves. She walks farther in and realizes that the noise is also different here. This forest's song sounds hoarse and rough—as if the trees are forgetting the words.

Croi lets her hearing expand, and instead of hearing the chittering of insects, she hears whispered conversations, laughter, screams, and cries. This forest is alive in a way the Wilde Forest wasn't. Here, the magick's song is subdued, but the forest is abuzz with a cacophony full of notes she itches to understand. The gringits are missing here. Instead, small lean figures, green-skinned with two curling twiglike horns on their heads, fling themselves from one tree to another. The Hag taught Croi about these creatures: they're treepers, rulers of the treetops in Talamh. They are notoriously reticent and keep to themselves unless provoked. Croi will, of course, restrain herself from provoking them.

She takes a breath and exhales fully for the first time in what feels like hours. The pixie meadow was beautiful, but the sky outside is too wide. It made her feel vulnerable in a way she doesn't like. Forests are where she belongs, where she feels the most like herself, whoever she turns out to be. She takes another breath and loses herself to the sounds of the forest. Croi doesn't know how long she spends standing there, in the middle of what seems like a well-traveled path, just listening, but suddenly fatigue comes crashing down on her shoulders and pulls her legs out from under her. She crumples to the ground, so weary that even her hair hurts.

She knows better than to rest here, where she'll make a nice snack for any predator looking for a meal. So she gets up and staggers away from the path and farther into the forest. It gets colder the deeper she goes. She hugs her pack close, hoping the SoulSeed will give her some of its fading warmth.

All of a sudden, Croi smells smoke. She follows her nose for a few minutes and is rewarded when she reaches a small clearing. In the middle is a fire burning merrily in a pit.

Go closer.

Her other self is a little bit too impatient. Even though there's no one else in the clearing, a cat is napping in front of the fire. It doesn't look like a wild Meow. Maybe its owner is somewhere around. Croi waits for a while, but no one appears, so she walks closer to the fire, ready to bolt, just in case. She should be more worried about whoever lit the fire, but she's so tired that she doesn't mind playing with danger for a few moments of peace. She makes it all the way to the fire and sinks down gratefully in front of the undulating flames.

Move closer. So bossy. Croi grumbles but obeys.

She scoots as close to the heat as she can without actually sitting in the pit. The Hag took great pains to ensure Croi didn't ever come in contact with fire. She cooked all Croi's food and even made her give her word that she wouldn't play with fire in the human city. It didn't occur to Croi then to wonder why, but she does now.

Several sticks lie beside the firepit, and at her inner self's behest, Croi drops a couple of them into the flames, enjoying the crackling sound they make as they burn. If only there were a plump rabbit she could catch. She'd roast it over the fire. Croi's mouth waters at the thought, and she pats her stomach sadly. Food feels like an impossibility in this forest. Perhaps her hunger will be sated in Talamh Caisleán.

She warms her hands over the fire, but it isn't enough; she brings her face closer to the flames and enjoys the heat on her cheeks. She looks into the depths of the flames and suddenly, instead of the crackling, hears a raspy, throaty song.

"Do you hear that?" she asks her inner self.

Yes.

The song is so soft that it is almost indiscernible. Unable to resist the beauty of what she *can* hear, she leans even closer to the flame, closer than is wise. The fire's song makes her breathless, so she takes a deep breath, and when she does, she inhales the fire into herself.

FIFTEEN

THERE IS NO INFERNO, NO CONFLAGRATION OF CROI, NO agony. Though the fire licks her insides warm, she doesn't burn. She's not singed, scorched, or seared. She's feverish, but that is due more to fear than the heat. Throughout the entire experience, Croi keeps hearing snatches of the fire's song, loud one minute and barely audible the next.

She takes another breath and feels the flames pour into the spaces within her that were created by the breaking Glamour. The heat reaches her core first and electrifies her other self. She takes a deep breath and is not surprised when it hurts. Then something unexpected happens: the fire creates a bridge connecting her to her inner self, and for a moment, just a tiny sliver of a second, she is a patched-up whole instead of two broken halves. But the sensation is too intense, and she can't help but exhale, breathing the flames back into the crude firepit. All that remains is the taste of smoke in her mouth, and the memory of once being complete.

She shifts away from the fire but is reluctant to leave it entirely. Breathing cautiously, she turns her face away so the flames don't jump into her once again. The fire writhes, its flames flickering toward her, and she, unable to resist, reaches out a finger and watches in wonder as a tendril of flame curls around it. Again there is heat, but it is banked as though the fire itself is trying not to burn her. Croi breathes the tendril of flame in, choosing to keep it.

"Hey!" She mentally pokes the other self.

What?

"Do you think we're turning into a dragon? Isn't that why the Hag kept us away from the fire? She wouldn't be able to control us if we turned into a dragon. It all makes sense now! The reason why our bones are rebelling and our eyes have that strange liquid shimmer! Why our face looks terrible! We're turning into a giant lizard. We're going to have a tail!" Croi doesn't know how she feels about having a tail.

We're not turning into a dragon.

"Yes, we are!" Croi is so excited that she jumps up and twirls around before coming to an abrupt stop when she sees a fae boy crouched on the other side of the clearing. A feral snarl has peeled his lips back to reveal sharp white teeth. When Croi blinks, the boy hisses. His magick has the red edge to it that Croi associates with hostility, but curiously, the boy seems to have misplaced all his clothes. Unless he doesn't ever wear any. Croi suddenly wishes the cat was around so she could use it as a shield, but if this boy is its master, she doesn't blame it for disappearing. If it were her, she would too.

The boy's skin is brown with black and yellow stripes overlaying it. His hair is a mix of the same black and yellow colors. He's slender to the point that his bones are poking out. When Croi's eyes drop lower, he hisses. She obediently raises her eyes back to his face.

Even though the snarl is doing its best to disfigure his features, it cannot hide his beauty. A sharp nose and high cheekbones accentuate amber eyes ringed by a deep, dark brown. Croi and the fae boy regard each other silently. Croi's not sure what to do next. Run away? Her feet don't seem inclined to cooperate. She is also extremely reluctant to leave the fire. The boy may not even let her leave. He's probably hungry and she's prey.

"Look, I'm sorry I inhaled your fire. I didn't do it intentionally. I just took a breath, and it jumped into me. I didn't know I'm a dragon—"

"You think you're a dragon?" The boy's voice is startled but warm, reminiscent of lazy days spent dozing in a patch of sunlight.

See. Even he is laughing at us.

Croi ignores her inner self.

With the snarl gone, he's even more beautiful. His beauty gives substance to her lack of it. In fact, his beauty is an affront to her ugliness. Croi grimaces and pulls the scarf tighter around the lower half of her face.

"What of it?" she responds haughtily. Dragons are infinitely more powerful than any creature or kin. They don't have to be beautiful. They don't need to be afraid of being magicked or bound. And no one *ever* tries to eat dragons.

"Nothing, nothing. Now turn around so I can put on some clothes."

The boy makes a shooing gesture with his hand that Croi finds very irritating. If he has so much modesty, why is he walking around naked in the first place? She turns her back to him anyway, and the flames warm her comfortingly.

"You may look now." He has dressed in a pair of green-and-black pants and a green shirt that seems to have been washed many times. The ensemble is strange when contrasted with the stripes on his skin. What kind of kin are striped? Those stripes look very familiar to Croi.

He's Catkin.

"Really?"

I can't lie either.

Croi turns and looks at the boy a little closer. He *is* Catkin! A type of fae who alternate between fae and cat forms. Uaine called fae with secondary forms Lesser Fae, which makes no sense to Croi. Unlike the so-called Higher Fae, the Lesser Fae have two forms, so shouldn't they be regarded as the superior beings?

The overgrown Meow is observing Croi with his head tilted to one side and his face filled with amusement.

Why is he amused? Is he amused by her ugliness? Croi sneaks another look at him and sees his lips twitch.

I don't like him.

Cats play with their prey before they eat them. Croi has helped many mice escape their predators in the human city. This Meow shouldn't think she's helpless. No matter what her inner self says, she's going to be a dragon.

"What makes you think you're a dragon?" the Meow asks in a perfectly nice tone that makes Croi dislike him too.

"I breathed fire, didn't I?" She tries to be as polite as she can. He can still attack her with those sharp claws.

"The dragon world is closed off to the Otherworld. All contact with dragons is forbidden. Especially after Nuala the Brave defeated their king," the boy points out.

"Who?" If the dragon world is unreachable through the Otherworld, how is she going to get home?

The dragon world isn't home.

"Nuala the Brave, the heir to the Forever King, the one who should be the queen right now," the Meow elaborates. His words make Croi think of her dream visitor. She wonders if he knows about Nuala.

"What happened to her?"

"She disappeared. Perhaps she, too, was the Usurper's victim."
The sorrow in his voice is deep. "Anyway, you can't be a dragon."

"Why not?" Croi scowls at him.

The boy smirks. "Dragonlings are hatched from eggs."

Croi pauses. She came from an egg?

"And they don't change forms," the Meow finishes.

"Why are you so determined to destroy my dragon-ness?!" Croi
jumps to her feet and glares at him. The boy is leaning against a pack
that is much like hers except that it is larger and the same color as the
ground it is resting on.

"How can I destroy your dragon-ness when you didn't have any to
begin with?" The Meow folds his arms.

Croi's eyes fill with tears. They're angry tears, she tells herself. She
does not appreciate the catkin breaking her hopes.

"I'm sorry. I'm just teasing you. What are you doing by yourself
in the woods? Didn't your parents tell you about the dangers that lurk
here?" The amusement trickles out of the boy's eyes, leaving him stern
and disapproving.

"I'd need to have parents before they can tell me what to do," Croi
replies, sniffing. "They threw me away when I was born," she adds,
just in case he asks something else.

The boy's eyes widen and fill with what suspiciously looks like pity.
Croi doesn't want his pity. She doesn't want anyone's pity.

"If it's so dangerous, what are *you* doing here?" The Meow doesn't
seem much older than her. "Don't *your* parents care?"

His face goes blank at the question before smoothing over.

"I'm older than I look" is all he says. Croi wonders how old
the Meow is. He looks about twenty winters, but fae stop aging
after they're twenty, so for all she knows, he could be a hundred.
Maybe two hundred. Maybe he's a grandpa. Croi chuckles to herself, but her mirth disappears when her stomach growls piteously.

Her cheeks burn with unexpected embarrassment.

The catkin's face gentles, and he says, "Sit down. Let's have a bite to eat."

Croi's sitting before he has finished speaking. She doesn't know where her next meal is coming from, so she may as well think with her stomach. When she looks at the Meow again, a laugh is peeking out from his eyes, but his expression remains cautious. He still thinks she's dangerous. Croi wishes she was.

He rummages in his pack and pulls out a pot, several small packages, and a flask. He pours the water that's in the flask into the pot that he sets atop the little fire. The flames spark their displeasure, and Croi grins. As the water heats, he adds many unfamiliar spices and greens before adding what looks like dried fish. Soon a delicious smell wafts over. Croi's stomach growls its impatience, and the boy chuckles. He stirs the concoction before closing the pot with a lid.

"We'll let it cook for a while," he says, and throws something at Croi. She catches it and finds a bright red apple gleaming in her hands. She looks at it suspiciously.

"It's fine. Eat it."

Croi tries to resist the allure of the apple. For all of two seconds. She decides to eat it, but then she realizes that she will have to take off her veil to do so.

"Look, I'm going to take off my veil now. I'm really ugly, so you should prepare yourself," she warns him. The Meow raises an eyebrow and gestures for her to go ahead.

Her hand trembles, but Croi pushes away all emotions. Being beautiful isn't everything. Ugly people have a place in the world too. She takes off the veil and very carefully doesn't look at the Meow.

"If you don't want to eat, return the apple to me," the Meow says, and Croi starts. She takes a big bite of the apple and almost weeps. It's that sweet.

"Do you have nothing to say to me?" She glances at him from the corner of her eye. He's not even looking at her.

"About what?" he asks.

"About my . . ." Croi gestures to her face.

"Your face is your business. I don't think it my place to comment on it," he replies.

"Why are you being so kind to me?" she asks between bites.

"You sound as if I'm the first person to ever show you kindness," the boy says, checking on the cooking stew. Croi deflates when he announces it not yet done.

"You are the second person," she replies, licking her fingers. Irial was the first. She looks at the pot on the flames hopefully before turning her attention to the Meow. "That's why I don't trust you."

He grins at that and shrugs, the mirth fading from his face. "Kindness doesn't take much. Besides, you remind me of my own siblings."

"Do you have many?"

"Oh yes. I have fifteen. Eight sisters and seven brothers."

Croi gapes at him. That's a lot of Meows.

He notices her shock and laughs. "Catkins always have large families."

"I didn't know." Croi suppresses the spurt of envy his words evoke. Where are the people she belongs to? Does she have siblings, aunts, uncles, cousins, an entire family? How does it feel to have so many people love you? See you? Recognize the sound of your voice? Know your name?

"Where are you from, kitten?" He casts an eye over her, and Croi tenses. But his face doesn't change; no expression of disgust mars his features. "And, this may be a rude question, but what kind of kin are you? I can't tell."

He's not the only one.

"I thought I was a dragon," she says sadly.

"You weren't jesting about that?" The boy sounds startled.

Croi gives him her fiercest look. She wouldn't joke about her potential identity.

"You don't know what your parents are? Who brought you up?" His concern is like a balm. Croi soaks it in.

"I . . ." She hesitates before taking the plunge. "I grew up on the other side . . . in the human world."

He doesn't reply and Croi peeks at him. A frown has marched itself to the center of his forehead and set up home there. It looks wrong on him.

"You came from the human world? Really?" His disbelief couldn't be more obvious if it stood up on a table and sang out loud.

"I don't care if you don't believe me," Croi mutters.

"I thought all doors to the human world were locked," he explains himself. "How did you enter? What is the human world like?"

"I followed the magick." Croi shrugs. "The human world is very much like this world except for the humans."

"What are humans like? Are they really monsters? Do they really have no magick?"

Croi thinks of the humans in the city. "We're all monsters in some ways," she says softly.

The boy stiffens, and a dark look slips into his eyes. He says nothing, but somehow Croi doesn't think he disagrees with her words.

"Who brought you up?" he asks again, changing the subject. He's very curious, for someone who hasn't even told her his name. Not that Croi has told him hers, either.

"I don't want to say," she replies.

He shrugs. "You can keep your secrets, but I'd like to know why the person who brought you up didn't tell you what kind of kin you are."

"I'd like to know that too. I asked her many times but she refused to answer. Perhaps she couldn't. Maybe she was bound not to." Croi shakes her head, not wanting to think about the Hag anymore. "Is the food done?"

He stirs the stew and shakes his head. "A little while longer." The boy looks at her again.

"What?"

"I don't know if this helps, but your eyes are very uncommon. The green ring pronounces you Talamh, but the orange ring asserts your Tine lineage. Having two rings around your eyes is not impossible, but usually the two rings are complementary colors of the same elemental magick, like green and brown rings both belong to Talamh. It's the first time I've seen eyes with rings from two different magicks. What magick do you use?" He looks at Croi expectantly.

Croi frowns, thinking. The only magick she can do right now is calling other people's magick to herself. Does that even count as magick? But she gave her magick to the pixie who cast a spell with it. "Magick has its own language, right? You need to know the words?" She remembers Uaine breaking the summoning spell and the words she used.

The boy nods. "Observe." He speaks a word and taps the ground. A blade of grass unfurls. "You try."

Excited, Croi follows his steps. She speaks the same word he did and taps the ground in exactly the same way. Nothing happens. She tries again. The result is the same.

"Clearly I can't do Talamh magick." She lies back on the ground and contemplates the forest canopy. Not yet, anyway.

"Maybe you can do Tine magick, but unfortunately I can't help with that." The boy dusts his hands and goes to the pot simmering above the fire, opens the lid, and tastes the stew. Croi's eyes widen, and her mouth waters. She sits up quickly. One more second and she's sure she'll drown in her own drool. "It's done."

All thoughts of magick are forgotten as the boy hands her a spoon while he uses the ladle he used to stir the stew. Croi's too hungry to talk, so they eat in silence. For the first time in her life, she is too impatient to fully savor what she's eating. The food is delicious: spicy, fragrant, and filling. It is gone too soon. At the end of the meal, they both drink long drafts of water.

"Is your name a secret?" the catkin asks after a while.

"I will tell you my name if you tell me yours," she tells him.

"Caolan," he says simply.

"Aren't you scared I will try to take your name?" Croi remembers what it felt like when Uaine tried to steal her name and shudders.

"No. All kin have a name they use and another one they keep hidden. You don't?" Croi's face must give her away because he grimaces, an apologetic expression in his eyes. "You don't have to tell me your name."

The catkin's attitude softens considerably after he finds out that Croi has only one name.

"I'm looking for my brothers," he says.

"Where have they gone?"

"Gone? They're just kittens. They wouldn't leave home by themselves." He laughs. It's an ugly sound. "They were taken by the Robber Queen's soldiers. They're being transported to dig for jewels in the mines the blue-horned fauns used to work at—before the disease killed them all."

"The Robber Queen?" Croi's eyes widen. Is he talking about Irial's mother?

How many Robber Queens do you think are in the Otherworld?

"But from Irial's words, she doesn't seem the kind to command her soldiers to kidnap kin from their families," Croi thinks to her other self.

He is her son. You really expect him to see her evilness?

"Yes!" Croi huffs.

"Have you never heard of the Robber Queen?" the catkin asks.

"I told you I'm from the human world. Is she important?" Croi opens her eyes wide and tries to look ignorant.

"She seems to think herself so." The catkin falls into an angry silence Croi doesn't feel the need to interrupt.

The forest is strangely quiet. The sun went down some time ago, and night creatures should have come out now, but they're absent.

Listen, Croi's other self suddenly says.

Croi listens, then gets to her feet without speaking. She walks out of the clearing, motioning for the catkin to follow her. The catkin gives her a puzzled look but walks after her without a word. Croi follows the sound and comes to a wide path in the woods. She stops behind a tree and waits.

First, the soft sigh of a lamentation fills the air. Then, accompanying wails rise and drown all other sounds in the forest. Half a minute later, a funeral procession passes by. It is led by two fae women, deerkin, dressed in brown and green with faces streaked by tears. Following them are four male deerkin, carrying a wooden stretcher on which the body of a child deerkin rests. No marks of violence or abuse mar his face; his eyes are shut as though he is asleep and not dead. A long line of mourners, all performing their grief in various ways, passes by. Croi and Caolan watch silently.

"This is the third funeral procession I have seen," Caolan says, his eyes bright with tears and his hands clenched. "It's true that the magick is running out."

Croi jumps at his words. "I . . ."

"It's because of the Robber Queen!" Caolan continues, his eyes bright with barely restrained pain. "It's because she's holding on to the Talamh throne when it doesn't belong to her."

He's not entirely wrong. If the HeartStone has been missing for a very long time, the Robber Queen probably hasn't been able to bond to the magick.

"Before, when kin faded, their bodies would fade as well, returning to earth. Now, as you saw, the bodies remain, empty shells the earth rejects." Caolan wipes his eyes with the back of his hand and stalks away.

Croi scrunches up her face, feeling the crown of her head ache. The pain is going to be visiting her soon. She shrinks into herself and returns to the clearing without speaking another word.

SIXTEEN

HAVING A LARGE TAIL CHANGES EVERYTHING. CROI shifts and fidgets, feeling extremely strange and awkward. Her forehead itches; she tries to bring up a hand to scratch it and realizes she has no hands. What she has, instead, are wings. The discovery brings excitement that deflates only too quickly when flapping her two wings has no effect on her ground-loving body. She wonders if she can breathe fire and growls, trying to create some heat in her throat. But alas. Not even an ember appears.

What's the point of dreaming about being a dragon when you can't even breathe fire? Croi, feeling resentful, looks around her surroundings and realizes that she's perched, very precariously, at the edge of a mountain. Will it hurt if she falls down in a dream? She'd much rather not find out.

Suddenly lightning flashes and the dreamscape trembles. A moment later, Croi hears familiar footsteps behind her.

"A dragon?" an amused voice says. "Why a dragon?"

Croi hangs her head, reluctant to turn around. Who other than her would meet a beautiful fae prince as a lizard? Her maiden heart is bruised.

"Hey . . ." Irial sounds uncertain now. "It *is* you, right? Can't you tell me your name? I can't keep calling you 'you' or 'the kin who changes bodies every time I see her.' I give you my word that I won't try to hurt you with it."

Croi backs her ungainly form away from the precipice and, after much maneuvering, manages to turn around. "Don't look at me. I'm a lizard."

"You're much more than a lizard. You're a dragon!" Irial grins at her, and Croi feels the stirrings of fire in her heart. She gets excited, but the fire fizzles out a moment later. "I've already given you my word. Tell me your name, huh," he cajoles.

"Should you give your word so easily? Have you seen what happens to people who break their word? I haven't. Is it really as terrible as everyone says it is?" Croi looks at Irial and finds that today he is wearing red flowers in his hair. In fact, every time she has seen him, he has been wearing flowers in his hair. Is it a prince thing? She decides not to ask.

"There's an area in the grounds of the Talamh Caisleán called the Stone Garden. Instead of plants, however, the place is filled with kin who broke their word and, as a consequence, were turned into living stone. Sometimes people who break their word are hit by a century's worth of bad luck at the same time, sometimes they disappear, but mostly they turn into living stone," Irial replies. "I will take you there when you arrive at the Caisleán."

Croi blinks at him. "That's all right. You don't have to bother."

"So? Your name?" His eyes are too warm. Too coaxing.

"Croi," Croi tells him. Maybe she shouldn't have given Uaine her word so easily. Did the stone maid break her word? Is that why she's stone? If she didn't break her word, what *did* she do to get turned into stone?

"Croi." Irial says her name, and Croi shivers, her attention drawn back to him. The way he speaks her name is intimate, a caress even. She shudders, her dragon body ruining the moment. "You're the only Croi I know."

"I . . ." Can dragons blush? Croi looks down to see her green scaly body turning red. The horror! The humiliation!

Thankfully, Irial is polite enough not to mention her changing color.

"Where are you now?" he asks instead.

"Oh! I'm in the Otherworld!" Croi tells him about the empty village and the beast in the mountain. About the pixie meadow and the catkin. When mentioning Caolan, she gets serious. "Don't get offended, all right? But the catkin said your mom is having her minions kidnap young kin from all over Talamh. Is that true?"

It is a gloomy afternoon in Croi's dream, and the wan light creates hollows and shadows on Irial's face. Her words evoke little emotion in the fae boy, and for a moment, Croi thinks her words have angered him.

He says something, but his voice is too low for Croi to comprehend his words.

"What did you say?"

"I said I don't know!" he bursts out. "I wish I could say no and get angry at the accusation, but now it feels like I don't even know her or what she's capable of. What reason could there be for her to kidnap kin? Young kin? If you say she wants them for an army, she already has soldiers at her command. To help her take over the Caislean? She's already the queen and one without any threats to her power. But this is all I know. She might be doing something I don't."

"What you're saying is that she *could* be behind these kidnappings, but she probably isn't?" Croi says out loud, her voice a dragon-roar. She winces. "Sorry."

"Yeah," Irial says, and suddenly sits down on the cliff. Croi, in an attempt to comfort him, covers him with a wing. He gives her a bemused look before his face lightens with a smile. "Thank you."

"I think I am a Tine kin," Croi confides to Irial. He is warm by her side. "I can hear the fire song."

"But weren't you a tree—"

"We decided we'd never talk about my tree phase again. Remember?" Croi growls.

"*You* decided. I never mentioned a thing," Irial mutters. "How far are you from the Caisleán?"

"I'm not sure. I'm waiting for the pixie to find me. I asked her to lead me there," Croi says to him.

Irial says something in response, but his words are drowned out by the scream in her mind. It's her other self.

WAKE UP!!!

The command is sudden and the dream breaks immediately. Croi's eyes open to an abrasive darkness that even her changed eyes cannot pierce.

"What is it?"

Look.

Spherical globes of ghostly blue suddenly push the darkness back, and Croi sits up, her chest hurting. Will-o'-wisps. If she remembers correctly, will-o'-wisps augur danger, doom, and sometimes death. Belatedly, she notices what they're illuminating.

The tree branches that blot out the sky are laden with night crows. They were the darkness that pressed against her eyes. With their sooty feathers and red eyes, night crows are a prelude to nightmares. They sit with unnatural stillness, looking down at Croi. The Hag said that night crows are portents of death. Are the will-o'-wisps present because of the night crows, or are the night crows present because of the will-o'-wisps? This is a puzzle Croi has no interest in unraveling. What she is sure of is that something is either already wrong or about to go wrong.

We must leave this place.

Right. Croi gets to her feet and runs across the clearing to where Caolan is curled up under his blanket.

"Wake up," she whispers. He doesn't move, so she shakes him. It doesn't seem to have any effect.

Leave him.

Croi looks down at the sleeping Meow and shakes her head. She won't leave him. He shared his food with her. How can she betray him? Wherever the danger is coming from, the villains are going to do as much harm to him as they would to her.

"I won't!"

Because he's your friend?

"He's your friend too. You are me." Croi doesn't think this is the correct time for this conversation.

I'm not. You are not me, either. You and I are both different halves of Croi.

"Can we talk about this later? I'm scared of the night crows."

Then leave.

"No!"

Croi sits down beside Caolan and puts her hand on his arm, intending to shake him once more. His skin is smooth, and his magick runs in a steady current under her fingertips. When she presses her fingers into his skin, his magick brightens and splashes out of his skin onto hers. He comes awake gasping and shoves away from her.

"What did you do to me?" he rasps, breathing hard.

"Woke you up," she replies, a frown on her face. "We need to leave here."

"What? Why?" He looks around.

"Look at the night crows. . . ." Croi points and Caolan looks up at the trees. He pales for a second before his eyes darken.

"Finally," he says.

"Have you been searching for them?" Croi doesn't understand.

"If the night crows are here, then the Redcaps are not far away," Caolan says.

"Redcaps?" Croi jumps to her feet.

Can we leave now?

"Let's go!" Croi urges the catkin. She is not sure what Redcaps are, but she's very sure she doesn't want to find out.

"I'm not going anywhere," Caolan says, and Croi looks at him. Should she leave without him? "The Redcaps kidnapped my brothers on the Robber Queen's commands!"

"So your plan is to rescue your brothers by getting abducted by these Redcaps as well?" Croi asks slowly, wondering if he can hear how ridiculous the plan is when it's spoken out loud.

"Yes. I *will* rescue them." Caolan gets to his feet.

As much as Croi wants to persuade him against this course of action, she recognizes from the look on his face that it will be a futile endeavor.

He is determined to be foolish. Leave him.

"All right. Good luck. I will be making my own way from now on." It isn't much of a farewell, but time is limited. Croi turns to go, but before she can take a step, the night crows descend. She brings up her hands to shield her face, but at the last moment before impact, the night crows cast off their physical forms and become smoke, forcing their way into her mouth, nose, and lungs.

The sulfurous stench of fear wakes Croi. It covers her skin and buoys her insides as though her body has been learning to be afraid while her mind was busy sleeping. She lies still, with her eyes closed, trying to orient herself. The last thing she remembers is the night crows turning into black smoke and violating, drowning, forcing her to unconsciousness.

She sends the mental equivalent of a poke to her other self. "Are you there?"

No thanks to you.

"No need to be crotchety. I didn't plan for this to happen," Croi grumbles.

She's in some sort of conveyance that is moving briskly over a rocky road. She opens her eyes and immediately wishes she hadn't because the first thing she sees are the bars of a cage. Bars she is on the wrong side of. Weak light barely illuminates the forest they're passing through. They must have been traveling awhile now. Nothing hurts too much, so Croi is sure no one has taken a bite of her yet. However, the scarf tied around her face is gone.

Croi turns her head and almost swallows her tongue. Caolan is slumped not too far from her in a corner of the cage. Is he dead? She stares at him and sees his chest rising. Whew. In front of her, just two breaths away, is another striped kin. In fact, the entire cage is filled with striped kin. About fifteen or so, not including Caolan. She wonders if they're all catkin. She can't tell as, like Caolan, they're all unconscious in their fae forms.

As the minutes pass, Croi becomes aware of a wrongness within her; her nose stings and her eyes prickle as if in preparation for despair. Her palms are sweating, and she's breathing in short gasps like she is in the process of fleeing from danger. Her chest hurts, but beyond the physical pain is a deep fear mixed with a feeling she can't pin down. Hopelessness. That's what this feeling is.

"What's wrong with me?"

I feel the same way.

Croi sits up gingerly, trying to move past the panic and peer through the wall of kin to see what's pulling the wheeled cage, but the kin are too densely piled, and she can't see through them at all. She tries to shove them away from her and notices that all of them have black patches on their arms. A liquid slime, coating small areas of their skin. She touches the patch on the arm of the kin directly in front of her and jumps when it coalesces into a night crow. It shouldn't be possible for it to be here during the day. The night crows are creatures of the night, the Hag taught, animated by the darkness.

The night crow Croi disturbed fixes a beady red eye on her. Malevolence fairly drips off it. Its magick is a shimmery black and has a discordant melody that grates on her nerves. Croi accepts the challenge in the night crow's red gaze and calls to its magick with a thought. The magick roils and the creature falters, losing its bird form and dissolving into smoke. It collapses back onto the skin of the sleeping kin. Croi stares at the patch in puzzlement when a noise makes her turn. Her mouth drops open at the sight before her.

Behind her cage is another cage and behind it, yet another. She's in a train of cages, all full of prisoners. Fear pushes its way to the surface, and Croi looks around for her pack. It's nowhere to be seen.

Croi breathes in sharply. She lost it. She has lost Uaine's SoulSeed. Uaine is going to die. If Uaine dies, no one will help her sister look for the lost HeartStone. Without the HeartStone, the Saol ceremony won't be completed. When the Saol ceremony isn't completed, Fionar's magick will fail. Her sacrifice will be for naught. And it will all be Croi's fault.

Don't be stupid. It's not like we asked to be kidnapped.

"If I had been more careful . . ." Croi trails off, shrinking into herself.

How could you have done that? So what if the world falls into chaos? Why should we care? No one has ever cared for us. The Hag only brought us up because we were a debt she needed to repay. Uaine only broke the summoning spell because she needed us to transport her SoulSeed to her sister. She took the risk, knowing full well the dangers of handing herself to someone who won't be able to guarantee her survival. As for Fionar, her sacrifice was her decision. We don't need to worry about the fate of the world. What we do need to worry about is ourself. Are we going to survive this day?

Panic envelops Croi at her other self's words, and for a moment she can't breathe. She grips the cage bars with her hands and pulls. Her helplessness shames her. Her chest feels like it's on fire. She tries breathing. It doesn't help. The pain spreads from her chest to her arms to her fingertips. She stares outside blankly, fists clenched, forehead damp with sweat, enduring the agony.

The forest on the other side of the bars doesn't seem quite real. The trees appear as though they were etched into existence by blunt crayons. The moss hanging off the branches is undefined, and the forest floor is made of darkness . . . just like her. She should not exist.

Stop.

The anger in her other self's voice pierces through the dark haze currently trying to overwhelm her. The little flame she swallowed burns through this haze, ruthless in its determination to excise it from her body.

Croi breathes out, suddenly relieved. Her head feels lighter.

Stop existing? Croi shakes her head. She doesn't want to die. She has so many things to do still. So many kinds of food she hasn't tasted, so many places she hasn't been. She still needs to find out who her parents are, what her body really looks like, what her *face* looks like. She needs to find a way to become whole. Fall in love. Find out the taste of kisses.

Croi shakes her head again. Her throat is thick with unshed tears, and her shoulders are bent with a sorrow that insists it is hers. However, this misery feels artificial.

"What is this haze?"

I don't know. It feels like a spell.

Croi brings up an arm to wipe away her tears and freezes. There's a black patch on her skin too. She scratches it, and her fingers come away with black slime on them. Irritated, she rubs at it with the edges of her dress. It smears instead of wiping off. How vexing. She scrubs harder and her skin reddens.

Another tear spills, and an insistent gloominess blankets her. Croi's fingertips heat again. Determined not to succumb to the misery, she rubs her arm against the white bars of the cage, hard enough that it scrapes and blood beads on her skin. When the blood comes into contact with the black slime, it dissolves with a hissing sound. A few minutes later, the black patch is gone, and Croi no longer wants to be death's bride. Relieved, she sits back, exhausted by the sadness.

The scenery outside the cage remains unchanging no matter how much time passes. Has time abandoned them, or does the cage train exist outside of it? The taste in the air—like burnt magick—scares her for reasons she does not care to examine too closely.

After a while, Croi gets up and makes a space for herself beside Caolan. He's warm, and even though it is because of his pigheadedness that they're in this situation, she is still comforted by his presence. The conveyance travels at a steady speed. Just when Croi has grown accustomed to its motion, the cage goes over a rut in the road and she's almost buried under an avalanche of kin. She pushes her way out and wrinkles her nose. They smell as ripe as she does and are probably younger than she is. How long have these kin been unconscious? From their faces, they seem to be male, but Croi cannot be sure. She wonders how they're fed and given water. They were kidnapped for some purpose, so they are probably fed.

There is no sign of their captors except for the taste of the burnt magick in the air.

"What do Redcaps look like?" Croi asks her other self.

I don't know, but I can tell you they're probably not beautiful.

Croi swallows and reaches out to pinch Caolan hard on the arm, but he doesn't seem to feel it. His lack of response is eerie, and she's tempted to pinch him harder, but she resists. Barely. It is his fault they're in this cage, on their way to either become dinner or something just as dire. If he had listened to her and run, they might have escaped.

He's not entirely to blame for our predicament. I told you to run, but you didn't listen.

"He is our friend! How could I leave him?"

Are you sure he thinks of you as warmly as you do him? Look around.

Croi looks at the bars of the cage and admits it. She was wrong. She should have run away as fast and as far as possible.

The catkin said the Redcaps are taking the kin to the mountain with the monster to mine for jewels. To him that's the truth, but we know it to be a lie.

Croi remembers the mountain, the monster, and the empty village. She shudders.

So where are we really being taken?

"Do we need to know the answers to everything? What if knowing is more terrible than not knowing? Can't I just remain ignorant?"

How have we remained alive until now with a brain like yours?

"Hey! My brain is your brain too, you know!" Her other self declines to reply.

Scowling, Croi turns back to Caolan. How did she wake him before? His magick is dull and unmoving underneath his skin. She puts her hand on his arm again and presses it into his skin. Nothing happens. Then she notices the patch of black on his upper arm. The infernal night crows. Just looking at the black makes her skin crawl. Suddenly furious, she looks at Caolan's black patch with renewed determination. As though it senses her regard, the black patch slithers

on Caolan's skin, trying to creep under his sleeve. Ha! As if that'll stop her. She grabs Caolan's arm and rubs it hard against the bars of the cage. The patch doesn't come off; if anything, it just spreads its sliminess even farther across Caolan's arm. That's probably not good. She rubs his arm hard enough that he starts bleeding, but again, there's no change. She pinches the skin on his arm where the patch has spread itself and thinks hard.

It was her blood that conquered the black patch. Maybe the alchemy in her blood destroys night crows. There's only one way to find out.

Croi looks at the sleeping Meow and purses her lips. It's just that she doesn't know why she should bleed for him. *He* should be bleeding for her, but Croi isn't sure she can get out of here without his help. She glances at the slack faces of the unconscious kin, all with their own black patches sinking roots into their skin. She hadn't noticed it before, but apart from the smell of ripe, unwashed bodies and the accompanying stench of fear, there's a darker, danker whiff of despair.

Croi picks up Caolan's hand. His fingers are calloused, but his nails are cleaner than hers. It's a strong hand, a capable one. Yes, this hand will help her escape. She puts Caolan's patch-infested arm on her lap and takes a breath. The wound on her arm is just beginning to scab, and this will hurt, but maybe if she kicks Caolan twice later, this will make them even. Squeezing her eyes shut, she gouges the wound, and when her blood beads again, she smears it on the black patch on Caolan's arm. The black patch reacts immediately. Ha! However, instead of dissipating into a cloud, the night crow reclaims its bird form and squawks loudly. It struggles to retain its birdiness but loses the battle and thins out into smoke that fades with the wind. Croi grunts. Filthy night crow. She smiles smugly and waves the air around her to clear it of the stink the night crow left behind.

Beaming, she turns to Caolan and finds him still sleeping. She pinches him hard again. Surely, he can wake up now.

As Croi is congratulating herself on a battle won, the temperature plummets, and her fear returns, becoming a living thing, beating frantically in her throat. Her chest twinges. She's still holding on to Caolan's hand and dimly realizes that it is clutching hers in a strong grip. Caolan turns so his body is shielding hers. Croi hides her face in his chest, somehow knowing the next few moments will test their courage.

They don't wait long.

First there's the sound of something like cloth being dragged on the ground, a soft sibilance that freezes the flame in her blood. Then there's the smell of decay. The stench of death is more rancid than the stink of fear—fear still retains small notes of hope. Death doesn't. Death smells like the end.

The sound stops beside the cage that, Croi realizes with some shock, has stopped moving. She senses eyes that travel over the prone bodies of the kin; these eyes stop when they reach her. She feels a gaze prickling her exposed limbs. She knows she should keep her eyes closed and pretend to be as unconscious as the rest of them. She knows this, but her eyes open anyway. Croi lifts her head, peeks over Caolan's shoulder, and freezes.

SEVENTEEN

NIGHTMARES WOULD LOSE THEIR POTENCY IN FRONT of this creature.

He stands tall, with limbs clothed in a dark material that seems to absorb all the light around it. His skin is as pale as moonlight, and his fingernails are crimson. White-blond hair falls down to his shoulders. The top of his head is a glistening red, like freshly drawn blood—he is a Redcap. His face is cold carved marble; the skin on both sides of his mouth and both his eyes is cracked, like the parched earth during a drought, revealing the flesh underneath.

She cannot see his eyes as they're hooded. The picture is incomplete—a small mercy.

The stench emanating from the Redcap is overpowering. Croi swallows twice to repress the bile climbing up her throat. Suddenly she is not as optimistic about finding her pack and Uaine's SoulSeed. The thought of being eaten by a creature such as this makes her shudder, and Caolan's arms tighten around her. Perhaps he is afraid too.

Croi shifts in Caolan's tight embrace and wonders if she should risk another peek over his shoulder. How long is the Redcap going to remain in the cage? Just when Croi is about to expire from the tension, the Redcap leaves with a curious clicking sound, taking with him both the arctic temperature and the smell of death. As soon as he is gone, Croi pushes against Caolan's arms and he eases his grip.

She moves back, but there's only so far she can go. The carriage is crowded. Croi busies herself for a few minutes by pushing away the unconscious kin. The cage starts moving again, causing several of them to slide in different directions. When she looks back, Caolan hastily averts his gaze. Croi pats her face. Has she become more hideous since the day before?

We should have run.

"We should have run." She repeats her other self's words, bolstering herself with false courage. Her insides are still quavering from the Redcap, but that doesn't reduce the sting she feels when she sees her reflection in Caolan's eyes. Croi takes a deep breath. There's nothing wrong with the way she looks. Nothing at all. Not everyone in the world, any world, can look beautiful.

"My brothers!" Caolan ignores her for the kin drooling behind her. He shakes one, and when he gets no response, he turns to her with imploring eyes.

"Can you wake him?"

"Maybe."

"How did you wake me?"

Croi refuses to answer his question. As if she's going to confess to bleeding all over him. "Look, if I start waking up the kin, that thing, the Redcap, will come back. He came when I woke you up, didn't he? Do you *want* to attract his attention again?" Actually, Croi's not certain why the Redcap came; it could have been because of the noisy night crow, but Caolan doesn't need to know that. There is more than one way to lie.

The catkin stares at her for a long second. Then he shoves her aside and clambers over the unconscious kin to a small form snuggled up against another.

"This is Aindriu." He speaks softly, patting the little catkin's hair. The little one has the same coloring and stripes as Caolan, though his skin and stripes are a darker brown.

"Were all your brothers taken?" Croi asks. She looks around the cage and wonders who else Caolan is related to.

"Four of them. They were out playing in the hills even though I had told them not to. I'd told them countless times to stay close to home. But they didn't listen. They don't like it when I tell them what to do," he says, rubbing a hand over his face. "I wasn't around. I went fishing. My da's dead, so it's my duty as the eldest to feed my family and keep them safe."

"Are they all here, then? Your missing brothers?" Croi asks.

Who is feeding his brothers now that he's here? Who is keeping them safe?

Croi doesn't repeat her other self's questions out loud. She doesn't think Caolan would want to answer them.

Caolan searches through the cage while she clings to a corner as though her life depends on it. It probably does because Caolan is none too gentle with the kin he's not related to. He finds an older catkin he calls Diarmaid and another one named Orrin.

"I can't find Bearach." He turns to her, desperation adding frenzy to his movements. The cage lurches and Croi stiffens, waiting for the Redcap to return. Thankfully, he doesn't.

"Maybe he's in one of the other cages," she suggests. Caolan looks uncertain. He tries to look into the cage behind theirs, but he can't see through the mass of kin to find his brother.

"Maybe, but what if he's not? Why would they put only him in a separate cage? What if they did something to him? He's the youngest! My mother will never forgive me if something has happened to him." He comes and kneels in front of Croi, catching hold of her hands in his much larger ones. Croi goes still, deciding that she doesn't like to be touched.

"You're too close," she tells him, trying to pull her hands from his grasp. It has no effect.

"Please, I beg you. Wake one of my brothers. Let me ask him what has happened to Bearach." Croi looks at his pleading eyes, not knowing how to refuse him. Unlike the Hag, she has a heart.

"Could you answer some questions before I do?" she says.

"Ask. I'll answer them all," Caolan replies immediately, finally letting go.

Croi rubs her hands. "Who are these Redcaps? Who controls them?"

"No one *controls* them. They choose who to serve. Right now they're the Robber Queen's soldiers." He looks grim. "She must have offered them something they couldn't resist."

"How do you know they serve the Robber Queen?" Croi asks, feeling uncomfortable with his continued assumption of the monarch's guilt.

"Everyone knows!" Caolan insists, not answering her question.

Just like everyone knows the kin are taken to the mines to dig for jewels?

"How do you know where the kidnapped kin are being taken?"

"I'm not certain, but there have been rumors. . . ." Caolan trails off and his jaw clenches. "All the blue horns died suddenly, and there's no one to work the mines. The strong and able Lesser Fae are being taken to provide labor and supply the Robber Queen with the precious gems she so loves."

His words are hollow.

"Yeah, but he believes in them," Croi thinks to her inner self.

His truth is not necessarily the only truth.

"You want to tell him that?" Croi retorts.

I don't want to poke a wounded tiger.

The catkin snarls soundlessly. "Are we done? Can you wake Diarmaid? He's the oldest among them, so he'll know what happened to Bear."

"Wait. I'm not done yet. I want to ask about the magick—"

"I can't tell you what I don't know, kitten. I've kept my end of the bargain. Please, before I slip further into mad worry, wake my brother."

Croi is about to protest, but a look at the cat's face has her giving in. "Which one do you want me to wake?" She steps on a foot and someone's hairy hand to get to the kin Caolan is pointing at. He looks about fifteen winters old and has black hair peppered with white. His skin is dappled with cream-and-black stripes in a manner identical to Caolan's. His sleeping face is tearstained and hollowed.

A feeling whispers tragedy to Croi, so she avoids Caolan's eyes just in case he reads hers.

"Go keep a look out for the Redcaps," she commands Caolan's chin. She waits until he has moved to the side before she kneels by the younger cat. She locates the black patch on his inner wrist. It seems to have sunk deep into his skin, leeching the color from the surrounding area, leaving it pale and magickless. Hmm. Croi lifts the hand of a neighboring kin, and the magickless area around the patch of that kin is larger. She checks the skin around other patches on other kin, and they all tell the same story. The night crows are consuming the magick in the kin bodies. Is that why everyone is sleeping? Because they don't have the magick to do anything else? If so, Croi wonders why she didn't stay asleep. What's so different about her? Not that she's complaining about being awake.

"Is he conscious yet?" Caolan asks from his spot in the corner.

Croi says nothing but gives him the most eloquent look she can manage. She turns her head back to the brother and looks down at his face. Sighing loudly to express her discomfort, she brings up her arm and gouges her wound yet again. It hurts. It hurts a lot. Croi decides to make Caolan serve her forever in exchange for the pain she's currently suffering. Two drops of blood do nothing, so she squeezes out another two, cursing the human curses she learned in the city. Four drops of blood seem to suffice. She watches as the night crow tries to regain its bird form before it fails and dissipates into noxious clouds. She waves her hand to clear the air, leans back on her haunches, and waits.

She doesn't have to wait long. The catkin's eyes flutter open, and the first thing he sees is Croi's face. His eyes widen in terror, and he opens his mouth in a scream, but Caolan is faster. He muzzles his sibling before the young catkin can make a sound.

"Diarmaid, calm down. She's a friend!" Croi beams at his words and feels mollified. Maybe she shouldn't be so grudging about spilling blood. They're friends. Friends spill blood for each other.

The younger cat sees his brother and sags, the fight going out of him. He hides his face in Caolan's chest and sobs, great gasping sobs as though his sadness were a rapid river and he, too small a vessel to ride it. Caolan holds the kin tight, patting his back and making crooning sounds. Croi looks away; the moment between the siblings feels too intimate for her to intrude upon.

Diarmaid's sobs subside after a while, but he doesn't move away from his brother. If anything, he clings to him even tighter. He keeps sneaking looks at Croi—she can read the disgust in the wrinkle of his nose and the fear in the flare of his nostrils. She gives him her most insolent stare, and the young catkin bows his head.

"Diarmaid, I see Aindriu and Orrin, but there's no sign of Bearach. Where is he?" Caolan asks, his voice hoarse with urgency.

The younger cat stiffens, his face going oddly still, as though he has been reminded of something he was trying to forget. He opens his mouth and closes it without uttering a word. And then he just folds over like his insides have suddenly been liquefied. He writhes on the floor of the cage, captive to some anguish the rest of them are not yet privy to.

"Mida, calm down! Breathe!" The last is a plea. Caolan grabs his brother by the shoulders and simply embraces him until the terror passes, until he stops shaking, until he can breathe again.

"Where's Bearach, Mida?" Caolan asks again.

"They ate"—the catkin breaks off in a choked sob—"Bearach. They woke us up when they took him. We couldn't do anything. I swear we couldn't. We tried, but they froze our limbs so we couldn't even move a finger."

"What are you saying, Mida?" Caolan shakes his head, drawing away from his brother. "Stop making up stories."

"I'm not! I can't! I would do anything to make this only a story. But it's not. Bearach's gone. The Redcaps . . ." The catkin breaks off, gasping, unable to complete the sentence. And at this point, he no longer needs to.

EIGHTEEN

CAOLAN'S GONE GRANITE; HIS RIGID SHOULDERS spell out his disbelief. Croi fumbles, uncertain what to do or say. Diarmaid pulls his knees to his chest, rocking back and forth.

"Caolan." Croi leans forward and, after hesitating, touches his shoulder. It isn't to offer comfort, not exactly. She doesn't know how to console someone. She simply needs to do something. Anything. Caolan recoils from her, losing his balance. He hits the cage bars hard, and the conveyance lurches once again. His eyes are wild. He looks destroyed. A sudden violence, a silent ruination.

Croi leaves Caolan to his pain and Diarmaid to his and retreats to a far corner of the cage. She cannot understand what it must feel like to lose someone that terribly. Actually, she doesn't even know what it feels like to have someone to lose. Her heart cannot fathom the horror, though her mind understands the depths of the loss.

Time passes. An hour, maybe two or three or five. What does time matter anymore? Croi is surrounded by kin, but she has never felt as alone as she does right now in this full cage, on this dark road, with the damp smell of grief and her broken self.

The road continues in front, and on either side of the conveyance, the forest remains unchanged. This monotony is difficult to endure, but endure they must.

"Have the Redcaps eaten anyone else since?" Croi finally breaks the silence and asks the younger catkin, who raises a tear-wrecked face to her, baleful glare in place.

"Isn't it enough that they took our brother?" he chokes out.

"For you it's not *enough*; it's too much. For them, it may be too little." Croi glances at Caolan, wondering if he'll ever be unbroken again. "They will need to eat again."

Diarmaid swallows before answering. "I don't know how long I've been asleep. They only woke us up when they took Bear."

Croi stares at him, willing him to say more. Surprisingly, he does.

"After, they left us awake for three days . . . so they could watch us grieve, I think. We were in shock for the first few hours. We couldn't understand it. The injury was too great. Then Aindriu started screaming. He screamed till he went hoarse. Orrin just went silent. Me? I cried. I'm useless. I was the one who made them come out to play, you know? I called Bear away from Mother. He didn't want to join us, but I told him he needed to play with the big cats now. He was only seven. I killed him. *I* killed him. You see? I should be the one dead. Not Bear. Me." His words crash into each other, slurring in their rush to get out, to be heard. As though confessing will vindicate him. He wants so badly to be told that everything will be all right. No one here will tell him that lie.

Croi turns to Caolan. No help is coming from that quarter. What should she say to this young cat?

Tell him he should be happy he wasn't the one eaten.

"He might hit me if I say that."

I don't have any other suggestions.

"You are terrible at comforting people."

You say that like you're any better. Tell him we'll take revenge.

"We'll avenge your little brother." Though she feels rather silly, Croi obeys her inner self's command.

"Avenge? We can't even escape the cage," Diarmaid says.

"That's true. But it's important to have goals." Croi shakes a fist at the little catkin.

"We will get out of here alive. We will survive this. I won't fail you a second time, brother." Caolan's rough voice interrupts Croi. She looks at him and flinches. His sorrow is written in the planes of his face, warning them not to ask about his pain. It seems a living thing, this grief, filling the empty spaces around them, stealing the air they need to breathe.

"It wasn't *your* fault!" Diarmaid bites out, looking as though he wishes it were.

"Can we argue about whose fault it was later? Maybe when we're not in a cage on our way to being dinner?" Croi says, and both cats turn to her with identically angry expressions. She ignores them.

"Can't you change form and squeeze through the bars?" She eyes Diarmaid. He should be able to do it.

"No, the bars are made of human bones. They prevent us from reaching our magick," Caolan replies.

Croi turns and looks at the bars with wide eyes. They have been smoothed by the passing of time and the elements, but there's not even an echo of magick. She had thought their lack of magick was because they were old and not because they were human bones. She suppresses a shiver and wonders how many humans died to furnish these cages with bars.

"Where did they get the human bones?" Croi knows this is not the time for the question, but she can't help asking it.

Caolan shrugs. "Sometimes kin steal human babies from their world into ours."

How dastardly evil. Croi decides to travel the Otherworld and save all stolen humans as soon as she has finished running Uaine's errand.

She turns her gaze outside. "This road just won't end. We've been traveling for hours without getting anywhere," she mutters, groaning her frustration.

"That's because we're on a Shadow Road. It's made by magick and lays out paths where none exist. It's bad magick. Redcap magick. We're probably halfway to the mines by now," Caolan replies.

"How long do you think it has been?" The Saol ceremony can't have passed, since the world hasn't ended.

Your attempts at humor are atrocious.

"I can't say," Caolan replies.

"We're slowing down!" Diarmaid hisses. They duck down into a corner as the wheeled cages slow down and arrange themselves in a semicircle. The road falls away and gradually disappears when the magick pops. The landscape shifts and comes into focus. They're in a large clearing somewhere in the forest. It seems to be afternoon. The sun is nowhere to be seen as the sky has been conquered by sullen gray clouds. There are more than nine cages in total, and all of them are filled with sleeping kin. A caravan with ornate trappings, pulled by creatures Croi would call horses were it not for their red eyes and sharp horns, stops in the middle of the clearing. The door to the caravan opens.

Five Redcaps, their cloaks flowing behind them, descend. Croi bites down the fear that rushes up her throat at the sight. She peers from behind a bulky kin as they walk to the cage farthest from the one they're in and start to examine the sleeping kin inside.

Caolan whispers an epithet and drags both his younger brother and Croi into an embrace. "Pretend to sleep," he hisses, his arms a shackle around Croi.

He's too close again. Croi is too scared to care about her inner self's discomfort.

The waiting is the worst. Leaden seconds pool into minutes punctuated by their breathing. The Redcaps draw nearer steadily, bringing with them the stench and the cold. Fear holds Croi still as the stench grows pronounced.

There is a series of clicks and whistles, a sound like paper tearing and then a laugh. The Redcaps don't seem to converse in Faerish. The cage door opens and Croi trembles, trying to stay as motionless as possible, even though the urge to run is nipping the soles of her feet. She can feel Caolan's heart racing.

The Croi-inside would like to kill the Redcaps; she's entirely confident that she can. Croi, on the other hand, is just as certain there's something very wrong with the one inside her.

There seem to be two Redcaps in the cage now and from the frequent clicks and laughs Croi hears, they're having a grand conversation. If they don't go away soon, she's sure she's going to do something stupid. Like open her eyes.

She feels them draw closer and can't help but tense. They're hovering over the corner where Croi and the two catkins sit, pretending to be unconscious. She can feel their attention, the same attention she gives chickens at dinner. Suddenly, unexpectedly, Croi is pushed forward, drawing the Redcaps' attention completely. Before she can react to this betrayal, she feels a touch on her arm. Ice follows, seeping through the fingertips of the Redcap and spreading to her limbs, freezing them. She gasps and opens her eyes to see a Redcap leaning over her. The creature meets her eyes and smiles. His teeth are chiseled to points and, like his fingers, tipped with red. He picks her up, slinging her over his shoulder.

Croi catches a glimpse of Caolan before they carry her away. His eyes hold hers for a blink before he looks down. His cheeks are red, perhaps he's ashamed, but his expression is resolute. Faced with the chance that the Redcaps would choose either him or his brothers, he chose to push her out. She's expendable; they're not. They're family; she's less than a stranger.

The Redcap carries her to the middle of the clearing where, in front of the fancy caravan, a fire is being built. Croi looks at the companion Redcap who is walking behind the one carrying her. Gazing at his face, she forgets to breathe because for the very first time, she can name the emotion darkening the Redcap's irises: hunger.

NINETEEN

THE MOMENT BURSTS INTO BEING WITH A WICKED clarity.

Here she is. About to be dinner. Numb, bound by ice this time. Powerless, yet again. There they are. Night terrors realized into day, preparing to eat her. The sun is high in the sky, hidden behind the clouds. Nary a breeze rustles the leaves of the trees. Will-o'-wisps flood the dark places in the forest surrounding them, waiting for another kin to do the death dance, waiting for another story to end.

A chalky, mindless fear grips Croi's limbs and breathes hotly over her skin. Not that she can feel it. She can't feel her body at all, and oddly enough, she wants to laugh. Even now, her body is not her own.

She refuses to think about Caolan's action. Her mind understands that he simply chose his sibling over the stranger he barely knows, but her heart. It's wounded. For someone without siblings, without parents, this betrayal is just another abandonment in a series of abandonments, but for some reason, it hurts the most.

The smell of the dead that clings to the Redcaps is even more rancid at such close proximity. A few night crows roost on the roof of the caravan. Their beady red eyes mock her.

"Is this it?" Croi thinks to her other self. "Is this really the end?" Croi fights her despair, but she's no match for the dread that holds her as tightly as the Redcap magick does.

What if it is?

"I don't want it to be."

Since when have we had choices in the things that happen to us?

"I'm tired of being a puppet for others."

Me too.

The Redcap puts her down a little ways from the fire, facing her toward the caravan and away from the cages. The ground is hard, and she cannot move, though she tries. Just like when she was under the summoning spell, her hands and feet don't obey her mind. The Redcaps, all five of them, stand in a circle and look down at her. They have a rapid conversation in clicks and whistles. One of them sinks to his haunches in front of her and lifts her chin with a long pale finger tipped in dried blood.

Croi looks up into his eyes. They're red with black irises. His magick lacks vitality; it looks washed out, like the night just before the morning sweeps away the darkness. The Redcap touches her cheek, leaving behind a trail of ice, and Croi shudders, feeling his desire for her flesh. No, not just her flesh. The Redcap licks the finger he touched her face with, and his magick brightens slightly. He wants what's inside of her. Something more potent than her flesh.

Our magicks.

The Redcaps are identical except for their sizes. Some are bigger than the others. The largest Redcap says something to the one kneeling before Croi, and the other inclines his head deferentially. The largest one must be their leader. The pit fire sparks, drawing her attention.

The fire is singing.

The fire song awakens the little flame in Croi's veins. It flares inside her and warms her body gradually, melting the ice magick encasing her limbs.

She pushes against the fear and thinks. If the flame melts the ice holding her, will she be able to run before she is caught?

Where can we go? How far can we run?

The leader issues a command in a staccato click followed by a sharp whistle. In response, a Redcap disappears into the caravan only to reappear a minute later with a rectangular wooden box in his hands. The wooden box has symbols carved on it, and a strange sort of magick weaves in and out of these symbols. The Redcap hands the box over to the leader, who opens it to reveal a large dagger with a dangerously curved blade. When the light hits its blade, the dagger wails. The hilt is bejeweled with rubies.

Croi's attention locks on to the dagger, and she realizes that her time has become finite. Her heart thunders in her chest, her throat goes dry, and her eyes prickle with unshed tears.

Though she has joked about dying, Croi has never considered it with any gravity before. What shape will it have? How much will it hurt? Will she just be gone? Will the pixie wonder what happened to her?

The Redcaps don't lift their gazes from her body, and she is too afraid to look away from them. What if she blinks and they pounce? She's food to them. Just like a chicken is food to her. Is that how it is for them? Is she just a chicken to them?

Croi tenses as the dagger-carrying Redcap approaches her.

This is it. This is the closest she has come to not being. The red

threads of magick wound around her feet and hands have been loosened by the little flame inside. Croi pushes against the magick with all the strength she has. Nothing happens.

Why can't she fight back?

We are always without power when it matters the most.

A wave of violent anger sweeps over her, taking the little flame that was in her veins and stoking it into an inferno, shoving the fear away. The numbness disappears; both her selves are angry. A moment later, "angry" is too puny a word to correctly describe the savagery of the emotion both her selves feel.

Call the fire to you.

Croi obeys, crooking her finger in a silent summons, and the fire burning in the pit responds. The Redcap nearest to her slams his hand down on her shoulder, intending to reinfect her with his magick and freeze her limbs again, but before he can, the fire oversteps its boundaries and comes to her, scorching the ground between them.

The fire's movements alarm the Redcaps, and they give off a series of whistles and clicks. She doesn't know what else they do because the fire slams into her, and for one long moment, she doesn't think at all. She can't. She simply burns. It is a glorious feeling, but the heat fades too soon. And just like that moment in the clearing when she first met the catkin, both of Croi's selves exist at once in a tenuous harmony. Her two selves unite.

She is fortified by the fire; it gives her the courage to withstand what will come and what will be. Because the fact is, there are five of the Redcaps and only one of her. Were she to fight, it would not be a battle but a massacre, and yet, her pride refuses to capitulate. Croi's skin heats, and the Redcap holding her is unable to endure it; he lets go of her with an angry sound. She stands then, a fawn testing her new legs, and faces her would-be murderers.

The red eyes of the Redcaps are trained on her body, glittering in the weak light of the day. She is Croi, the united halves of the broken whole, and she will fight.

The Redcaps have no expressions on their faces; the flesh visible through the cracks in their skin is bleeding now. They, aware of how terrifying they are, look toward Croi as if waiting for her to falter and quail.

Croi smiles at them, gleeful and giddy. The circumstances are terrible, but she's whole right now. All her questions have found answers. She's one whole person and not aching halves. She is not anyone's prey. She raises her chin, takes the heat from the fire burning in her; her smile glitters, and she waits for the Redcaps to make a move.

She knows they will. They have too much hunger and too little patience. A few seconds later, the leader of the Redcaps brings up the dagger, slices the air, marking the ground underneath. It's a ritualistic gesture Croi doesn't understand. Nor does she care to. Done marking, the Redcap takes a step toward her. She burns more fiercely. Death may be imminent, but so what? She's whole. She will have no regrets even if she dies at this moment.

A chant flows through the three Redcaps who have moved to stand behind her, waiting to catch her if she runs. The leader is followed by another at his shoulder. As the Redcaps approach, Croi sees now what she didn't before.

One red strand of magick links the Redcaps to each other; it weaves in and out of the body of each Redcap. They're five bodies, united by one magick, and that magick appears to be failing. Croi watches as the Redcaps stumble when the magick within them sparks and goes still for a moment before moving again.

She calls to the Redcap magick, to see if she can. She croons to it. She tempts it with the strength of the two magicks racing around her body.

The Redcaps' magick listens to her call; it is tempted by her promise of power. The red magick's desire for her is thick in its faltering song. It sees her as fruit, ripe and luscious, to pick, to eat, to suck dry.

It is no surprise the magick accepts her invitation.

The Redcaps jerk to a stop when they feel their magick move out. The leader throws back his head and screams—the sound nightmares would make had they voices. The Redcap magick is rooted in the leader's chest, so it hurts him most when it tries to leave.

The Redcap on Croi's right moves then, faster than she thought he could. He slaps her left cheek, his nail tearing her lips. She falls to the ground, unable to withstand the force of the strike. There's pain. There is *always* pain. But she cannot stop to savor the hurt. She looks up at the Redcap who struck her as he leans over her supine body. He sticks out a finger, wiping the blood off her lips. He licks his finger. Hums his pleasure.

Croi tries to get up, and another Redcap pushes her down and holds her there. She struggles, but the Redcaps are too strong. They keep her prisoner in that position. The fire still burns within her, but she cannot burn anything outside. The Glamour hasn't broken enough yet.

The leader of the Redcaps kneels before her, and their eyes meet. He pauses at whatever he sees in her gaze. The moment has come. A Redcap behind Croi pulls her head back, exposing her neck, treating her as a lamb to slaughter. She looks up at the sky, wondering when the clouds moved in. The dagger, heavy with magick, approaches the pulse gone wild in her neck.

Right before the blade touches the skin on her neck, the air is torn apart by an arrow. A moment of confused chaos follows. The Redcaps shove away from Croi; her head falls forward, her breath remains in her throat, her heart continues beating. The leader of the Redcaps falls, an arrow protruding from the center of his head. There is no blood.

The night crows leave the sleeping kin, rise up as smoke, and reclaim their bird shapes. They squawk loudly and join the remaining Redcaps as they take up strategic points around the clearing. They're protecting the fallen leader even though his wound is fatal. Croi looks closer at his prone form and sees that though his life is ending, the magick rooted inside him is still pulsing. The other Redcaps are keeping him alive.

A rain of arrows falls, and the night crows speed off in various directions. The Redcaps pay Croi no attention as their eyes sweep the surroundings, trying to pinpoint the direction from which they're being attacked. This moment comes as mercy, as opportunity, and she seizes it.

She builds a command into her call and sends it to the Redcap magick. The Redcap magick doesn't hesitate; it leaps to her. As the Redcap magick flows into Croi, she connects to the other Redcaps. She feels the leader die when the magick leaves him and roots in her. She hears the mind voices of the remaining Redcaps—the sound of a winter wind—she feels their hunger, their grief for their fallen brother, their need for vengeance. She feels the things the Redcaps don't say— the evil in them flushes her cheeks red—she learns to fear the same thing the Redcaps do, light and heat. She becomes the Redcaps and the Redcaps become her.

Croi fills herself to the brim, and still the Redcap magick pours into her. There is no end to it. It threatens to shade in the deepest spaces within her. She has only one way to destroy the magick before it takes over.

She commands the fire in her to burn the Redcap magick. The fire obeys instantaneously. The Redcaps sense their magick dying and turn to Croi, rushing to kill her, but before they can, they fall to the ground, clutching their chests. They keen, guttural sounds of pain. Croi watches the Redcaps die along with their magick, and she smiles.

She doesn't burn all the Redcap magick. She keeps just a little bit of it to flavor her own, to give her a bite, to make her a little more dangerous.

The death throes are over in minutes, and the Redcaps are gone. Their magick is less than an echo—except for the bit she keeps. The night crows are smoke, as are the horselike beings that pulled the carriage. Croi sits on the ground, at the center of the chaos, and breathes.

TWENTY

UNLIKE HUMANS, KIN AREN'T BURDENED BY THE weight of souls. Instead, they have magick. Human lives are meteors in the night sky, but their souls are immortal. On the other hand, kin lives are usually measured in a collection of eternities, but their ends, when they do come, are absolute.

But if Croi doesn't have a soul, why, then, does she feel hollowed out by the deaths of the Redcaps? If she hadn't killed them, they would have killed her. And yet, the feeling, too layered to be simple grief, persists.

She kneels among the corpses of the Redcaps, concentrating on breathing. She holds on to the fire inside tightly, knowing that once it leaves, she'll be severed again. She'll become broken again.

Dusk is fading. The imprisoned kin are awake and struggling to get out of cages that remain locked. Pain rends her insides with every breath she takes, but Croi remains stubborn, not willing to let go, not willing to break.

She looks at the body of the Redcap nearest to her. He was about to plunge the knife into her when he fell. His pale features, contorted in a snarl, are frozen in death. Are Redcaps truly evil, or are they victims of their nature? Croi felt their hunger; it ruled them in the end. Would she, too, steal the magick of others in order to satiate herself? Would she, too, feast on kin flesh to fill the void that defies filling?

Of course she would. Hunger would give her no other choice. How, then, can she judge the Redcaps for the things they did? For the things they were about to do? Very easily, it seems. She doesn't just judge them. She loathes them.

The cries of the imprisoned kin get louder, and Croi looks at the forest around them. The trees seem anxious to swallow up the clearing, encroaching on its uneven periphery. What will happen to them when night falls? A lot of hungry horrors must live in this forest. At the thought, Croi tries to get up, but her feet refuse to cooperate.

A frisson of danger lights the air, and Croi stiffens, her hands clenching. She raises her head to see a fae girl rushing toward her. The fae's red hair is streaming behind her as her long limbs eat up the distance between them. Her skin is a burnished orange-brown, glowing with health, vitality, and magick. A grim look decorates the delicate features of her face, and her mouth moves, as do her hands, readying a spell with which to attack Croi.

When she's five steps away, the fae flings something in Croi's direction. Croi smells smoke before she sees the ball of fire rushing toward her, its heat so intense, the air shimmers. The orange in Croi's eyes deepens. She gets to her feet, easily this time. She does not avoid the fireball. Rather, she opens her arms to it, stepping back at the impact. The flames sink through her skin and into her veins.

The red-haired fae comes to a sudden stop, stumbling when her body reacts more slowly than her mind. Shock steals all expression from her face, and her eyes learn the color of fear.

Croi smiles at her. "My turn."

The red-haired fae's magick, a robust red and gold, coils around her body in plentiful abundance. Croi's smile widens.

She doesn't bother to sing to the fae's magick; she doesn't need to make an effort for such a trifle. She simply crooks a finger to it, commanding it to obey, and the fae's magick is helpless to do otherwise.

The fae screams like Uaine did. Like the Redcaps did. Her eyes meet Croi's for all of one terrified second. Then Croi lets go of the magick, and it trickles back to the fae, pale and subdued. The fae crumples to the ground. In the next moment, there's a shout, and Croi senses a sword slicing the air before arriving sharp at her neck.

She tilts her head to the side and looks at the soldier holding the sword. He is dressed in a black tunic and pants of the same color; his face is beautiful but stern. He meets her eyes for half a second before his hand trembles. The sword falls first, then he follows, dropping to his knees before Croi. At that point, a number of similarly dressed fae slip out of the forest and into the clearing, keeping Croi and the other two fae at the center.

"You're alive!!!" A high-pitched musical voice pierces the air, forcing the black-clad soldiers aside. The pixie comes to a stop, hovering in the air above them, looking around in bewilderment. "What happened to Ceara? Daithi? Why are they on the ground?"

At her words, Croi turns to look at Tinder, and the fae soldier on the ground immediately gets to his feet and rushes to the red-haired fae, or Ceara, as Tinder named her.

"Your friends?" Croi whispers. She can barely deny the fire's desire to leave. The pixie nods. "Let them not attack me." Before the final word is fully out, Croi falls to the ground and writhes as the fire burns through her skin before leaving. She is severed again. Broken once more. The fire flows back to the pit, burning brighter, replete

with Redcap magick. Croi lies on the ground, smudged by the ash, convulsing with the pain.

Breathe.

"I suddenly no longer want to," she thinks to her other self.

Breathe anyway. Think about this. The Hag knew of our severed self all along.

"What do you mean?" Croi regains some sense of self, some measure of anger, and breathes deeply.

Have you forgotten? She didn't let you touch fire ever. She went as far as to make you give her your word to never play with fire in the human city. Because she knew the fire would join our halves into one, even if only for a brief period.

Croi thinks of her last few minutes with the Hag, then sneers. "Does her knowing surprise you? She has already betrayed us."

I loved her just like you did.

Croi feels the wetness on her cheeks and hides her face. First the Hag, then Caolan. Who will betray her next? The pixie? The fae prince? What is life when all your memories are tinged with pain? When your hours complete themselves on your ability to endure hurt?

We can't give up. Not yet. We have to find the kin who halved us. We have to hurt them as much as we are hurting. I refuse to give up like this. You owe me this.

Croi closes her eyes, acknowledging the truth in her other self's words, and continues enduring.

When she opens her eyes again, it is full dark. A small fire is burning in front of her, and when she sits up, she sees several small fires flickering merrily around the clearing. The kidnapped kin, having been freed, are sitting around these fires, which often have meat sizzling above them. All signs point to them recovering their spirits as they wait for the food to be ready.

"Are you there?" Croi reaches for her other self and sits up, wincing as pain lances through her chest.

Yes.

Croi breathes out, comforted. She takes inventory of her aches and finds that her head feels heavier than it used to. She raises a hand to touch her head, and some of her hair falls forward. Frowning, she gathers her hair and brings it to the front. It grew from her shoulders all the way to below her waist. The color also changed from a muddy brown to gold, red, and brown. Croi braids it with aching fingers.

"What should I do next?" she asks her inner self.

You *gave our word to the dryad to get her SoulSeed to Talamh Caisleán.*

"That was the only way to break the summoning spell, you know that," Croi grumbles.

Go look for the pack. I don't want to be living stone.

Croi attempts to get to her feet but fails, so she sits back, trying to muster up energy for another attempt. Her movements attract attention, and soon the pixie flies over.

"You're awake!" Tinder's bright voice startles Croi. The pixie is flitting up and down in the air in front of her, a worried look on her face. "Are you . . . all right?"

Instead of answering, Croi looks at the fae called Ceara who is standing a safe distance behind Tinder. Accompanying her is the dark soldier who tried to defend her from Croi. They are both staring at her with complex gazes that she doesn't care to decipher.

"I will live," Croi replies, looking away from the fae couple.

"This is Ceara, and with her is Daithi," Tinder says, rapidly making introductions. "They helped me track you. Ceara saw you and mistook you as part of the Redcap group."

"Because all ugly things must be evil?" Croi asks faintly.

"I apologize," the red-haired fae says, stepping forward and sketching a bow. "I should have known better than to act on assumptions." Ceara's voice is husky, and she brings a smell of spices with her. Something piquant. It's not an entirely unpleasant smell.

Should we forgive her?

Croi nods at Ceara, indifferent to her apology.

"*I'm* not going to apologize," the soldier, Daithi, says.

"I don't recall asking you to," Croi says. Daithi thins his lips and turns away, as if looking at her is beneath his dignity.

"How did you get caught by the Redcaps?" Tinder asks.

"Are you asking me if I did anything to attract their attention?" Croi asks.

"I guess?"

"Does eating a hot meal count?" Croi replies.

"How long were you on the Misery Train?" the red-haired fae asks, moving closer to Croi. Seeing her blank look, she explains. "That's what the train of cages is called."

"I don't remember. Time didn't seem to move outside."

"That's because you were on the Shadow Road. It's a good thing the Redcaps love comfort. If they hadn't left the Shadow Road, we would never have been able to catch up. The archers climbed the trees on the north side of the clearing to aim at the Redcaps, but then the night crows attacked and put some of the weaker ones to sleep. Thank Fionar Ceara was there. She set them on fire, but there were too many of them for her to handle. For a while I was sure we were going to end up in the cages right beside you, but all of a sudden, they just"— Tinder waves her hands around—"dissipated. It was really strange. What happened?"

"Presumably the Redcaps died at that moment," Croi replies, wondering if she should tell them that she was the one who killed the creatures.

Tell them. The knowledge will make them wary and less likely to trouble you.

"How did they die?" Ceara's eyes are a light orange ringed by amber and surrounded by long, curled lashes. She's wearing a tunic and leggings of a fine silver material Croi has never seen before.

"I killed them," Croi says. Her words fall heavily in the space between them, stark in their simplicity and certainty.

"How?" Daithi asks, the contempt on his face finally shifting to something more, something that looks a lot like respect.

"I burnt their magick." Croi looks up at him and quirks her lips. "Do you need a demonstration?"

"Why did my magick not hurt you?" Ceara asks, not letting Daithi respond to Croi's provocation. "Are you Tine? Why do you have two rings around your eyes? How can you hold that much fire? Why were you in so much pain at the end?"

"Why do I have to answer your questions?" Croi counters, her earlier spirit returning. She tries to get to her feet and succeeds this time. Tinder yelps.

"You grew taller! Your hair changed!" She makes rapid observations, flying around Croi at a dizzying speed.

"You should know that if you continue to buzz around me, I will be tempted to smack you. I'm not really up to resisting temptations right now," Croi warns, and the pixie pouts, returning to perch on Ceara's shoulder.

"Do you want to join the rebel army?" Ceara says without any warning. Daithi looks at her, a displeased expression flitting across his features.

"What rebel army?" Croi stares at the red-haired fae a bit incredulously. "Never mind. Don't tell me. It's better if I don't know any details." She waves her hand, preventing the fae from answering. "Is there anything about me that says I'll make a good soldier?"

"No," Daithi replies. Croi ignores him.

"You are stronger than me," Ceara says, her face excited. She ignores the soldier too.

"I don't even know what you are fighting for," Croi says. She glances at Tinder, her one constant in this phantasmagoria. It's too bad the pixie's attention is fixed on Ceara.

"For the death of the Robber Queen," Ceara says without hesitation.

Croi takes several steps away from her. "Why do you want to kill the Robber Queen?"

"She killed my entire maternal family!" Ceara says, her magick sparking dangerously.

"Tinder, I feel like there's something I am not understanding," Croi says a little desperately.

"She is Ceara, daughter of Aodh, the Tine King, and Mabh, the younger daughter of the Forever King." Croi takes in Tinder's words and looks deeper at the red-haired fae. She is the kin Irial has been looking for. Introducing them to each other might not work out for the best, however, considering Ceara *does* want to kill his mother.

"The Robber Queen killed the Forever King and his family?" Croi asks.

"No, the Robber Queen's father did, but *she* inherited his sin," Tinder says softly.

"Does inheriting his sin make her guilty?" Croi's head aches, and she really can't understand why she has to have this conversation minutes after being assaulted by murderous kin. But then again, when have people ever asked her what she wants?

"Why wouldn't it?" Ceara demands, obviously not wanting to consider otherwise.

"Because though this Robber Queen inherited the sins of her father, she did nothing directly. *She* didn't kill your maternal family. If what I've heard is the truth, all the actions you are condemning her for were undertaken by her father, so *he* is the guilty person. Yet you seek to kill her. Why? As an expression of your filial piety? Why did the Robber Queen inherit his sin anyway?"

"The Usurper—I mean, the Robber Queen's father—was too injured, and living had become too unbearable for him. But he wouldn't be able to die until he paid back, in pain, what he owed for spilling blood in the Caisleán. By inheriting his sin, the Robber Queen allowed her father to die," Tinder answers, instead of Ceara.

"So, you are saying that she is already being punished for what her father did. The Caisleán is punishing her, which means no one is else is allowed to. At least, not until she's done paying for her father's sin. Once she has been punished for the sins her father committed, what right do you have to take her life? Unless she has done something else? Has she? Has she committed other sins that move you to end her?" Croi asks Ceara.

The fae princess doesn't answer, so Croi continues speaking.

"Also, could you tell me what her death will achieve? No matter what justifications you give it, killing someone is murder. If you kill her, how will you be any different from those you say you are fighting against?

"You are Tine, so you can't rule this kingdom. If the Robber Queen dies, who will replace her? Her heir? Will you kill him, too? Will there be a war as people vie for the throne? Do you think kin will thank you for the pain that a war, if there is one, will bring? I don't know much about ruling or royalty, but surely the primary motive of anything a monarch does is to benefit the subjects they serve. How will *you* be serving Talamh kin by killing the Robber Queen?" Croi ends her monologue with a dry throat. She looks around for a water flask, but there isn't one to be seen.

"You are an outsider! What do you know of the oppressions Talamh kin suffer? Who do you think is kidnapping these kin from their homes?" the Fire Princess says, fairly spitting out the words.

You won't be able to convince them. Give up. Consider, too, that you are biased in your opinions because of your friendship with Irial.

"You are right. I am an outsider." Croi holds her head, squeezing it to lessen the agony of the ache. "Therefore, you should leave me out

of whatever plans you are making. I am not interested. Not in you and not in this kingdom."

She ignores the angry expressions of the fae surrounding her and looks around the clearing. The Redcap caravan is still standing dark, seemingly untouched. Strange, she would have thought that it would be the first place these rebel soldiers explored.

She takes a step toward it, and Daithi's hand goes to his sword.

Croi turns to look at him and narrows her eyes. She is too tired for more of his nonsense. "Do you really think you can stop me?"

TWENTY-ONE

THE PROMISE OF BLOOD FILLS THE AIR, TURNING IT COLD.
A deadlock has been reached: the taciturn rebel soldier and the kin with the face of nightmares. The soldier, beaten once, refuses to be intimidated again. No one can predict what the ugly kin will do next.

"Must you?" Croi thinks to her inner self.

Yes, I must.

"Let me pass. I need to look for my pack in the caravan," she says, not hiding the fatigue in her voice.

"What caravan?" Tinder asks. The pixie seems a bite muted; her friendliness has been banked by Croi's earlier outburst.

"The one behind you. It's too big for you to not be able to see it." Croi points, then looks at them. Neither the princess nor her soldier seems able to see the caravan. Croi looks at the pixie, who gives a quick shake of her head. "How did you track me here?"

"I gave you my necklace. . . ." Tinder trails off, her face brightening. "Oh! I can sense my necklace, but it isn't on you." She looks around the clearing. "Is it in this caravan?"

"I don't see where else it could be." Croi holds up her hands to show their emptiness. "The caravan must have some sort of invisibility spell on it." Croi looks at Daithi. It is quite unsettling to look at someone who absorbs light instead of being illuminated by it. "Will you get out of my way by yourself, or should I shove you?"

The soldier stares at her for a long moment before reluctantly moving away. He stands protectively in front of the princess as if to prevent Croi from attacking her.

"What do you think the princess's relationship to the soldier is?" Croi asks her other self.

Do you really think this is the right time to be nosy?

"Right." Croi rolls her eyes at the soldier and starts walking.

"How come you can see it but we can't?" Tinder demands, following Croi as she makes her way to the caravan.

"I can also kill Redcaps. Can you?" Croi says with a twist of her lips. When Tinder gives her a look, she sighs. "I don't want to tell you my secrets, all right? I don't trust you enough yet."

The pixie deflates but doesn't say any more. She grabs a ride on the Fire Princess's shoulder, and the three of them follow Croi to the caravan.

They reach the caravan, and its gaping door yawns before them. Well, only Croi can see it. She glances at the two fae accompanying her. "Some light would be nice."

Ceara snaps her fingers, and little balls of magick coruscate in the air in front of them. Handy trick. Croi wonders if she could learn to do that too. She puts a foot on the step leading up to the entrance of the caravan and turns back to the fae hanging on to her every move. She raises her eyebrow and pats the side of the caravan, making a loud thump.

"See, I didn't make it up. I don't know what kind of spell it is or how to break it." There's no magick around the exterior of the caravan, so presumably, the spell was cast on the inside of it.

"I'll go first," she says to the two fae and Tinder.

"I'll go with you," Daithi says, moving forward. When the Fire Princess moves to follow, he stops her. "We don't know if it's safe. Let me go see if there's anything that could present a danger to you"—he pauses for a moment—"my lady."

The princess struggles, but she ultimately obeys him.

The rebel soldier looks up at Croi. "I can't see the steps. Can you give me a hand?"

No.

Croi looks at the soldier. His eyes have a thick brown ring around the iris, and his magick is a strong and healthy green-flecked brown. "Figure it out for yourself."

The caravan is invisible, but it's still a tangible item. The soldier finally makes his way up the steps to the door by touching the sides of the caravan. Croi has him stop at the entrance. "Can you see the interior?"

"No," Daithi admits a little sullenly.

"Wait for me here. Let me see if I can break the spell." Croi takes a breath, pushes all thought away, and enters the caravan, expecting monsters to emerge from the darkness and finish what the Redcaps started. Nothing happens. There's darkness, then there isn't. She hears some shouts behind her, but she doesn't turn to investigate. Lights flicker on in sconces on the wall. Croi looks around. The entrance widens into a room the size of a small field. The interior is far larger than the exterior suggests.

She can see lines of magick running along the perimeter of the room, stretching it longer and wider than it really is. But this magick is not at all like the Redcap magick Croi is familiar with; the magick

worked on the caravan is of the woods and the earth, brown and green. What makes it strange, though, is the tinge of red in it, like it has been washed in blood. There are holes, too, in the magick, with blackened edges as if it were burnt. Croi sucks in a sharp breath. The person who magicked the Redcap caravan is also the person who cast the summoning spell on her. Croi tilts her head, ignores the fae soldier waiting at the doorstep of the caravan, and thinks. If the Redcaps are the Robber Queen's minions, then the Robber Queen is the one who cast a summoning spell on Croi, but somehow this doesn't seem true.

The Robber Queen needn't do everything personally. She could have just directed a minion to do it for her.

"Then why would the Hag say, 'Tell the princess,' and not 'Tell the queen'?" Croi counters. Her other self has no answer.

The hall, which is what Croi is calling this room, looks more like a chamber in a cave than a room in a caravan. The ceiling is high, and the walls are made of stone. The earthen floor is covered with furs, and a cold breeze chills the air. Croi catches a whiff of the stench native to the Redcaps. The furs need to be burnt as soon as possible. No pieces of furniture dot the room.

A knot of magick up on a wall catches Croi's eyes. The magick extends into thin filaments that cover the entirety of the room. Croi gets up on her toes and is barely able to reach it. She simply touches it, and it unravels with a slithering sound common to snakes. A second later, she hears exclamations of surprise coming from outside and assumes the invisibility spell has broken.

"I'm good at this," Croi tells her other self.

Maybe we can get a job as a spell-breaker.

Croi doesn't see her pack anywhere in the main hall, but it branches off into five smaller rooms, so she still has hope.

"Wait." Croi doesn't know when Daithi walked in to find her, but here he is, trying to control her movements.

She raises an eyebrow and says, "No." She walks until she reaches the closed door to the first room. She looks down at the knob, wondering if it's locked. It looks harmless, and for that precise reason, she doesn't trust it.

"Are you attempting to communicate with it?" Daithi comes up behind her.

"Yes, I talk to doorknobs all the time," Croi replies.

"You must have scintillating conversations," he replies. Croi angles him a look. The soldier is still wary of her, but that inexplicable hostility has faded somewhat. He catches her look, and his brown cheeks deepen with color. He still won't apologize, but Croi doesn't need him to.

"Do you want to try opening it?" She moves aside to give Daithi access to the door. He gives her an amused look but doesn't refuse.

He puts his hand on the knob and Croi tenses, but it turns easily, without him bursting into flames or being hit by a lightning bolt.

"They weren't worried about burglars, were they?" Croi says to Daithi's back as she follows him into the room.

"They were Redcaps," he replies. Point.

There's nothing extraordinary in the room. Just a sleeping pallet in the middle with a tankard of some noxious brew beside it. The fear in Croi's stomach starts to climb her throat. Is the SoulSeed really gone?

The next two doors open to reveal the same malodorous pallet and, once, a pair of pants that neither Daithi nor Croi dare to get close to. By the time they reach the fourth room, Croi is almost sick with anxiety.

There's magick on the knob of this door, a complex net created from the damaged magick that has been worked on the rest of the caravan. Croi stops Daithi when he reaches for the knob.

Be careful.

"Magick," Croi says, pointing to the knob, and he brings out a glove made of black wool. He drops it onto the knob, and it sizzles. They wince and watch the magick destroy the glove completely before resettling.

"How do we remove the spell?" she asks.

Daithi thinks for a second, then touches the door instead of the knob. The magick net immediately jumps off the knob to make its way to where Daithi had touched the door, leaving the knob unprotected. Croi turns it and the door swings open. The magick net dissolves with a hiss.

"I didn't know we could trick magick," Croi says.

"Neither did I," Daithi replies, walking into the room. It's clear that this room belonged to someone more important than the other Redcaps. For one thing, there's an actual bed covered with luxurious bedding. Which is probably smelly, but Croi isn't going to check. The room is decorated with wall hangings, and there's furniture, a chair and a small table beside the bed, both made of pale brown wood. But what commands her interest is the open chest in front of the bed.

The chest is inlaid with precious jewels. Ornate carvings ornament the sides and the lid of the chest. Croi sidles nearer to it, looking for her pack but scared to touch the other contents just in case they're magicked with malevolent spells. At first glance, she doesn't see her pack, and her heart sinks right down to her feet. She does see a large crystal, the kind pretend fortune-tellers use in the human city, and scrolls jostling for space with, bizarrely enough, cutlery. Considering how close she came to being dinner for the Redcaps, Croi is not impressed.

There! Wedged under a plate with only a strap peeking through is her pack! She grabs it before Daithi can react and clutches it to her chest. The slight warmth emanating from it reassures her of the presence of the SoulSeed. Despite her ambivalent feelings for the dryad,

Croi is relieved that she has recovered her pack and hopefully the contents within it. She sits down on the ground with a thump; opens the pack; and takes out the wrapped SoulSeed, Tinder's necklace, and the book the Hag gave her. The scarves have not been touched. Satisfied, she replaces the SoulSeed into her pack and has just picked up the book when a noise makes her pause.

"Why do you have that?" Ceara stands in the doorway, Tinder riding on her shoulder.

"I told you not to follow us," Daithi says to her, his eyebrows coming together in an irritated frown. Then, as an afterthought, he adds, "My lady."

"You are mistaken if you think that I take orders from you," Ceara tells him, her chin at a haughty angle.

Daithi's lips tighten at her words, and he turns away. The Fire Princess comes to stand in front of Croi, who scrambles to her feet.

"Why do you have that book?" The Fire Princess looks at the book before her eyes return to Croi's face. Her gaze is complex and confused.

Croi looks down at the book in her hands. "Should I not have it?"

"It belongs to the Forever King's library, which was thought to be destroyed in the fire during the Great Betrayal!"

"How do you know it came from the Forever King's library?" Croi gives the book a quizzical look. Apart from the ornate cover and its dense weight, it doesn't seem to have any special qualities that set it apart from other books.

"Look at the drawing of the flower crown on the spine. That's the symbol of the Forever King," Ceara says.

Tinder flies over for a closer look, and Croi rubs the slightly raised symbol with her thumb.

Ceara looks Croi over, her eyebrows drawing together. "Tinder said you came from the human world. How could *you* have it?"

"Someone gave it to me," Croi replies. She didn't ask for it.

"Can . . . ?" The princess hesitates and licks her lips. "Will you give it to me?"

"Ceara!" Tinder exclaims, her face red.

"I know it's rude, but . . ." The Fire Princess clenches her hands into fists. "I have nothing from my maternal grandparents. Not even memories. That book would be something to hold on to. To remember them by."

Croi narrows her eyes, thinking.

"Please?" The entreaty is soft and sounds awkward on the princess's lips.

TWENTY-TWO

THE QUAVER IN THE PRINCESS'S VOICE CONVINCES CROI. The tightness in her shoulders and the sheen in her eyes all point to a sentiment Croi knows too well. She hands the book over without a word.

It doesn't mean anything to us anyway.

"Yeah. Our pack will be lighter and our shoulders will hurt less," Croi agrees silently.

The pixie gives Ceara a reproachful look, but the princess doesn't pay her any mind, cradling the book in her arms with a reverent expression on her face. Daithi pretends he hasn't seen anything, immersed as he is in the items he keeps unearthing from the Redcap chest.

"Thank you," the princess whispers after a moment.

Croi shrugs. She doesn't particularly want Ceara's gratitude. Her stomach growls indignantly, and Croi remembers that her last meal was a very long time ago.

"My stomach must be hungry. I shall go feed it," she says to no one in particular, and walks briskly out of the room, through the hall, and out of the caravan without waiting to see if anyone is following her. Soldiers, with swords extended, are standing at attention outside the caravan. One of them squeaks when Croi emerges and immediately blushes. These rebel soldiers are very young, too young. Croi wonders how they were recruited into the rebel army—don't the families of these young kin have anything to say about them risking their lives? The sound of wings comes from behind her, and the faces of the soldiers ease. They put down their swords and back off. Oh, so they'll trust a pixie, but not her.

Croi leaves the caravan and walks farther into the clearing, looking around at the little campfires dotting the landscape. The clearing is sizable; it would have to be to accommodate the cage train and the caravan. The surrounding forest looks inky in the night. Not a place Croi would want to spend any time in. For a second, she misses the familiar paths and turns of the Wilde Forest. She longs for the warmth of the flower sprites.

Before she can truly wallow in self-pity, however, her stomach grumbles again. She chooses a campfire farthest from the rest and walks over. Only two kin sit around this fire. One is solidly built with red hair peppered with brown, while the other has the most intriguingly striped skin Croi has ever seen. He has black hair tipped with silver. When they see her approach, the kin duck their heads and touch their right hands to their chests. Then they leave, joining the campfire closest to this one. They seem not to care for the whole hare roasting on a spit on top of the fire. Croi looks after them with not a small amount of puzzlement.

"Word has spread that you killed the Redcaps. This is their way of showing you gratitude," Tinder, who followed Croi, explains.

"They'd willingly leave food?" Croi finds that difficult to believe.

Not everyone is as enamored of food as you.

"They'd much rather leave food than *be* food," Tinder replies dryly. "Listen—"

"Let me eat something before we talk." Croi interrupts the pixie. A conversation is inevitable, and she doesn't intend to avoid it, but only after she has stuffed herself.

Without waiting for a reply, Croi picks a large leaf from a nearby bush to use as a plate. Tinder picks a smaller leaf that suits her size. Croi chooses to attack the meat with her hands while Tinder fashions a fork and knife out of a twig. As they eat, Ceara emerges from the caravan, followed one beat later by Daithi. The rebel soldier immediately turns to his compatriots and starts talking to them intently. The princess looks over to where Croi and Tinder are sitting but ultimately decides not to disturb them, sitting instead at another campfire and browsing through the book Croi gave to her.

Tinder puts down the twig she was using and looks at Croi, an uncomfortable expression on her face. She flies up so she's hovering in the air in front of Croi's face and bows. "I'm sorry. I didn't think Ceara would act in the way she did."

"Are you talking about her attacking me or her asking for the book?" Croi swallows her last mouthful of food and takes a draft of water before wiping her lips with the back of her hand.

"Both of those things," Tinder says. She looks at the red-haired fae girl in the distance and frowns. "It's not like I don't understand why she wanted the book, but she should know not to covet what is not hers."

"But she thinks it should be hers," Croi points out.

"But it's not," Tinder insists. "Why did you give it to her?"

"I know what it's like to want to feel close to your family," Croi replies. "I can't because I don't even know the identities of my parents. She does, and through this book, she can."

I just realized that we are good people.

"No, *I* am good. I don't know about you." Croi smirks at her inner self.

"Hey!" The pixie pinches her, and Croi starts.

"What?" Croi rubs her cheek. The pinch hurt.

"I asked you your name."

"Do I have to tell you?" Croi asks.

"What should I call you if you don't?" Tinder asks.

"I don't care what you call me." She told Irial her name, but that doesn't mean she's going to tell others.

"In that case I will call you Fiadh," Tinder pronounces after a minute of thinking. At Croi's raised eyebrow, she explains, "It means wild. Unfettered. Free."

"I like that." Croi smiles truly for the first time in a long while.

Me too.

"How do you know the Fire Princess?" Croi asks. She looks around the clearing.

"There's a school in the mountains of Talamh where scholars from all four elemental kingdoms study and collaborate. The scholars who attend the school create extraordinary objects of art by working magick together. I met Ceara there a year ago when we both attended the school for a time." Tinder's voice is muted, as is her magick.

Croi stiffens at the mention of the school. Irial talked about a school too. Was it the same one? She wonders if Tinder knows Irial but decides against asking her. To her he is an enemy.

"I know this was said before, but help me understand—what happened to the Forever King?"

"Do you want the long version or the short one?"

"How long is the long version?"

"Give or take five hours."

Croi stares at the pixie, who grins unrepentantly. "The shortest version."

Tinder clears her throat. "According to songs and legends, the Forever King ruled Talamh for centuries. His reign wasn't always peaceful, but whenever wars were fought, Talamh was guaranteed a victory. These victories weren't due to him alone; his advisor, Lugid, deserved just as much credit, for his strategies led to triumphs without excessive bloodshed. The stories claim that the two were closer than monarch and subject; though they shared no blood, they loved each other like brothers.

"No one thought that Lugid would betray the Forever King. He killed not just the Forever King but also the king's consort, sons, and their families. The water in Talamh Caisleán ran red for days afterward. The Forever King's younger daughter, Mabh, was present in Talamh at that time; she was accompanying the Tine King for the Saol ceremony. She got separated from the king during the melee after the ceremony was completed and was attacked by Lugid's allies. She was heavily injured and faded after giving birth to Ceara. Monca, Ceara's brownie mother, brought Ceara to Aodh along with the news of what had happened to Mabh." Tinder lapses into silence, leaving Croi to ponder upon her words.

"Why did Lugid betray the Forever King?" she finally asks the pixie.

"Eh?" Tinder looks startled by the question. "Obviously because he coveted the throne."

"Would killing the king automatically make him the next monarch?" Croi purses her lips.

"No, the person wanting to be the monarch would need to hold the HeartStone first. Only if their magick is strong enough to hold the HeartStone would they be able to put on the Talamh crown," Tinder explains patiently.

"So where is this Lugid now?"

"Ah? He died. You know that already," Tinder says hesitantly, perhaps realizing the logic is a bit skewed.

"You mentioned that he was the Forever King's strategist, so presumably he knew the risk that came with fighting and killing in the Caisleán. Being proficient at nefarious scheming, I don't believe he couldn't have thought of other ways to lead a coup than to attack the Forever King in the Caisleán where he is the strongest."

"What are you trying to say?" Tinder asks, her wings whirring.

Croi scrunches up her face. "I'm saying that if Lugid was aware of the consequences of his action and still went ahead and spilled blood in the Caisleán, that means the Forever King did something to incur his hatred. So, the question I want answered is, what did the Forever King do?"

Tinder's eyes widen. "Shhh," she says, looking around. "Talamh kin will not tolerate anyone doubting the Forever King's goodness."

That is how tyrants are made.

"Surely people *have* questioned him before?" Croi raises her eyebrows.

Tinder shakes her head. "Everybody knows that the Forever King was good and Lugid, bad."

"Doesn't that seem strange to you?" Croi asks. The pixie doesn't respond. "Several things don't add up. The catkin said the Redcaps were taking the kidnapped kin to work in the mines at Areed. To replace the blue-horned fauns who all died suddenly." Croi rubs her forehead. "You and I both know that isn't true. The village is empty, and I didn't see any signs of an active mine. Did you?"

Tinder shakes her head. "But that doesn't mean there isn't a mine."

"Where would the mine be if not in the place we saw?" Croi counters. "What is the Robber Queen doing with all the kidnapped kin if they're not being used to mine? Look at these rebel soldiers. Doesn't it strike you odd that they are all so young? How did they come to be rebels? What led them to become soldiers? Have you asked?"

Tinder's magick is dyed in the blue of anxiety, and she flies up. "I'm going to talk to Ceara!"

She flies off in a blur, and Croi draws her knees to her chest, hugging them. She is so exhausted that even breathing feels like a chore. She rests her head on her knees and closes her eyes. A little bit of peace returns to her, but it is fated to be short-lived as footsteps sound behind her.

Croi turns to see the one person she had hoped she never would again. Caolan.

"Can we talk?" Clad in the colors of the night, the catkin presents himself to Croi in the same way a criminal would to his executioner.

"Do we still have something left to discuss?" It's not a question, though Croi dresses it up as one.

"Please?" The catkin seems determined.

"If I ignore him, will he go away?" Croi asks her inner self.

Smelly things tend to linger.

Caolan doesn't move, nor do his eyes shift from Croi's figure.

The quiet between them is dissonant.

"The crickets are loud tonight," Croi says, turning to look into the depths of the forest, startling a pair of eyes blinking back at her.

"I'm sorry." Caolan makes his apology from a distance.

"Are you? Really?" Croi looks at him. "What are you sorry for?"

He doesn't reply, so she decides to help him.

"Are you sorry you pushed me? No, you'd do the exact same thing if something like that happened again. Hmm. Perhaps you are sorry for the situation that led you to decide that my existence is less important than your brother's?" Croi's face clears when Caolan flinches. "I'm right, aren't I?"

"I won't make any excuses," Caolan says.

"If you won't make excuses, why are you here?" Croi frowns, annoyed by the situation. "Let me guess—you want to appease your conscience? You think yourself a good person, so your actions, your ruthlessness, make you feel uncomfortable? To make yourself feel better, you came to seek my forgiveness?"

"I have a responsibility to my siblings, but I shouldn't have done what I did. For that, I apologize." Caolan bows. He won't acknowledge her words.

"I understand what you did." Croi doesn't need him to.

But understanding doesn't mean forgiveness.

"But I won't forgive you. I will never forgive you. If you really are sorry for what you did, please never let me see you again."

No rancor makes barbs of her words. Croi knows that she cannot compare to his siblings. Perhaps it would hurt less if she had a family of her own. But she doesn't. Her words are a weary plea that is, perhaps, more cutting than her anger would be. Croi doesn't turn around to watch the catkin stumble away.

Hours pass.

Embers rule where fires burnt, and the only conversations that can be heard around the clearing are those of crickets riding the moon to midnight. The kidnapped kin willingly slip into sleep, though there are some who lie still with their eyes wide open; they're the ones stalked by nightmares. Rebel soldiers are strategically placed around the clearing, though whether they are keeping danger out or everyone in is not something Croi wants to think about.

Tinder returns with eyes full of questions, but she has learned by now not to ask them. Whatever the princess said in response to Croi's questions doesn't seem to have appeased her. Her magick is still carrying flashes of anxious blue. "Ceara didn't have any answers to your questions, and she told me not to listen to you because you are clearly on the enemy's side." The pixie sits on the ground in front of Croi and sighs glumly. "But I feel like your questions poke holes in the story everyone insists is the truth. I feel like I've been complacent and naive, accepting everything that has been fed to me without asking questions or thinking for myself."

Croi doesn't say anything. Neither does her other self.

"On a completely different note, if you want, we can travel with the Tine envoy to the Talamh Caisleán. Ceara is accompanying her father and his entourage there for the Saol ceremony." Tinder preempts Croi's opposition. "Listen to me before you object. It will take us three days, four at the maximum, if we travel with them. It will take a lot longer if we go by ourselves. Do you have that much time? Even if you do, consider this. Many Redcaps wander the forest, and other horrors, the kinds which you haven't ever seen before, thicken the nights in this world. How many of them will we kill? How many can we kill?"

Why would the Fire Princess allow us to travel with her when she thinks we stand against what she's fighting for?

It's a good question, so Croi asks the pixie. Tinder seems contemplative. "I think she thinks she can persuade you to join the rebel army. Whatever her purpose is, I guarantee that she won't harm you."

We need to get the dryad to her sister before the Saol ceremony. We don't really have a choice in the matter if we are to accomplish the task Uaine set for us.

Croi is still deeply reluctant, and her expression illustrates this fact.

Tinder tosses her a quick glance, reading her face. "I've talked to Ceara. She owes you for the book. Let her compensate for it by letting us travel with her."

"I'm going to sleep," Croi says out loud. She refuses to answer either Tinder or her inner self. They can wait until she has talked to Irial.

Why can't you make your own decision? What's the point in talking to him? Admit it, you just want to see him again.

"I do. What's wrong with wanting to see him? He is my friend."

You want him to be more than a friend. He has someone he likes. Have you forgotten?

"I don't even know what my face looks like. Do you think I have the luxury of time and mental capacity to romantically pursue someone I have only met in my dreams?"

Yes.

Croi refuses to talk to her other self anymore.

She settles down in front of the flickering fire, using her pack as a pillow. The sky above is crammed with stars, some falling, some flickering. Croi feels Tinder making a nest for herself in her hair and resolutely refuses to think about the tangles she'll leave in it.

The pixie's decision to stay with her is a surprise, especially considering her friendship with the princess. Croi doesn't complain, however. She'll take whatever warmth she can get.

Her eyes grow heavy and close. A second later, she opens them again, convinced that she doesn't want to know the shape her body has changed into. She looks around her surroundings; the dreamscape is the clearing she went to sleep in. Tinder and the Fire Princess are nowhere in sight, however. The dream version is much more exaggerated; many more rebel soldiers stalk the perimeter of the clearing, their bearing not in the least like the saviors they are dressed as. Croi brings up a hand and is confronted by sharp, red-tipped fingers. Her breath rushes out.

She doesn't dare touch her face; if she doesn't know and cannot see, she can pretend she isn't.

"You . . ." Croi is so absorbed in being disgusted by her new shape that she doesn't hear Irial's approach. As a result, she whirls around, gets dizzy, and falls to the ground. It is a good thing she has no attachment to dignity, as she currently finds herself lacking any.

The dream-Irial is standing over her with a horrified look on his face. "Why do you look like a Redcap?" he demands.

"I ran into some," Croi explains. She loathes her shape, but she cannot change it, not until the dream breaks. She looks at the fae boy. "Do I stink? I can't tell. *They* did."

Irial sniffs. "No. I don't smell anything. Is that why I haven't been able to enter your dream for the last two days?" he asks, squatting down beside her so she doesn't have to look up.

"According to my pixie friend, we were on a Shadow Road. I was almost dinner, you know?" Croi complains. "I came this close!" She pinches her fingers together to show him.

"How did you escape?" Irial asks.

"I killed them," Croi says in a very small voice. "Don't ask me how."

"Are you all right?" he asks instead. "Did they hurt you?"

"Just some bruises and scratches. But"—she swallows, remembering being enclosed in ice—"they scared me."

He gives her a long look, and Croi ducks her head, not wanting to see the disgust her form evokes. To her surprise, he simply gives her a hug.

"Am I not disgusting?" Croi asks.

"You're not really a Redcap," he replies with a crooked smile. He has red flowers in his hair again today.

"Thank you." Croi's eyes are hot, and she feels her nose sting. "The catkin betrayed me. He pushed me out so I'd attract the Redcap's attention instead of his brother. I understand why he did that. I understand that to him, his brother is more precious than me, but—"

"It still hurts. I get it. He's unimportant. Don't care about him," Irial says, holding her Redcap hand. Croi looks at her red-tipped nails and shudders, pulling her hand away from him.

"I can't stand this shape," she grumbles.

Irial nods, taking no offense. He looks around the dreamscape. "Where are you now? Did the pixie find you?"

Croi straightens up, her resolve strengthening. "I met the Fire Princess. She was with the rebel soldiers. Do you know about them? Does your mother?"

"Yes." The word is uttered softly, entirely without inflection. Croi tries to peer at Irial's face to see his expression, but he turns away, not letting her.

"Then do you know what their goal is?" she demands.

"Probably to overthrow, possibly kill, my mother and me." Still the same flat tone. As if what he's saying has no relation to him.

"How can you be so calm about this?" Croi hops up, forgetting that she's a Redcap. She points a red-tipped finger at him. "They're conspiring to kill you without any clear knowledge of what led to your mother becoming the Robber Queen!"

"Of course they have the knowledge," Irial counters. "My grandfather and his allies killed the Forever King and everyone related to him."

"But *why* did your grandfather kill the Forever King? What drove your grandpa to take such drastic actions?" Croi asks. "What did the Forever King do that incurred such hatred?"

Irial looks surprised at her questions. "Everyone says my grandfather desired the throne."

"Am I everyone?" Croi sneers. "Where is your father?"

"Dead," Irial says without any emotion.

"Who killed him?"

"He sacrificed himself to save my mother and me when the Forever King's soldiers attacked us," Irial replies. There is a crack in his expression. A secret pain.

Croi sits down with a thud and swallows her words. A moment heavy with unsaid words passes. "Who else did the Forever King kill?" she asks in a whisper.

"My grandma, aunts, their children and their husbands. My

grandfather went mad and attacked the Forever King. Nobody expected him to succeed in killing him. They all forgot that he was the king's strategist. Because he failed to keep his family safe, they thought he was defeated." Croi reaches for Irial's hand, and he holds hers tight. "I don't know why their relationship broke apart, though. If my mother knows, she hasn't told me."

"How did she become the queen?"

"There was no one else," Irial says. "I was only two, but I remember the chaos of the time. She simply did what no one else wanted to. No one else dared to."

"And the HeartStone?"

Irial looks at her sharply, his face pale. "How . . . ?"

Croi waves a hand. "Don't ask."

"Yeah. It's missing. It has been missing since the happenings after the last Saol ceremony. My mother has been searching for it for the last seventeen years without any success." He laughs a bit. "You don't know how relieved I feel to share this with someone. I told her to just tell the court kin about the missing HeartStone, but she insists on keeping it secret, scared of the chaos that will erupt once people find out that it's lost."

Croi squeezes his hand, not knowing what to say or how else to comfort him.

"How far away from the Caisleán are you now?" Irial asks.

"I have no idea. Tinder says that I should join the Tine envoy because it will be safer and get me to the Caisleán faster. Do you think I should?" she asks him.

"The Tine King has arrived in Talamh quite early," Irial muses. "There is still five days before the Saol ceremony. The monarchs of the other kingdoms usually arrive in Talamh the night before the ceremony."

"Perhaps he has another purpose," Croi says.

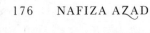

"Perhaps. I think you'll be safe with the Tine. At least you won't be abducted by the Redcaps again," Irial says, a slight grin lightening the melancholy on his face. "I will be able to see you sooner."

"I'm not much to look at," Croi says with a twist of her lips. "But hey, I look better awake than I do as a Redcap." She cheers up.

The rest of the melancholy melts away from Irial's face, and he chuckles at her. "Thank you for being my friend."

"Say that to me when we are both awake," she counters.

"I will. Listen, I probably won't come into your dreams anymore. I need to conserve my magick in preparation for the Saol ceremony. I reckon something big is going to happen on the day."

"All right."

"Be safe," he exhorts her. "Don't take risks."

"I never do." He looks like he doesn't believe her.

"Sleep. I will see you soon," he says, and offers her a soft smile before disappearing.

TWENTY-THREE

THE FIRST RAYS OF THE SUN SKIM THE TIPS OF THE trees, dusting them orange. A low hum, full of birdsong, is a prologue to the cacophony that will come with the ripening of the day. Croi's body aches fiercely, and her lips have swollen to twice their usual size, or so she feels with her tongue. The only reflective surfaces around are eyes, and no one seems to want to look into hers.

At this moment, she is standing, a bit horrified, in front of a beast. The Fire Princess insists that it is a horse, but Croi has seen horses before, and this beastie is nothing like one. To begin with, it is not made of flesh and blood but sand forged by fire. It has big, fiery eyes that are fixed, malevolently, on her. The princess calls the sand-horse a birthday present from her father, Aodh, the Tine King. Croi would be suspicious of anyone who tried to gift her such a thing, but that's just her. The sand-horse answers to the name Dahy. Croi thinks Beastie would suit it better, but no one is asking her.

"Will you get on already?" the Fire Princess says with no small amount of exasperation. She's already astride the beast, not in the least bit concerned about its sharp teeth, evil eyes, and flaring nostrils. Croi saw it belching smoke. Perhaps it, too, fancies itself a dragon.

Tinder is nowhere to be seen. She flitted off with the dawn to regions unknown. The princess approached Croi just after breakfast, when she had sadly put down what looked like porridge because her mouth hurt too much to eat, and told her that Tinder had confirmed that they are going to the Tine camp and, subsequently, to Talamh Caisleán with her. The plan is to pick Tinder up along the way.

"We're wasting time." The princess levels a look in Croi's direction. Her words are sharp, smudged with hostility that is curbed by an unwilling respect. Ceara might not like Croi, but she defers to the power in her magick. "Do you have to say goodbye to anyone?"

Croi looks over to where the kin are piling into the caravan. The interior of the caravan remains large enough to fit all the kin and rebel soldiers. Croi doesn't know where they're being taken, though she's pretty certain none of them are being sent home.

"These rebel soldiers—were they once kidnapped kin?" Croi asks instead of replying to the princess's question.

Ceara looks flustered by the question. "What do you mean?"

"Look at them." Croi nods at the black-clad soldiers. "I'm not sure how old they are, but I'd be willing to bet none of them are over twenty-five summers. Now look at the kidnapped kin. If they were to put on the uniforms of the rebel soldiers, would you be able to tell the difference between them and the soldiers?"

"What exactly are you saying?" Ceara narrows her eyes.

"How are the rebel soldiers recruited? Who leads them?" Croi pushes for an answer. Not because she cares but because things don't make sense.

Are you sure you don't care?

"There's no reason for me to care," Croi thinks to her other self.

"Why do you care so much about the rebels and the rebellion?" Ceara raises her chin, her eyes gleaming. "Have you changed your mind about joining us?"

No.

"Of course not."

"In which case, get on. We need to go." The princess sounds impatient, and her beastie whickers, as if anxious to be on its way.

"I'm not exactly sure how I'm supposed to get up there," Croi tells the princess. Ceara sighs loudly and offers her a hand. Croi looks at the proffered hand, raises an eyebrow, and grasps it with a shrug.

She settles on the beastie before looking around with some fascination. The world looks completely different from this height; it gives her a false sense of prominence. The sand-horse feels strange and Croi squirms, trying to get used to the feeling of being on an animal. Usually, the things she sits on aren't alive, but the sand-horse isn't really an animal, is it? Nor is it alive. It's fae-made, so maybe being on a real horse feels different. Croi vows to find out one day. She will start off with a small horse. A really small one that doesn't look at her wrongly.

"Don't you have to make your farewells?" Croi asks the princess.

Ceara doesn't reply but looks over at Daithi, who is standing on the side, ostensibly talking to one of his subordinates. He senses her gaze and looks up, his eyes lingering on the princess, sweeping over the gentle rise of her cheeks, leaving red blossoming in its wake.

"No. Hold on tight," the princess says, digging her legs into the sides of the beast. It starts running; Croi feels the bit of breakfast she did manage to eat slosh around her stomach. She concentrates on keeping it inside where it belongs.

The beastie speeds through the forest, tearing through pockets of darkness that still cling to the nooks and hollows like cobwebs. They battle with the wind and almost win. Croi's half drunk with glee and wondering how she can procure a beastie of her own when the princess brings the sand-horse to a sudden stop. Croi's flung forward and would have fallen had she not clung to the princess. After directing a dirty look at Ceara's back, she peers around in confusion. They're in the middle of nowhere.

The princess relaxes her hold on the reins and whistles a call that is picked up by the birds in the canopy.

"Wait here," she says brusquely, and slides off the beastie without offering any other explanation.

"Where are you going?" Croi calls, but the princess doesn't answer. She watches the fae walk farther into the forest and deep into the shade of an oak tree. There, dressed in a cloak that obscures both face and body, is a kin.

Croi doesn't care too much about the princess's business, but the cloaked kin's magick makes her freeze. The magick circulating the body of this kin is the same magick as the summoning spell on her. It is also the same magick that was present on the Redcap caravan, turning it invisible. The magick is shades of green, brown, and gold, but what sets it apart, what makes it recognizable, are the holes in it, as if something corrosive touched it. Like dragon magick touched it.

Do you think that's the Robber Queen?

"Why would Ceara meet with the Robber Queen in the middle of the forest? She wants to kill her, not secretly rendezvous with her."

Could this kin be a servant of the Robber Queen?

Croi looks at the way the two kin are standing together. Ceara's body is leaning toward the older kin, the expression on her face soft and yearning.

No. She wouldn't be so soft on someone allied with her enemy. Maybe this kin is the leader of the rebels? But why would the leader of the rebels, if she is indeed that, summon us? Why would she have kin kidnapped from all over Talamh?

"Obviously to build an army," Croi thinks. "Evil genius, isn't it?"

We need to find out who she is. She might know the princess the Hag mentioned.

"How? It's not like we can ask Ceara," Croi replies to her other self. She stares at the princess and the kin, her intuition telling her that the identity of this kin is important.

As if sensing Croi's intense curiosity, Ceara and the unidentified kin look toward her. Croi shrinks in on herself, her heart burning in her chest, unwilling to be recognized as a not-brownie. She isn't yet ready to confront the kin who cast the summoning spell on her. Who severed her into two. Her strength is still too little, though her rage feels hot enough to engulf all of Talamh. While enduring the gazes of the other two, she makes plans to flee should they try to take her prisoner. Her endurance pays off as Ceara returns not a minute later. The Fire Princess doesn't say a word about the kin she met, nor does she explain the sudden stop. She simply touches the reins, and the beastie is galloping again.

They travel for a little longer and stop at a silver-leaved tree Croi has never seen before. The leaves glint in the sunlight, blinding in their radiance.

"You're late!" a familiar voice yells, and Tinder flies out from where she was hidden in the leaves of this tree. The princess straightens and glances over her shoulder at Croi.

"Someone couldn't decide whether she wanted to come with me," she says. Croi meets her eyes with no expression in hers.

"That's because *someone* disappeared without a word," she retorts with a meaningful look at Tinder, who ducks her head.

The pixie has no idea about the identity of the kin the princess rendezvoused with. Croi's other self is more astute than her. Why else would the princess not mention her meeting, which led to Croi, unwittingly, keeping it secret as well?

"I had to return to the meadow and let my family know that I'll be away for a few days," Tinder mumbles.

"How did they take it?" Croi asks interestedly, remembering the attitudes of the pixies in the meadow.

Tinder makes a face. "The less said, the better."

"We must go. Tinder, settle on my shoulder. I need to talk to you," the princess commands, and Tinder complies after a guilty look at Croi. Oh? What's the point of trying to have a secret conversation? Croi simply listens harder and hears their words as if they are speaking in her ear.

"What did your mother say?" the princess asks.

"I told her I'm going to the Caisleán with you," Tinder replies.

"Why didn't you tell her about the creature?"

"Do you think she would have agreed to let me accompany some-one whose origins are a mystery? Besides, it's not like I lied. I *am* going to the Caisleán with you."

"Do you really know so little about the creature?" the princess asks, her tone cajoling. "I'm scared she means harm. There's some-thing about her that doesn't sit well with me."

"Call her Fiadh. . . . Anyway, you like her enough to want her to be part of the rebellion," the pixie says.

"That's because she was able to best me. Not many kin can. She's strong and I can use her. However, her politics are too radical. She spoke for the Robber Queen! If I can't use her, I have to keep her close so no one else can either!" The princess's voice is righteous. Croi curls her lips.

"Do you think of everyone in terms of their use to you? Is that how you see me, too?" Tinder's voice is small.

"No, you know how much you mean to me. But that's not the point here. We're talking about that c—Fiadh."

Croi tunes them out as their conversation cycles. Seeing their familiarity with each other gives her a strange, wistful feeling that makes her chest hurt. Their easy camaraderie, the genuine concern they have for each other, how they can argue without worrying they'll break the bonds between them. How does it feel to have someone who likes you? For what you are and for who you are. For someone to want to spend time with you for no other reason than it gives them pleasure to do so?

I like you.

"You are me. You have no other choice but to like me." Croi rolls her eyes.

I could have easily hated you. You get to be in the sunshine while I'm stuck in the darkness.

"I'm sorry."

I'm not angry at you. You didn't choose for us to exist in halves.

"I didn't, but I'm still sorry."

Don't be sorry. Be angry. Anger will serve us better than sadness.

A few hours later they reach a thickly wooded area just shy of the Tine camp. The princess informs them that the journey would have been twice as long had they been on a normal horse, but since Dahy, the sand beastie, is not a normal horse, it is able to travel great distances without needing to stop and rest.

The princess, Tinder still on her shoulder, slides down the beastie with an ease that almost turns Croi crisp with envy. Reacquainted with the ground, the princess stares up at her. Croi stares back.

"What?"

"Do you not plan to get down?" the princess asks pleasantly.

Croi looks at the ground and shakes her head. "I think I'll just stay here. The view is . . . Well, all I see are trees, but they are . . ." Croi trails off and looks closer at the magick filling the trees. The magick in the trees is unraveling. The color of it is pale and the movement sluggish, not at all similar to what she saw in the human world and by the pixie meadow. The sound of the earth magick is faint and tired. Croi frowns and slides off the beastie without pausing to consider the consequences of her action. Fortunately, apart from a jarring thump when she reaches the ground, there are none.

She walks closer to an oak tree and extends a hand to touch its magick. It barely prickles. A shattered feeling fills her chest; Croi places the palm of her hand on her chest and presses. It hurts.

Do you think the dryad will be able to locate the HeartStone?

"Didn't we not care?" Croi thinks to her other self.

Perhaps we do. Just a little bit.

"Here." The princess hands Croi a lacy cloth, triangular with string ties on both sides. Croi takes it and looks askance at her.

"Put it over your face," she says.

"Why? Does my ugliness hurt your sensibilities?" It hurts hers. Thankfully, Croi doesn't have to look at herself all the time.

The princess rolls her eyes and refuses to answer.

Croi glares at the veil but puts it on in the end. It hides her nose and mouth, leaving only her eyes visible to the world. Tinder flies over to sit on her shoulder, but she doesn't say a word, and neither does Croi as they follow the princess and the beastie through the forest. Gradually the trees thin, and the princess stops abruptly. Croi peers from behind her to see what the problem is. Considering her luck, Croi wouldn't be surprised if there are swords involved. However, all she sees are three female fae, half hidden in the gloom of the forest. Two of them have uncovered their faces while one is veiled like her. They are wearing dresses in varying shades of red, and the two with faces visible are beautiful. It seems that to be fae, one must be beautiful.

"Wait here," the princess tells them tersely, and, pulling her beastie along, she walks over to where the fae maids are standing.

"Do you know them?" Croi whispers to Tinder, who is a warm weight on her shoulder.

"They are Ceara's handmaids," Tinder replies.

"All of them?" They're very well dressed for servants.

"Yes, they were handpicked from the Tine nobility to serve the Tine princess."

"Do pixies have handmaids too?" Croi can't understand such a custom where one fully capable person needs to be served by another person. Kin, after all, are not humans who need whole hosts of servants to do their daily work.

"The pixies do not believe in such servitude," Tinder answers haughtily, and Croi nods sagely. The pixies have once again demonstrated their excellence. She decides that she, too, doesn't believe in such customs.

"Fiadh!" The princess beckons Croi over, giving her no more time to think. The trio of fae maids look at Croi and Tinder with expressions ranging from curiosity to suspicion. Their eyes linger on Croi for long moments, and she stares back at them defiantly. They turn away first.

"You all have met Tinder. This is . . . Fiadh."

The hesitation is accompanied by a look Croi ignores.

"These are my companions, Caoimhe, Aislin, and Fiona." Caoimhe has a long face with red-ringed amber eyes and orange skin, while Aislin's features are delicate apart from her lips, which are generous, and hint at a tendency to curve. Fiona's green-ringed brown eyes are sharp, piercing, and entirely out of place.

"Fiona will return to the rebel camp, and Fiadh will take her place," the princess is saying when Croi finally deigns to listen to her again. The green-ringed eyes belonging to Fiona make a lot of sense all of a sudden. She is the messenger between the rebels and the Fire Princess so she is of Talamh origins.

"Why can't I just join your group without pretending to be someone else?" Croi doesn't want to be a handmaid. Like Tinder, she doesn't believe in them.

"Do you think just anyone can be part of the king's entourage?" Caoimhe asks stiffly. She seems to have taken an instant dislike to Croi. "Everyone, from the cooks to the horse goblins, is carefully vetted before they're allowed to exist in the proximity of our royalty."

If the handmaid gets any more pretentious, she might die. Or Croi might ask Tinder to pix her.

"Will you Glamour her, my lady?" Aislin asks the princess, and Croi takes two steps back. No one is Glamouring her ever again.

"How else will we convince everyone that you are Fiona?" the princess says, correctly interpreting Croi's actions.

"I don't know and I don't really care," Croi replies.

A tense silence follows as the princess considers her words. Then she shrugs, her features smoothing over. She removes a set of the dark uniform common to Daithi's soldiers from her saddlebag and hands it to Fiona, who takes a minute to change before handing the dress she was wearing to Croi.

"Put it on," the princess commands.

For once, Croi is happy to obey. She changes behind a tree, slipping gleefully into a dress the color of a sparking fire. Croi wonders if the shine of the dress will rub off on her, but when she rejoins the group, all of them, even Tinder, take one look at her, and their faces turn politely blank. Their reaction makes Croi smile brighter.

"Fiona had no conversations with anyone and kept her eyes downcast. She never took off her veil, so if we're careful, no one will notice," the princess says to Croi, and turns to Fiona, who bows her head deferentially.

"Find Daithi, tell him we're all right and that . . . I . . . We will see him . . . soon." Fiona nods once and is gone.

"Why didn't you give her the beastie?" If the rebel soldiers are still at the Redcap camp, they are hours away.

"She's a fleet-foot," the princess replies, rubbing the beastie's flank.

"She'll be able to reach the rebel camp in less than the time it took us to reach here." She turns to her remaining handmaids. "Did Monca go to Lorcan?"

"Yes, my lady," Aislin says, "but we must hurry. She warned us that she could not keep him occupied for more than an hour—"

"Monca?" Croi interrupts. "The brownie who brought you to your father?"

"Yes. She's my brownie-mother," the princess clarifies.

Croi squelches the sudden spurt of envy she feels. The fire princess didn't just have a mother; she also has a brownie mother. Then she comes to attention. A brownie. A *real* brownie.

"A real brownie," she says breathlessly.

"Are there any other kinds?" Ceara rolls her eyes.

If only she knew.

Croi smirks.

"Let's go!" The princess clutches the beastie's reins and, with a smile so brittle that glass would covet it, leads the way into the camp.

Tinder has concealed herself in Croi's hair, seemingly preferring it to the princess's cleaner cloak. According to the princess, the camp contains fifty Tine soldiers, ten horse goblins, seven cooks, seventeen Tine courtiers, one monarch, and countless imps. Imps, Tinder informs Croi, are pixie-sized fire-breathers who attach themselves to Tine fae. She doesn't like them at all.

They enter the camp through the area set aside for the horses. Croi sees her first horse goblin here. They are short kin, with sharp faces, gentle eyes, and an affinity for horses that make them the perfect stable hands. The horses are kept in an enclosure fenced by red-orange threads of Tine magick. At the rear of the enclosure, they meet a horse goblin the princess calls Min to whom she hands the beastie's reins. Freed of the beastie's conspicuous presence, the princess starts walking with furiously quick steps.

The first glimpse of the camp surprises Croi. She had expected something similar to the Redcap camp, but what she sees here is more of a tent city than a camp. Colorful tents have been erected in a circle with the largest, and grandest, smack-dab in the center. An organized chaos choreographs the movement of the Tine kin as they all perform whatever duties have been assigned to them. Round creatures Croi doesn't recognize tend cooking fires. The air is fragrant with the smell of food; Croi's stomach rumbles rudely.

The Tine soldiers have on dark uniforms similar to the ones worn by the rebel soldiers. According to Aislin, the Tine fae sitting in small groups, dressed in billowy shirts and pants, are soldiers who aren't on duty. They are talking in hushed voices. The royal guards contain both male and female kin, mostly fae, three quarters of whom seem to be on duty. The atmosphere in the camp is restless and watchful; even those soldiers not dressed for duty seem tense and ready for danger.

The princess tries to hide herself among her handmaids, but that is difficult to do as she is the only one with red hair. Croi wonders if she should have introduced the princess to mud. A little page kin with light orange skin and curly black hair notices Ceara first, and his exclamation garners the attention of the older soldiers.

The princess gives a resigned sigh, puts her head up, and walks as though she expects everyone to get out of her way. The soldiers bow in her presence; some even sink to their knees. But behind the deference, Croi hears a wave of whispers; all of them are mutters of surprise at her appearance. Hmm. It seems that the princess's trip away from the camp isn't common knowledge. However did she conceal her absence in the first place?

"The Glamour wore off me this morning," Aislin whispers. Ah. Though the soldiers whisper among themselves as the princess and her companions pass them, not one of them moves to stop the princess and demand an explanation from her. Croi's vastly relieved because the soldiers have swords with serrated edges, and she doesn't fancy finding how they will feel cutting into her skin.

They're almost at the tent in the middle, a pavilion really, and Croi has begun breathing easier, when the princess comes to an abrupt stop.

TWENTY-FOUR

IT IS NOT WITH A WORD OR A SPELL THAT THEY ARE halted; it is the mere presence of a Tine fae that causes the princess and her companions behind her to come to a standstill. Croi would have continued walking had Tinder not pinched her. The fae soldier in front of them is much older than they are but not as old as either Uaine or the Hag. He is wearing magically enhanced armor over the dark tunic and pants common to the Tine soldiers. His eyes, a light brown ringed by orange, are narrowed to slits and trained on the Fire Princess. Anger emanates from this fae, scorching in its intensity. He is tall and broad, with a narrow face, a pointed chin, and a sharp nose; his skin is a dark burnished orange, and his hair is the exact same red as the princess's. His magick, too, is a shade similar to the princess's. Croi looks at him closer, wondering if he and the princess are related. The similarity in their bones is distinct.

So fierce is the fae soldier's regard that Aislin and Caoimhe move closer to the princess, while Croi edges away from her. If there are going to be flying arrows or daggers or whatever this kin handles, Croi doesn't want them hitting her accidentally.

"You were told, were you not, that leaving the protection of the guard is forbidden?" The fae's voice is low, measured, and without inflection. Yet anger hisses through it. "I will not ask where you have been because I fear I know the answer only too well. You send your brownie mother to distract me? Do you think I will fall prey to her tricks?" His anger builds until his voice is a roar. "You willfully involve yourself in matters that don't concern you! Your guards"—his gaze flays the soldiers who have just arranged themselves around the princess—"will be replaced and doubled. You will not be allowed—"

"You forget yourself, Lord Lorcan," the princess says icily, cutting him off. "*You* do not have the right to tell me what I am and what I am not allowed to do." She is brave, this princess, to ring her voice loudly in front of this angry soldier. She doesn't see that her words sit ill with the soldiers this Lorcan calls his comrades.

"Your father—" Lorcan starts.

"Exactly. *You* are not my father."

Croi wonders if she has imagined the spasm of pain that distorts Lorcan's face for a second.

He seems a tad bit sensitive to the word "father."

"Until I hear directly from my father about what I can and cannot do, I shall keep my own counsel. As you persist in reminding me so often, I *am* the Tine princess." With that, Ceara walks past the angry Tine kin, face smooth and head held high. Croi and the other two handmaids follow her. Croi cannot resist looking back, however, and in Lorcan's eyes, she sees the frustrated words his mouth is not allowed to utter.

She puts him out of her mind and focuses on the kin she is most curious about. The princess's brownie mother, or Monca, as she is called. She looks around but doesn't see anyone that looks like a brownie. Mouths shut and eyes looking directly ahead, the princess and her entourage walk past more tents, soldiers, and fires. Just before they reach the tented pavilion, the princess stops again, and everyone tenses.

"Monca!" the princess exclaims, her voice fuller than Croi has ever heard it before. Ceara moves to hug a short, plump kin with faded brown hair and wrinkled brown skin. Croi stares at the bits of the kin that haven't been enveloped by the princess's taller frame, and as though the brownie feels her gaze, she looks up, and Croi sees her eyes. They're exactly the same size, shade, and shape Croi's were before the Glamour started breaking.

Croi is struck mute; looking at her is like looking in a mirror at a past Croi given color by her experiences, and fine lines by time. She hadn't been a complete lie. She had been a true brownie, at least on the outside. This knowledge is both sweet and bitter.

Croi ducks her head to hide her tears. She cannot explain her sorrow, and she would rather not reveal it.

"Who is this?" The brownie mother has a rich voice. It makes Croi think of nutmeg, hot drinks, and the Hag.

They have paused before the curtained opening of the pavilion, and a look at the tense faces of the guards tells Croi that the angry Lorcan has followed them here. When the kin soldier hears the brownie mother's question, he turns in Croi's direction. She tries to look as harmless as possible.

"You've met Fiona before, have you not?" The princess's voice is disinterested as if Croi's presence is common knowledge and does not warrant comment. Monca's eyes sharpen, and she gives Croi a closer look.

"Avert your eyes!" Tinder hisses in Croi's ear, and she hurriedly looks down at the ground, putting in more effort to seem timid and handmaidlike. Croi doesn't know if she succeeds, but the princess avoids any further questioning by marching into the tent. Croi follows her with her eyes still averted. As soon as they're inside, Tinder flies out from under Croi's hair with a relieved sigh only to yelp loudly. Croi looks up to see everyone, even Tinder, sinking to the ground in a curtsy.

The object of their deference is a fae man of Lorcan's age, with hair much like a lion's mane, yellow sprinkled liberally with red. His body is tall and strong, and his arms are corded with muscles. His skin is a mixture between orange and brown, gleaming with health and power. He's dressed in an embroidered white tunic and black pants. His boots are made of a supple brown material that molds to his legs. A crown made of phoenix feathers and gold filled with flames rests on his head. Croi wonders that it doesn't burn him.

She turns to her companions and sees that each one of them has bowed their head. Something in her resists looking at the Fire King's face, but she overcomes that reluctance. His face is lightly bearded and boasts thin lips, high cheekbones, a narrow forehead, and thick eyebrows that frame densely lashed tawny eyes ringed with red. His face is unlined, but his eyes give his age away.

His magick is so powerful that it shocks both Croi and her other self. *We know him . . . don't we?*

"We've never seen him before today. How could we know him?" Croi keeps her eyes on the king, almost greedy for his attention.

His magick feels familiar. Too familiar. I don't like this feeling.

Croi doesn't bother replying. She knows exactly what her other self means. This is Ceara's father, Aodh, the king of Tine. That much is obvious.

"Who are you?" His words are a command, demanding that Croi respond. She, however, doesn't feel the urge to tell him any of her secrets.

Frowning when Croi doesn't reply, the fae king gives the kneeling kin permission to rise, and they, especially Monca, rise gratefully. Then he starts walking toward where Croi stands, at the back, near the entrance.

Be careful.

Croi stays still, waiting for the king, barely breathing as he approaches.

"You are familiar to me," the king says, looking down at Croi from his greater height.

Croi doesn't respond. What can she say that will make sense? There's a roaring in her ears.

"Who are you, child?" the king asks again. His voice sounds like crackling fire.

Instead of replying, on a whim, Croi reaches out and touches his hand. At the moment of contact, both the magicks inside her are shocked awake. One of her magicks sings the same song as the Fire King's magick; it undulates to the same tune.

Croi finds the word for this fae king, and she knows by his surprised look that *he* knows the word for her as well. He holds her hand tight in his for a second before he lets go and walks, almost flees, away. Croi ignores the questioning looks everyone directs to her and follows a servant kin to her living quarters. The room Croi is given is empty of all furniture except for a bed. She has never slept on a bed before, so she takes one long moment to luxuriate in its softness. She places her pack beside the pillow and takes off the veil she was wearing. The windows in the room are curtained, making the room dark. She walks over and pulls the curtains aside, and a breeze, unlike any other she has ever felt before, wafts in through the windows, tracing eolian fingers over her skin. Unlike the cold earthy breezes of the forest, this breeze has an underlying heat to it, like a promise from the sun fulfilled. Croi lifts her head, looks outside, and blinks twice.

As far as she can see, there is dry, arid sand, and a bright blue sky, uninterrupted by clouds. Not a single tree sways in sight, not even a miserly bush. Croi can see no green, just shades of red and brown stretching on for leagues. The little flame in her veins, the one she has almost forgotten, exults at the sight; the Croi inside trembles as well. She takes pleasure in the desert while Croi recoils from it.

The view outside seems real, but a flash of magick thread gives it away. Croi can see the Tine magick winding round and round the room before spilling out the open windows and weaving the living picture she sees outside. The fire magick is familiar, the song muted, but brilliantly shaded. The desert is an illusion created by the Tine King; it is his magick that pulses softly around the edges of the enchanted horizon.

The thought of the Tine King brings a confused frown to Croi's face.

"Is he . . . ?" she thinks to her other self.

Don't say it.

Both Croi and her other self felt an affinity, a kinship, for the Tine King. How is that possible? How can the Tine King belong to her when he's obviously Ceara's father?

Croi's chest hurts again, and she rubs it. She picks up her bag and pulls out Uaine's SoulSeed. She unwraps it carefully. Its heat has substantially faded, and its light has grown dimmer.

"What are you doing?"

The voice in the doorway of the room startles Croi. She turns her head and sees Monca standing at the door. The brownie has an impressive scowl on her face and is looking Croi over as though she is a stain that has to be removed.

"Who are you?" the brownie asks. She has a gruff manner of speaking. Her voice is low and rough, as though she has spent her life whispering and has forgotten how to speak normally.

Croi sighs at the same old question. A question that she still has no answer to. She doesn't respond, and the brownie comes closer, shutting the door on her way in. Is she supposed to be frightened by the brownie's actions?

"You are not Fiona." Indeed. Croi wonders when the brownie noticed. "Why are you here?"

"My business is my own," Croi replies.

Monca glares at Croi, her contempt obvious in the curve of her lips. "If you hurt my Ceara," she hisses, drawing even closer, "I will . . ."

Have we harmed this brownie mother in any way?

"You will?" Croi stares at this brownie, who gives her all her thorns. Did she think that just because she used to be a brownie and Monca is a brownie, some kind of bond would exist between them? A shared appreciation of being small and helpless? Croi is more likely to find that with Tinder than with Monca.

"You will see what I will do," Monca says, doubling the gruffness. "Now follow me. It is dinnertime. The king wants to see you." The one inside jumps at this tidbit while Croi frantically thinks of excuses. Seeing the king before she comes to terms with her relationship to him would be folly.

"I don't feel too well. Can't I take a nap instead?"

The brownie sniffs haughtily. "No one refuses the king's summons, child. That is the first lesson you should have learned." She walks to the door and pulls it open before looking at Croi over her shoulder. "What are you doing? Hurry up and follow me!"

Croi puts on the veil with a sigh. Clutching her pack tightly, she follows the brownie through a myriad of corridors. The magick used to increase the space inside the pavilion runs underneath her feet in thin orange strands. The floor is covered with a carpet and feels firm, like wood. The inside of the entire pavilion has been woven by magick, yet the outside is, Croi's sure, made of some kind of canvas. How do these fae play so easily with space?

She looks at Monca as they walk, wanting to ask her many things.

Like, how does it feel to be a true brownie? If she knew, maybe she could quantify her loss, but she doesn't know what to say. How does she translate this void inside her into words? What tone does she use to present them to the brownie? Can one question contain her entire query, and if not, what parts of "who I was" are the most important and should be included?

In the end, Croi asks nothing and follows her quietly into the dining room. A large chandelier hanging from the ceiling gives the room a golden glow. Croi glimpses Tinder sitting next to the Fire Princess's plate on a table in the center of the room. She sees Croi and nods. Croi knows they're playing parts here; Tinder is the honored visitor and Croi, the inconsequential servant. The princess sits on one side of the Tine King and Lorcan on the other.

A chair remains empty beside the princess, possibly for the brownie. Other Tine kin sit at the table besides these four, but they're thrown into shadow by the king.

"Take your place," the brownie says. Croi notices Caoimhe and Aislin standing at attention behind the princess's chair.

"We don't get to eat?" This is crueler than if they'd just lashed her with a whip. How is she supposed to endure watching food that she can't eat pass right in front of her? Croi looks at the brownie with wounded eyes.

"Servant kin eat later," the brownie says, and pushes her farther into the room. Croi is tempted to turn on her heels and go, tempted to take her chances with the unfriendly forest, but the slight warmth emanating from Uaine's SoulSeed makes her stay. So she grits her teeth and takes a place behind the princess's chair, but not before she sends a glare her way. The princess doesn't look at Croi, nor does she give any indication that she has even noticed her, but the Tine King does. He gives her an indecipherable look before turning back to his conversation with Lorcan.

Then the torture begins.

Platters of food are carried into the room by the same rotund creatures Croi saw before. They are a kind of kin Croi doesn't know and has never seen. They aren't important at the moment; the food is. Different types of meat, gravy, fruit, and dishes she doesn't recognize but wishes she did find their places on the table. Artistically arranged desserts and colorful drinks in pewter jugs are carried out. The aroma of the food nearly makes her swoon, and Croi furtively wipes the drool from the sides of her mouth.

Her attention is caught by the princess and her father. A father—the thought is novel. Croi shapes the word out, confident that no one can see her lips moving beneath the veil. The word has a weight to it, a resonance, like the peal of a brass bell. There's a reason the Tine King's kindness to his daughter makes Croi want to weep. He speaks to the Fire Princess and pays attention to her replies. He offers her choice bits of meat, and she glows as though he has given her the world. Her other self aches and aches, and suddenly the sorrow twists into white anger. Croi knows she should shift her attention, but her eyes refuse to look away from the two of them.

Don't covet what doesn't belong to you.

"I'm not!" Croi is aggrieved. "I just think that if our life didn't go awry, we, too, would have had a family, a f—" She snorts to herself and shakes her head. "I don't want to see this."

Perhaps it is the turmoil that accompanied meeting the Tine King or the fight with the Redcaps that lowers her defenses, but the pain attacks at this moment. Croi utters a whimper and falls to the ground, not seeing Tinder's yell, the king's reaction, or Ceara's panic. All she knows at this moment is the pain tearing through her insides.

TWENTY-FIVE

"HOW ARE YOU FEELING RIGHT NOW?" TINDER'S FACE is creased with concern. She's hovering in the air in front of Croi, her magick an erratic orange.

Croi struggles to sit up; someone returned her to the room she was shown earlier. The pain has faded, but it stole all her energy. Croi licks her lips and feels the rawness in her throat.

You screamed a lot.

"How about you handle the pain next time?" Croi thinks sourly.

"You . . ." Tinder trails off, her eyes widening.

"What?" Croi croaks out. She follows the pixie's gaze down to her bosom, and her eyes widen too. "What is that?"

They both stare at the rather obvious bumps on Croi's chest. Croi pokes at them and then flinches. "Ow!"

Tinder swallows, looking at a loss for words. "That . . . They weren't this prominent an hour ago, were they?"

Croi blinks.

"I will call Ceara!" Tinder flies away.

Croi gets out of bed and walks to a mirror in the corner of the room. "I don't want to look at my face," she complains to her other self.

It's just an in-between face.

Croi takes off the lacy veil and looks at herself in the mirror. Once again, she's taken aback by the jeweled colors of her eyes. Her face . . . It hasn't changed much. Still hideous but a more acceptable sort of hideous than it used to be.

The most dramatic change is in her body shape. She now has curves. She used to be completely flat in the front, but now . . . Croi looks down at her bosom again and makes a face. What is she supposed to do with them?

"I'm back!" Tinder announces from the doorway. Croi looks up to see Ceara behind Tinder. Following the Fire Princess are two servant kin holding trays filled with food.

Ceara looks Croi up and down, her face betraying her shock. "You . . . Why have you changed so much? Has your hair grown longer?"

Croi hadn't even noticed the length of her hair, but the princess is right. It did grow longer. Now it is almost to her knees.

You have to give them some sort of explanation.

"The truth?" Croi doesn't know if it is possible for her to hide her situation anymore.

Parts of it. Don't tell them about me.

Croi waits until the servant kin have placed the trays of food on a short table in the sitting area on the side of the room. Once they leave, she settles in front of the food, intensely aware that she is the focus of two unblinking gazes. "Can I eat something first?"

"No," Ceara replies immediately.

"I might die." Croi whimpers.

"You won't die." Tinder is heartless too.

"Fine. Do you know why I am so resistant to having Glamour put on me?" Croi crosses her arms and looks grumpy. The other two stare at her without replying. "It's because I'm already under a Glamour. How I am is not how I really am—does that make sense?"

"The Glamour spell on you is in the process of breaking?" Ceara frowns. "How long have you been Glamoured?"

"Almost seventeen years," Croi says, distracted by the food on the tray, specifically by the meat, cooked in gravy and served with tiny puffy grains. There are nuts and other strange but obviously delectable things on the plate. It smells delicious.

"Seventeen years?!" Tinder exclaims, startling both Ceara and Croi. "I didn't know Glamour spells could last that long!"

"Neither did I." Ceara looks thoughtful. "Do you know who cast it on you?"

The kin the princess met didn't tell the princess her secrets.

"Are we that kin's secret?" Croi thinks.

We seem to be.

"Well?" Ceara prompts.

"No," Croi replies. She picks up a fork and scoops up some puffy grains. It tastes as delicious as it looks. "I don't know who gave birth to me or how I ended up in the human world. The person who took care of me wasn't all that forthcoming with answers."

"Does it hurt every time the Glamour breaks?" Tears sparkle in the pixie's eyes. Croi feels strange when she sees them.

Is she crying for us?

"Probably not." Croi feels awkward at the thought.

She shrugs at the pixie.

"I will ask my father to see if your magick is similar to any Tine kin he knows. Kin can identify their family by the similarity in their magicks," Ceara says.

Ask her why her magick is so similar to that fierce Lorcan's.

"No!" Croi sends a mental glare to her other self.

"Isn't there any way to alleviate the pain?" Tinder asks worriedly.

"Did you finish eating?" Croi pointedly changes the subject. "Can I eat all this?"

"No! I'm still hungry!" Tinder immediately grabs a little fork provided for her and a piece of meat almost as big as she is and commences eating. Ceara does not partake of the meal. Instead, she cradles a glass filled with red liquid that smells like flowers and spice and sips.

They eat for a while, all of them sunk in their own thoughts.

"How come you didn't bow to the Tine King?" Tinder asks after swallowing a morsel. "Didn't you feel compelled to?"

"No?" Croi takes a bite of a pastry and finds raisins inside. She makes a face but continues chewing. "Why?"

Ceara and Tinder are staring at her with that dumbfounded look again. "What?" Croi puts the pastry down, feeling nervous.

Did our face change again?

"You seriously didn't feel compelled to bow to my father?" Ceara asks, a shrill tone in her voice.

Croi winces. "No. Why? Is bowing that important?"

Tinder swallows. "No one can meet a fae monarch's eyes without bowing first," she explains. "Unless they are another monarch."

"Do I look like a monarch?" Croi asks with some interest.

Neither the fae nor the pixie deign to answer the question.

"Your brownie mother . . . Has she been with you all along?" Croi asks after an awkward pause. "What is a brownie mother anyway?"

Ceara shakes her glass, watching the liquid catch the light and taking that moment to gather her thoughts. "Before the Great Betrayal, brownie mothers were a common practice among the Talamh royals. Every child born to a Talamh royal had a brownie mother; they imprint upon the child at birth and remain completely loyal to them for the entirety of their lives. Monca was actually my mother's brownie mother originally." She sees Croi's questioning face and elaborates. "Mabh, the Earth Princess and the previous consort of the Tine King."

"Monca was the one who brought you to the Tine King?" Croi tries to piece the princess's history together.

How many times do you need to ask that question? Is the brownie that important?

"Don't you think it is about time we wondered *why* the fae with the damaged magick was trying to summon us to her side? What does she want from us? The brownie might have answers," Croi points out to her other self.

Why would she have the answers?

"She was the last person who saw Mabh," Croi thinks to her other self.

But what does her seeing Mabh last have to do with us?

"What if Mabh isn't dead?" Croi's words echo in her mind, and her other self falls silent.

"Yes, my mother extracted a promise from her to do so. Otherwise, she would have faded when she lost my mother," Ceara replies, not noticing Croi's blank gaze.

"Oh." The response is inadequate, but Croi doesn't know what else to say. She pours herself some of the drink the princess seems enamored with. She takes a cautious sip of it and widens her eyes at the taste. It is sweet but not cloyingly so. The floral notes are tempered by a spice Croi has never tasted before. She takes a deep draft and sighs happily before pouring herself another glass.

"Don't drink too much of the sun-drink," Ceara warns. "You'll have a headache tomorrow morning."

"Who is looking after Tine now that your father is here?" Croi asks drowsily.

"His new consort," Ceara says, the tone of her voice warning her not to ask more. Croi and Tinder exchange looks.

"How are you related to that angry soldier who stopped us before—what was his name?"

"You mean Lorcan." Tinder shudders, expressing her feelings directly.

"I'm not related to him!" Ceara bursts out, looking horrified at the idea. She jumps to her feet. "I'm going to bed." She leaves without another word. Croi blinks at Tinder.

"How did I offend her? Are they really not related?" Croi says.

"Lorcan is the general of the Tine soldiers and the Tine King's close friend. I don't think he and Ceara have any other relationship." Tinder rubs her slightly protruding stomach.

"They're really not related by blood?" Croi narrows her eyes, remembering the similarity of their magicks. "How is that possible?"

"Ah, but if Lord Lorcan's wife and child had survived the Great Betrayal, his daughter would have been the same age as Ceara currently is," Tinder says.

Croi, who had just taken a bite of a squishy fruit, chokes, and fruit juices dribble down her chin. Her chest aches as if it's going to split, and her face contorts.

Pay attention. This is important.

"Who was Lorcan's wife?" Croi asks.

"Mabh's lady-in-waiting. A fae woman by the name of Lilia. Not much is known about her. Only that she accompanied Mabh to Talamh with her daughter and unfortunately fell victim to the Usurper." Tinder yawns.

Do you think Ceara is Lorcan's daughter?

"Their magicks are too similar for her to be anyone else's." Croi's chest is throbbing.

Why would the Tine King accept his general's daughter as his own?

"Do you think I have any answers?" Croi grumbles to her other self. "All I have are questions."

Tinder is snoring on the table, her face content. Croi picks her up gently and carries her over to the bed. She places her on a pillow, slips off her shoes, and climbs into bed too. Quiet descends upon the room as the torchlight wanes. Everyone else has retired for the night since the camp will be broken down at dawn the following day. Croi wonders if the princess is asleep. According to Tinder, the sleeping arrangements in Ceara's room are complex. Apart from the two guards who stand in front of her room, the handmaids Aislin and Caoimhe sleep on either side of the bed, protecting her from midnight assassins. The brownie mother has a pallet at the foot of the bed just in case the other four kin fail to keep the princess safe.

Croi feels a watery compassion for Ceara; if she really is not the princess, then her life has been as much a lie as Croi's has been. Croi sighs loudly, and the pixie mutters a string of curses in her sleep. In revenge, Croi pokes her cheeks and giggles at the pixie's attempts to swat her away.

I had thought the Tine King would ask to speak to us. Surely, he was able to see the similarities in our magicks.

Croi shrugs, not wanting to think about Aodh. She will not covet things or people that don't belong to her. Instead, she thinks about the menu for breakfast before drifting off to sleep.

Morning arrives too quickly, and Croi gets happily acquainted with a type of bread made of nuts and gold raisins and a hot drink made of bitter chocolate and sugar that serves as breakfast. Soon the camp is broken up and they're riding hard and fast on a path toward the Caisleán.

Croi and Tinder ride with Ceara on her beastie, flanked on either side by Tine soldiers. Croi looks at the increasing lassitude in the

magick as they get closer to Talamh Caisleán and pats her pack. Why haven't more people noticed the state of the magick? Does no one suspect that the Talamh HeartStone is missing?

"What is a HeartStone made of?" Croi asks out loud. If the dryad is not able to find it in time, would she be able to replace it with another one? Would that be possible?

Ceara answers the question. "Fionar and her companions crystallized the purest form of whole magick, refined it into elements, and then broke the sphere according to the saturations of the elemental magicks in the sphere. The HeartStone of Talamh contains the purest form of earth magick, the HeartStone of Tine contains the purest form of fire magick, and so forth."

A HeartStone is not something one can simply replace or re-create. Croi can feel her other self rolling her eyes at her. Well, if she had eyes, she'd be rolling them.

"So the monarchs of each kingdom get to hold the HeartStone of the kingdom?" Croi tries to see the Tine King, who is riding at the head of the procession.

Tinder, sitting on Ceara's shoulder while facing Croi, nods her head. "Remember, I told you before. To be the monarch, you need to have the strength to hold the HeartStone. Only a few among the fae have this strength. Other kin can't hold the HeartStone at all."

"I remember. So magickal strength is of utmost importance in a monarch?" Croi asks.

"Yep," Tinder says. "The Saol ceremony requires the monarch of an elemental kingdom to infuse the HeartStone with a percentage of their magicks. If the monarch is unable to do so, the Saol ceremony will be unsuccessful."

"Oh . . ." Croi takes a breath. "What happens if a HeartStone is lost?"

Both Ceara and Tinder look at Croi.

"I'm just asking!"

"Don't ask. The consequences of a missing HeartStone are not something the Otherworld can bear," Ceara says, her voice grim.

They stop at midday for food and an hour's rest. After munching on meat and vegetables wrapped in thin bread that tastes of fire and sesame seeds, Croi leans against a tree and watches Tinder juggle seeds she harvested from a nearby bush. A breeze that smells like ripe apples plays with her too-long hair that rests in a braid down her back; a rare sense of well-being envelops her.

If only this could be our every day.

"Someday," Croi says, comforting her other self.

"Let me show you something." Tinder flies over, her eyes sparkling. She places a seed on her palm and sings a word of earth magick. The seed sprouts until it is a small plant. "Are you impressed?" The pixie giggles.

"Can I try?" Croi asks. Her last attempt at Talamh magick was unsuccessful, but who knows—she might be successful this time around.

"You can do Tine magick, not Talamh," Tinder retorts, but hands over a seed anyway.

Croi, mirroring Tinder, places the seed on her outstretched palm. She can see a bit of green magick housed in the center of the seed. Tinder woke the magick by singing to it in the language of earth magick. Croi doesn't know how to do that. Instead, she sends a thought to the magick, and it stirs slowly.

"Bloom," Croi commands it silently. It doesn't react. *"Bloom!"* she commands it again, this time infusing the command with a bit of her will.

In the next second, the seed sends a tender green shoot out. Tinder gasps in shock. The seed, however, isn't done. It continues growing until it grows into a plant that is too big for Croi to hold.

She places it on the ground, her eyes not moving from it as it sends roots down into the ground and shoots up into the air, growing into a tree. It sprouts dark and vibrantly green leaves. Half a minute later, yellow buds appear on the tree, which then bloom into large yellow flowers that exude an intoxicating fragrance that attracts bees and birds.

Perhaps you shouldn't have done that.

Croi has to agree with her other self when she realizes that Tinder isn't the only one who is staring at her as if she has grown another head. Everyone is looking at her, but the sharpest gazes come from Ceara, her brownie mother, and Lorcan.

"Weren't you Tine?" the princess asks sharply. "You clearly handled fire magick. I saw you doing so."

You really shouldn't have done this.

Croi looks at Tinder in desperation. The pixie, correctly reading the plea in her eyes, flies up to the bush. "There's something weird about this plant. The seeds come from that tiny bush. How could it be a tree?"

Tinder directs attention away from Croi, and the Tine fae crowd around the verdant tree, exclaiming at the lushness of the blooms it contains. Croi slinks away from the crowd, trying to blend into the shadows, but instead bumps into the Tine King, who has been standing at a distance, observing her.

However, apart from a complex look, he doesn't say anything to her, and soon they are on their way again.

The Tine King and his retinue stop again in the evening for dinner and sleep. The camp is set up by magickal means, and all the soldiers do is look fierce and ready for anyone with sinister intentions. Their attentions go unrewarded as the Tine procession is not attacked by anything or anyone. In fact, not even a rabbit crosses the road on which they travel.

At the end of the day, Tinder informs Croi that the Caisleán is near, but even if she hadn't, Croi would have known. She can feel it, hear it, even. Just as the summoning spell tugged on her limbs, the Caisleán tugs at her limbs, at her heart, which aches at all times now. Sometimes Croi thinks that her heart wants to liberate itself from her body and fly ahead to the Caisleán.

The royal pavilion, with all its luxuries, is set up first, and Croi is sent to the bathing rooms with stern orders. Tinder accompanies her, not because she enjoys her company, but because the pixie wants to ensure that Croi does actually scrub herself clean and doesn't just pretend to. Croi is slightly offended that she's not trusted to clean herself, but she doesn't make too much of a fuss. The truth is, the royal pavilion, with its many rooms and impossibilities, unsettles her.

"Take a bath," Tinder commands, wrinkling her nose.

"I am!" Croi scrubs extra hard and finds that under the dust, her skin has turned from brown to orange-brown, but her fingernails and toenails are a light green. She puts on a pale yellow dress Ceara lent her and goes out of the bathing room to an anteroom where Tinder is waiting.

The pixie looks her up and down, her eyes lingering on Croi's nails. The lightness flows out of her features, replaced by a rare solemnity. "You must make sure not to do Tine magick in the camp."

"Why?"

"Nobody can handle both Tine and Talamh magick. Being able to do so makes you a threat to the Otherworld," the pixie says.

"Because it harkens back to before Fionar's time?" Croi asks.

"Yeah. A time ruled by blood and greed. You may not intend harm, but your intent won't matter. Do you understand?" Tinder whispers.

Croi nods.

"I will talk to Ceara tonight. Ask her to help you hide your ability to command both fire and earth magick," Tinder says.

"Thank you," Croi says, turning to hide the sudden sting in her eyes.

"We're friends!" Tinder grins.

Friends.

Croi smiles secretly, holding the word close. A friend.

Much later, when she's in bed and holding her pack tight while trying to infuse the SoulSeed with her warmth, she takes the word out and considers it again. Friends and friendship. She tried it with the catkin and got betrayed. Surely not everyone will betray her. Surely Irial, wherever he is right now, doesn't mean her harm. Surely the pixie is sincere. She looks at the empty space beside her pillow. Tinder decided to bunk with Ceara for the night in order to talk to her about keeping Croi's secret.

I miss her.

"She's *my* friend," Croi says proudly.

She's our friend.

Croi spends a while bickering with her other self before the day's fatigue pulls at her eyelids. She's almost asleep when they come. The shadowy soldiers do not give her a chance to scream, cry, or defend herself. A piece of cloth wrapped around her mouth gags, silences, and overpowers her. Her hands and legs are tied; she's trussed up like the turkey humans like to sacrifice during feasts. Her attackers are Tine soldiers, though none of them are ones she knows. It takes two of them to carry her out of the room, through the corridors, out of the royal pavilion, and into the night. The guards around the pavilion avert their eyes when they see her. Fear prickles her insides; Croi reaches for her other self, finding her quiet and wary.

The soldiers carry her some distance away from the camp to a little clearing where a tremendous fire is burning. This fire is malevolent, with red flames and a smoky breath. Fear drums harder in her chest. Croi looks around and sees a dark figure detach from the trunk of a nearby tree and walk into the light. Lorcan. Why would he kidnap her from her bed?

The soldiers place her on the ground before the fire. Croi gleans some comfort from the earth pressing against her skin. Lorcan drops to his haunches before her and with one hand rips the gag out of her mouth. She takes a deep breath, wheezing as the cold night air stings her throat on its way in.

"Tell me who you are," Lorcan says softly, almost kindly.

Croi stares at him stupidly. She still doesn't understand why he brought her here. Did the princess order him to do this? Or was it the Tine King? Did she trust Tinder wrongly? But why would he do this? Croi doesn't mean anyone harm.

"I heard that you hurt the princess, almost killed her," he continues in that eerie voice, and Croi shudders. He is not wrong. She did do that. "How much pain do you think she felt?"

Without warning, he pushes Croi into the fire. She barely has time to gasp a breath before the flames reach for her. The heat has no bite, but the flames feel solid; they feel like they have the serrated edges of the swords beloved to the Tine soldiers. Lorcan holds up a hand, and the fire stills. This fire is unlike the other fires Croi has played with; its song is crooked. Still, both she and her other self wait for its heat, knowing that it will allow her broken self to be one again.

"Will you not tell me who you are and why you're going to the Caisleán?" Lorcan whispers, his voice losing its soft edges for the first time.

"I don't owe you any answers," she tells the Tine general. She tightens her lips, grits her teeth, and readies herself for pain as Lorcan waves a hand, letting it flow toward her. The flames gain tangibility, become solid, and rush at her, cutting her skin with their edges as they continue through her skin and into her body. Croi screams at the

pain; she didn't think the fire would cut her like a knife.

She doesn't realize she's bleeding until the first drop of her blood falls into the earth.

It's just one drop, but the effect is instantaneous and immense. Both Croi's selves are shocked still when the earth reacts to the blood with an enraged roar. She sees Lorcan pale and the soldiers pull out their swords. She sees stooping trees stand straight. Monca's shocked face flashes before her as a soldier pulls the brownie out from under the leafy shade of a rowan tree. Another drop of Croi's blood falls to the earth, and the roar resounds. Her back arches as pain slices through it in two different spots.

Croi feels like her world is ending and she's going to go to glory in an inferno. There's fire within her and fire without her. Anger spreads from her fingertips to her toes. The fire heats her blood and creates a bridge between her two selves, joining her two halves into one whole.

When the world shrinks to Croi and the pain she feels, a hand presses on her shoulder, and the chaos inside her retreats. The cadence of the magicks within her harmonizes with the magick of the kin holding her. She knows before she turns that it is Aodh, the Tine King, standing behind her. She sags as he wraps a cloth around her arms, staunching the flow of blood.

"Give me the fire, child," the king says, expecting to be obeyed.

Croi straightens up and pulls away from his embrace. "No," she replies, her voice brittle and sharp. "No," she repeats. She looks at the Tine kin surrounding her.

Lorcan has fallen to his knees, as have the soldiers. There's no sign of Monca, but Croi knows she was here; the trees will not keep secrets from her.

"I do not recall asking you to do this, Lord Lorcan." The Tine King is angry; his words create welts on Lorcan's face.

"We were told that she harmed the princess, sire." Lorcan's voice is even and controlled, betraying none of the darkness that colors his swirling magick.

"Did you not ask your princess what she was doing when I harmed her?" Croi walks closer to the kneeling fae. He lifts his head at her approach and his irises flare, hatred filling the red depths. Croi does not understand why he hates her, but she cannot let his actions go unanswered.

She looks at him, and Lorcan's magick stills, sensitive to her attention.

"Do you know what I did to her? Would you like to find out?" In the next second she rips the magick out of him. Lorcan crumples to the ground with a scream, unprepared for the agony unfolding within him. Croi watches him convulse. She watches him weep. He begs for mercy, but no one moves to intercede on his behalf; nobody dares. When his voice thins out with exhaustion and the light of his magick is almost extinguished, Croi rescinds her call, and his magick slithers back under his skin.

"Is it because she is your daughter that it hurts you more?" she whispers to the fallen fae. Lorcan tries to speak then but coughs blood instead.

The fire heats her skin, bites her insides, and demands release. Croi bows her head and clenches her fingers so her nails leave half-moon gouges on her palm. A moment later, she turns and looks at the king with the fiery eyes and the wild hair; she looks at the shell-shocked soldiers; she looks at a little cat on the side, snacking on a careless bird.

The moment of breaking approaches once again.

Croi closes her eyes for a brief second, savoring the feeling of being whole, before she loosens her hold on the fire and it flows back, scalding her, tearing her, on its way out. The Tine King first catches the flames with his fingers, absorbing them.

Severed once more, Croi leaves the clearing, holding herself

together until she reaches her room in the royal pavilion. She changes out of the nightgown the princess gave her and into the dress she is supposed to wear the next day. Then she lights a candle and sits in front of the window.

Will he come?

"We'll wait until he does."

TWENTY-SIX

THE CANDLE FLAME FLARES WHEN THE TINE KING arrives.

Croi is sitting in front of the window, gazing out at the desert that has been painted with the colors of the night. A full moon commands the horizon. Looking out at the sand dunes, she wonders which one is the true illusion. The desert outside the window or her.

He's here.

Warned by her other self, Croi is ready when the knock sounds on the closed door of the room. It opens after a short pause, and the Tine King enters the room. She looks at him, choosing not to speak.

What can we say to him anyway? "Surprise"?

The king's eyes have no smile in them. His lips are a thin line, and his body is tense.

Surely, he has something to say to us.

He comes to stand in front of her; Croi remains seated, feeling no need to show him obeisance. His eyes look her over carefully, raking over the planes of her in-between face; he flinches when he meets her gaze.

Our existence seems to hurt him.

"I must ask you, how do you come to be?" His first words surprise Croi.

"Should you not be asking *who* I am? Or is that a question you already know the answer to? As for how I came to be, surely *you* know that better than I do?" Croi has no expectations of warmth from the Tine King. *She* knows better now.

"Will you not answer my question, child?" the Tine King asks.

"Why should I? What right do you have to command me?" Croi gets to her feet, desiring to put physical space between herself and the king, but she forgot the pain her body has suffered in the past hour. She stumbles, and the king reaches out to catch her. Once again, their magicks align and sing together. A choked sob escapes Croi, and she wrenches herself away from the king.

Breathe. We will get through this.

Croi breathes. Deep breaths that do little to dilute the hurt her heart feels. She rubs her chest, the pain physical.

The king clears his throat, perhaps to speak, but before he can say another word, there is a knock on the door. A servant kin pushes it open after the king gives his permission.

"The healer is here, sire." After speaking, the servant kin moves aside to allow another kin through.

This kin has white skin upon which are traced, in the darkest green, drawings of vines, flowers, and tendrils. On a closer look, these tracings are actual plants that grow on the inside of this kin. They twist and twine under Croi's gaze, aware of her attention. The kin's magick is solid green. The kin has a sharp chin and high cheekbones, and their hair is kept hidden under a headpiece decorated with the feathers of colorful birds. Their green eyes are ringed by a deep, dark brown.

"This is Maon," the king says, looking at Croi with an intensity she doesn't reciprocate. "They're a healer."

"A healer?" Croi looks at the kin with renewed interest. "Can they mend me? Put my halves back together?"

Maon says nothing for a moment. Perhaps they prefer to be silent, or perhaps they cannot speak. Croi retreats to silence as well, content to let it rule their gathering.

"I need to taste your magick first. Will you let me?" Maon finally speaks.

"Before you do, we will have your oath of silence," the king says, and unexpectedly the healer smiles, the expression ill-suited to their somberness.

"You have it, sire." The healer bows their head.

"Why should we listen to them?" Croi thinks to her other self.

Maybe this healer can mend us. It will not hurt to let them try.

Croi hesitates but finally extends her hand, waiting to see what sorrows the healer will taste in her magick. The healer cups their palms underneath her hand, and Croi lets her twin magicks spill over into them. Her magicks disappear into the healer's skin, and they gasp at their potency. The healer's magick blooms with the infusion of Croi's, and they drop to their knees, trying to endure what they have not been made to.

Croi and the king wait for the healer to regain their equilibrium. They don't wait long. The healer gets to their feet. Breathing heavily, they look Croi over once again. Their gaze is complex, containing awe, fear, and pity.

"What is wrong with the child?" the king asks. Croi tilts her head, waiting for the healer's answer.

The healer hesitates, perhaps uncertain if they can speak frankly.

"Don't worry. Your words will not harm you," the king says.

The healer takes a breath, glancing at Croi. She meets their stare without flinching. "According to her magick, the child was born Tine, but a spell was cast on her birthday. This spell, from the dregs that remain in her magick, seems to be a complicated one. Generally, Glamour spells create illusions, but the spell cast on this child didn't just truly change her form but also separated the magicks within her." They pause and frown. "She has very strong Tine magick, and had she been allowed to grow naturally, I daresay her fire magick would have rivaled yours, sire. However, the magickal interference has led to her earth magick becoming many times stronger than her fire magick. I cannot speculate on the reasons behind this, but I can tell you that dragon magick was involved."

Ah. The fire magick speaks to me. Croi's inner self relaxes slightly.

"Does that mean you are the true self and I'm the artificial one?" Croi asks her, feeling guiltier. Her inner self doesn't reply.

"What causes her pain?" Croi raises her eyebrows at the king's next question.

"The Glamour spell on the child is in the process of breaking," the healer replies. "Her body is changing too rapidly; brownie physique is vastly different from fae. She is having to do the amount of growing in a month that other fae children do in seventeen years. I should tell you, sire, that the breaking of the Glamour is dangerous.

"Glamours are not meant to be cast long term. They erode the self, repress the true, and champion the false. Both her Tine and Talamh selves are extremely strong. Both of them will vie for dominance in the end. Unless these parts can be equalized and merged into one, her core will not survive the breaking." The healer speaks softly, but their words are very clear.

"Is there no way to help her through the breaking of the Glamour?" the king asks. No expression mars his features; he might as well be made of the same stone as the Hag.

The healer closes their eyes, and when they open them again, the answer shines through. The king flinches, and Croi feels the absurd urge to laugh. Or cry. Or both.

I don't want to die. I haven't even felt the sun on my skin yet. You've been living on the outside all this time while I've been spending my days in the dark. How can I die?

"Can you not do it? Can you not make her whole again?" the king asks, and the healer shakes their head.

"That requires a magick far older, far stronger than I have . . . than what remains in this world." The healer's words linger in the silence that follows. "I'm sorry." The healer bows once and leaves.

Croi stands beside the king, her eyes not moving from the illusion of the desert outside. Death has been on the horizon for so long, but the end Croi grappled with was a result of violence. Of monsters. A tremulous possibility when the wrong turn is taken. But the healer's words promise that death is not a possibility but a probability. A conclusion that will be reached long before the embers have burnt out.

"I will not give up," the king says suddenly, grabbing hold of Croi's hands. "I will—"

Croi pulls her hands away. She does not want his sentiments. She understands his need to express them, but she will not accept them. It is far too late for him to assume responsibility for her.

"I am your father," the king finally says, and Croi winces. She did not want him to name their relationship.

Just like the word "mother," the word "father" is complicated for her. When she was still in the human world, she was desperate for parents to call her own. She saw how humans loved theirs. She thought that a father was someone who protects, someone who heals, and someone who makes things right. She was wrong. For Croi, a father is just another person she cannot call her own. Just another way she has been betrayed.

"You are Ceara's father. Not mine," Croi tells him. The Tine King frowns, clearly dissatisfied with her words. "Perhaps it was your seed that created me, but your absence in my life pronounces you unfit for the position of my parent."

"I didn't know you existed!" the Tine King says.

"Then where did you think your child went? Did you ever try looking for me? Surely you are not going to tell me that you thought Ceara was your daughter?" Croi challenges him, her arms around herself. The king looks away. "See, you know she isn't your child, but you are content to let everyone think she is. Why is that?"

"Things are much more complicated than you realize," he says.

Croi snorts. "You found out yesterday that I am your child. Yet you didn't call for me or come to me. It wasn't until your general tried to kill me that you made an appearance. How complicated is that?" She tilts her head and looks at the king, unimpressed by his majesty. "Tell me, how are you going to punish Lorcan?"

"Didn't you take your revenge on him?" The king frowns at her. "Aren't you satisfied with the pain you caused him?"

Croi laughs at his words, the sound ugly and broken. "He hurt me because I hurt his daughter. A daughter he doesn't dare claim. He just might be a better father than you." Croi turns away from him, her rejection loud in the silent room.

A moment later the king leaves. The candle flame sputters out.

TWENTY-SEVEN

CROI SKIPS BREAKFAST THE NEXT MORNING, PREFER-ring to stand outside and watch the soldiers take down the camp in preparation for the final leg of the journey. The ones who took her the night before are nowhere to be seen. Neither is Lorcan, for that matter. Croi's hungry, but she'd much rather endure the hunger than eat with those who have betrayed her. Someone told Lorcan about the happenings in the Redcap camp. It was either the princess or Tinder.

It probably wasn't the pixie.

Croi is surprised by her inner self's evaluation. "Why do you say that?"

She's too scared of Lorcan to go telling tales to him. Besides, we know her personality by now, don't we?

"We thought we knew Caolan, didn't we?" Croi reminds her other self.

No, we didn't. That was only you.

Croi grimaces but can't deny her other self. She has been careful not to think about the healer's warning or her rapidly approaching death. Perhaps she is in denial right now. Perhaps rage will follow denial, which will eventually fade to acceptance. Her life, finite though it is now, has three goals. One, get to the Caisleán and meet Irial; two, find someone to go to the human world and rescue her stone maid; and three, fulfill Uaine's errand. Truly, she doesn't care in the least if the HeartStone is found or not. She won't be around to see the chaos if it remains unfound. If she can fulfill the first two of these goals, she will fade, if not happily, then contented.

Fatalistic.

"Stop reading my mind. It's rude."

It is my mind too.

Croi flushes at her other self's words. If she could, she would be willing to let her navigate their body for a while, but it doesn't seem to work that way.

"You didn't come for breakfast!" Tinder's high-pitched voice reaches Croi, and she turns to see her exiting the pavilion perched on the princess's shoulder. The handmaids and Monca follow close behind. The princess regards Croi with a tranquil expression, her eyes clear. The brownie mother, on the other hand, has her eyes downcast. Is her refusal to meet Croi's eyes an admission of guilt?

"Why do you look at Monca so?" the princess asks coldly. The brownie mother looks up and puts a wrinkled hand on the princess's arm, to quiet her perhaps. Croi can't presume to know the workings of a brownie mind.

"Ask her what she was doing last night under the cover of a rowan tree. See what she says, and then tell me you blame me for the look I'm giving her," Croi replies, surprised by the sound of her own voice. It sounds different, deeper and hoarser. Like something that has been burnt.

"Monca?" the princess says, turning to the brownie mother.

The brownie's face drains of color, and she retreats a few steps, nearly falling in her haste to be away from Croi.

"What happened?" Tinder flies over to Croi, looking uncertain. Croi's suddenly glad for the veil covering her face and hiding her expression. No one will like what it shows right now. She gives the pixie a quick glance but keeps her silence and is glad she does so when she spies Lorcan over the princess's shoulder. Even though he can't see her smile, the fae soldier's eyes widen and his nostrils flare when he sees her. For a minute it is unclear whether he will join the group, but then his lips tighten and he moves toward them with long, unhurried strides. He looks rather worse for wear; the night left its mark on him.

"My lady, we will be leaving in fifteen minutes. Please prepare yourself." Lorcan meets Croi's eyes, perhaps thinking it unbecoming of a fae of his stature and authority to give in to fear, but whatever he sees in them adds to his disquietude because he turns on his heels and leaves abruptly.

Tinder looks at his retreating back, then at Croi. "Did he do something to you? Did you do something to him?" The brownie mother flinches at the question, and the princess's eyebrows draw together.

"He found out that I am not entirely as weak as I look," Croi says, and turns to the horses.

"You don't look weak at all, though," Tinder says. Croi glares at her, and she hurriedly flies to Ceara.

The princess is having a whispered conversation with her brownie mother. Monca finally excuses herself. "I'm not sure what happened between you and my brownie mother, Fiadh, but if she offended you in some way, I apologize on her behalf," she says when it becomes clear that Monca is not going to confess. "Will you still ride with me today?"

"That won't be necessary, Ceara," the Tine King says from behind them, and once again, everyone sinks to their knees. Apart from Croi,

that is. This time, though, the slight is noted by everyone present. The king looks at her, and once again, there is no smile in his eyes. Instead, there is a deep, dark sadness that neither Croi nor her other self knows how to respond to. So she pretends not to see it. Instead, she focuses on the reins he is holding. The king leads a sand-horse over. Softly golden with large orange eyes that have a strangely gentle look in them, this sand-horse is as magnificent as the princess's Dahy. Croi watches as it whuffs, releasing smoke into the chilly morning air.

Do you think the Tine King is trying to bribe his way into our heart?

"Will it work?" Croi asks, keeping her eyes on the sand-horse.

Of course it will. You are already almost persuaded.

"I'm not, not really. But if I'm going to die soon, I may as well live the best I can in the time I have."

You have already lived a lot. But what about me? Are you asking me to accept ending in the darkness I've been living in?

Croi has no reply for her.

The sand-horse swings its head to look at her; Croi feels a curl of its magick in her mind. Rather than being invasive, the magick is pliant and questioning, as though looking for a place to anchor. Croi pounces on the magick and binds the sand-horse to herself swiftly. At that moment, the sand-horse ceases being an "it" and becomes a "he."

"Father, are you gifting the sand-horse to Fiadh?" the princess asks, looking puzzled. "Why do you show her favor when she shows you disrespect?"

How did we disrespect the Tine King?

"Probably by not bowing to him," Croi answers.

"I like her courage," the Tine King says, and no one moves to question him. Who will deny a king his peculiarities? "Well, child, will you try riding him?"

All eyes swing to Croi, and she, shining at the attention, nods and steps forward. The sand-horse makes a growling sound, and she stops, midstep, unsure. She glances at the king, and he nods, so she takes a deep breath and walks until she's standing close to the sand-horse. So close, he could take a big bite out of her. Croi hopes the horse resists any biting urges he may have. She stares into his very red eyes and rethinks her enthusiasm.

Name him.

"Why don't you do the honors?" Croi says, feeling generous.

Call him Enbarr.

"Why Enbarr?"

You should have listened to the Hag's lessons.

"I name you Enbarr," Croi says out loud.

As soon as she names the beastie, he bends his knees and bows his head. Through the bond between them, Croi feels his wordless devotion to her. It's a strange feeling, this bond; it tastes rather like the tears at the back of her throat when she's trying not to cry.

"Is he mine now?" she asks the king, who is looking at her with a curious expression Croi doesn't particularly feel the need to decipher. Croi glances at Ceara and finds her looking over with narrowed eyes and a displeased face.

"Not until you ride him," the king says. All right, fine. Now that her limbs are almost as long as the Fire Princess's, Croi is able to get herself on Enbarr's back easily. The saddle is soft and supple, and when she's comfortably seated, the sand-horse rises to his feet. She grabs his mane as she wobbles in her seat. Tinder alights on her shoulder, keen and curious. Croi surveys the world around her, satisfied by the loftiness of her current position.

"How do I make him walk?" she asks her other self, because she doesn't want to ask anyone else.

Try sending him a request to walk through the bond.

Croi finds the bond stretching between her and the sand-horse, a thick thread of amber magick, and sends a mental picture of walk-

ing, slowly. Enbarr obeys her thought-request and takes a few steps. Elated, she beams at the world. She will no longer have to hold on to the princess.

"He's mine now," she tells the king. From the mutterings of the kin around her, Croi can tell that her words and the way she delivers them are not received well. But what to do? She doesn't care. Life, she has discovered, is much more livable when your emotions aren't involved.

"The sand-horse is yours," the king pronounces, and it becomes fact.

While they were talking, the camp was completely packed up, and after the traditional ritual of gratitude to the earth for shelter, they are on their way. The king is at the head of the procession with the princess beside him. The handmaids and Croi follow with the rest of the Tine fae behind them. The carts containing diminished supplies bring up the rear of the procession. Soldiers are in place all around the group.

"Fiadh," Tinder says in her ear. Croi doesn't respond. "Why did the king give you a sand-horse?"

"How could I know the Tine King's thoughts?" Croi shrugs. "Perhaps he wants me to be his daughter."

Tinder starts, her eyes flitting from the king on his horse to Croi. She leans closer and asks in a whisper, "Really?"

Croi snorts. "Do you really think I'm that lovable?"

"No," Tinder replies immediately.

Hey.

"How rude," Croi says with a sniff. "Now that I'm the owner of a sand-horse, you should be kinder to me. Who knows, I might be a princess tomorrow."

"Being a princess is not a lot of fun," Tinder offers, a glum look on her face.

"How would you . . . ?" Croi's mouth drops open. "Are you a princess?"

Not another one!

Tinder ducks her head, blushing. "I didn't plan to be one! I'm just the youngest daughter of Titania, the queen of the pixies."

"Youngest? How many siblings do you have?" Croi asks warily.

"I have eleven sisters," Tinder says mournfully. "Do you know how awful life is when you have that many siblings?"

Life is even worse when you don't have any.

"You're lucky. You have so many people who love you," Croi says, keeping a tight hold on the reins. "I have no family. No one loves me."

At that moment, the Tine King glances back. Croi turns her face, determinedly not meeting his eyes.

"Do I sound pitiful?" she whispers to the pixie, who is quiet on her shoulder. "More importantly, Lorcan attacked me last night."

"What?" the pixie shrieks, garnering attention. She flushes and lowers her voice. "Why?"

"As revenge for what I did to the princess in the Redcaps' camp. He kept on asking me who I am." Croi pulls up the long sleeve of the dress she's wearing. The places where the flames cut their way in are puckered red and angry. They hurt, but the pain is negligible.

Tinder's magick turns red when she sees Croi's wounds. Without saying another word, she flies over to the Fire Princess.

They continue on their way. Though the forest gets denser as they travel uphill toward the center of Talamh where the Caisleán lies, the road they're on is well kept. No obstacles, magickal or otherwise, block their way. There are things hidden in the underbrush. Things that don't show themselves. Muted sounds of roaring animals and other beasts reach them, and for once, Croi is glad to be surrounded by soldiers. The scenery is peaceful and wouldn't be worth commenting on were it not for the increasing lassitude in the magick.

"What happens when we reach the Caisleán?" Croi asks Tinder, who flew back with a grim look on her face.

"I believe they will enact the Welcome of the Three," Tinder replies.

"Who are the Three?"

Tinder gasps. "How can you not know the legend of the Three? They were the most influential figures in kin history!"

"Tell me," Croi says.

Tinder clears her throat and sits down in her favorite position on Croi's shoulder.

One soft silence later, she begins.

"The legend of the Three is so old that the lines between make-believe and truth have been blurred. It is up to the listener to decide whether the legend is fact, fiction, or a mix between the two." Tinder glances at Croi and deepens her voice. "The books say they came to life at the same time that Talamh did. That the green of the forests owe their verdant nature to the glory of the dryads. The books also say that when Fionar the First and her company separated the Otherworld into the four elemental kingdoms, she gave to Talamh not just the strength of magick but also the Guardian dryads, the only ones of their kind."

"The books say quite a bit," Croi comments, and gets a pinch for her efforts. "Why did Talamh get the Guardians but the other kingdoms didn't?"

"Talamh is the largest kingdom and, more importantly, where magick originates. If Talamh falls, all other kingdoms will be affected. Is my answer sufficient?" Tinder glares.

Croi clears her throat and waves a hand. "Please continue."

"Uaine, the oldest of them, was the protector of Talamh." Croi get chills when she realizes that she has met this Uaine. The dryad's great age and her greater power make more sense now. "She meted out justice to Talamh royalty when they crossed lines forbidden to them. Blanaid, the middle sister, was the negotiator. She soothed ill feeling among the royals and ensured that the hot blood of the fae did not redden the grounds of the Caisleán. Enya, the youngest dryad sister, presides over the magicks of the Otherworld. She is the one who leads the Saol ceremony."

"How can you speak the names of these powerful kin without dying?" Croi can still feel the thorny edges of Uaine's name in her chest.

"The dryads are—or were, I suppose—our elders. No other kin, royal or otherwise, are more powerful than them, so no one can impose their will on them by using their names. Because we don't have the intent to control them through their names, we can take their names without coming to harm. My mother told me that the dryads used to present their names dipped in magick as gifts to those they chose to protect."

Oh.

"Can I continue with the story now?" Tinder demands.

"I'm not stopping you."

"Enya was the keeper of the HeartStone of Talamh. She still is, I think. It's not a position you can give up or hand over to anyone else. However, no one has seen her since what happened seventeen years ago, but then again, she usually only appears during the Saol ceremony."

Wouldn't the Guardian dryads have tried to protect the Forever King? Ask the pixie.

"Wait. If I interrupt her now, she's going to yell at us."

"The stories say that for millennia the dryads guarded Talamh from ill intentions and danger; they defended the magick and the Caisleán from those who would exploit them for their own gain. They would give magicked keys to visitors from other kingdoms, keys

that read the intent of the visitors and acted accordingly. Those with malevolent intentions would find themselves turning the key to enter rooms outside the Caisleán, or in dungeons to await the rulers of the Caisleán. They carried out their duties fairly because above all, the dryads were created to be impartial in their dealings with royalty. They were bound to be objective, to place the well-being of Talamh above the well-being of any of the fae ruling it."

Croi senses a twist coming, but she doesn't say a word. Tinder's pinches are painful.

"There are many truths to the story, and some of these truths say that Blanaid fell in love with a young prince, an ancestor of the For- ever King's. They say she helped him survive a plot to take his life and by doing so broke her vow of objectivity."

"Is objectivity an important thing to the Guardians?" Croi asks.

"Yes, according to my mother, the Guardians defend the Caisleán and the kingdoms but rarely, if ever, come to the defense of individual kin."

"Even if they are dying in front of them?"

"Even then. Can I go on with the story, or do you have any more questions?" Croi wisely shakes her head, and the pixie continues. "Dryads can live forever, but if their tree is destroyed, they will die. Blanaid's preference for the young prince made her a target for his enemies. One account of the night the dryads fell says that Blanaid was with the prince when the enemies burnt down her tree. She would have died had it not been for Uaine, who was forced to break her neu- trality to save her sister. Though she succeeded in saving Blanaid, a large portion of the Caisleán was destroyed in the fight." Tinder stops speaking.

"Why are you stopping? That can't be the end! How can you stop?"

"I just paused to catch my breath! Anyway, the prince Blanaid was in love with gave her a new tree, but one that cost her the heart with which she had loved him. Her new body was made from wood and stone."

"What?" Croi's voice cracks, and she has a hideous feeling she knows who Blanaid is.

The Hag.

"I know. Songs are still sung about her sacrifice because though she lived, she could no longer love. Her relationship with Uaine soured, and they become estranged. Uaine blamed Blanaid for forcing her to break her vow and left the Caisleán, unable to carry on protecting what she helped destroy. Blanaid left next; the reasons for her departure are not recorded by the books. The youngest dryad, Enya, retreated to the heart of the Caisleán, no longer venturing out to walk the grounds and sing the songs of magick."

"So only the youngest dryad was present when the Forever King was killed during the last Saol ceremony?" Croi asks.

"I would assume so. Uaine and Blanaid haven't been in the Otherworld for centuries." Tinder sighs. "Do you think things would have been different had they been present?"

No. Uaine wouldn't have interfered in the business of the kin—not unless the Caisleán was threatened.

Croi says as much, and the conversation fades.

Why do you think Uaine chose us to bear her SoulSeed?

"Because there was no one else. She said as much."

Surely you didn't believe her. There may have not been anyone present, but do you think she really needs a kin to transport her SoulSeed? She has enough magick to figure out a way to get her SoulSeed to her sister without us.

"So she wants something from us?"

But what could it be?

"Perhaps the same thing the kin who summoned us does."

Croi sinks deep into her thoughts and rides silently, watching the trees that she passes by. The magicks of the various flora are pale in color, and that is concerning enough, but the magick of the earth in which they grow is also weak. The strands are slow and sluggish, thinning in places they have no business thinning.

Suddenly a keening cuts through the diminished Talamh song; the sound pulls at Croi's heart so intensely that it burns hot in her chest. She gasps, and Enbarr, her sand-horse, reacts to her pain. He, entirely of his own volition, steps out of the procession. Though the Tine kin and the soldiers watch her leave, no one makes any move to stop her. Croi closes her eyes against the pain and allows Enbarr to move off the road and into the forest.

Her other self is quiet and wary, as Croi tries to endure the pain in her chest. Enbarr moves through the underbrush, the bushes not presenting an obstacle to him. The pain grows as Croi and her sand-horse get closer to wherever the keening is coming from.

Finally, Enbarr stops moving, and Croi takes a shallow breath. She opens her eyes to face whatever lies in front of her.

Wood nymphs, the Hag taught her, live in small gatherings of trees within the forest. Unlike dryads, whose primary form is a tree, wood nymphs have fae-shaped bodies that are bonded to trees. They can leave the tree and travel, but their health depends on the well-being of the tree they are bonded to. The copse in front of Croi is full of dead trees, and beside each dead tree is a wood nymph, their bodies hard and hollow. They are still in death.

A young wood nymph stands in the middle of the copse, crying. It is her keening that pulled Croi over. The nymph, scared by the sand-horse, hides behind the wooden body of an older nymph. Her grief clouds the air, turning it dank.

Do you think anyone will cry when we die?

Croi swallows at the question. She is not ready to think about her own end. Thankfully, the sound of horses behind her saves her from having to. She turns to see the Tine King, Lorcan, and Ceara, each on their own horse, looking at the copse with varying degrees of shock on their faces. The pixie is sitting on Ceara's shoulder and flies over when she sees Croi.

"What happened here?" The pixie looks around. She darts over to the young wood nymph, who doesn't seem as fearful of Tinder as she is of the others.

"I woke up this morning, and they were all gone," the little nymph says. She's shaking. "My sisters felt dizzy yesterday, so we rested early, but when I woke up this morning, they . . ." She sobs.

"Is it because of the missing HeartStone?" Croi thinks to her other self.

What other reason could there be?

Croi rubs her head and considers. According to what she has been told, the HeartStone, apart from keeping the elemental kingdoms separated, also facilitates the magick cycle. Kin are born with magick within them, they live with this magick, and when they die, the magick is returned to the element—in Talamh's case, earth. In turn, the earth allows more kin to be born. If the HeartStone is no longer present, the magick cycle is broken. She looks at the wood nymph standing beside the dead trees. Is this what happens when the cycle breaks?

"We can't leave her here by herself," the princess says suddenly. "Father, how do we help her?"

"Would you like to come with us to the Caisleán?" Tinder asks the wood nymph.

The nymph starts at Tinder's question before looking at the bodies of her sisters. "Will I be abandoning them if I go with you?"

"They're already gone," Croi says. "You should save yourself."

The Tine King must hear something in her voice because his brows draw together and he gives her a look. A look that Croi ignores.

"We will take your tree along with us," Tinder says. Perceiving the question in Ceara's eyes, she explains. "She can travel without taking the tree, but I'm sure she'd much rather not return here. Right?"

The nymph hesitates, then nods.

Lorcan returns to where the retinue has stopped and brings back two soldiers, who dig up the young nymph's tree and replant it in a pot. The tree is as young as the wood nymph. She follows her tree back to the Tine procession, anxious to keep it in her sight at all times.

Tinder returns to Croi, hiding in her hair without speaking. Nobody in the group speaks. The Tine King seems lost in his thoughts while Lorcan seems alert for any kind of threat to Ceara's safety. Croi is just glad her chest has stopped hurting.

How long do you think we have remaining?

"Can we not think about this until we reach the Caisleán?" Croi replies sourly.

Not thinking about our upcoming death won't magickally make it go away.

Croi ignores her. At this point, Tinder regains some of her spirit and whispers, "Ceara said she mentioned your strength to Monca and how you proved yourself against her. Perhaps the brownie mother considered you a threat. . . ."

"I knew she looked at me wrongly," Croi mutters.

The rest of the journey is remarkably uneventful. Three long hours have passed when Croi feels the Calling for the first time. It calls the deepest parts of her, the parts where she exists only in thought. The feeling spreads until her body is straining toward whatever is calling. This calling is not a sound she can hear but something unspoken she can feel. She urges Enbarr to go faster, but they are hemmed in by the kin around them. She wriggles impatiently, nearly upsetting Tinder from her perch on her shoulder. The pixie snaps her annoyance, and her wings almost slice Croi's cheek open. Croi mumbles an apology, but she flies ahead to find another shoulder to shelter on. Croi doesn't call her back. This is not an experience she can share or even translate into words.

The trees they pass, though lacking vibrant magick, are taller and more imposing, perhaps aware of their exalted positions near the center of the kingdom. The forest feels like it continues for eternity. Croi is almost out of patience when the trees suddenly fall away.

The entire group comes to a standstill on the edge of a mountain. The Caisleán is in a valley surrounded by mountains. Numerous waterfalls cascade down their sides, joining a river that meanders its way through the valley, dipping below ground, then reappearing until its path is hidden by a dense wall of trees surrounding the Caisleán. From their vantage point, Croi can see the Caisleán fully. Its beauty is more than her mind is capable of comprehending.

A warm glow suffuses the white-stoned buildings of the Caisleán. From this distance, she can see wide arches opening into well-dressed balconies surrounded by exquisitely crafted railings, sheer curtains teasing at the treasures hidden within, and moon windows. Flower vines climb up the walls of these buildings while trees interrupt the stone every so often. Unlike the human city, the Caisleán isn't built against nature but as an extension of it. The massive living trees that punctuate the stone have a curious green magick that displays the same lassitude as all other magicks here. The gardens of the Caisleán aren't manicured and lifeless like those in the human world. They are wild, yet maintained. Brightly colored bridges provide pathways over the lone river. Numerous towers try to reach the sky. Scattered courtyards and arbors are overflowing with flowers; pergolas and gazebos dot the gardens.

The forest that forms a wall around the Caisleán breaks in two places, once to allow the streams to join the river that leads into the mountains, and again to allow for gates.

A happiness so potent that it feels like pain fills Croi. Her other self

echoes this feeling. Croi's chest heats again, and a sense of homecoming infuses her.

The soldiers, with the Tine King at the forefront, lead the way down the mountain. Croi, holding on to Enbarr, follows with her eyes open wide so she doesn't miss anything.

The road they're on leads to the large, imposing gates Croi saw from above. The gates—made of wood and magick—are guarded by several fae soldiers wearing shades of green and brown. They all have bows and arrows, although a group of them carry swords as well.

Croi ignores them, greedily savoring the glimpses of the Caisleán visible through the gaps in the gate. A stray ray of sunshine glints off a golden bell that hangs in the belfry of a tower just inside the gate.

The Caisleán beats like a heart. Croi can feel it, a ponderous boom in her chest, like a knock on a door.

What is that? Are we dying already?

"I think this must be what home feels like," Croi thinks uncertainly.

As they approach the gates, the Tine soldiers tense and strengthen their grip on their swords while the Talamh soldiers remain stoic and silent, looking stiffly in front of them. They betray no awareness of the Tine procession. Croi is so intent on peering through the gates that the Caisleán catches her unawares.

She feels a rush of emotions: gladness, despair, and sorrow. The emotions are followed by mind-pictures, just like the ones Uaine showed her, of male kin with long solemn beards and merry eyes, of female kin with dresses made of flower petals and jewels, of laughing faces and crying ones. She is inundated by these images, moving from happy times to sad ones to those of blood and horror. When she is one image away from being overwhelmed, a gravelly voice that is not her other self whispers deep in her head.

Welcome.

Thank you, Croi's other self replies. The Caisleán hums with pleasure at the response. When the procession is perhaps ten steps away from the entrance, the large golden bell in the tower begins to peal crystal notes that echo throughout the valley.

The Talamh soldiers who had remained stone-faced at their approach are undone by the sound of the bell. They start, and some of them look over uneasily, their eyes lingering on the Fire Princess, who holds herself straight and proud on her beast. She's the picture of deposed royalty returning home to claim her heritage. The gates remain barred, though the Caisleán extends her welcome with the ringing of the bell.

Croi waits impatiently for the Talamh soldiers to move aside and pull the gates open. They don't move. Minutes pass by without action. She grumbles to the Caisleán, asking her to hurry the Talamh soldiers.

The Caisleán does not disappoint. She throws the gates open, and the bell peals anew. The Talamh soldiers scatter from the path, and the Fire Princess leads the way into the Caisleán. It pricks Croi to let her go first.

I told you not to covet the things that don't belong to us.

Croi scowls. "I know."

She makes sure the veil is tied on and obscuring her face, pats Enbarr, takes a deep breath, and follows the Tine King through the gates into Talamh Caisleán.

ACT THREE

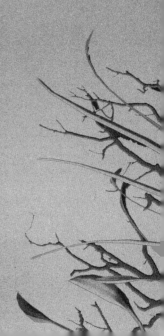

TWENTY-EIGHT

THE GATES OF THE CAISLEÁN OPEN UP TO A NARROW path lined by more Talamh soldiers. Unlike their muscular Tine counterparts, the Talamh soldiers are slender and wiry, carrying bows and arrows instead of swords. The Tine kin, with the king and Ceara leading them, are directed up a path flanked by stately beech-trees and into a wide courtyard in front of the entrance to the largest building in the collection of buildings that make up the Talamh Caisleán.

These buildings are connected to each other through roofed corridors and flower paths. Croi looks around avidly, trying to absorb as much detail of the place as she can while also trying to see if she can catch a glimpse of Irial. He should know the Tine King and his retinue is arriving. He told her he would see her when she came to the Caisleán.

Or it may all be your wishful thinking. Do you think you dreamed him up . . . ? Wait, you did *dream him up.*

"Don't talk to me."

The air has the smell of roses, though there aren't any blooming that she can see. Murmurs increase at the approach of the Tine kin. Croi looks around and is startled by the number of kin amassed in and around the courtyard. It seems as though all the kin in the Caisleán have turned out to welcome the Tine royalty. They fill the corridors, gardens, pathways, and patios; they're peering out windows and crowding balconies, each of them shining bright, each of them becoming the word "beauty" and moving beyond it. All the Talamh kin are shades of green, brown, gold, and gray. Some have wicked antlers with sharp prongs, and some have leaves instead of hair. They wear strange and beautiful clothes fashioned from the petals of flowers, the silk of spiders, and the barks of trees. Several of them are veiled like Croi, though in their case, it is to increase their mystique rather than to hide their flaws.

Their whispers crest and fall. Waves of emotions, hidden and stark, flavor the air. All eyes are on the Fire Princess, and she, in turn, looks at no one; her back is straight, and her face must be devoid of expression. She has probably made this journey a million times in her dreams, walked these unknown paths to the center of the Caisleán and asked it to confirm her existence.

The Caisleán won't talk to her. Will it? Not like it talks to us.

Croi shrugs. Ceara remains the Fire Princess no matter who her birth parents are. Croi and her inner self do not have the luxury of time nor the desire to challenge Ceara's position. The thought makes Croi's chest ache; she places her hand above her heart, pushing against the pain.

The spectating kin whisper louder as the Tine kin get nearer to the center of the courtyard where several servant-kin are preparing to receive them. Croi steals glances at the gathered kin, enamored by their color and their sparkle, their shining magicks, and their feverish energy.

Most of her attention, however, is on what normal kin aren't able to see: the Caisleán's magick, which is like a song that has lost its tune. Or a scarf whose threads have come undone. She, not it—though the Caisleán perceives gender in a very fluid way—is mourning. What or whom she's mourning, Croi can't tell, but her grief is immediate and urgent. Perhaps it is related to the missing HeartStone. Croi slips a hand into her bag to make sure the SoulSeed is still there once again, wondering if the dryad will be able to find the magick stone before the Saol ceremony.

The Tine King and his retinue come to a stop in the center of the courtyard, and Croi lifts her head to see Aodh looking at her, a concerned expression on his face. Croi looks away from him. She doesn't need or want his concern.

Why do no birds sing here?

Croi widens her eyes and listens, and indeed, her other self is right. Unlike outside the Caisleán gates, no birdsong fills the air here. Below, the whispers of the Talamh kin are a trembling silence, one that not many kin seem able to comprehend. Croi shakes away a feeling of unease and gingerly slips off Enbarr, patting him on the side. He nuzzles her, and she gives him a hug. At this moment, Tinder flies over to her, almost a blur in her excitement.

"Haven't you been to the Caisleán before?" Croi murmurs to her, holding on to Enbarr's reins.

"Not in a very long time!" Tinder exclaims. She settles down on Croi's shoulder. "And certainly not for the Saol ceremony!"

Croi looks at the kin milling around; the servant kin appear to know what they are doing, but Aodh and Ceara seem to be waiting for something or someone.

"What happens next?" Croi whispers to Tinder.

Murder and mayhem would be nice.

"I'll pretend I didn't hear that," Croi admonishes her other self.

Technically, you didn't.

Croi doesn't dignify the comment with an answer.

The Tine servant kin unload carts full of gifts brought for the Talamh court; Croi wonders what Aodh feels for the Robber Queen. More importantly, where is Irial? Croi cranes her neck, looking at the many faces present, wondering if there are any among them that she recognizes.

"The ceremonial Welcome of the Three. Remember I told you about them?" Tinder replies to Croi's previous question. "Who are you looking for?"

"I'm trying to see if there's a familiar face in the crowd," Croi replies, her attention caught by a kin wearing a dress made of peacock feathers. His hair, too, is in the same shades as his dress. Another kin is dressed in a sheet made of tiny gold stones linked together by some kind of filigree. Her headpiece is made of emeralds.

"Look, they're here!" Tinder says, hopping up and down on Croi's shoulder.

Three fae women, wreathed in garlands made of small red flowers, approach the fire king and princess, who stand at the head of the procession. The fae women are dressed in gowns made of scraps of trees: twigs, leaves, vines, and bark. Their skins are dark brown with a filigree of gold that Croi recognizes as their magick. Their eyes are the same gold ringed by a thick green. They stand shoulder to shoulder in front of the king and the princess, their backs straight and their eyes downcast. They have delicate, slightly avian features, and their hair is a speckled nimbus, with patterns that resemble the feathers on sparrows.

"Who are they?" Croi whispers.

"Half-kin. One of their parents is from the Aer kingdom. They're enacting what the Guardian dryads used to do in the ancient times."

The fae women start singing, taking care of the whispers that

buzzed like bees and were just as annoying. They sing pure, crystalline notes, coaxing up the magick from the earth. Croi watches with some fascination as the women try, and fail, to manipulate the earth magick into the shape of a physical key. Though their song is more beautiful than any Croi has ever heard before, their magick is weak. Finally, the women cast a tenuous Glamour on a pair of pebbles that were concealed in the hands of the one in the middle, making the stones look like ornate keys. The last notes of the welcome song tremble as the fae women finish their singing. Many of the gathered kin, Tine and Talamh alike, dab at their eyes. Even Tinder's voice is thick as she waxes poetic about the magickery of the singing fae. The singers hand a Glamoured pebble each, with great solemnity and ceremony, to the Tine King and the Fire Princess, and depart the courtyard with small, unhurried steps.

"What's the point of the keys?" Croi asks Tinder. She had been expecting a truly sacred ceremony, not the pretense of one.

"It's symbolic of the Caisleán's welcome to allies," Tinder replies. "The real keys used to open all the doors in the Caisleán that visitors are allowed to go to."

Right after the three half-kin leave, quiet envelops the surroundings. The Talamh kin stop whispering, and the Tine kin go still. Croi rises to her toes, trying to see what is bringing about this change.

"The Robber Queen has arrived," Tinder says in a low tone. "Along with her attendants."

For a while Croi sees nothing. There are many taller kin in front of her, but entirely of their own volition, these kin start retreating. Croi stays put, her curiosity overriding all other emotion. Tinder, too, seems reluctant to move.

They first see two female fae, dressed simply in green clothes with headpieces made of wildflowers, clearing the way. Their magicks are pale green, and their faces are wan. Following these two, entirely without ostentation, is someone who can only be the Robber Queen. She is dressed starkly: a shapeless brown ankle-length dress without any flounces or frills covers her body. Gloves, the same color as her dress, hide her hands and arms. On her head is a simple crown made of lilies. Her unadorned black hair flows down her back to her waist. Her face is expressionless, her lips are pale, and her eyes . . . Croi takes a breath.

The rings around the pale brown irises of the Robber Queen's eyes are black. As black as the magick coiling around her body. Every breath this fae monarch takes is a lesson in pain. Croi thought that *her* pain was excruciating, but this queen's suffering has an intensity she cannot fathom. Each breath must hurt; the black magick has imprisoned her original magick. Not enough to kill but enough to torture.

Croi recognizes the choked feeling in her throat as compassion. She has been so focused on the Robber Queen that she has ignored the kin following her.

Someone's looking at us.

Croi heeds her other self's words and looks around. There, just behind the Robber Queen, is a fae boy, one with the sun in his eyes and a spring-green magick with yellow running through it. His beauty announces itself in his high cheekbones, serious and sad eyes, full lips, and curly black hair. His skin is tawny brown. Croi forgets to breathe while looking at him until the lack of air makes her gasp. The dream-Irial was beautiful, but the real Irial is so vivid and so bright, she cannot take her eyes off him. Croi feels her other self's disgust, and her cheeks flame.

"I'm appreciative of beauty, all right?" she thinks.

That's a little bit more than simple appreciation. Your drool could make a river blush.

"Hey!" Croi protests silently.

Perhaps he feels her ardent gaze because Irial turns to look at her

again. However, his gaze is cool and dismissive; he only spares her a very brief glance before turning his attention to the rest of the Tine envoy.

"He doesn't recognize us!" Croi wails to her other self.

Why are you so surprised? He has never seen our true form.

Croi deflates. What her other self said is not a lie, but for some reason, she still feels let down.

"Hey!" Tinder tugs Croi's ear again.

"Ow!" Croi hisses. "What is it?"

"It's time to go!" While Croi was looking at Irial and conversing with her other self, the Robber Queen and the Tine King have exchanged greetings. What their actual conversation was, Croi doesn't know. She's a bit regretful that she didn't think to eavesdrop.

She takes one last look at Irial, who is gazing at the Tine kin with a disappointed look on his face, before she's herded, along with the rest of the Tine envoy, to a circular pavilion in the grounds, away from the largest building of the Caisleán, which is home to the Talamh royal family; a roofed corridor connects the pavilion to this building.

The Talamh attendants leave the Tine party at the door, their courtesy showing that everything in the pavilion, despite being in the Talamh kingdom, falls under the purview of the Tine guests. Before they leave, the wood nymph and her tree are given over to their custody, and they promise to locate a group of wood nymphs with whom she can make a home.

Croi follows the Fire Princess and her handmaids through the wooden doors of the pavilion and comes to a standstill, her eyes widening to take in the vista inside. No matter how many times she sees it, she is always stunned by the liberties fae take with space. The inside of the pavilion is a hundred times larger than the exterior of the building suggests. It has five floors; the first is for the soldiers and the animals, the second has the kitchens and rooms for the servant kin, the third one is for the Tine nobles who have accompanied the king, the fourth is for the princess and her attendants, and the fifth for the Tine King and his attendants. Though, Croi notes, the Tine King doesn't seem to have too many personal attendants around.

Croi pities the servant kin who work in the kitchens. Perhaps they can magick the cooked food from the second floor to the tables on the upper floors. She hands over Enbarr's reins to a horse goblin and follows the other handmaids up to the fourth floor. Accompanying them are the princess, Tinder, Monca, Lorcan, and, of course, Aodh.

The living quarters on the fourth floor consist of five bedrooms and one large central living room that is furnished with chairs and low tables, all made of wood. Lorcan moves from room to room, with Croi following him, unable to suppress her curiosity. The rooms are spacious, with large windows, open to allow the green in. Thick rugs soften the hardness of the stone floors, and leaves appear intermittently to remind the inhabitants that the trees composing this pavilion are still alive, still growing. There are no flowers, but once again, the air is redolent with the fragrance of roses.

Croi is enamored by the Caisleán. She touches the walls that boast blue stones in one part and are living wood in others. The floor in the parts not covered by rugs is a mosaic of patterns, shifting and changing, earth one minute and stone the next. Trees bend themselves to provide canopies for birds; tapestries on the walls give color to wars fought a long time ago; windows open up to balconies that look over gardens where the Talamh kin are making merry. Were it not for the weak and dying magick here, Croi could almost believe the idyllic scenery before them.

As soon as Lorcan pronounces the rooms safe, the handmaids scatter to ready the princess's clothes. They are scared of the soldier general and do not understand why Croi isn't. Monca clings to the princess and Lorcan to the king. Tinder is sitting on Croi's head

because she likes the view from there; Croi, having long given up any efforts at dignity, lets her.

Croi expects the Tine King to leave with Lorcan. Instead he sends his attendants ahead to the fifth floor. A sense of disquietude seeps into the atmosphere at the king's continued presence.

"Monca, I would like to talk to you," the Tine King says, and the brownie flinches, her face paling.

"What do you need Monca for, Father?" Ceara immediately asks, looking at the king warily.

Not the sentiment a daughter in harmony with her father would evince.

"We all pretend," Croi thinks to her other self.

"I believe Monca knows very well what I mean to ask her. Don't you, Monca?" Aodh's voice is as soft as silk and more lethal for it. Tinder trembles on Croi's head.

Maybe it's a good thing we grew up without him. Imagine all the rules he must have in place for his children.

Instead of replying to her other self, Croi angles a look at Lorcan. The Tine general, as if aware of her attention, immediately retreats a step. Heh.

"Monca?" the Fire Princess prompts her brownie mother.

"It's all right, child," Monca replies, a look of resignation on her weathered face. "I shall follow your commands, sire."

The Tine King moves to leave but pauses, glancing at Ceara, Tinder, and Croi. "Be safe. If you leave the pavilion, make sure to take some soldiers with you. Don't expect friendliness or kindness from either the Caisleán or the kin who live in her. Saraid has given us this day to rest, and all events will start tomorrow."

"Who is Saraid?" Croi whispers.

"That's the Robber Queen's name," Ceara replies.

"You," Aodh addresses Croi, "especially. Be careful. If you can help it, stay inside."

With that, he strides out of the room, followed by Lorcan and a reluctant Monca.

"My father shows an inordinate amount of concern for you," Ceara says suddenly, eyeing Croi with a definite unfriendliness. "Why?"

TWENTY-NINE

YOU SHOULD ADDRESS THIS QUESTION TO YOUR father . . . unless you are implying that I know the workings of his mind?" Croi answers the Fire Princess, a lazy smile accompanying her words.

Well said.

Ceara's cheeks flood with color. She flings herself onto a chair in the living room, looking disgruntled with the world.

"Why are you so upset?" Tinder flies over to her and sits on the arm of the chair she has claimed.

Croi follows the pixie and takes a chair opposite the princess, resigned to the conversation that is going to happen whether she wants it to or not.

Ceara is silent for a long while before she sighs. "It is easy to hate people when you don't know them. When all your thoughts of them have been shaped by rumors and hearsay." She bites her lip. "The

Robber Queen was a fae-shaped monster in my mind. She might not have directly killed my maternal family, but I felt that she was guilty anyway because she has the same blood as those who did."

"And now?" Croi prompts.

"Now I don't know," Ceara bursts out. "She appeared in front of us so simply, without ostentation or vanity, without pride, and"—she chokes—"without guilt. She welcomed us to Talamh and wished us a peaceful stay."

"That's it?" Tinder asks.

"That's it," Ceara answers. "She doesn't feel evil, which confuses me. If she's not evil, then what have I been doing all this while? Who have I been fighting against?"

Ask her about the kin she met in the middle of the forest.

Croi clears her throat, wondering how best to word the question so she's not pricked by the thorny princess. "When we were traveling to the Tine camp, you stopped to meet a kin under a tree. Who was she?"

"Eh?" Tinder perks up and stares at Ceara. "Who did you meet?"

Ceara looks discomfited by the question and fidgets on the chair. "That's none of your concern."

"Well, it sort of is," Croi replies, leaning forward.

"Should I tell her?" Croi asks her other self.

It'll be a risk.

"Let's live dangerously," Croi tells her.

"Elaborate!" the princess commands.

"Don't rush me. You might not like what I have to say," Croi warns her. Ceara sneers but settles down. A breeze curls its way through the open doors of the balcony, and the glass chimes hanging above move, as if heralding the upheavals Croi's words will bring.

"Say it already!" Tinder is impatient.

Still, Croi hesitates. Perhaps she ought to let them be. After all, she's going to fade. What's the point of creating chaos when she won't

be around to fully enjoy it? A moment later she shakes her head. Why shouldn't she create chaos before she leaves?

"First, I'll tell you a secret." She smiles at them, and when the pixie and the princess look confused, she continues. "I can see magick. It appears to me like a river rushing around the boundaries of a body or object." She licks her lips and gathers her words. "I saw the magick that cast the summoning spell that compelled me to begin my journey from the human world to the Otherworld. I saw the magick that made the Redcap caravan invisible. I saw the magick of the kin you met under the tree in the forest. Guess what all these three things have in common?"

Tinder's eyes widen, and she turns to Ceara, who has gone pale.

"Are you going to say I'm lying? But what to do, kin can't lie," Croi continues, blithely ignoring the Fire Princess's distress. "So, tell me, who is this kin? Why is she summoning me? Why is she casting spells on Redcap caravans? Why are you consorting with her?"

Instead of answering, Ceara gets up and stalks to her room, slamming the door on her way in. Tinder and Croi are left to stare at each other.

"She likes to run away when she doesn't have the answers, doesn't she?" Croi muses out loud. She gets to her feet and dusts off her dress—not that there's any dust on it.

"Can you really see magick?" Tinder flits after Croi as she walks over to a room on the far side of the living room, directly opposite the one Ceara calls her own.

"Yes."

Croi opens the door and glances into the room; she immediately falls in love with it. A magnolia tree peeks in from the open window across from the entrance. The bed is made of living wood, and flowers bloom along the sides of it. Croi places her bag on a small desk in a corner and moves the scarf-wrapped SoulSeed from it to a pocket in the dress she's wearing.

"What color is my magick?" Tinder asks, her wings going a mile a minute as she flutters in front of Croi.

"A piercing shade of green, though it changes color depending on your mood," Croi replies. She pats her pocket and glances in the mirror in the room. Her orange dress is not dirty, and her dark blue veil is firmly in place. Her eyes are incongruously bright. Croi drags some strands of her hair forth to draw attention away from them. Her body has become curvier in the past few days; she still has narrow hips, but the shape is much more feminine than it was three days ago. Plus, the bumps on her chest. Croi looks down at them and feels uncomfortable. "Let's go."

"Go? Where? Didn't the Tine King tell you to stay in place?" Tinder asks.

"This is the first time I've come to Talamh Caisleán. There is no way I'm staying inside." Croi tweaks Tinder's nose. "You can come with me to explore the Caisleán, or you can accompany the princess."

"Obviously I'm going to go with you," Tinder replies without hesitation. Croi grins.

Are you going to look for the central hall? Her other self is concerned about the errand, but Croi pretends she hasn't heard her question.

"Let's go, then!" Croi, with Tinder riding proudly on her shoulder, saunters out of the room and down the flights of stairs without being stopped or noticed by anyone. The soldiers at the door do glance at them but very briefly.

Croi breathes in deep of the air outside the pavilion and beams at the bright blue sky. There are no kin cavorting near the pavilion where the Tine are housed, but shrieks of laughter come from a distance, siren songs to both Croi and Tinder.

"Should we go see what's so fun?" Tinder whispers.

"Not yet. Let's go this way first," Croi says, pointing in the opposite direction. There's an intriguing smell coming from that direction, and

she would very much like to know what it is that smells so fragrant.

"You're hungry," Tinder grumbles.

"As if you aren't," Croi replies.

"Walk faster, then," the little tyrant commands.

Croi walks through the corridor connecting their pavilion to the main building of the Caisleán and, following the aroma, turns a corner into another corridor. Several Talamh kin are walking around, occupied with their own business. Nobody pays much attention to Croi, who keeps her eyes lowered, not wanting to attract attention or comment. The few kin who do stop her do so mostly because they want to speak to Tinder—either they are acquainted with another pixie or just want to get acquainted with one.

You are a glorified pixie-carrier. Heh, you are Enbarr.

Croi sniffs but refuses to reply—it's not like her other self is wrong.

Soon Croi comes to a building that feels more like a forest; its walls are trees growing tightly together. The entrance to it is framed by two rowan trees leaning toward each other. Though there are no kin at the entrance, Croi and Tinder can hear the hum of multiple voices coming from inside.

"Let's go!" Tinder hops up and down on Croi's shoulder, nearly falling off in the process.

Croi takes a step toward the entrance, then pauses when a laughing maid runs out of the building and toward her. She's being chased by another fae maid whose face is bright with glee. Croi tries to move aside to avoid colliding with the first maid, but she needn't have bothered; both the maids run through her as if they are insubstantial—or perhaps *she* is. Croi turns around swiftly and sees the fae maids turn into smoke and dissipate, though their laughter echoes.

"What was that?!" Croi demands out loud.

"What was what?" Tinder says in a perplexed tone.

Were we the only ones who saw those fae maids?

"Were they ghosts? Are we haunted?" Croi thinks, shivering. "Why do I think we've seen the one who was being chased before?"

The Robber Queen before she wore sorrow like a second skin.

Croi stops short at her other self's words and looks back again, as if hoping to see the fae maids once more.

"What's wrong with you?" Tinder demands.

"I've just had an experience," Croi says. "Have some patience with me."

"What experience?"

"A ghostly one."

Need I remind you the Robber Queen is still alive?

"What?" Tinder exclaims.

"No, never mind. Let's go see where the aroma leads us," Croi says, and quickens her steps. The forest building encloses a large, open space within its walls. A silver peal of laughter comes from above, and they look up.

"Flings!" Tinder exclaims.

Flings are tiny kin, smaller even than the pixie. They have dragonfly wings and flower-shaped bodies. Instead of clothes, their bodies are covered by colorful petals that grow out from their skin. There are as many types of flings as there are flowers. Instead of being born, these flings grow from mother plants. The ceiling of the building they are in is made of the branches of the trees that form the four walls of the structure. Multitoned fuchsia flings roost in the branches of these trees, brightening the space with their jeweled forms.

But Croi is not looking at them. Her attention is on the exhibits set up in the center of the building around which many kin rotate, tasting, viewing, admiring, and on occasion purchasing, either with favors or spells.

"Ah! It's the School fair!" Tinder, in her excitement, flies up in the air and shoots forward like a crazed star, leaving Croi behind.

Rude.

Croi is a bit more hesitant, waiting a while before wading into the multitudes of kin present, a bit overwhelmed by the magicks swirling through each individual. Still, her curiosity about the things being displayed at each stand will not be denied.

We don't have time for this.

"We don't have time for anything, but that's not going to stop us from living while we still can," Croi replies to her other self. "Don't pretend you aren't curious, because I won't believe you."

Croi takes her other self's silence as acquiescence and moves forward with the crowd of kin, all of whom are too immersed in the experience to pay attention to her. She feels as invisible as she did in the human city. The first stand Croi visits is filled with exquisitely crafted string instruments, most of which are strange to Croi as she has never experienced kin music before. The fae in charge of the stand tells visitors that these instruments are a result of a collaboration between Aer and Talamh artisans.

One of the kin present at the stand is a musician, and she plays several to demonstrate their high quality. The first one she plays makes the sound of the wind haunting a full-moon night. The next one spills the sound of raindrops hitting the surfaces of leaves. Yet another expresses the giggles of a river flowing over rocks. Croi is instantly enamored.

"If we live, I'm going to learn to play one of those," she says to her other self.

I don't indulge in impossibilities.

"Bah."

The next stand displays jewelry made of glass beads with tiny flames captured within. These were made by Talamh and Tine artisans combining their magicks and are in high demand. From the conversations Croi overhears, the living flames in the glass beads are not just beautiful to look at but also serve practical purposes. For one, they provide warmth, and for another, they are an alternate source of energy should the kin wearing the jewelry happen to be running low.

The flame jewelry is sold in exchange for Tine spells. Croi, of course, has none to offer, so she moves on. Before she can reach the third, and the most anticipated, stand, she catches a glimpse of a fae boy with the sun in his eyes.

"Should I follow him?" Croi asks the one inside.

Will you listen to me if I say no?

"No."

Torn between her desire to explore the delicious and savory aromas emanating from the next stand and talking to Irial, Croi finally chooses the fae boy. Only because she can't afford to buy any of the food. She follows the Irial-shaped figure out of the building, up a flight of stairs, down two, and across a pergola full of sunflower flings doing somersaults in the air. Somewhat abruptly, she finds herself in a strange garden without any kin around. The Irial-shaped figure is nowhere in sight.

All sounds fade, and gloom drapes itself over the stationary figures populating the garden. Croi looks around the place and is shocked still by a moment of horror. She recognizes this garden—not because she has been here before, but because Irial spoke of it when answering her question about what happens when kin break their word.

She looks at the numerous frozen figures and identifies various species of kin: fae, brownie, troll, nymph, goblin, even a centaur. There are some with panic-stricken expressions and others with faces permanently contorted in pain. A moment passes, and Croi hears a moan on the tails of a breeze, as if someone is crying in despair. She shivers.

You've been avoiding the SoulSeed for a while now.

It is easy to forget the SoulSeed. Everything that has happened, that Croi has found out about her identity and origin, has been much more immediate and urgent.

Stop making excuses. You just don't want to complete Uaine's task.

That is true. What does it matter to her where the HeartStone is or if it is found? Death waits for her regardless.

I'd like some dignity in my last moments.

Croi looks at the nearest grotesquerie and shudders. She can't deny her other self's words or desire. She'd like some dignity too.

"Fine, I'll go search for the central hall now."

Croi retraces her steps to the forest building; as soon as she passes through its door, her right shoulder sinks under the pixie's weight.

"You disappeared!" Tinder accuses.

"Do you want to check your conscience and say that again?" Croi rolls her eyes.

"Sorry. I got too excited. Where did you go?" Tinder sounds guilty.

Croi refuses to reply. The less said about that garden, the better. Instead she asks, "Do you know where the central hall of the Caislean is?"

"The central hall only appears the midnight before the Saol ceremony and disappears the midnight after," Tinder replies promptly. "It will appear tomorrow at midnight."

Croi brightens at the answer. She doesn't have to think about the SoulSeed until midnight tomorrow.

"I heard some kin talking about a revelry that's happening right now. You want to go?" Tinder says in her ear.

Croi perks up. "Yes! Where?"

"We have to go through the grape garden and to the center of the maze!"

"Let's go!"

They ask the friendliest-looking kin nearby for directions to the maze, but Croi finds that she doesn't really need them. The Caislean guides her, letting her know which corners to turn and which paths to walk on. The grounds of the Caisleán are wild, unfettered by gardeners who insist on artificial order and manicured beauty. Instead, honeysuckles grow where they want, roses climb over short walls, and trees appear where the earth suits them. The grounds of the Caisleán are chaotic, championing color and fragrance.

The sound of laughter attracts Croi's attention, and she walks through a moon gate to find a garden filled with female kin dressed in multihued flowy dresses. At the front of the garden in a swing dressed up in small white flowers is an older fae woman with a crown on her head. She is surrounded by kin of a similar age who show her obeisance and respect. She has a beautiful face on which age has made infrequent forays in the form of faint lines around her eyes and lips. Thick green rings around the irises of her eyes label her Talamh. The crown marks her as royalty. The garden is full of grapevines heavy with clusters of white grapes made transparent by the sunrays piercing them.

Suddenly a clamor rises up among the women, and Croi watches as they separate to allow another fae woman through. This woman looks familiar. Croi watches her smile and realizes that she just saw a younger version of her earlier, chasing the younger Robber Queen. This fae woman, whoever she is, walks quickly to the older woman and embraces her. Following this woman are a bunch of other kin who look very much like the handmaids that follow Ceara. One of these handmaids is expecting and walks slowly and carefully.

"Mother!" the fae woman says, beaming at the Forever King's consort. At least that's who Croi assumes the queen is. The only person she can be. "My womb has quickened! I'm going to have a child!"

The older woman is overcome with happiness at her words and springs to her feet with an agility that surprises Croi. "How long has it been?" she asks her daughter, cupping her face in her hands.

"Two months!" the younger woman says, laughing gleefully. "If

Lilia hadn't asked me to check, I wouldn't have realized until much later!"

The expecting handmaid smiles at the other two.

"My lady is glowing as if the sun lives inside of her." She caresses her stomach gently. "My child will serve my lady's child as faithfully as I serve my lady."

Good wishes pour forth; the atmosphere in the garden is frothy, indicative of a happiness Croi isn't familiar with. She blinks, and when she next opens her eyes, the garden has changed. The grapevines that were lush not a moment ago are now withered, and the grass is dry as if unfamiliar with rain. No gaiety lights the air. No kin, fae or otherwise, frolic in the spaces not covered by the withered vines.

"Oi! Why have you been staring into the distance for the last five minutes?" Tinder says, tugging at Croi's ear.

"Stop that! It hurts!" Croi shakes her head, dislodging the pixie.

"What happened?" Tinder demands after regaining her seat on Croi's shoulder. "Did you see another ghost?"

Croi shakes her head, not wanting to speak about something she hasn't made sense of yet.

The Caisleán is showing us the past. What's complicated about that?

"Was that Mabh and the Forever King's consort, do you think?" Croi thinks.

Who else could they be?

"The pregnant handmaid was called Lilia . . . Lorcan's wife?" Croi remembers the gentle face of the fae woman.

The Fire Princess resembles her.

"Hurry up! Otherwise, the revelry will be finished by the time we reach there!" Tinder urges.

Croi, still a bit dazzled by what she saw, starts walking absentmindedly. A few minutes later, they reach the maze, and she's stunned all over again. The maze in front of her looks nothing like the maze in the human city. That maze was a series of manicured hedges with nary a leaf out of place. The maze before her is constructed of trees instead of hedges, paths appearing here and there, inviting the traveler to take a chance. Wildflowers tumble over each other; their fragrance sweetens the air. Croi follows the paths randomly, shimmying between trees to cross to the side when she walks wrong. Tinder chatters relentlessly along the way, telling Croi everything she knows or has heard about revelries.

As they get nearer to the center of the maze, they meet other kin on their way to the revelry. All of them are young and dressed in bright colors, often with flowers and feathers embellishing their already glittering appearances.

We are woefully lacking sparkle.

"If we want to surprise them with our appearance, I can just take off my veil," Croi thinks to her other self, grinning.

"What's so funny?" Tinder asks.

"I just realized that we are very underdressed for the occasion," Croi says solemnly.

"You are, not me!" Tinder says, and flies in front of Croi so she can take a look. The pixie is dressed in a gown woven with brown and gold threads. Little daisies decorate her hair, while gold pollen gives her face a soft glow.

"Glamour?" Croi asks flatly.

"Yep!" Tinder replies. "Forgive me my vanity. Do you want me to—"

"Nope."

"Sorry."

Their conversation peters out as they reach the two trees that construct the entrance to the center of the maze. Croi stops behind the tree and peeks into the space. The center of the maze is much larger than she thought it was, and it is full almost to the point of choking

with kin. A trio of musicians are playing on one side, and people are dancing in the middle. Tables laden with food are located on the sides. Kin talk, laugh, and flirt; they all appear deliciously free of worries.

Croi looks at them and feels her entire being ache with a feeling she cannot find the words for. Is it grief, envy, or sadness? The taste is bitter in her mouth; her eyes are hot, and her chest hurts like her heart is breaking, one crack at a time.

"Aren't we going in?" Tinder asks.

"You go first," Croi replies. She senses the pixie hesitate and nods at her. Tinder launches off Croi's shoulder and plunges into the crowd. A long moment passes before Croi takes a step inside and then only because she can no longer deny her hunger.

She walks over to the food tables, wondering what delicacies they offer. The first thing she sees are clusters of white grapes, the kind she saw in the garden. These are moon grapes; they are ripened by the light of the moon rather than the sun. Breads of several kinds, sweet and savory, occupy a large portion of the table. Desserts made of sugar and cream, cakes with filigreed icing, candied dates, edible flowers stuffed with meat, fish thinly filleted kept fresh on ice, chilled wishing water, and so much more.

Croi takes a grape and pops it into her mouth discreetly. Sweetness bursts in her mouth, and she hums in delight. Maybe she will fill a plate and leave, eat somewhere else with her mask off.

"Come here!" someone says in a loud whisper in front of her. Croi opens her mouth when she recognizes Mabh, whom she saw not an hour ago in the grape garden. Now Mabh is pulling a younger Aodh by the hand. Food forgotten, Croi follows them out of the center of the maze to a more secluded corner not far away.

I feel like we shouldn't be witnessing this.

"Shush," Croi says, her eyes not moving from the entwined figures in front of her. They certainly seem to love each other passionately.

"My father is in a good mood. Talk to him about marrying me today," Mabh says.

Croi watches the complex look in Aodh's eyes as he looks down at Mabh. She's not convinced he wants to marry Mabh.

"I will," he says with a slight smile.

"Do you love me?" Mabh senses his hesitation and moves away from him. He catches her hands in his and draws her back into his embrace.

"I do. You know I do." He hugs her tightly. The figures flicker and fade, and Croi is left staring at the empty space.

She goes back to the center where the revelry is going strong and looks around for Tinder. The pixie is nowhere to be seen. Shrugging, she returns to the tables and starts filling a plate, but her hunger has disappeared now.

As she's picking up and putting down food, someone clears his throat behind her, and Croi jumps, surprised. She turns and sees Irial standing before her, an uncomfortable look on his face.

Well, this is a surprise.

He is dressed in a creamy white shirt and black pants that hug his long legs. No crown decorates his head, but little white flowers with yellow centers are woven in and out of his hair. His eyes have no smile in them, however. He is entirely too solemn to suit Croi's taste. "I'm sorry to bother you, but are you part of the Tine retinue?" he asks before he looks at her eyes and his own widen with shock. Croi immediately lowers her gaze.

"Yes," she replies.

"Is there a brownie in the Tine retinue?" he asks eagerly.

Croi smiles a little, mollified that he's thinking of her. The brownie was the first form he saw her in. "There's Monca, the Fire Princess's brownie mother. Is she whom you're looking for?"

"No one else?" His shoulders droop.

"No. But—"

"Irial! You came!" A light, fluttery voice interrupts Croi at this moment. A fae maiden with lustrous eyes and waxen cheeks runs over to Irial. She grabs his arm, holding it close to herself.

Croi feels another crack in her heart.

"Brianna." Irial looks uncomfortable. He allows her to hold his arm for a moment before extricating himself. "Caleb is looking for you."

"I don't care for him. You know that. If it weren't for your mother . . ." The fae maid trails off. She glances at Croi. "Who is she?"

The fae maid's hostility is inexplicable.

Don't take it personally. Anyone female is a threat to her.

Croi glances at Irial and then at merrymaking kin, still seeing no sign of Tinder. "I'll take my leave now." She is no one.

She turns to walk away when Irial reaches out and catches her hand. He holds her gently but firmly for about three seconds before letting go.

"Croi . . . ," he whispers, his eyes finally flooding with the smile she has been waiting for.

He is not ours. He will never be ours.

"That's not up to you," Croi tells her other self.

"My lady, the king is asking for you." Before Croi can reply to Irial, a Tine soldier appears in front of her. The look on his face says that neither he nor his king will be denied.

"Find me," she tells Irial before following the soldier out of the center of the maze.

THIRTY

THE LATE AFTERNOON SUN WASHES THE WORLD golden, giving it a deceiving warmth, but Croi, as she trails after the Tine soldiers, knows better. The scent of roses is heavy in the air, but it cannot hide the stench of despair that roils underneath. Every kin here, no matter their status or power, is pretending that nothing is wrong: not with the magick, not with the Caisleán, and definitely not with their monarch. No matter how loud the lamentations of the kin outside the walls of the Caisleán are, they will not hear them. The revelry Croi attended is just another way the kin fool themselves and keep fear at bay. They will abandon themselves to merrymaking because the alternative is too heavy to bear. They would much rather not watch a monster they know will eventually eat them approach.

Motes of magick swirl beside Croi as she walks through the maze before coming together to create the tremulous form of a fae. But before the figure of the fae can fully come together, it collapses inward, and the magick motes dissipate.

What was that?

"How would I know?" Croi quickens her pace, walking closer to the soldiers. Not that she expects them to move to protect her in case of danger. She just feels that if she's nearer to them, the chances of them getting attacked first are higher.

They emerge from the maze, coming out onto a cobbled avenue Croi has never seen before. Court kin, dressed for the night, march past them, their noses (of those who do have them) high in the air.

"Move!" a hoarse voice suddenly commands, and Croi turns around sharply to see a group of Talamh soldiers herding an elderly blue-horned faun up the avenue to a path lined by trees with dark green triangular leaves. The faun walks slowly, his head drooping.

Then, just before they all disappear, the faun looks back, and Croi sucks in a startled breath. It seemed like he was looking back at her. But how could that be? He was a part of the past, and she's very much in the present. How could he see her through all the time that has passed between his presence in the Caisleán and hers?

Why would that be an impossibility? Humans would say magick is an impossibility. Kin would say our broken self is an impossibility.

"You don't understand. If he saw us, really *saw* us, does that not mean we owe him something?" Croi is very close to panicking.

Why would we owe him anything?

"Because we have the possibility of knowing the truth behind the blue-horns' disappearance. Of figuring out the real reason they no longer exist." Croi swallows, her throat dry, her hands cold.

Why would that be our responsibility?

"If not us, then who?"

Whoever. Our time is limited as it is. What do you think we could find out before we die?

"Shouldn't we at least try?"

Why should we bother?

"Why shouldn't we?"

"Follow me." For all that she has been in a tizzy, Croi has been walking behind the soldiers all the way back to the pavilion. She realizes that she's standing dazed at the foot of the stairs leading to the fifth floor where Aodh's wrath awaits.

She just saw the Tine King kissing his previous consort. Croi is not in the mood to converse with him.

"Why does he want to see me? Is it not enough that I'm back?" Surely the Tine King doesn't think he can assert paternal authority over her.

You shouldn't have accepted Enbarr.

"I should have known he would give no gifts unconditionally," Croi mutters out loud.

"It is not up to me or you to know the thoughts of the king," the Tine soldier with magick the color of dusk replies.

Croi snorts rudely but stomps all the way up the stairs, where she's stopped by yet another soldier who excuses himself to inform the Tine King of her arrival. She is left to cool her heels for about five minutes before the soldier returns and gestures for her to enter.

The Tine King is leaning against the balcony railing right outside the central living room when Croi enters the royal quarters. Seeing her, he straightens up and walks inside. There are thunderclouds in his eyes, and she can tell he is simply waiting for the right moment to storm.

Does he expect us to quail in front of him?

"I'm not sure. Is that what the Fire Princess does?"

I've never seen him get angry with her.

"Did I not tell you to not take a step out of this pavilion?" Aodh asks, his fury announcing itself through the scowl on his face.

Croi raises both eyebrows. "I don't know what gave you the idea that I take orders from you. Do you think that because you are the king of Tine, you can tell me what to do?"

Aodh bristles; his aura as king is mighty, and the Tine soldiers standing in front of the entrance fall to their knees, their magicks reacting to his power. Croi, however, is unaffected and blinks at him.

"Our relationship—"

"We have none," she interrupts him.

"Can you not understand how dangerous it is for you here?" he demands.

Croi laughs at his words, genuinely amused. "Where were you when I was almost a meal to the Redcaps? Where were you when my body was being torn apart by the summoning spell?" All amusement fades from her face, leaving her eyes cold. "It is a bit too late for you to show concern for me. If your conscience is uncomfortable, just endure me for a little longer. I have a feeling in my bones that my end is just a few breaths away. Once I'm gone, you can go back to pretending I never existed."

"I realize that you are angry," Aodh says, a conciliatory note in his voice.

"Angry?" Croi whispers.

We are past anger.

"It would be easier if I were simply angry," she says.

"Your mother—"

"I don't have a mother, either," Croi cuts him off again. "Two people who shared their bodies happened to create me. One of them tore me in two and threw me to the human world, and the other pretended I never existed until he no longer could. What do you want from me?"

"I want you to be safe!" Aodh bursts out, and a wall hanging catches fire. He looks at it, and the flames falter before disappearing.

"Safe?" Croi scoffs. "You want me to squander what few moments

I have left in this world in pursuit of a nebulous safety? I'm going to die, King. Whether it is by the mischief of whatever powers that brought me here or by the breaking of the Glamour, I am going to *die*! Do you not understand that? Whether I cower inside the walls of this pavilion or provoke every single kin outside, death will come for me. I refuse to sit here and wait for it. Save your concern for the Fire Princess. *She* might appreciate it."

Croi turns and leaves the room. No one dares to stop her.

Back on the fourth floor, Croi decides it is high time she washed her hair. She chooses a dress from the many the princess gave her and makes her way to the door of a washing room. She opens the door and is suddenly, impossibly, by a riverside complete with a gentle waterfall and large stones on which to sunbathe. The sky above is blue; the rich green flora on the banks boasts fragrant blooms. Croi spends an hour playing in the river before her stomach growls a complaint. She puts on a yellow dress that shimmers like liquid sunshine and returns to the living room, where she finds a pale-faced Tinder curled up on the arm of a chair.

"Hey." Croi walks over to her. "What's wrong?"

Tinder gives a low hum, her wings drooping as she gets to her feet.

"Tinder?" Croi picks her up gently, placing her in the palms of her hands, and brings her up to her eye level. The pixie avoids her eyes, bowing her head to look down. "Did someone hurt you?"

"I saw Daithi in the Caisleán," the pixie whispers after a moment. "At the revelry. I flew over to him and saw that he wasn't alone. The catkin is with him."

"Which catkin?" Croi has a feeling she knows which one.

"I don't know his name, but he's the one who came to talk to you in the clearing after the whole mess with the Redcaps," Tinder says, sneaking a look at Croi.

Didn't I say bad smells tend to linger?

"Why does his presence upset you?" Croi makes a note to warn Irial about the rebel presence in the Caisleán.

"Because it made me realize I have been a fool," the pixie bites out.

"Elaborate," Croi says, sitting down. She wonders where Ceara and her handmaids are.

"Your words earlier, about how the same magick is responsible for so many different things, made me think about everything that I thought I knew about the Great Betrayal and the politics of Talamh. It's like accepting the sky is blue because I can see it is blue and everyone else agrees it is blue. Then you come along and say the sky is *not* blue, and we are only perceiving it as such. Of course I wouldn't believe you."

What does the sky have to do with anything?

"Let's just continue listening."

"When I saw the catkin, two questions popped into my mind: One, what does his presence here mean, and two, were you right all along? The catkin was wearing the uniform of a Talamh soldier, but I'm sure that before that, he put on the uniform of a rebel soldier. You wondered, didn't you, where the rebel soldiers came from? Why they were all so young? Furthermore, the magick in the Redcap caravan belonged to the kin Ceara met, the one whose identity she won't tell us." Tinder takes a deep breath. "What if she is the one who is instigating the Redcaps to kidnap kin from all around Talamh only to send her own forces, the rebel soldiers, to rescue these kidnapped kin? What if her purpose is to blacken the Robber Queen's name and let the rescued kin and their families idolize *her*? In this way, she is responsible for both the sickness and its cure."

Bravo.

Croi grins under her veil. "She has been playing you all for fools."

"Who do you think she is?" Tinder scowls, the expression sitting wrongly on her delicate face.

"The only person who can make the Fire Princess refuse to accept reality. The only one who could convince Monca to blur the facts. The only person who would summon me, though for what purposes is still beyond me." Croi thinks about the glimpses she has had of the "princess" the Hag mentioned before she set off on this journey.

"Who?" Tinder thinks, then pales. "Mabh? But she's dead!"

"Did anyone see her die, Tinder?" Croi asks. "Everyone assumed she did." Croi rubs her chest, her heart aching again.

"Monca brought word of Mabh's death. Kin can't lie, remember?" Tinder argues.

"Do you know the exact words Monca spoke when giving news of Mabh's passing?" Croi asks.

Tinder starts shaking her head, then stops, her expression complex. "Ceara told me about this. According to her, Monca said, 'The Talamh princess is no more.'"

Croi sneers. "She fooled everyone so easily."

"What do you mean?"

"I mean, the brownie mother didn't lie. The Forever King died, so Mabh was no longer the Talamh princess . . . but just because the Talamh princess was no more doesn't mean Mabh is dead."

Tinder blanches. "Don't you think Monca would have considered that?"

"Nobody clarified what her words meant. They all just assumed that she meant Mabh was dead . . . as she wanted them to." Croi barks out a laugh.

"If Mabh is still alive, and I'm not saying she is for sure, but if she is, she has been hiding for the past seventeen years, waiting for the Saol ceremony to arrive before she makes a move. For what reason? What can she do?" Tinder wonders out loud.

What use does she have for us?

"I don't know, but I am sure the Saol ceremony is going to be very exciting, and not for the reasons everyone expects it to be," Croi replies.

The HeartStone needs to be present for the Saol ceremony to be successful, and for the HeartStone to be present, you need to deliver the SoulSeed to Uaine's sister. Why are you dragging your feet on the errand?

Croi touches the pocket in her dress where the SoulSeed lies, wrapped in a tattered scarf. "You said it, didn't you? We have too little time. We'll be dead, so why should we care about the Heart-Stone?" Croi replies to her other self, more muted than ever before. She knows she is wrong, but she cannot suppress the contrariness that rises up in her every time she thinks about how the world will continue unchanged even when she's no longer in it.

You . . . Croi can sense her other self's exasperation. *If we can help get the HeartStone back to the Caislean, we should. Don't you remember what we have learned? The magick cycle will be broken without the HeartStone, and if that happens, Talamh will fall, and if Talamh falls, so will the Otherworld. Do you really want the Otherworld to fall? Can your conscience handle it? Mine can't.*

Croi's heart twinges, and a suffocating blankness fills her. She clears her throat and shakes her head. "There's no point quibbling over this matter. I will do what I gave my word to. Anyway, the central hall, where Uaine's sister is, isn't even open yet. Once it is, which is tomorrow at midnight, I will hand the SoulSeed over and fulfill my end of the bargain. That's all I have to do, isn't it?"

It's not like I was telling you to go search for the HeartStone under your bed.

Croi doesn't dignify the comment with a reply.

The sun has sunk, and with darkness comes light; torches with living fire burn in the Tine pavilion, but out in the Caislean buildings and grounds, thousands of fireflies keep the night at bay. The heavens are heavy with stars, and a pendulous moon commands the horizon. The fae are luminous, illuminating the surroundings with their glow. The Caislean pulses underneath Croi's fingertips, injured, yes, but still alive in all the ways that matter.

Tinder and Croi enjoy a light repast of bread, meat, and wishing water from the pavilion kitchens on the second floor. When they return to their rooms, they find Ceara and her handmaids in a flurry, getting ready for a banquet in the evening.

"My father doesn't think it a good idea for you to accompany us," Ceara tells her haughtily. She seems to have withdrawn from her after their conversation earlier. Perhaps it is easier for the Fire Princess to avoid the stone that would break the glass castle she has so painstakingly constructed. Croi shrugs, not particularly troubled by the princess's hostility.

"You should come with us, Tinder," Ceara says to the pixie. "There is no reason for you to shut yourself up with her."

Tinder doesn't react to the Fire Princess. She fixes her eyes on Croi instead, as if asking her what the best course of action is.

Croi shrugs. "You might as well go experience a Caisleán banquet so you can tell me all about it."

"You want me to believe you'll honestly stay in after we're gone?" Tinder whispers in Croi's ear.

"What you don't know can't hurt me," Croi replies. "Perhaps you can get Ceara to confirm our speculations about the identity of the mystery kin."

Tinder grimaces before nodding. "I will try."

An hour later everyone on the fourth floor of the pavilion apart from Croi are dressed and ready to attend the banquet. Croi sits cross-legged on a chair in the living room and watches them.

The princess has outdone herself; she has on a dress so darkly green, it is almost midnight, silver shoes that sparkle, and hair tied in a complex style so that some of it cascades down her back while the rest of it is in a braided crown around her head. Her lips are red, and her orange cheeks are flushed. She looks beautiful, but she barely spent any time in front of the mirror admiring herself. Croi glances at her and sighs; if she looked like the princess, she would spend at least an hour staring at herself.

Tinder has on a green dress that she procured from somewhere; there are red flowers in her hair and sparkles in her eyes. The handmaids are, as they are wont to be, looking glorious but understated in their expensive gowns.

Monca looks muted, as though someone has stolen her light; she hasn't leveled a single glare at Croi.

I wish I knew what she and the Tine King talked about.

"You and me both," Croi thinks to her other self.

A knock sounds on the doors opening into the princess's quarters before they open to reveal Aodh and Lorcan along with their attendants. They have stopped on their way downstairs to pick up Ceara and her entourage.

The Tine King looks at Croi, but she refuses to attend to him and makes it a point to stare out the window.

The ugly child is left home alone.

"I'm no one's ugly child," Croi growls at her other self.

"Someone will bring you food. Be good and stay inside," the Tine King, seemingly impervious to Croi's hostility, tells her.

She doesn't reply to him.

"I'll tell you how my investigation goes," Tinder whispers in Croi's ear. A few minutes later they're gone, and Croi is alone.

She takes out the wrapped-up SoulSeed, which was in the pocket of her dress; it is warm and heavy in the palm of her hand. She unwraps it carefully. The SoulSeed pulses weakly; its light has diminished gradually until its glow is all but gone. She taps the seed, wondering if Uaine is conscious of her actions. What game is the dryad playing, and what kind of pawn has Croi become? She rewraps the SoulSeed and returns it to her pocket.

Without considering anything else, she jumps to her feet and marches to the doors leading out of the fourth floor and down the stairs. She pulls them open to find two extremely large Tine soldiers barring her way.

"The king told us to ensure that you stay inside," the gold-magicked one says. Croi slams the door in his face.

He wants to make prisoners out of us.

"He is annoying."

Did he really think placing soldiers outside the doors would stop us?

"He is too used to kin obeying him," Croi says decisively, moving toward the other side of the room. She steps out onto the balcony, peering right and left, just in case the king has left some kind of winged beast to foil her escape.

Croi noticed earlier that the walls of this pavilion are covered in vines, and when she checks, she finds them sturdy enough to support her weight if she shimmies down. The ground is far away, but Croi has climbed enough trees in the Wilde Forest to be reasonably confident about reaching the bottom. She takes off her shoes, drops them over the railing, and pats her pocket to reassure herself of the SoulSeed's presence. Once satisfied, she swings herself over the railing and grabs the vines next to the balcony. She perches, for a moment, like a lizard on a wall, then starts descending. She realizes, only when she's on the wall, that climbing in a pretty dress is not just inconvenient but also very annoying.

She's about halfway down and rethinking the entire venture when a dragonfly flies directly into her face. Startled, she lets go, and though she grabs wildly for the vines in the next second, it is too late. She hurtles through the air straight toward the ground's hard embrace. Croi squeezes her eyes tightly and is hoping death won't hurt too much when someone catches her. Someone with wide shoulders, someone who smells like the sun on golden summer days when the grass is green and life is full of honey.

Croi looks up to see a fae boy with the face she has been dreaming about for a while now. His eyes are as beautiful as she remembers them, and at this moment, they are full of her. He has arched eyebrows and unruly black curls. His lips are full and look very soft.

Croi looks at the fae prince holding her and grins. "Hello, Irial."

THIRTY-ONE

WE CAN'T LOVE HIM.

"Perhaps we already do."

The realization has Croi abandoning the smile she gave Irial so easily. She jumps out of his arms and stands at a cautious distance from him.

"Croi?" he says uncertainly.

"Yes! How could you not recognize me earlier, when you first saw me?" Croi frowns at him. "You looked through me as if I were air. That hurt."

He ducks his head, but not before she sees his reddened cheeks. "I'm sorry. I didn't know your true form. I only know that you were a brownie before your Glamour started breaking."

"How did you figure it out?" she asks him.

She studies him for a moment and then reaches out and pokes him. He is so satisfyingly real and warm. He is still dressed in a creamy white shirt made of the finest material Croi has ever seen. His long legs are encased in snug black pants. Small white flowers, this time with red centers, nest in the mass of black curls on his head. An air of sorrow clings to him; despair is present in the shadows under his eyes and in the hollows of his face.

"Do you want to know what I look like right now?" she asks him. It's only fair that he gets to see her when she has been wanton with her gaze.

"Can I?" he replies, his eyes lighting.

Feeling brave, aren't you?

"What's the worst thing that could happen? He won't revile me because I'm ugly."

He won't do anything else to you either.

"I never expected him to."

"First, can we go somewhere else? If the Tine King finds me missing, he is going to go on a rampage. He has become very annoying since the last time I talked to you. I'll tell you why when we get to a place we can be alone." She looks around, trying to pick a direction in which to walk.

"I'll take you to one of my favorite places in the Caisleán," Irial says. He holds out a hand; Croi looks at it and then at him.

Don't.

She takes his hand.

"I've never held anyone's hand before," Croi says, bringing their linked hands up. His fingers are as long as hers, tipped by pearlescent nails. She squeezes his hand and grins. "It feels good. No wonder human lovers always held each other's hands."

She looks at him and finds him staring at her with even redder cheeks than before.

"Oh, I don't mean that we're lovers. I know you are in love with someone else. I just . . ." She trails off, not knowing what else to say. Her cheeks are hot, and the flustered feeling makes her stomach queasy. "Don't worry. I have no ideas about you." She coughs. "Where are we going?"

"You'll see," he says, instead of replying to her question.

The surroundings around her ripple, and Croi is deluged by Irial's magick as it wraps around her for a second before retreating. She looks around to find that they are now on top of a green mountain, looking over a sea that glints silver under the light of a full moon. The long grass on the mountain sways under the persistent attentions of a breeze. The air smells sweet.

"Are we still in the Caisleán?" Croi asks. The mountain is empty of all kin except for the two of them.

"Yes," he says, sitting down, legs dangling over the edge of the mountain. "Sit." He sees her hesitating and grins. "Don't worry. You won't fall. I won't let you."

You are a fool if you believe him so easily.

"We're going to die anyway, remember?"

Croi sits down. A minute passes and neither of them speaks. Their eyes are full of the sea in front of them. She can feel him warm beside her, and for just a flicker of a second, Croi is racked by a fierce yearning. What if she could call him hers?

"Can I see you now?" Irial asks, breaking the silence.

"What if you hate the way my face is at this moment? What if it scares you?" Croi asks. "I don't want you to be scared of me."

"I saw you as a Redcap, remember?" Irial replies. "Your current face can't be any scarier than a Redcap."

"Hey, that's true!" Cheering up, Croi unties the veil around the lower half of her face. "Ugly, huh?"

She closes her eyes and allows him to look his fill of her.

"Does it hurt?" he asks, his fingers glancing off her cheeks. His eyes are filled with such compassion that Croi's chest twinges. She lowers her head, willing her heart to settle.

"Does what hurt?"

"The breaking Glamour."

"Yeah. It hurts. A lot." Croi bites her lips, then confesses without looking at him. "The healer said I'm going to die. That my body is not going to be able to tolerate the final breaking."

Irial goes still. He even stops breathing for a moment. "What?" His voice is hoarse. "Which healer?"

Croi blinks. Her eyes are suddenly wet. "First, tell me how you recognized me. We'll get to my future, or the lack of it, later."

"No, that's not important, Croi," he says, holding her by the shoulders. Why is it so easy for him to touch her? Why does she want to cry every time she hears him say her name?

"Give me a moment, all right?" she beseeches him. "Tell me your secrets first."

"It's my magick," he says, letting go of her. "Every time I touch something or someone, I can see their past. When I touched you, I saw myself in your dreams and realized who you are. Can you tell me now? Who was the healer? What did they say?"

Croi takes a breath to speak but stops before the words gain form in her mouth. She looks at the roiling sea, and the immensity of what is to come crashes down on her.

You're crying.

She keeps her back to Irial so he can't see her tears. "Do you know, I found out who I am when I met the Tine King?" She looks over her shoulder at Irial, his figure blurry through her tears. "I'm the child he had with Mabh."

"What?" Irial grabs her hand and makes her turn to face him. "You're the Fire Princess?"

Croi shakes her head. "No, I'm just the child he had with Mabh. Ceara is the Fire Princess; I have no desire to take over the position. You should tell your mother that Mabh is probably not dead. She is probably the rebel leader whose soldiers have infiltrated the Caisleán."

Irial's face grows taut. "She's not dead? How is she not dead? Didn't her brownie mother report her death? You don't know for certain that the rebel leader is Mabh, do you?"

"I don't, but who else other than the kin who birthed me would do such a thing to me?" Croi asks. "She considered me nothing more than an extension of her body, so she felt comfortable casting a Glamour spell on me that would hurt me. Who else but she would cast a summoning spell on me, knowing the pain the spell causes? No one else even knows I exist other than her and Monca. As for Monca's report, you know kin have more than one way to lie. Who is to say the brownie mother didn't simply suggest that Mabh was dead instead of saying so? If she appeared with bloody clothes and a newborn baby, who would question her about the life of the mother? Everyone would assume without asking."

Irial's eyes are hooded as he considers Croi's words. After a while, he asks, "Did the Tine King accept you as his?"

"Does it matter if he did? *I* don't accept him. I don't want him." Croi is shaking from the force of her utterances.

Irial puts his arms around her, holding her close, trying to comfort her. Croi stays in his embrace for a few moments before pulling away. She doesn't want to get used to his warmth.

"I'm all right. Just, the healer the Tine King called said that the magick required to piece me back after the Glamour breaks is no longer in this world. So my minutes and hours have become finite." Croi offers Irial a watery smile.

"Are you giving up that easily?" Irial demands.

"If not? What am I supposed to do, Irial?" Croi gets to her feet and marches away from him. "Do you think we want to die?"

"We?"

"The one inside me. The Tine side of me. *She* has lived all this

while in the darkness while I, oblivious to the truth, have been nothing but a pawn on the chessboard that is my life. I don't know what Mabh wants from me, but I daresay I will find out at the Saol ceremony."

"Do you think she'll appear there?"

"Don't you? If it were me, there is no way I would let the ceremony pass without creating chaos."

Irial gets to his feet and walks over to Croi. "My mother probably knows that Mabh isn't dead. She's waiting for her to make a move. That's why she lessened the number of soldiers in the Caisleán. That's why she walks with no guards."

"Is your mother in danger?" Croi thinks of the Robber Queen with her pale cheeks and her black magick.

"My mother accepted the sins of my grandfather so he could die. She suffers in his place, and until she has paid her due in pain, no one will be able to kill her," Irial replies flatly. "Blood spilled in the center of the Caisleán has consequences."

"You have no such protection!" Croi looks at Irial in panic.
Mabh will kill him.

Croi grabs Irial's hand. "You should leave the Caisleán right now. Escape while you still can."

The lips Croi is an ardent admirer of quirk too bitterly to be a smile. "I guess both you and I are in for a number of difficult days."

"My death is a certainty, but yours need not be," Croi says. "You should live for me. Live hard and live free. *Live.* Find . . ." She stops abruptly.

Love? I didn't know our heart was so accepting.

"Shut up."

"Find love," Croi says, even though she'd much rather he didn't. "Perhaps you and that fae maid can be together after all this is over."
And I'm not here.

Irial looks at Croi with eyes that feel like they are looking through her words right into the part of her where she stores things that she can't say out loud. She looks away from him, not comfortable with his gaze.

"Do you mean that?" he asks, smiling slightly.

"No." Croi shakes her head promptly, then laughs. "I'm being absurd. Who you love has nothing to do with me. I just hope you will live a long and happy life. As your friend, what more could I wish for?"

"If you can think of me, why can't I do the same for you?" Irial demands. "I can't leave my mother to face what's coming all by herself. I won't leave *you*, either."

Do you believe him?

Croi stares at the fae prince, confused by the feelings currently holding her heart captive. He, lit by moonlight and magick, is somber and earnest. She ducks her head, once again grappling with feelings she doesn't have the time for.

"All right." She finally shrugs. "You have the right to make your decisions." She looks at Irial, silhouetted against the heavens, his curls blowing in the wind, his eyes deep, and his face determined. Sorrow realizes itself in a tremor in her beleaguered heart. Croi musters up a smile. "As beautiful as this place is, I'm hungry. Shouldn't you feed me?" Spending time alone with the prince makes her keenly aware of all the impossibilities she is pursuing.

The smile Irial gives her in return is lighter. "Of course. Let's go." Irial reaches out and takes her hand again, and one dizzy moment later they're on a cobbled path in a different part of the Caisleán from where they left.

They haven't taken more than five steps, however, when Irial is stopped by five Talamh soldiers. Croi recognizes two of them and stiffens. Caolan and Daithi, dressed in the dark green uniform of the Talamh soldiers, stand stoically among the other soldiers and don't give any indication they're familiar with her. The catkin, however, is

not as able to control his expressions as Daithi and gives her a closer look.

"Your Highness, the queen requests your presence in the banquet hall," one of the older soldiers says, glancing at Croi as he speaks.

Irial hesitates.

Croi rises to her toes and pulls him down to whisper in his ear. "Two of these soldiers are from the rebel forces. Be careful."

Irial stiffens and looks at the soldiers again. His fists clench. "I'll come get you for breakfast tomorrow. We'll figure some things out. Be careful."

"You too." Croi hesitates. "Maybe I should go with you." She doesn't think Daithi will do anything to Irial in the Caisleán, but what does she know?

"No, I will be all right. I'm not entirely helpless," Irial says, squeezing her shoulder. "Follow this path to the kitchen. They'll give you something to eat. We'll have breakfast together tomorrow. I will take you to my favorite places in the Caisleán. I'll go now?" Croi nods and steps back.

She watches him leave before following the cobbled path to a room that opens up to an herb garden. She crosses the garden to a room that looks, feels, and smells like the paradise the humans in the city spoke so reverently about.

It is a large room, with wide windows that open up to the herb garden. Green pots of fragrant bushes line the windowsills. Croi can see no silverware as one would expect in a kitchen, no metallic pots and pans. Instead, there are cauldrons and stoneware. Enchantments are used to bake and cook. A dozen or so kin dressed in uniforms bustle around a red-faced brownie, the cook, who barks commands and occasionally sends kitchen-hands scurrying. Croi wishes she could bottle the smells coming from the bubbling pot.

There's also the aroma of a cake in the air, something filled with honey. The next moment the savory smell of roasting meat rises from the hearth. Vegetables, chopped and ready, line the table in the middle of the kitchen, and jugs of nectar sit pretty on a corner table created from a block of ice. The kitchen kin are preparing for the evening banquet, which means her arrival is extremely timely.

One of the kitchen kin notices Croi standing in the doorway and comes forward. "Can I help you, lady?"

"Could I get something to eat, please?"

"Of course, please follow me." The little kin leads Croi to a small room right beside the kitchen without asking questions and seats her at the only table in the room. Soon the table is laden with dishes containing savory and sweet delicacies. Croi is overwhelmed with the flavors. She feasts until she can't eat any more.

An hour later Croi steps out of the kitchen, wondering what to do next, where to go.

I don't want to return to the pavilion.

Croi is in accord with her other self. She'd much rather not return there either. "Let's look around the Caisleán. We didn't see much of it during the day."

Thus begins her exploration of the Talamh Caisleán. She finds rooms laid out warmly in invitation, and rooms empty of furniture and light, cautioning any who thinks to trespass. Doors open to cavernous chambers filled with tall trees, stuck in the middle of winter. Other doors lead to corridors that become filled with forest paths in autumn. She follows a narrow hallway that culminates in silver doors that move apart to reveal a garden thick in the middle of spring, overflowing with the fragrance of flowers and the buzzing of bees. A staircase leads down to a pergola in the middle of a lake. Fireflies hover over the surface of the water, and a full moon holds the sky and the stars captive.

When she emerges from a room that turned into a garden full

of peonies in full bloom, the Caisleán shifts suddenly. Croi stumbles, barely managing to keep from falling. When she finds her balance again, she is in front of the path lined by trees with triangular leaves, the path the elder blue-horned faun was led up. Down this path, a little ways in front of her, motes of magick swirl, coming together to shape a fae form. This time the magick is a bit stronger and the fae figure lasts longer.

The Caisleán's fae form is dressed in a bloody white dress; her hair is long, tangled, and snow white in color. The pupils of her eyes are also white but thinly rimmed by dark green. Her skin is brown, a deep earth brown. She stands on the path and beckons to Croi.

Should we?

"How can we not?"

Croi follows the Caisleán down the path, which leads into a courtyard that splits off into three different hallways; not one kin is present in this part of the Caisleán. While the Caisleán is millennia old, the parts Croi has seen of it are well maintained. In this section, however, decay rules. The air is stale and dusty, making breathing an interesting exercise. Croi suddenly hears voices talking and walks down the first hallway all the way to the end, where it opens up into what looks like a throne room. Torches burn on sconces on the wall, and a large chandelier illuminated by multitudes of fireflies hangs from the high ceiling. Several kin fill the room, but they are all shadowed by the two standing in the front. The first one wears a crown made of living wood complete with thorns, leaves, and flowers. The skin on his face is stretched tight, and his eyes tell tales of his ruthlessness. The crown makes his identity obvious. The second fae is also male, with black hair and thick eyebrows that resemble Irial's. Croi identifies him as Lugid, the king's strategist before he became the Usurper.

Everyone's attention is on the elderly blue-horned faun who stands in front of the king and his strategist, head bowed in deference.

"The beast in the mountain is called Ocras, my lord. According to the teachings of our elders, he was trapped in the mountain by kin from before Fionar's time. As long as the amount of magick in the mountain doesn't lessen, he will remain asleep, but as soon as the magick level decreases, he will awaken. We cannot risk waking him; the consequences will be more than we can bear. Have mercy on us, sire."

"We have heard you," the Forever King says, the kindness on his face at odds with the look in his eyes.

Everyone in the throne room disappears in the next second as if the Caisleán is choosing what to show Croi. Only Lugid and the Forever King remain in the throne room. "Sire, it is better to heed the words of the faun elder," Lugid says, breaking the stiff silence between them.

"Do not presume to tell us what to do, Lugid. You have no comprehension of the amount of magick it costs us to hold the HeartStone," the Forever King snaps, abandoning the facade of the benevolent king.

"If the crown is too heavy to bear, sire," Lugid says gently, "perhaps it is time to take it off."

"You dare?!" The Forever King's lined face grows cold. "I could have you beheaded for your words, Lugid."

"I know that what I say is what you least want to hear, Your Majesty. However, I must speak. If you keep asking the blue-horned fauns to mine the magick stones in the Ocras Mountain, the monster *will* awaken, and the consequences of his wakening are not ones we will be able to endure." The Forever King is silent and Lugid continues. "Nuala's magick is strong, and she's physically ready to take on the burden of the crown, sire. I beseech you to allow her to do so."

"I do not have the time to continue listening to your nonsense, Lugid. Due to the friendship between us, I will pretend this conversation hasn't happened. Do not let me hear you speak of this again." The Forever King is gone with a swish of his robes. Lugid stays awhile in

the empty throne room, the look on his face bleak, but after a moment he, too, fades.

Croi finds herself standing in the dark, her chest aching. The why of the Great Betrayal has almost been answered.

I'm afraid to learn more.

Instead of replying to her other self, Croi returns to the courtyard and looks at the two hallways she hasn't explored. Footprints appear on the floor of the second hallway, clearly inviting her to follow. Before the fear can stop her, she steps into the hallway and, ignoring the frigid temperature in it, follows it down to the end, where it opens up to a courtyard filled with flowers and fountains, lit by the stars in the sky and the two glowing fae immersed in their argument.

"How could you, Father?" a fae woman screams at the Forever King, her features contorted with anguish. "They all died due to your avarice! All of them! Not a single blue horn remains in this world!"

"Calm yourself, Nuala. As my heir, you should understand that sometimes power requires sacrifice." The Forever King reaches out a hand, perhaps to caress Nuala's face, but she turns away, rejecting him.

"They are *all dead*, Father," Nuala repeats, her shoulders shaking. "All the blue-horned fauns that ever existed, even those who were nowhere near Areed. They are all dead! Your actions have killed an entire species of kin, Father. Their deaths are not sacrifice; they were not martyred! They were murdered due to your greed and your refusal to accept that your time is over."

"You are determined to oppose me in this?" the king asks, his voice so cold that Croi shivers.

"You should be punished for your actions." Nuala sucks in a breath. "In fact, I will ensure that you are punished for them."

"I am your father."

"You are a murderer. What will the kin say when they realize what you have done? Do you think you can hold on to your reputation? To your grace? Do you think history will remember you warmly?"

The king tilts his head. Nuala's eyes sharpen. "Why ever do you think I would allow you to speak freely?"

Nuala starts running before he has finished speaking, but it's too late. He says a word and she freezes. A second later stone covers what was flesh.

The Forever King clicks his tongue, and soldiers appear in the courtyard. "Take her to the human world. Give her to the human king in the castle outside the forest. Tell him to keep her safe. Someone will come for her eventually."

Croi sinks to her haunches when the stone maid dissipates into smoke. The kinship she felt with the stone maid makes sense now. It turns out the stone maid hidden in the human castle in the human world is Nuala, the Forever King's heir, Mabh's sister, and Croi's aunt. Croi rubs her chest. All that while she had been yearning for a family member, and one was present, right beside her.

Croi rubs her eyes and looks around the courtyard, abandoned now and showing the neglect it has suffered in the wildness of greenery, the broken cobblestones, the dirt and mold on the fountains. Dried rosebushes creep over the decaying surfaces of the courtyard; though the rose's branches are desiccated, dry blooms still cling to the stems. Croi moves to go, then realizes that her dress is entangled with rose thorns from a nearby branch. She tries to pull it free, but suddenly the rose branch holding her dress retracts. Croi watches, shocked, as all the rose branches around the courtyard are pulled back to the rosebush. They weave round and round to first form a tall pillar before this pillar is further shaped into the figure of a woman whose skin is decorated with thorns and who sports withered roses instead of hair.

The fragrance of roses is emanating from her! The creature's eyes are red, and her skin is a black-green, gleaming in the starlight.

"You . . . ," the creature whispers through dry lips.

Is she real, or are we still seeing ghosts?

Croi takes a deep breath. "Who are you?"

"Do you know Nuala?" the creature asks. "I'm her Rosen. I have been waiting for her return. Everyone says she will never come back, but I don't believe that she would abandon me."

"What's your name?"

"You can call me Roisin," the Rosen replies. "When I had a mother, that's what she called me. Do you know where Nuala is?"

"Yes," Croi replies.

The Rosen's eyes widen, and she walks closer to Croi, her fragrance overpowering. "Where?"

"In the human world," Croi replies. "She was turned into living stone. She has been there for as long as I can remember—almost seventeen years."

The Rosen breathes in sharply, and her thorns become more prominent on her emaciated form. She looks at Croi more closely. "Who are you?"

Croi shakes her head at the question. Once she didn't know the answer to it, and now she wishes she didn't. "Who I am isn't important. It is imperative that you find a way to rescue her."

She doesn't have to specify who. The Rosen nods her head, her face determined. "Where in the human world is she?"

"In the castle in the city outside the Wilde Forest. I cast an invisibility spell on her, so she should still be safe. But if I die, my magick will fade, and I don't know what her fate will be."

"You are dying?"

"Almost. Will you rescue her?"

"Even if it takes my life."

"Thank you."

"No, thank *you*." The Rosen leaves Croi in the courtyard filled with the fading scent of roses.

Croi makes her way back to the pavilion because she doesn't know where else to go. She could ask the Caisleán for shelter and it would oblige, but she doesn't feel safe sleeping anywhere other than in the walls of the pavilion the Tine are currently sheltering in.

The Tine King hasn't returned from the banquet when Croi saunters back, surprising the soldiers who are stationed in front of the door on the fourth floor. They give her narrow-eyed looks that she ignores. She places the SoulSeed back in the pack and hides the pack under her bed before taking another bath, a quicker one this time. Afterward she falls into bed, completely exhausted. She has no idea when the princess and Tinder return, no idea of the chaos that fills the Caisleán in the wee hours of the morning.

She wakes to a strange atmosphere. Tinder is sitting on her pillow, staring blankly into the distance.

"What's the matter?" Croi asks, rubbing her eyes. "When did you come back last night?"

The pixie doesn't reply.

"Tinder?" Croi pokes her.

"The Robber Prince is dead," Tinder whispers.

"What? Who?" Croi frowns.

"The Robber Queen's son and heir. Irial. The Robber Prince. He's dead. He was killed last night."

THIRTY-TWO

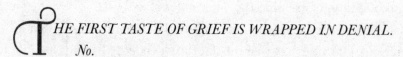*HE FIRST TASTE OF GRIEF IS WRAPPED IN DENIAL.*
No.

"What do you mean?" Ignore the trembling heart. Ignore the panic. Hold fast to the remaining thread of reason. "Who is dead?"

No.

"The Robber Prince. Or Irial as he is called."

A mountain falls on Croi. "How? When?"

The pixie shrugs. "I don't know the details, but I heard that though the prince's body has faded, his blood still colors the floor of the corridor outside his rooms." Tinder breathes in deeply. "I saw him leaving the banquet hall last night. He smiled at me. The soldiers in his escort included Daithi and the catkin I told you about." She grips Croi's hand. "You don't think they had anything to do with his death, do you?"

Croi pulls her hand away. A chill originating from somewhere deep inside of her makes her shiver. "I don't know." She lies back down in bed. "I'm going to sleep some more."

"Why? Fiadh?" Tinder tries to come closer, but Croi waves her away.

"Because I want to. Let me. Please."

"Are you all right?"

"No. I'm going to sleep."

The pixie, giving Croi a concerned look, reluctantly leaves the room.

Croi closes her eyes and pulls the blankets overhead, trying to coax herself to sleep. Perhaps her other self aids her, because it doesn't take more than a minute before her consciousness fades and she yields to Morpheus's grip.

Her dreams are color and chaos and entirely bereft of Irial.

The second taste of grief has the bitter notes of despair.

Croi opens her eyes again, unaware of the time that has passed in the interim, knowing only that the day hasn't ended. She finds her pillow wet and her cheeks damp. She sits up, feeling like an old woman. Her heart is hot in her chest; every single breath hurts.

We should have held him tighter. Looked at him longer.

"It is easier to die than to be left behind." Croi stares down at her hands and remembers that not more than twelve hours have passed since she held Irial. Now he's nothing more than a name in her heart and a picture in her mind. His warmth has faded, and the sun in his eyes has set.

Is he really just gone? What do we do?

"What can we do?"

Give the SoulSeed to Uaine's sister. Then, probably, die.

Croi's face sharpens at her inner self's mention of the SoulSeed. With some difficulty, she drags her pack out from under the bed and

removes the wrapped SoulSeed from it. Without feeling the need to check on it, she places the SoulSeed in her pocket. "What's happening outside?"

It is far noisier outside the pavilion than it should be considering the Robber Queen's only son was murdered in the wee hours of the morning.

Possibly the envoys from Uisce kingdom and the Aer kingdom have arrived. After all, the Saol ceremony will go ahead no matter who dies. More importantly, why do you think Mabh summoned us to the Otherworld? What possible use could she have for us? When will we find out?

"Soon enough, I should think. You don't think our mother will let us die in peace, do you?"

Are we going to let her do what she wants with us?

Croi squeezes her hands into fists, not even feeling the pain of her nails digging into the tender flesh of her palm. "How do we resist her? She will take whatever she wants from us whether we want to give it to her or not."

Are we giving up so easily?

"Why not? What's the point of continuing to live in this world? It has no space for us."

Is it because Irial is gone? We barely knew him.

"We wanted to, though. You can't deny that. We could have known him. He could have known us. We could have loved him. Maybe he would have loved us had he the chance to. But he didn't. *We* didn't."

And now we never will.

No longer wanting to think about Irial, Croi gets out of bed and takes one step toward the door leading to the living room when pain, more intense than anything she has ever felt before, tears through her. Her vision fails and she falls forward, her head hitting the sharp edge of a table by the door. She throws her hands forward to break her fall, but her bones seem to have softened. She can feel the stone floor against her cheek and a sting on her lips telling her they were cut on impact. A sticky wetness against her forehead tells tales of blood. The pain deepens into agony, and her consciousness succumbs.

Croi doesn't feel the Caisleán quake when the first drops of her blood come in contact with the wooden part of the floor. She doesn't hear it wail when she stops breathing for a moment. The door to her room is smashed open, and the Fire Princess, with Tinder following behind her, enters the room. Tinder cries out when she sees Croi's unconscious form. Ceara freezes for a second before she whirls around and runs up a flight of stairs to call the Tine King, who is already opening the doors to his rooms.

Croi is unaware of the fire that lights her form just as she doesn't see the flowers that suddenly bloom in her hair. She is like a broken doll with uncoordinated limbs when Aodh picks her up from the floor and moves her to the bed. She is oblivious of the people who enter and leave the room, checking on her, talking about her. She doesn't see the anguish in Aodh's eyes when the healers all shake their heads and pronounce her rapidly approaching death. She doesn't see Tinder's red eyes or Ceara's clenched fists.

A sliver of moonlight hits the magnolia flowers on its way through the window into the room, turning them luminescent. Croi opens her eyes to the greeting of the moon-drunk blooms. Her body is racked with fever, but her mind is sharp and clear.

"Are you there?"

Yes.

"What has happened?"

The final breaking of the Glamour has begun.

"How long do we have? Do you know?"

Enough time to get the SoulSeed to Uaine's sister.

Croi sits on the bed and looks down at her hands. Her fingers are

swollen, the joints misbehaving. "The end is coming soon, isn't it?"

The most difficult thing to accept is that the world is so much more than us. A long minute passes without either of them speaking. Then Croi's other self whispers. *Remember what Uaine said about everyone and everything being words that come together to form sentences that eventually tell stories?*

"Yes."

Perhaps even though we will no longer be here, the words we are will have helped to construct sentences that tell other stories. Many other stories. The stories of the trees, the land, the flowers. Kin that will continue living, and we will be a reason they are able to do so. Our story will end, but theirs won't. Because of us. Perhaps as long as their stories continue, so will we.

Croi bites her lips and inhales, holding back tears. She wraps her arms around herself. "I'm glad I don't have to face whatever is coming by myself. I know you are me and I know this makes no sense, but I'm glad you exist."

Her other self doesn't reply. Then again, she doesn't need to.

Croi glances at Tinder, who is asleep on the same pillow she used. The pixie's face is gentle and innocent in repose. Croi leans down and gives her a butterfly kiss on her cheek. "Thank you for being my friend."

Straightening, she shivers and looks around. Finding a shawl on the blanket on the bed, she wraps it around her shoulders and watches the shadows congregate in the corners of the room that the moonlight is not able to reach.

Minutes pass before midnight arrives. Lamentations fill the air, mourning the passing of the Robber Prince. Croi squeezes her eyes shut, determined not to cry.

It is time.

Knowing that walking to the central hall is an impossibility for her broken body, Croi sends a wordless plea to the Caisleán.

For a moment, nothing happens. Then the air pops, and Croi sees gold and green magick motes coming together to form a wavering female shape that blinks in and out of existence. After a moment or two of flickering, the shape stabilizes, and the corporeal form of the Caisleán appears.

The Caisleán's fae form stands a cautious distance away from Croi, as if afraid. Her face is blank, as though she doesn't know how to twist her features into expressions, but her emotions are so strong that Croi can taste them. Right now, the taste is the sour lime of panic.

Croi's magicks spark feebly in her presence.

Help us.

The Caisleán's fae body hesitates before she walks to the door leading outside and looks over her shoulder. Croi takes two breaths and feels the air burn its way down her throat. She pulls the shawl tighter around her and tries to get to her feet. She fails. Then she grabs the back of a chair close by and tries again. It takes her a while, but she finally regains her feet. Croi staggers after the Caisleán, and when she gets close to her, the Caisleán reaches out and opens the door before disappearing through it.

Croi follows her, choosing to trust her. At this point, the Caisleán is perhaps the only ally she has. Besides, choices are a luxury Croi can no longer afford.

Croi finds herself at the top of a grand staircase that leads down into a hall that is in the process of decay. Ivy has died over walls that used to be covered by finely woven tapestry. The tattered remains of moth-eaten tapestries lie on the ground at intervals. Light green moss carpets the floor of the hall, while the ceiling has been reclaimed by bare branches, trees stuck in perpetual winter. Grief permeates the air.

Croi clutches the banister of the staircase and pants. The effort it took her to just walk a few steps from her bed to the top of the stairs has nearly spent her. The pain inside is electrifying every nerve in her body. She closes her eyes briefly, trying to muster up the courage to walk down the stairs.

Suddenly the air in front of her shimmers. Croi raises her head to see the central hall changed.

No longer is it in a state of tragic disrepair. Now it is illuminated by light stones embedded in the wall, powered by magick. The tapestries on the walls are untouched by dirt and wildly growing vines. The trees are verdant, their leafy branches raised proudly to cover the vaulted ceiling. The floor is gleaming wood, and the tree growing in the middle of the hall is no longer withered.

Croi sees four monarchs standing around a pedestal on the dais in the center of the room. A dryad stands at a distance from them, presiding over what appears to be the Saol ceremony. Croi watches as each monarch places the HeartStone of their kingdom onto the pedestal and takes a step away. The four HeartStones tremble before they are pulled together and unite to become a whole. Then, one by one, each monarch steps forward and infuses the HeartStone belonging to their kingdom with the elemental magick native to them. Croi recognizes the Forever King and watches him ingest a magick stone before he infuses the HeartStone with magick, but even then, his face empties of color. Once all monarchs have filled the HeartStones with their distinct elemental magick, the dryad sings words of magick. The united form of the HeartStone breaks into four once more. The other three monarchs disappear with their HeartStones, but the Forever King lingers, not picking up the HeartStone. The scene fades and the air shimmers again.

In the next moment, Croi hears the metallic sound of swords colliding with each other coming from the bottom of the stairs.

Two fae men are engaged in a sword fight. There are other kin also present in the hall, also fighting, but they are blurry figures. The identities of the fighting fae are obvious.

One is Lugid, the Usurper, and the other is the Forever King. At this point, Lugid has the upper hand. The Forever King is gray with exhaustion; his magick is low and sluggish. Croi watches Lugid feint a move with his sword. The Forever King, probably more used to fighting with magick, is deceived. Lugid seizes the chance and stabs the king right through his heart.

The Forever King screams, as does the Caisleán.

"Despicable," the Forever King says through bloody lips. "Attacking me at my weakest."

"*I'm* despicable?" Lugid laughs hysterically. He is also heavily injured. "You claimed it a sign of your favor when you sent my entire family to the Grace estate while I was away doing your work. There, you had them all killed so that no one would know the atrocities you have committed! Generations of my family! All gone." A choked sob punctuates Lugid's words. "You didn't even spare children, and *I'm* despicable? You sent soldiers to attack me when I was returning home. The only reason I'm alive is because your soldiers have more heart than you do." The man sneers, the emotion fading from his eyes. A terrible coldness fills them instead. "I'm not despicable, Collum. I'm just returning the favor. You believe in the old adage, don't you? An eye for an eye? A family for a family?" He spits at the Forever King and takes a few steps away, disappearing.

The Forever King falls to his knees, hand pressed against the wound in his chest, trying to staunch the flow of the blood.

"Father!" A scream comes first, followed by a heavily pregnant woman. Mabh grabs the Forever King by the shoulders, supporting him clumsily. She sobs, trying to give him her magick and failing.

"The HeartStone is still on the pedestal near the dryad tree. Get it. Keep it. Avenge me." The Forever King gasps loudly and fades in

the next moment. Mabh is left clutching the air. Nothing remains of her father except for the blood on her hands and clothes. She doesn't give in to the grief present on her face. Instead she gets to her feet and runs as fast as her girth will allow to the pedestal in front of the tree where the HeartStone remains untouched.

She picks it up, then staggers as if the burden is too heavy for her to bear. Without being stopped by anyone, she rushes to the far wall opposite the staircase and knocks on it until it slides open. She disappears through it, and the wall slides shut.

The lights in the central hall fade, and it returns to its original appearance. Croi breathes out, drained by what just unfolded in front of her. She moves down the staircase, falling down twice. Each time, it gets more difficult to get back up, but giving up is out of the question. When she gets to the middle of the hall, the Caisleán returns to her incorporeal form.

Croi looks at the tree on the dais in all her dying glory. Her branches must have been majestic in happier days but are now bare, the knots on the joints mourning the absence of the green. An empty pedestal stands in the barren shade of the tree. She moves past it to the trunk, which she touches, trying to reach into the tree to reach the dryad within.

Enya.

The youngest dryad sister, dressed in coarse gray material, emerges wordlessly and without spectacle from the trunk. She is as withered as her tree. Tall and ethereal, she has a pointed face and eyes the color of faded late-summer grass. Her hair is mostly dead twigs, and her skin is the color of parchment. Her magick is pale and dim.

Without speaking a word, Croi hands the SoulSeed to her. The dryad takes it, unwraps it, and buries it in the soil a small distance from her tree. Not five minutes later, Uaine's tree stands, oddly resplendent, in the decrepit central hall of the Talamh Caisleán. Uaine steps out of the tree, this time without pomp, and falls into the embrace of her youngest sister.

"Sister, the HeartStone," Enya, the Guardian dryad, says.

"Worry not. I've brought it with me," Uaine replies, turning to look at Croi.

⊕HIRTY-THREE

CROI'S BODY FEELS AS IF IT IS FREEZING FROM THE inside out.

Step gently. Carefully.

"I have fulfilled my word, Uaine," Croi says, grasping what little dignity she has tightly in her trembling fingers. She takes a few steps away and manages to get to a small bench set against a tree growing right beside the wall. She wraps her arms around herself and sits at the edge of the seat.

"Indeed you have, child. But the story isn't over yet," Uaine replies.

"How could it be over? I'm still alive," Croi says, turning to look at the stone wall.

How long do you think it will take for her to arrive?

The wall slides open, and Croi swallows her reply. Mabh, the daughter of the murdered Forever King, steps through, but this Mabh has changed so much from the coddled maid she was in the fragments Croi saw that she might as well be a different person.

This Mabh has a destroyed kind of beauty. She wears her hair short, cropped close to her skull, bringing her delicate features into stark relief. Her eyes contain the wreckage of a tragedy, and a gleam that promises retribution. She is dressed in a plain black tunic and black leggings on top of which she wears complicated fae armor. On her feet are black boots. On her hands are fine silver claws with sharp, pointed tips, delicately crafted but deadly nonetheless. A scabbard hugs her back. She looks like she has scrubbed the softness out of herself. Croi looks closer at her and notices the rock Mabh's fingers are clasped around. The magick in the rock is decreasing as Mabh absorbs it; this magick filters into Mabh's body, repairing her dragon-damaged magick. But the repair is tenuous and temporary. Croi sucks in a cold breath when she realizes that the magick in the rock looks familiar. She saw it last in the mountain where the monster sleeps.

When the magick in the rock is drained, Mabh tosses it to one of her companions. She, of course, hasn't come alone. Unlike the rebel soldiers who are all young and inexperienced in battle, the kin following her all look fierce, as if they are well versed in the art of spilling blood. They are all armored with sharp weapons.

Has she not told these kin the consequences of spilling blood in the central hall of the Caisleán?

"I wouldn't have if I were her."

Mabh looks over at Croi; her gaze is a violation. "My daughter. I have been waiting a long while for you."

Croi's temper stirs. She tries to access the power that allows her to call kin magick to herself, but, unsurprisingly, she can't feel her magicks at all. In this moment of broken bodies and divided souls, she has become emptied of power and agency. She might as well be human.

The doors of the hall open with a bang, admitting the wraithlike form of the Robber Queen, but unlike Mabh, she comes alone. Croi would applaud her courage, but she is uncertain of her ability to raise her arms.

The opponent is onstage. The scene is set.

The Robber Queen's eyes are red, and her face is wan and lifeless. Seeing her makes Croi think of Irial. She is dressed even more plainly than Mabh, her black dress and black gloves complementing her black hair.

"Hello, Mabh. I've been waiting for you for a long while," the Robber Queen says, echoing Mabh's words.

"Why? Has your guilt troubled you all these years?" Mabh replies, her face distorting for a moment.

"What guilt is that?" The Robber Queen's expression doesn't change.

"Are you truly asking because you don't know?" Mabh takes a step forward, but a horned kin pulls her back, reminding her of reason.

The Robber Queen remains standing beside the door.

Not as impervious to danger as she would have us think.

Croi doesn't reply to her other self. She is waiting to see what Mabh wants from her.

"If you're talking about the massacre of your family, I will remind you that your father killed my family first. Do you remember those twin maids, my nieces, you used to call Apple and Orange? Their bodies were in three pieces once your father's soldiers were done with them. My husband sacrificed his life to save my son and me. Were it not for him, we, too, would have been victims of your father's tyranny. What am I guilty of, Mabh? Surviving?"

"The throne doesn't belong to you," Mabh says, as if the Robber Queen hasn't spoken.

"Neither does it belong to *you*—or have you somehow forgotten your older sister, the true heir to the Talamh crown?"

"Why bring her up? She's dead. Your father killed her too," Mabh screams, her calm facade breaking.

"My father's sins are many, Mabh, but that one doesn't belong to him. Have you never wondered why my father went against yours?" Contrary to Mabh's hysteria, the Robber Queen seems calmer with each passing moment.

"It is not my place to question my liege, Saraid," Mabh replies, suddenly regaining her composure and becoming all the more dangerous for it. "If you want to sow discord, it is far too late."

The Robber Queen lifts an elegant shoulder. "Your father is dead, so yes, it is far too late to sow discord. You've waited a long while for your revenge. What do you intend to do? Kill my family? I don't have any. Kill me? You can't. At least not until I'm done repaying the sins of my father. If you do manage to find a way to kill me, I will thank you for it. What else? Take the crown of Talamh? By all means, take it. I have never possessed it in the first place."

"How could you be the Talamh monarch without the HeartStone?" Mabh scoffs. "You searched for it hard enough. Turned Talamh upside down looking for it. I heard you even invited trackers from Tine."

"Do you think I looked for the HeartStone because I wanted the Talamh crown?"

"Why else would you be so desperate for it?" Mabh spits out.

The Robber Queen laughs. The sound is weary. "You are exactly like your father. Have you seen what is happening to Talamh without the HeartStone? Have you seen how many kin have died from the breaking of the magick cycle? You don't care, do you? You are *just* like your father. All that mattered to him was power, and all that matters to you is revenge." She bows her head and heaves a sigh. "So take it. Take your revenge. Take the crown."

"The Talamh crown will belong to the kin who can bond to the Talamh HeartStone," Enya interjects.

Mabh turns to face Croi. "Come here."

We'd much rather die, thank you.

"Come here!" Mabh says again when she gets no response.

Croi doesn't move.

Mabh sighs. "You made me do this. Remember that." Her eyes glow for a second, and then she says once again, "Come here!"

This time Croi's limbs move entirely without her permission. Her feet step forward despite her struggle to stop them. They carry her all the way to Mabh's side.

She used blood compulsion on us.

The use of this spell, possible only between people who share blood, is forbidden. It intensifies Croi's pain and exacerbates the final breaking. Croi stumbles, and Mabh grips her by the arm, her grasp punishing.

"Do you know who this is, Saraid?" she asks the Robber Queen.

The Robber Queen shrugs. "Does it matter who she is? In your hands, she is probably nothing more than a pawn."

"My daughter, Saraid. Years ago, you said you wished to see her. Remember?" Mabh says. Croi bows her head so she misses the startled look on the Robber Queen's face.

"Where is the HeartStone?" Enya, not caring for the matters between the fae, asks. "If it isn't present when the hour for the Saol ceremony arrives, calamity will follow. It won't be just a handful of kin who will die. The Caisleán will also fall."

Mabh cups Croi's face with her hands. The contact is cold and repulsive. Croi tries to shrug her away, but two of Mabh's companions come forth and grab each of her hands. She doesn't even have the power to struggle.

This is it.

"You *will* forgive me for this," Mabh tells her. Then, without giving her a moment, she plunges a hand, tipped with sharp metal claws, into Croi's chest and tries to tear out what feels like her heart but is actually the HeartStone that has been hidden in her chest for seventeen years. Croi screams, but Mabh isn't moved to mercy. Croi can feel the HeartStone lodged in her heart. She can feel it being pulled. She feels it crack; a fragment of it remains embedded in Croi's chest while the rest of it is torn out.

"Here it is!" Mabh crows victoriously, raising the blood-covered HeartStone in a gesture of triumph.

As soon as the HeartStone is visible, the Robber Queen's soldiers pour into the hall. Mabh pushes Croi away, and her soldiers surround her, protecting her and the newly harvested HeartStone.

Croi lies on the stone floor, convulsing with pain. Her clothes are bloody, her chest bare to the world. The chill spreads, and her eyes darken, but just before they do, Croi raises her head and meets Uaine's eyes.

A wordless plea rises from her, but the dryad turns away.

Mabh raises the hand containing the HeartStone, and the soldiers around the Robber Queen still.

"The Talamh crown belongs to the kin who holds the Heart-Stone." Her words are sharp, piercing the stale air of the central hall. "Take her into custody." The Talamh soldiers don't move. "Immediately!"

"The HeartStone is broken," Enya suddenly says. Mabh lowers her hand and looks at the artifact she is holding. The dryad is right. A sizable fragment of the HeartStone is missing. Croi knows where it is. She can feel it inside her chest, the only source of warmth in her body.

Mabh's eyes turn on her currently prone body. Croi is conscious of the second ruthlessness lays claim to the expression in the older fae's eyes. She will dig out the fragment that remained behind.

"Mabh!" A roar comes from the open doors of the central hall, halting Mabh in her steps. It is Aodh.

The pain surges and Croi closes her eyes, weak against it.

Is this how we end? We didn't even get to find out what our face looked like in the end. Still, it will be good to stop hurting.

Just when Croi is ready to let go, a slight warmth lands on her shoulder. A voice soaked in tears calls her. "Fiadh! I'm here. Hold on! Ceara, hold her for me. Hold tight. We need to get her out of here."

Croi smells the scent of spice and feels someone embrace her. She hears swords being drawn, words being thrown. A burst of magick envelops her, and in the next moment, the familiar smell of the Wilde Forest. She's so cold. So very cold.

"Set me on fire. Please. Please," Croi begs whoever might be listening. No one responds, and she thinks no one will, but in the last moment before the cold wins, before she is gone, there is a crackle, then heat, blessed heat, and then. Oblivion.

EPILOGUE

THE TOUCH OF A HAND ON MY ARM AND THE SMELL OF orange zest wake me. I open my eyes to the curve of Irial's lips pursed above mine, a peach ripe for the taking. Some regret tangles me. Would he have touched those lips to mine had I remained asleep a little longer? Should I close my eyes again and pretend? But alas, he knows I am awake.

A flowery bower is my current home; a canopy of roses dances above me while long vines full of pink and cream blooms sway around me. I should be intoxicated by the fragrance of the flowers, and yet, all I smell are oranges.

Irial's eyes are green, yellow, and full of wonder. He is sitting so close to me, I can feel the warmth of his skin and, dare I say, hear the pounding of his heart. Does it beat for me? I wish it would.

The question at this moment: Which one of us is the ghost?

A pulse beats rapidly in his throat, a butterfly batting its wings.

When I look at him closer, he swallows. I wonder if he tastes like oranges. I lean forward and press my lips to the pulse in his throat. The salt is in his skin. I lick it.

He shudders. "You kissed me!"

"You can do things like that in dreams," I tell him, as solemn as the priest I once saw in a human church.

He whispers my name. Then adds, "You are alive."

"You're not." I wrap my arms around him and hold him as tightly as I had wished to when I first learned he was gone. "I wish you were."

"But I am," he says, and the smile in his voice tugs at my lips. I pull away from him, shocked.

"You are?" I trace my fingers over his face. His eyelids fall to aid my ministrations.

"Yes." His voice is a whisper. A confession. "My mother orchestrated the show of my death."

"To save you from Mabh." I remember the fae woman in the armor with the damaged magick and the cruelty in her eyes. "I hate her."

In response Irial hugs me tight. I hold him gently as you do those precious to you.

"Where are you now?" he asks, his face buried in my neck.

"I don't know."

"Find me. I'm in the School in the mountains," he says, his voice growing faint. I try to keep hold of him, but the dream fractures and I wake.

Has it always been so quiet inside me?

I open my eyes, and the shadows around me retreat as if I've frightened them. When I sit up, the world spins. I let it; one must always indulge the world. It stops after a minute.

A gentle daylight, filtered through the tree branches above me, illuminates the room I am in. The dwelling I once called home shelters me again. Little has changed in the time I have been gone. A light coating of dust that calls into question the Hag's housekeeping abilities and a new growth of ivy are all that is different. A familiar forest breathes outside the door.

The chitter of gringits is loud outside, and above that is the hum of two very familiar voices. I ignore them and the questions that surround my presence in the Wilde Forest for the moment. My attention is fixed on the handheld mirror lying on a tree stump in a corner of the room. My face is an imperative question I have to answer. However, to reach the mirror, I must challenge walking.

Well, I survived certain death, so I'm sure walking is not going to be too difficult. I stand up and find empathy with newborn colts before I master the art of putting one foot in front of the other. I walk over to the mirror and wipe its surface with my sleeve.

The first thing I see is the very dirty blue dress I'm wearing. The front of it has been patched together for the sake of decency, but the bloodstains tell tales of my brush with death. I look at the blood and once again feel the metal claws sink into my skin, break the bones of my rib cage, and pluck the HeartStone out.

Two breaths and one suppressed scream later, I am calm again.

My hair is a wild mess; long, right down to my knees, it is made up of brown, gold, and red strands. It, too, is dirty. My skin is a shade between brown and a light orange. I save my face for last. My eyelashes are long, thick, and green, surrounding my peculiar eyes; my mouth is wide and my lips are full. My eyebrows arch while my cheekbones are high.

I am ridiculously beautiful.

I bring up my hand and admire the length of my fingers and the pearl of my nails. Two magicks run wild in me: the green of Talamh coils around my body in vines, and the orange of Tine manifests as fire lilies crowning these vines. A fire lily buds on my cheek, and when I look at it a little longer, it bashfully blooms.

After admiring myself for a while, I turn to go outside. My foot hits something, and I look down to see a very familiar volume on the floor. I pick it up and carry it out. The Fire Princess and Tinder are playing with the flower sprites. Someone, probably Ceara, has dug a firepit a small distance from the front garden. Three fish are cooking on spits above the fire. My stomach growls in eager anticipation.

"Fiadh!" Tinder sees me first. She flies over, hovering in the air in front of me. I put out my palm and she jumps on it, her wings tickling my fingers. Her magick is pale, almost spent. Were it not for her, I would probably be nothing but a smear of blood on the floor of the central hall of the Caisleán. Mabh would not have let me keep the fragment of the HeartStone, without which I would most probably be dead.

How can mere words adequately express my gratitude?

"My name, my true name, is Croi," I tell her. My name is all I can call my own in either of the two worlds.

"Croi," she says, then smiles at me. This smile is unlike any other she has given me over the course of our acquaintance. It's almost shy.

"The fish is ready," the Fire Princess calls. I walk over, still holding Tinder. Ceara rises to her feet when I reach her. I am taller than her now, so she has to look up to me. I grin at her with all my teeth. She grimaces at me.

"I owe you a lifesaving debt," I say to her, and she waves her hand, dismissing my words.

"I am the cuckoo in the magpie's nest. If we are to speak of owing, I might never be able to pay you back." She holds my eyes for half a moment before looking away.

"Do you resent me?" I ask her.

"A little bit," she replies, her discomfort obvious in the twist of her lips. "I would have continued living my life a fool, had it not been for you. I did some ill-advised things because I swallowed everything

Mabh said as the truth. I thought she was my . . . mother." Her yearning reveals itself in the word she breathes out while I shudder at it. I never want to hear that word again.

"You should be glad she's not. She doesn't treat her daughters very nicely. Look at what she did to me," I tell her, settling down on the ground beside them. The flower sprites immediately surround me, nesting in my hair, nuzzling my arm. Sticky things. "How are we here?"

"My father—the Tine King," Ceara corrects herself.

"He's still your father. You don't have to share blood with him to be his family," I interrupt her, plucking a sprite out of my sleeve.

The Fire Princess takes a deep breath. "The Tine King's soldiers attacked Mabh's mercenaries, giving Tinder enough time to chant the world-moving spell. We were deposited in the middle of the Wilde Forest, and you were begging for me to set you on fire. So I did. While you were burning, the forest Guardian found us and brought us here. We've been waiting for you to wake up for the last three days."

"Do you know what has happened in the Otherworld? Was the Saol ceremony successful?" I ask Tinder.

"Yes. My mother sent me a message and told me so. She also advised us to stay hidden for a while. She told me that Mabh bonded to the HeartStone and has been crowned the queen of Talamh. The Robber Queen has been imprisoned. It seems that Mabh is searching for you," Tinder replies.

"Oh." I tease the flower sprites who are weaving flower petals into my hair.

"Are you scared?" Ceara asks.

I shrug. "What else could she do to me that she hasn't done already? Besides killing me, and it's not like she hasn't tried to do that once."

"What are we going to do now?" Tinder asks, a quaver in her voice.

"Look." Instead of answering, I give the book I found to the Fire Princess, and she takes it with a frown.

"*The Talamh Crown?*" She reads the title out loud and gasps. "Do you know what this is?!"

"A book." I stare at the Fire Princess blankly.

"It's not *just* a book! This is the living record of the Talamh crown! It is magicked to record the history of Talamh as it occurs without needing any kin to write it down. Everyone thought the book was destroyed when the Forever King was killed. Has it been with you all along?" She doesn't seem to require an answer. Holding the book reverently, she sits down beside me. Less than half a month ago this book didn't recognize me as kin and wouldn't allow me to read it. Now it opens easily.

The first few pages detail the actions of Fionar and her companions, which we all know already, so Ceara flips to the last few pages, which narrate the reign of the Forever King.

"His magick was running out!" Tinder exclaims softly.

"'To replenish his decreasing power, he had the blue-horned fauns mine for magick stones in the mountains of Areed, ignoring the repeated warnings by the blue-horned elders about Ocras, the monster in the mountain. His refusal to heed their warnings led to the occurrence of what the blue horns were most scared of: Ocras, realizing that his magick was decreasing, woke up. In a fit of anger, the monster killed all the blue-horned fauns and drained their magick,'" Ceara reads out.

"'The Forever King's refusal to heed the warning of his depleting magick and abdicate created a rift between him and Lugid. The Forever King, in an attempt to assert control and stop him from revealing his misdeeds, had Lugid's entire family killed. Lugid managed to escape assassination and returned the favor by killing the Forever King's family. He left Mabh alive because she was pregnant and he still had a conscience," I say without needing to read the book.

"Ah, look," Tinder says. "The book speaks of Mabh's actions. She . . ." Tinder trails off and looks at me.

"She broke me in two and used me as a vessel for the HeartStone," I say with a brevity I do not feel. "But, see, the book doesn't call *her* the monarch of Talamh. Nuala, the eldest daughter of the Forever King, retains the title."

"Nuala?" Tinder frowns. "Didn't Nuala die?"

"She's not dead. She was just turned into a stone maiden."

"If you are Aodh and Mabh's daughter, then who am I?" Ceara suddenly asks, as if the question has just occurred to her.

"Do you really want to know?" I ask carefully. The Fire Princess narrows her eyes at my words, then shakes her head.

"I think I already do," she whispers, something orange flickering in her eyes, something that looks a lot like rage. I know the feeling well.

"Do you know how all monarchs have titles besides their names? Like the Forever King and the Robber Queen?" Tinder says, ignoring the undercurrents in the air. She smiles grimly. "Mabh should have one too."

"What do you think it ought to be?" I smile at Tinder.

"The False Queen. Fitting, don't you think?"

"Indeed. She should love it." I turn toward the forest, my attention caught by the sound of nearing footsteps. I will recognize these steps anywhere. Ceara and Tinder stiffen beside me, alert to danger, as the Hag emerges from the forest.

When I see her, I remember Uaine and the apathy in her eyes. I remember how she manipulated me, and I, fool that I was, danced to her tune without even knowing my feet were moving. The fire in me burns hotter, and I get to my feet. The time that has passed since I

last saw the Hag is less than a month, but now I am as tall as her. She, who was a mountain to me, has become nothing more than a hill I can walk over.

"Hello, Blanaid," I say to her, and watch with pleasure as she flinches at the name. She can't be entirely bereft of emotion if she reacts to her name. "It has been quite a while since we last saw each other. Have you missed me?"

She doesn't answer.

"What am I saying? How could you miss me? You have no heart." I take a step closer toward her, and the scent of the forest fills me. "Shall I grow you a new one?"

The magick within me comes alive at my words as if aware of my desires. I see through the Hag's wood and stone body to the damaged SoulSeed nested artificially in her chest. A curl of magick holds the SoulSeed together. I don't even need words to command the magick in me. One thought and the magick shapes itself like an arrow, plunging into the Hag's body, filling her SoulSeed, repairing it.

The Hag's eyes widen for a second before she makes the sound of trees creaking in a windstorm. She clutches at her chest. The Soul-Seed pulses bright green inside the Hag's chest, burning hot and cold, bringing to life the emotions she has lived without for so long. She falls to her knees and keens.

"Do you love me now?" I ask her. She gives me a look that contains something other than indifference for the very first time. However, it is not love that fills her eyes but horror. "No? Shall I give you a new body as well?"

"No," she pleads, but it is my turn not to listen. I whisper a word, and her metamorphosis begins. Flesh fills out what was once stone, and green sap runs through hollow wood. Her hair lengthens; her cheeks plump. The dress she has on her body tightens as her curves appear. Minutes, punctuated by her screams, pass as her body is re-created.

It takes only a quarter of an hour before she stands in front of us, a dryad once again.

"Will you not thank me?" I give her a sad look. "I gave you a heart and a new body. Aren't they enough?"

"I didn't ask you to do this!" she spits out.

"You speak as though permission is important." I click my tongue at her. "I don't recall anyone asking me before they put the Heart-Stone in my body."

"I had nothing to do with what happened to you. I was simply repaying a debt!" Blanaid hisses at me.

"Indeed," I say, and smile at her. "Since you raised me for almost seventeen years, consider your new heart and body repayment for the grace you showed me. I, too, am simply repaying my debt."

Blanaid, no longer the Hag, stands before me. Her face is streaked with tears, and her flesh-and-blood body is bent under the heavy weight of her emotions.

She is in pain, yes, but this pain is far from enough.

"You should go join your sisters in the Talamh Caisleán. Bring them news of me. I'm sure they're anxious about the HeartStone fragment that remains inside me."

"Croi." Blanaid catches my hand in hers. This is the first time she has touched me of her own accord. I fling her hand away, repulsed by the touch of her skin on mine. "Take the heart away. Please."

"I begged you, too. Remember?" I think of the Croi I was. That poor creature, bewildered by the world around her. Stepped on, manipulated, beaten.

I lick my lips and remind myself of reason. I cannot set fire to everything at once. What will be the fun in that?

Dismissing the dryad, I turn to Ceara and Tinder. The morning is fading under the heated attentions of the sun. The pixie and the Fire

Princess are staring at me as if they don't know me and are not sure they want to.

I grin at them. I will not apologize for the things I have done and will do in the future. "Have you ever been to a human city?"

Tinder's eyes round, and she forgets her wariness. "No."

"Do you want to go?" I ask.

"Can we?" Ceara asks, looking at Blanaid, who hasn't moved an inch from where I left her.

"Yes." I turn and start walking, talking over my shoulder. "Follow me. I'll show you a prince who dresses like a peacock, a market full of color, and a stone maiden who has been waiting for me to save her for a very long time."

ACKNOWLEDGMENTS

FIRST, I'D LIKE TO THANK ALLAH (SWT) FOR GRANTING me the ability to bring stories to life. This grace has comforted me and kept me alive thus far.

Croi came to life in the wilds of a small village in Fiji called Vitogo. I dreamed her up in the company of my cousins, so they deserve my thanks. In no particular order, thank you to Shabrina, Wahfiqa (who read *Road of the Lost* back when it still had a "The" attached to it and told me it was BRILLIANT), Faaiza, Shafeen, Zaynah, Ziyad, Aliyah, and Hina. Thank you to my maamu, Azeem Khan, who lugged a suitcase of Enid Blyton books to Fiji from New Zealand because I was starving for new stories. Thanks to my late naana who took me on long walks (and walked faster than me every single time), accompanying me without complaint to libraries and secondhand bookstores. I don't know if I deserved you, but thank you for loving me. Thank you to my big sisters, Sanna bubu, Bina bubu, and Rifu bubu.

Thank you to my family: Amma; Abba; my brothers, Izaz, Isharaaz; my sisters-in-law, Robina and Farzana; the demons—I mean kids—Pakeeza, Waaizh, Zara, and Ruwaiz. (As you can see, my family loves the letter *Z*.) My aunts, Sadrul and Samrul Buksh, thank you for keeping things real. Thanks to my cousin Shaina for the long-distance support.

Thank you to Professor Maggie de Vries, who was my thesis supervisor and guided *Road of the Lost* through its painful first draft. Thank you to Rebecca Hales and Jeffrey Ricker, whose comments about Croi and her story in that writing class so long ago kept me from despair and made me think of myself as a writer. Thank you to Yashaswi Kesanakurthy, whose particular brand of wit has me putting down the knife on many dark days. Thank you to Jane Whittingham, who has served as a willing ear so many times when I felt the world was ending. Thank you to Janet Eastwood, whom I can text message when in a grammar crisis (it happens far more often than it should). You all read Croi when she was but an amorphous mess of words and didn't let me give up on her. Thank you.

Thank you to Rossi Hyunh, who has been through thick and thin with me. We'll keep our dark history under wraps, of course. Thank you, Teng, for all the foodie dates and for being willing to share the huge pajeon with me every single time. Thank you to Jasdeep Deol. You mean the world to me. Thank you to Amparo Ortiz, who is the warmest person I've encountered; Gabriela Martins, who is a pleasure to talk to; Sabina Khan, who tells amazing stories. To Karuna Riazi: I love you, little sister. Axie Oh and Kat Cho: thank you for the support. Thank you to Kate Elliot for your stories and your kindnesses. Thank you to also to Lana Wood Johnson, Julian Winters, Mason Deaver, Melody Simpson, Natalie C. Parker, Rena Barron, Ronni Davis, Becca Coffindaffer, and Lu Brooks. You've let me vent, comforted me, and cheered me on so many times. Thank you to Natasha Deen for the Zoom coffee dates and the giggles that accompanied them. A warm thanks to Roselle Lim and Judy Lin.

Thank you to my agent, Katelyn Detweiler, who didn't give up on Croi. Thank you to Karen Wojtyla and Nicole Fiorica, whose unique insights on *Road of the Lost* have helped the book become what it is. Thank you to Sonia Chaghatzbanian, who designed the jacket and made it look amazing. Thank you to Irene Metaxatos, who did the interior design of the book. Thank you to Sophia Seidner and Denise Paige from Jill Grinberg Agency, for their graciousness and kindness.

Finally, thank you to my readers, for being willing to dream with me.